ADVANCE PRAISE FOR
LUNA

"A great adventure for Sci-Fi readers. This book shows an immense source of J. Carl Hudson's inspiration and creativity. His writing technique is very inspiring and keeps the reader interested and not wanting to place the book down until it's finished. Never underestimate brilliant children as they play a large part in the running of this extraordinary society. He has it set up well for a sequel if he wants to write one. Great job and hope to see more!"

—Eliza Lynn Taylor, author; "Murder So Convenient."
ElizaLynnTaylor.com

"…Good action scenes!"

—iUniverse Editor, Publisher's Review

Marilyn Haight, recommended in the Washington Post and numerous publications nation-wide recommends, "Buy a copy, then find a quiet place to read where you won't be disturbed. Pay attention to the backgrounds of multi-national, exotic characters and then hold onto the edge of your seat! J. Carl Hudson delivers a riveting story replete with all the elements of an engaging, intelligent read: intrigue, escalating conflict, action, romance and a satisfying resolution…for now. You won't want this story to end, so don't be surprised to find yourself looking for a sequel - as well as a movie version so you can actually see all the fabulous special effects!"

—Marilyn Haight, author; "Who's Afraid of the Big, Bad Boss"
(www.bigbadboss.com)

READERS LOVE *LUNA*

"J. Carl Hudson's extraordinary ability to tell his story compelled me to stay home, undisturbed, until I finished reading it to completion. Carl is a gifted writer who has been able to capture experiences and weave them subtly into this exciting action packed story. His hero's yearning for a better world is something that can be found in all of us, and he actually delivers to us how it can be done. His characters are believable and charismatic. I highly recommend this engaging epic journey. He's given us hope of what can be… if we pursue our dreams and find individuals of like mind and purpose. I'm ready to fly to "Luna"… and beyond. Give me my boarding pass."

—I. Lignos, Peabody, MA

"Amazing, imaginative, and fascinating… is this our life yet to come? I thought this book was great, and at times felt I was there with the characters. Shame on J. Carl Hudson for leaving me hanging; he has done a wonderful job on Luna. There must be a follow up book coming!"

—S. Samuels, Chicago, IL

"Really cool! I bring it to work to read during lunch. I like what I've read!"

—S. Candrea, Casa Grande, AZ

"Luna is a superb book, I would recommend it both to Sci-Fi lovers like myself, and to anyone who wants a refreshing, mind-expanding read."

—D. Morris, Lavant, West Sussex, United Kingdom

"Enjoyable writing, believable and easily understood with a clearly defined story. Obviously told by a great storyteller; makes me believe you are there and put yourself into the story. One would want all people to have the desire to live as your characters; no bad war; no destruction to human life; no anger. I am thankful you chose to share with me."

—B. Strabenski, Carlisle, PA

"What a fun read! If only our real world would wage wars of inconvenience instead of death and destruction. I was fascinated by the fact that everything talked about in this science fiction story is technically possible with the knowledge and technology presently available to us. The story was thoroughly enjoyable and held my attention from beginning to end. When LUNA becomes a reality, I will apply for citizenship! Thanks for allowing me the privilege of previewing your book. When LUNA is on the best seller list, I'll be able to say I knew Carl when…"

—D. Romero, Cottonwood, AZ

"It has been my pleasure to be one of many with whom J. Carl Hudson has been able to share the beginning, middle and the end of this writing. It has been joyful to the heart to know that his dedication in following his dream and making it a reality shows that thoughts are really things if you believe in yourself. Good job Carl, and keep up the wonderful work and dedication."

—B. Silva, San Francisco, CA

ACKNOWLEDGEMENTS

A sincere thank you to a wonderful friend and true professional, Ms. Darlene Romero, who graciously donated her time to review the book in its entirety with an editor's eye while acting as an impromptu storyline consultant and overall sounding board.

A very special thanks to Contributing Graphic Artist Scott A. Hudson, B.S. EMF., Northern Arizona University, Flagstaff, Arizona.

A very special thank you to Shirlene Kelly Shirley of the Houck Navajo Nation, Houck, Arizona, for her invaluable input concerning Navajo culture and customs.

To the last mainstay of true independence, good moral fiber and a shining community I truly admire, thank you with all my heart to the wonderful Amish people of Lancaster County, Pennsylvania, for allowing me a touch of poetic license while including their ambience throughout my humble scribbling. Herr Stoltzfus, thank you for the buggy ride!

One direct quote is taken from the International Court of Justice 'General Information,' found at: http://212.153.43.18/icjwww/igeneralinformation/icjgnnot.html.

LUNA

J. Carl Hudson

This book is a complete work of fiction. Events and characters portrayed herein are fictitious or are used fictitiously. Certain objects and real locations are mentioned to provide feelings of authenticity, but all other incidents, places, and names are not to be construed as real, being products of the author's imagination.

LUNA

Cover Design by J. Carl Hudson

ISBN 9781976842689

For those among us who still possess the imagination to see science a little closer to home, and to my sister Sue Ellen, whose kind and beautiful soul prematurely left this world on July 18, 2004.

dramatis personae

Jake Starnes	Council Lead	American Male	68
Alahn Starnes	Assistant Council Lead	American Male	26
Kelly Akamatsu	Administrator	Chinese Female	58
Donah Morning	Assistant Administrator	Russian Female	35

Youth Council members

Abigail	Selene/Hydroponics	Hebrew Female	14
Raul	Cordial/Habitat, Environments	Hispanic Male	12
Walwyn	Cordial/Technology	British Male	17
Chaylen	Prexus/Engineering	African-American Female	14
Chidi	Selene/Special Services	African Male	13
Chateauleire	Prexus/Starflyer, New Hope	Canadian French Female	11

Adult Council members

Maralah	Selene/Exploration	Native-American Female	81
Iawy	Selene/Geology	Egyptian Male	70
Natalya	Cordial/Life Support	Russian Female	71
Singe	Cordial/Medical	East Indian Male	64
Yoshko	Prexus/AlSys	Japanese Female	57
Anoki	Prexus/Defense	Native-American Male	60

Five Years Ago

Twin spires of a coal-fired kiln added to a riot of haze-birthing pollutants where once clear light and heaven reigned. Relatively high temperatures and a gentle westerly wind did little to overcome noxious contributions of too many compact cars, small buses and motorcycles. However, while clear breathing would normally require battle against air pollution and dust... this day seemed blessed to provide more clarity than usual.

"Namaste," Prabidhi said to the gathering in general, slightly bowing her head with pressed palms as she took her seat at the table. She had lived her whole life in the Nepalese capital city of Kathmandu, and was considered to be one of the wisest voices within the group taking lunch at a street café adjacent to government offices at Singha Durbar. Working for the Department of Mines and Geology, she had arrived late and sat down quietly as Najju continued.

"I am saying to you, I saw this with my own eyes. Such strangeness has never been seen in the Office of Land Revenue," Najju intoned, holding off her next bite just enough to build an aura of suspense. "Ever."

Surrounded by curio shops and handicraft stalls, the café table was an island haven in the midst of chaos. Noise from the shops combined with social intercourse from tourists and passersby to isolate the group as effectively as soundproofing. The others were as eager to build on the excited foundation laid by Najju. An incredible invitation had been made to the heads of half a dozen major government offices some days ago, all having dealings with land and the mountains.

It was said the invitations were written in gold with borders of precious stones, and rumored that Tashi from the Department of Inland Revenue had actually seen one, although none of the others had. Each one sitting

3

at the table worked closely with their office ministries, so had been privy to at least some aspect of the meeting which had taken place the day before.

"How is the dal-bhat-tarkari today?" Prabidhi asked. The mixture of black lentil soup, rice and vegetable curry was a staple enjoyed by all.

"It is good, and you will enjoy it," offered Biscotti, signaling that another portion should be made available for their new arrival. His work for the Foreign Investment Board first brought the event to light, and he was quick to include his fellow conspirators in one of the most curious episodes any of them had encountered within the collective memory of the entire group.

Completing the assembly were Jambayang and Sagamatha from the Departments of Hospitality and Industries.

Tashi spoke up, denying the invitations were as glamorous as rumor would have them. "There were no stones, but let there be no mistake about one thing," he affirmed. "The invitation delivered to our office was in the form of a business card, and it was struck from solid gold, of this I am sure. I held it in my hand and was permitted to examine it closely. Most curious was the inscription on its face; a date, the word 'Luna,' time of ten-thirty p.m., and nothing more."

Silence enfolded the group as each in turn pondered the enormity of wealth that would allow one to present common calling cards made of gold. Nepal was a poor country, with a per capita income of about one hundred and seventy dollars per year.

"Acamba!" exclaimed Najju with a heavy sigh. "My family would eat the King's food for years from the proceeds of such a card." After a moment's reflection, her eyes grew wide with wonder as the enormity of her next thoughts caused her to stare off into the distance as she continued, "I could have a maid. I would command that water be brought to me!"

"Do not place your feet so close to Heaven, Najju," a smiling Sagamatha stated evenly. "The cards were not presented to us."

Najju's whimsical fantasy united with Sagamatha's grounded good nature to elicit chuckles from everyone. She went on to describe the strangers who had arrived so late at night to speak with the department heads. They were dressed in suits of color, somewhat akin to that worn by those who would climb the mountains, but not so bulky.

"And their heads were behind glass, although I could not determine why they would want to hide their faces from the world. I was asked to stay late and be available to serve refreshment, although they took none. I only saw a little from the table where I worked, but it was enough to see how they were dressed. What do you make of it all, Prabidhi?"

"They wanted to buy a mountain… Kangchenjunga, to be precise."

Comprehension was slow in coming, as each in turn struggled to fathom the meaning of Prabidhi's words.

"Forgive me, Prabidhi," said Jambayang. "I do not understand why anyone would want to do that. I do not understand *how* anyone can do that."

"Our Himalayan mountain range is considered to have the highest peaks located anywhere," Prabidhi answered. "Kangchenjunga is the third highest at eight thousand five hundred meters, or more than twenty-eight thousand feet. The summit does constant battle with high winds. Excessive rains, avalanche and mudslide dangers have claimed a number of international climbers in the past."

Tashi interjected impatiently, "Yes, yes, this we know, and as a result tourist trekking is limited to about five thousand meters," closing this thought with a dismissive wave of his hand. In a more speculative tone he added, "Because of that limitation, true adventurers prefer to focus on the more challenging higher peaks and leave the third highest to relative obscurity as far as climbing is concerned. Perhaps that is why they desire this particular mountain, although the remote Jannu north face possesses a sheer drop precipice; staggering in proportion."

Refocusing her thoughts, Prabidhi continued, "Obviously, neither our King nor government would allow foreign interests to purchase such enormous amounts of land. The strangers have therefore made an offer to lease the Jannu north face for an altitude and extreme environment research facility; an offer accompanied by an incredible sum for renewable lease options. Some aspects of the lease are strange, but can be accommodated without much difficulty."

She went on to explain that tourism was to be routed to other peaks, and the curious kept away. This made sense anyway, as death and injury on the mountain only served to draw embarrassing attention from the international community, taxing already strained local resources for search and rescue. Besides, there were other areas of the mountains just as appealing, so scarce tourist dollars could still be reaped by gently steering those with such interests to less dangerous, but still tantalizingly challenging venues. Sweetening the deal with assistance to local schools and medical facilities ensured the offer would be eagerly embraced and just as quickly approved.

The balance of their communal meal time was spent in silence, as each considered Prabidhi's words and the impact that such an arrangement and influx of foreign wealth would have on the lives of the everyday citizens of Nepal.

The common room had all the ambience of a hangman's scaffold. Inmates present there were close, crowded, and wore an air of fatalism as tangible as their orange jumpsuits. All four walls were painted cold battleship gray, with shadows being chased by scintillating rays of first light sunshine that pierced the room from open windows.

A spray of early morning air sending tiny dust motes dancing about would have seemed idyllic in another setting, but only succeeded in highlighting the stark reality of prison bars blocking the view.

Why they had been brought there was the primary topic on every tongue. Nothing more was known beyond the fact that each had been taken from their cell late at night, and told by their respective Wardens that they were being transferred. After two, or in some cases three days of travel, they had been placed in holding cells until this morning.

Even more curious was the absence of armed guards within the room. And even stranger was removal of the entire heavy chain set each had been wearing when brought in... and the guards had foregone the normal strip search routine!

One bewildered guest with a heavy French accent turned to his nearest neighbor and inquired, "Mon ami, what is to happen with us?"

"No idea whatsoever," returned his stoic bench mate, idly glancing around the room as if to assess the possibilities of being somewhere else. However, such speculation was quickly put to rest as the door opened. Four individuals walked silently to a small raised platform located at front center of the room.

"All right, listen up, roll call," said the first. "My name is Sergeant Wright and sing out when I call your name." After a quick check confirmed the proper head count, Wright continued, "You ten men have been handpicked to be here today." Indicating the men on his left, he said, "This is Police Commissioner Terrick and Federal Marshall O'Donnell. There are half a dozen heavily armed Federal guards in the hallway outside this room, and there's only one door in and out so don't get any ideas. You've got a special visitor here to talk to you today, so be polite."

With that, the three officials stepped off the platform and left the room, leaving one mystery standing there... an individual dressed in a dull gray protective suit of some kind.

"Good morning. My name is Jake." As he spoke, the door opened, admitting a guard pushing a refreshment cart. "Please help yourself to coffee, fruit and donuts as the cart is brought around."

A murmur of surprise swept the inmates at this unexpected turn of events, but none were slow to help themselves as the treats were brought within reach.

"Hey," spoke up one of the bolder fellows, in a slow and not too belligerent tone. "What's this all about? I'm rousted three days ago without so much as a by-your-leave. Here I am with these other guys, and I'm death row; no company now for over two years."

At this, other but somewhat more subdued voices began to echo similar sentiments.

Gesturing for silence and asking patience, Jake explained they had all been picked due to similar backgrounds and fates... granted terminal status, either death row or life sentences and had been gathered here from many different places. What separated them from others in the same circumstances were the specific reasons behind their sentences. Each had enjoyed a fruitful life with a future, and some had family and loved ones. None had a violent past or were prone to confrontation prior to the acts that separated them from society.

"You're stable, educated and highly skilled men who found themselves faced with impossible choices. That your particular circumstances led to the death of a violent perpetrator was unfortunate, but that tragedy has brought you together today. Of particular interest to us is your heavy engineering or similar backgrounds. I represent a business entity that wishes to remain anonymous. That entity has contributed heavily to enrichment of prisons as a whole through the Federal Prison Administration. In return, that Administration grants access to a select few specialized individuals on occasion to assist in certain, shall we say, *projects*."

"So, we are to be your esclaves de prison... your, how is it said, chain gang? This must be very good for you," spoke up Gautier with marked skepticism. "And exactly what have you sacrificed for our good names?"

"We donated five million dollars for each man in this room," responded Jake.

Gautier sat straight up in his chair as the silent attention of every eye in the room was instantly riveted on the speaker. The only sound was a slurp of coffee washing down one last sugary bit of frosted donut.

"You will be given an opportunity this morning to make a life changing decision. If you choose to accept, you will be granted full pardons. Those of you who still have families will be reunited, should they desire to accompany you on this adventure. Those of you who wish to journey alone will be given opportunities to mix socially with others so that you can start again.

"Know this from the onset. The decision you make today will place you in harm's way. You will work in an environment requiring a suit similar to mine, but only while you're on the job. Your new endeavors will require an initial six week stay at a facility we call 'Q,' short for 'Quarantine.' After that, you will journey to the site of your new home and jobs. The only concession we have been forced to make is to demonstrate that we have the ability to control you as a work force."

With that, Jake gestured, and two of the tallest human beings that anyone had ever seen walked into the room. Dressed in casual wear, they were obviously Asian in appearance and twins. Each one over seven feet in height!

"Allow me to introduce the brothers Zieng and Wiang, from the Chinese providence of Fu-chien." Jake's follow on comment that he had made a better offer than professional ball clubs drew snickers and chuckles around the room. "Each has attained the highest level of skill in self defense arts and will work with you daily during your stay at Q. There will be no need of arms or weapons of any kind."

"And would some manner of compensation be forthcoming in your offer?" asked a tentative Gautier, by now the unofficial group spokesman.

"That's an excellent question, and I'm glad you asked. We do not deal in currency, or monetary exchange of any kind. You will earn one day of barter credit for each full day's work. All medical and dental care is free, including commissary, housing, and transportation. As mentioned previously, you will be permitted free socialization with others of your choosing."

As a roaming gaze took in supporting glances and positive head nods from his fellows, a somewhat bolstered Gautier then spoke out, "Oui, yes, all very nice in the telling. And now instruct us what occurs when someone makes the screw up?"

"Our community... everyone in it," here Jake paused for effect, "has taken a vow of nonviolence, and you would be expected to follow suit. As a result, our policies apply to all equally. Incidents are to be dealt with on an individual basis, and could result in loss of privilege or provisional credit, depending on the infraction. I point out that since our beginning there've been no problems, no infractions; no incidents.

"There are no bars or cells. You will have the same rights as all others you meet in your new home. However, I do need to advise you of the necessity to renounce your citizenship in favor of your new benefactor. Once you leave this room, gentlemen, there can be no turning back. If you decide to reject this offer, you will be allowed to leave at this time, and will be returned to your place of origin. So I'm asking you to decide now. Those that stay will be given more details about your new assignment, but I can't go into that detail with anyone who doesn't want to sign on."

Jake allowed the inmates ten full minutes to discuss what had transpired so far. "All right, gentlemen, is there anyone who wants to leave?"

No one left their seat, and twenty eyes were still glued to Jake when he announced, "Welcome to Prexus."

Lloyd smiled from his seat at the table, fondly looking at the woman he had married fifty-eight years ago. They were celebrating their wedding anniversary with a quiet evening at home having tied the knot on their twentieth birthday, which coincidentally fell on the same date for both.

After visiting well-wishers all day, they had returned to a late dinner. He and Emma were everybody's favorite grandparents; gray headed, kind, and wonderful with children. He recalled that they were single children themselves, and suffered the curse of having to bury their parents over the years.

However, the two of them never felt alone; cherishing each day as a new life experience and seeing joy in companionship with others while relishing new found friendships.

"What an excellent meal, love," said Lloyd, as he hugged Emma and kissed her cheek. "You want to get a regular job here, little girl, just speak up. I'll put in a word with the boss and see if we can squeeze you in," saying this as he gently patted her right buttock.

"Stop, Lu," she protested weakly with a big smile and kissed him back. "How are your knees, honey?"

"Oh, fair to middling, not too much pain today. Doc said the arthritis medicine should start to work pretty good now."

Truth was that both of them were suffering the down side of growing old. Emma's stoop was more pronounced now, although he was bent somewhat more than she. His hands were at a point where it was difficult to pick things up, and driving had become a chore to avoid rather than the pleasure it used to be.

Air quality was getting worse, what with pollens and all, so he had hired a contractor to install special filter systems in their rooms to combat the irritation. Lloyd remembered when the two of them moved into an assisted living facility in Oklahoma, a five hundred acre ranch with up-scale multi-unit care home that provided for all their needs.

Lloyd had retired as a respected and highly successful engineer. Together with Emma's pension from the school district, they had more than ample to cover their expenses. He thought a moment about his local reputation for having quite a green thumb. Getting things to grow had never been a problem for him, and he especially liked working with orchids and roses, although any type of flower was appealing.

He had written several well-received books on the subject, and was sought after to speak at luncheons and gatherings of like-minded amateur horticulturists. He was glad that Emma was equally welcome to substitute at local schools, bringing a lifetime of teaching experience and love of children into each classroom.

That continuing opportunity kept the spark in her and she dearly loved working with children. They had made some sound investments together along the way and lived in comfort, denying themselves nothing during their retirement years.

"What did you make of that gold colored card, the one with the word Luna on it?

"I don't know, Lu. I put it on the dresser and haven't looked at it since," Emma replied. The doorbell caught her off guard and she glanced at Lloyd, neither one expecting anyone at this hour.

"It's late, Lu, should I answer the door?"

"Well, see who it is first before you unlock anything," he cautioned. Emma opened the door as far as the safety chain would allow, then turned to Lloyd and said, "Is it time for Halloween, Lu? I think we have a trick or treat guest."

Shuffling to the door, he removed the chain and pulled it open; startled into silence by the personage standing before him.

"Good evening, Mr. and Mrs. Boxe. I've traveled quite a distance to meet you, and I apologize for the hour. My name is Anoki, may I come in? I have some important information for you about an opportunity in the beautiful city of Selene."

Both stood in mute astonishment at the person who stood before them; hand out in greeting and wearing the most colorful getup either one of them had ever seen.

Present Day

Eleanor reflected on the history of the law firm of Ernst, Long & Stein, which occupied a top floor suite of offices in the Danville building, just outside Washington, D.C. in Brentwood, Maryland. Started by her greatgrandfather Howard Ernst in 1873, the firm had stood for one hundred and thirty years to become one of the premier houses of jurisprudence to be found anywhere.

The Old Man had spread out his eggs, ensuring the firm was capable of practicing law in a number of directions. She was confident in the fact that at a moment's notice, E, L & S could muster expertise in criminal or civil arenas with equal alacrity, as they maintained a stable of the brightest young legal minds to be found.

Some notoriety had been gained in the past with successful arguments before the Bench of the Supreme Court, and a number of highly publicized and quite lucrative class action settlements had provided solid financial stability. Being located at the heart of perceived governmental power strengthened a carefully nurtured image of bed rock representation.

Five generations removed from Old Howard, Eleanor Beatrice Ernst now stood at the pinnacle of career success, having shattered every glass ceiling that stood between her and the top chair of that venerable law firm. Referred to as 'Miss Bea' by everyone in the office, Eleanor was an egregia cum laude graduate of Harvard Law School. The forty-two year old Chief Executive Officer counted few intimate friends, and had no time for the male social gadflies that hovered around her as moths to light.

Having as her closest friend Jennifer Long, daughter of Carlton Long, ensured her turn at the helm would not be politically affected by the descendants of Randolph Stein. She intended to manage the firm with a level headed serious application of management skill that ran all the way back to the founder, confident that she had the right combination of initiative and chutzpah to accomplish that task.

The company's fortunes were at a turning point at the moment, and this was the primary point of discussion at a board meeting held the previous week. While it was true that a rising tide moved all ships, the reverse was just as applicable. The stock market roller coaster had taken its toll and now it seemed that Davy Jones might be looking for legal assistance at the bottom of the financial ocean's depths.

If something didn't turn up soon, the bean counters in the firm's accounting section would start the inevitable rounds of cost cutting, probably starting with some of Eleanor's pet projects.

She was a believer in youth and sponsored a high number of internships from some of the best University law schools available. Several youth organizations and adult care facilities had benefited as well, and Eleanor intended that such sponsorship should continue. After all, Old Howard himself had started the projects, adamant that something should always be given back to the community that built his house. He looked down at her from his place on the wall as if to admonish her to stand strong and not be bullied by such distractions.

Her height was exquisitely proportionate and housed in an immaculate blue and white business ensemble. The pendant she wore had been handed down from Old Howard himself, having been a gift for his wife, the first 'Miss Bea.' It was an elegant match to her bright green eyes. Parted, lustrous brunette hair had been given another touch up at Ginivino's on the second floor, and she had taken extra pains to ensure her makeup demonstrated the right professional finishing touches.

Presentation notwithstanding, Miss Bea had inherited from Old Howard the same mental toughness that had set him apart from his peers before the turn of the century. She was as capable of holding her own in a corporate boardroom brawl, going toe to toe with some hard headed jackass, as she was of being feminine when the time called for it.

"Ooh wee! Hot damn, Bea, look at you!" called out Randolph, passing her office on his way home. After another quick up and down appraisal, he continued, "Sizzling date tonight, huh? Give yourself a raise, or did you finally talk some stingy old bureaucrat into coughing up for a really serious dinner?"

Sparkling laughter acknowledged the offhanded compliment as she replied, "Neither. But remind me later this week and I'll do exactly that. This is something quite different. Do you remember that odd business card we received last week?"

"You mean the one that looked like gold?"

"Yes. I had it checked at Cartier's, and it is gold." Handing him the card, she continued as he examined it more closely. "Solid twenty-four karat gold, to be exact. Mr. Florence remarked that it was a very fine type, something he hasn't seen before. He offered to buy it. It was engraved with today's date, 'Luna,' and ten-thirty p.m.

"I intend to hang around and meet the owner. Anyone who sends that kind of greeting card may have something of importance to discuss, although they keep peculiar hours. The envelope didn't have a return address per se, just Luna as well," she said.

"Makes you wonder if they have that kind of money, what they need us for?

"Well," responded Eleanor, "you might want to consider that the price of Swiss gold is about twelve hundred and eighty-nine dollars per ounce at the moment. Mr. Florence weighed that card at three full ounces, making it worth over thirty-eight hundred dollars. But I bet the novelty value would shoot the price much higher than that."

As he returned the card, Randolph spoke with apprehension, "You know Eleanor, there's a lot of weirdos out there. You sure about this? Just about everyone else has left for the day. I could have security come up to the office and be close by."

"Don't worry about it. No one comes through the front door without being recorded on a dozen cameras. The Danville has fourteen security guards on duty every night, and five of them are in the front lobby. I'll be all right."

"OK," said Randolph, turning and walking toward the door, "Just give me a call if anything happens; I'll come back in."

Eleanor's association with Randolph was close and she liked him a great deal. Their working relationship was open, honest, and always focused on what was best for the business. Comforted by his concern, she listened to his footsteps as they receded down the hallway, then sat down at her desk. Picking up the first brief from a stack left there by the office assistant, she thumbed the pages.

Might as well catch up on some reading while I wait for Goldilocks. It's going to be a long four hours.

At about ten-twenty p.m., Eleanor placed the third brief on her desk, moistening her lips with a drink of bottled water. Standing up to stretch, she glanced out the window and took note of the traffic bustle; everyday people going about their affairs, heading home after yet another late day at the office. Setting the bottle down drew her attention to small vibration rings dancing on the liquid. A noticeable raise in the level of background noise caught her full attention.

Didn't know jets from National flew this close so late at night.

As the sound level increased, she noted it was more of a 'whoosh' than the typical roar of a jet engine, but wasn't overly concerned at the moment. The helo pad was located on the opposite side of the Danville building roof so the sound shouldn't distract too much from her reading. But fifteen minutes later she wasn't able to ignore the phone's sonic animation.

"Eleanor Ernst, may I help you?" she asked politely.

"Miss Bea, this is Hamilton, aviation security. There are two parties up here claiming they've got an appointment with you. They landed something that looks like a B-2 bomber on the helipad, and are dressed like divers. Options are the dog, the police, or you. Do you want to see them?"

"Do they speak English?" she asked.

"Yes, they do."

Hamilton's description of the visitors caused Eleanor to pause for a moment and reconsider Randolph's offer. D.C. and the surrounding areas had their share of people from numerous cultures, ethnicities, and backgrounds, so being dressed differently wouldn't usually be cause for much concern. She mulled over the options presented by Hamilton. He was an original fixture at the Danville and held the position of Chief Guard for helo operations. She trusted his judgment.

Damn. Bad enough dealing with one eccentric, now there's two.

She was aware that any number of famous, read 'rich,' personalities tended to purchase off-the-wall vehicles with armored limousines, military styled Hummers, and high dollar helicopters heading the list. Asking herself if these two had bought a jump jet wasn't as far-fetched as it sounded, given the outlandish expenditures of some celebrities she could think of.

Recalling the gold card, she replied "Escort them into the office foyer, Hamilton, and stay a moment until they've been properly introduced."

"Check," he replied. "We'll be there shortly," and broke the connection.

Eleanor made her way to the foyer, a huge room more properly suited for entertaining large groups than making intimate introductions. When Hamilton ushered his two charges into the area, Eleanor visibly stiffened, startled to see what accompanied him.

Standing to one side of Hamilton were two individuals dressed in striking environmental suits.

These two must spend their nights partying in some strange places.

Mentally running through whether she had read anything recently about movies being filmed in the city or the recent arrival of a circus, she looked them over. Both were short, one being somewhat over five and a half feet, and the other even shorter, maybe five feet exactly. The suit's material seemed to suggest an athletic and muscular build, but gender couldn't be determined.

While the interior of the helmets was not lighted, and the faces of both were somewhat hidden by the helmet visors, she could make out reflections from some sort of lightly colored instrumentation on the left side of each face. Focusing, she ran through the obvious. No weapons in sight. One head with acceptable looking features, two arms, two legs, two hands with a total of ten digits showing.

The suits themselves were not the bulky elephantine items usually seen on astronauts, but were instead quite elegant. The material appeared to be supple, and reinforced areas seemed to be incorporated directly into the fabric. The exteriors were brightly colored, being predominantly light sky blue with accents of purple and deep cobalt blue.

"Miss Eleanor Beatrice Ernst?" the taller one asked in a warm baritone voice, extending his arm toward her and offering his hand. "My name is Jake, my associate is Donah; we have an appointment."

While she couldn't immediately place the accent, she put her hand into the gloved one and with a firm grip stated "Yes, I'm Eleanor Ernst, Chief Executive Officer of Ernst, Long and Stein. Let's go into my office where we can speak privately.

Trusting her intuition, she spoke to Hamilton, "Thank you. I'll take it from here."

Turning, she led the duo through the foyer to her office.

The two visitors settled themselves as best they could on the office settee, sitting upright and angling their bodies to face her.

Once she was seated, Eleanor inquired, "How can I be of assistance, gentlemen?"

"Actually," the shorter one said in heavily accented English, "I'm female. My name is Donah, and I assist Jake in the day to day administration of Luna."

"My apologies. It's difficult to determine gender given the uniforms you're wearing," said Eleanor. "What sort of business is Luna? I noticed it was the only item listed on your unusual business card," adding, "Why use gold in that manner?"

Smiling, Jake explained, "I'm sure that before we leave, we'll have generated more questions than answers. We needed a medium that would attract attention at the proper levels… the card does that for us. I ask that you be patient and hear us out. We have something of significance to share with you and I'm certain you will be quite impressed with what we have to say."

"Thank you, Jake. Is that your full name?" asked Eleanor. "The office staff refer to me as Miss Bea after the Founder's wife. But please call me Eleanor if you feel comfortable with that."

"Thank you as well, Eleanor. Yes, Jake only," he said.

"I'm not familiar with the equipment you have on. What's its purpose, if you don't mind my asking?"

"Not at all. They're environmental, or E-suits; our own design. They protect us from your environment and biological problems here; are individually powered and self contained."

He went on to explain the suits could quite easily withstand much harsher environments and incorporated a number of advancements. A wearer could live comfortably for up to a week if needed, and extremely low bulk protein and other supplements were provided as well as air-water recycling and waste storage. The suit fabric itself was a marvel in engineering, capable of resisting certain radiation types for a surprising period of time while capable of sealing small punctures.

Donah joined in by pointing out the absence of any awkward backpack type assemblies; the form fitting support unit carried was quite small in comparison, yet capable of infinitely more functionality.

She added, "The colors are a concession to our young people, who much prefer more variety in their environment. By comparison, your Apollo type suits weighted about one hundred eighty pounds. Ours weigh less than one forth of that."

"I noticed some reflections on your faces," said Eleanor. "What's that from?"

Donah replied, "The face plates have heads-up displays, or HUDs, built into them for monitoring the suit's functions as well as other instruments for communication, navigation, and so on."

"I note you said 'your environment and biological problems.' Where exactly do you call home?"

"Well, straight to the point, I see," responded Jake. "We exist on what you refer to as the moon, and have been doing so for the past five years."

There was a moment of awkward silence while Eleanor considered that statement. She narrowed her options down to calling nine-one-one and having the medicals remove these nut cases, or continue to hear them out to see just how far their act would go. Glancing back at the Old Man on the wall, she wondered how many oddballs had rolled into his office over the years, figuring he would have put on his best game face and heard them out. She decided to do the same and tough it out for a few minutes more; leaning back into her chair and folding her hands in her lap.

Taking a deep breath while looking at Donah, she smiled. "Ooh kaay, I heard your aircraft but didn't see it… and I did have your card checked out. So. Please continue and I'll reserve judgment."

"Thank you," said Donah, "why don't we just have Jake start at the beginning?"

"We are, for the most part, originally from Earth. My son Alahn is an extremely gifted individual when it comes to computers and other sciences. He and his rather unique friends have the rare ability to see aspects of a problem from angles you and I wouldn't normally consider, and then find unique solutions to those problems.

"Approximately fifteen years ago, at the age of eleven, he was involved in a parallel study of hydrogen extrapolation for what you refer to as hydrogen fuel cells."

"Eleven!" exclaimed Eleanor, raising her eyebrows.

"That's correct," said Jake. "Something of a genius. He completed his doctorate soon after. The primary research was bogged down in the usual commercial system approach to such projects. Milk it out for as far as it would go. Stretch it to support the company for the next few decades. He, I, and others had grown weary of the 'company first' attitude of all such research. Alahn made a mind boggling discovery that was as far beyond current fuel cell research as man is above the amoebae."

Jake pointed out that fuel cells operate similar to a battery, but won't run down or need recharging. They produce electricity and heat as long as fuel is provided, which in this case is hydrogen. Two electrodes are placed in an electrolyte; a liquid solution that conducts electricity. Oxygen is passed over one electrode and hydrogen over the other, producing electricity, water, and heat.

"You must, of course, supply your own oxygen and hydrogen. Your current technology permits you to electrolyze water to produce hydrogen and oxygen. That process gives you about forty-eight cubic feet of hydrogen and twenty-four cubic feet of oxygen from one liter of water... extremely inefficient and wasteful by our standard."

He went on to explain that Alahn had discovered a phased tri-catalytic process that could extract hydrogen directly from water or any source of H2O, completely bypassing such cumbersome procedures. It was able to do this on an efficiency scale exceeding any known parameter; a virtually inexhaustible source of clean burning fuel whose only byproduct was, interestingly enough, plain water vapor.

"That's an incredible claim, Jake, how does it work?" asked Eleanor.

"We and the Council have made the decision to withhold that information, and we refer to it as the Alahn System, or 'AlSys', for short," he said.

Eleanor thought she could see where they might be going, and interposed with, "My sense of this is that you could be rich beyond your wildest dreams by patenting your discovery. Is that why you've come here? And please, what is this Council you refer to?"

Interjecting somewhat passionately, Donah made it clear they did not count their riches as Eleanor did. AlSys wasn't the end of Alahn's achievements. He and his team developed the ability to produce oxygen just as efficiently. While similar in technology to his original hydrogen process, the phased tri-catalyst permitted transfer of oxygen ions only across its structure. These discoveries gave them an unlimited fuel source for propulsion and power generation, as well as breathable oxygen.

Once AlSys was perfected in these three areas, the decision was made to destroy all research related materials, reducing the designs to one small but safely guarded data chip. At the heart of their philosophies was the desire to be separate, not above... to provide an environment free from violence and struggle encountered daily here. To move an elite mankind into an arena that has been their destiny from the beginning; exploration of space, and do it in a manner that demonstrates Homo sapiens is more than the animal he presents himself to be on planet Earth.

AlSys gave them the ability to put their philosophies into action.

"And I can assure you that none of the continuing violence that you experience daily exists on Luna," she ended.

After a moment of reflection on Donah's words, Eleanor placed her hands on her desk and leaned forward.

"Well, that was refreshing. Apparently, you've made a number of significant discoveries that could benefit mankind as a whole. Yet you withhold them in order to better your small group of, dare I use your own word, elitists? Hypocrite isn't a very impressive point of view from where I sit."

"Eleanor, please hear us out. We govern ourselves somewhat uniquely, our Council being composed of twelve members. My son and I were voted to head that Council. Six members are represented by youth; the other six members are composed of adults. A majority vote of both sides of the Council can overrule the leaders. We met a number of times to discuss and reflect on your reaction to us," explained Jake.

He continued by offering that as a group, they were aware their philosophy would be seen as isolationist, yet decided to accept that risk. They were resolute in their determination that to share such science with Earth would be to provide a recipe for serving up greater and more horrific portions of the same old soup. They had no faith that taking such a course of action at this time would result in anything but global infighting by various governments, vying to outdo each other with bigger sticks conveniently provided by them.

"We sought out an industrialist with the means to help us get started; someone who would embrace the same ideals we had and possessed the manufacturing capability to make it happen. Kelly Akamatsu, sole owner of Akamatsu Industrial Manufacturing in Sendai, Japan, was that person. A remarkable Chinese woman and world class businessperson who quickly grasped the potential of our discoveries and produced our first craft, complete except for the engines and computer systems.

"We built those ourselves and mated them in secret. You should be aware that our approach to every avenue of our venture is to accomplish tasks using the most simplistic process or means possible. We are present in every institution of higher learning on your planet, and actively recruit the brightest young minds we can find. Our fellow adventurers have made significant discoveries in severe habitat accommodation far more advanced than anything your own space program will posses for quite some time. It goes without saying we have made wonderful discoveries in other areas as well."

Eleanor stared at the two of them with a blank expression on her face, her sense of unease gathering momentum with each revelation. Still unsure of where any of this was going, and equally unsure as to how her firm fit into their scheme, she took a deep breath.

Controlling her voice, she stated, "Let me play devil's advocate and point out something to the two of you. If I understand you correctly, and lead a little into some of the statements you've made, I think I can say with certainty that there are governments and powerful individuals here who would have you arrested and charged for sedition, rebellion, kidnapping, brainwashing, and dare I add unwilling servitude or outright slavery?"

Pausing a moment to let that soak in, she added, "That would be their short list. They would take from you by force what you seek to have through secrecy, and convert it to their own use *for the good of the people*," she emphasized.

"You, and all your followers, would be separated and thrown into the far reaches of the most remote prisons they can find—never to see the light of day or tell your stories to another. That's assuming you survive any nasty interrogation surprises they may spring on you, claiming you resisted in some way."

"She understands our concerns so completely," Donah said wryly, "Perhaps the Council was right after all in selecting her for our needs." Sensing Eleanor's growing apprehension, she added, "We took the liberty of obtaining your medical dossier. We know your height, weight, and metabolism factors. Please don't be angry with us. I assure you the only person who looked at your file was our own Doctor Agave."

Surprised, Eleanor asked, "What could you possibly need that sort of information for?"

Jake clarified Donah's remarks, adding, "We anticipated your skepticism and apprehensions. We have designed an E-suit for you. There's more to tell, but sometimes the best way to convince someone is to simply show them. If you have vacation coming, would it be possible to take some time off? I'm sure we could then satisfy your curiosity within a week or less. We would like to start by inviting you to take a ride with us around the neighborhood."

"Why would I need a week to see a neighborhood?" she asked.

Donah offered, "There's a city named Cordial that we believe will do more to answer your questions than simply sitting here. Please come with us. You can stay in contact with your fellow workers and family at all times while you're away. We can provide phone and video conferencing if needed. I assure you, the trip will be well worth your time, and could be potentially quite rewarding for your firm."

"You must see us with different eyes, Eleanor," said Jake. "We are accomplishing now what present day mankind can't. You owe it to yourself and your firm to accept our offer and come with us."

After a moment of silent reflection and another glance at the Old Man, followed with a quiet sigh, she answered, "Being a product of our times I try to keep an open mind, but this is a real stretch." Coming to a decision, she leaned forward to pick up the office phone and dial her friend, Jennifer Long.

"Jenny? Hi, it's Bea. Something's come up. I'm with the clients I told you about. Yes, there's two, and I know how late it is. Listen, I'm going to take a week off for a business trip. Could you take the reins? I'll email Randolph and the department heads. Great, thanks. Where? Oh, just a short trip in the neighborhood. Looks like an opportunity for the company, and I'll need to look into it personally. I'll call you with an update and keep you all in the loop. Thanks again for filling in. Take care."

As she hung up the receiver, Eleanor said, "Well, fat's in the fire now, as they say. I'll need to stop at the apartment and pick up an overnight bag and a few extra things. Will that be a problem?"

"That won't be necessary," replied Donah. "We took the liberty of arranging everything. You only need to come with us."

The night wind was light and humid, and as she accompanied the two to the building's roof, she could see their aircraft sitting on the helo pad. It certainly wasn't a helicopter, a jump jet, or anything else she was familiar with. She wasn't sure if 'air' craft was an appropriate term either.

As they angled toward it from the front, it appeared deep black and flattened; slopping down in front and sitting on the flat of its belly. There was a tail of sorts on an extension from the rear. She could make out nozzle openings on the body and nose, but couldn't see any windows or other openings.

The nose and body were somewhat aerodynamically shaped, with gentle curves. There were no proper wings or other surfaces that one would normally associate with something that flies through the air. She watched as Jake placed his face near the ship, and slipped his right hand into an opening that she was sure hadn't been there a moment ago.

Thinking he had addressed her in some way, she said, "Pardon me, I didn't make that out."

"Sorry, I was responding to the ship. Come on in and I'll explain," he replied.

A panel moved silently up into the top of the ship. As all three proceeded inside, Jake turned to the left and made his way to one of two forward seats… that faced nothing other than a dark, gently sloping wall. Donah guided Eleanor through a narrow aisle way to a small room at the rear. She noticed two rows of seats as they passed, capable of seating twelve. Assuming two pilots, the ship could carry fourteen people.

Donah asked Eleanor to remove her clothing and placed it in a webbed harness, then assisted her in putting on the E-suit. Properly fitting two waste recovery systems was awkwardly invasive at first. Once she understood the functions, Eleanor was able to accommodate the anatomically designed catheters while Donah explained the helmet instrumentation. However, she stopped prior to actually fitting the helmet.

"Eleanor, I'm going to ask that you take this medication I have for you. It's a powerful combination of newly developed antibiotics, cultivated by Doctor Agave and his teams. We provide a less powerful version that's administered over a period of weeks while at our quarantine facility, but we don't have the luxury of time on our side at the moment." With no outward reason to distrust either one, Eleanor took the container and swallowed the liquid, then completed donning the suit helmet.

"Press your cheek on the left pad, and you can drink from the tube that will be provided. Press it a second time to have it retracted. Press back on the right pad to dispense a high protein low bulk paste that you may find surprisingly tasty. You'll note some basic instruments in front of your left eye. You can adjust the brightness in the same manner by pressing up on the right pad.

"To communicate, simply start talking. The voice unit will automatically transmit for you. The visor is light sensitive, and will adjust itself for varying light intensity conditions. The support unit will keep your internal temperature at seventy-four degrees, but you can ask the suit to adjust the temperature to suit your own comfort zone. Our seats are shaped to accommodate the support unit so you should be comfortable. If you feel the need to go, the suit will automatically store and recycle the waste products. It doesn't take long to acclimate."

Donah led Eleanor back into the main cabin, and had her take a seat in the first row, centered between the two pilot seats. "Now that you are isolated in your own suit, we will remove ours," said Donah, as she and Jake made their way aft.

Returning, Eleanor noted they were now dressed in soft, tan, one-piece unisex type coveralls. Both had short hair, conservatively styled. Donah's complexion was of a type that thrived without makeup; possessing expressive brown eyes, ash blonde hair with matching eyebrows and full lips.

Jake was equally striking, a mature man who had aged well. Complimented by bright blue eyes, his short gray hair lent quiet dignity to a healthy, mature image. She noted that he carried himself with a military-like bearing as he made his way to one of the pilot compartments.

"Our roles are somewhat reversed now," commented Jake. "We get to relax while you acclimate to your suit." As he said this, he placed his hand on a dimly glowing area on the left arm of his seat.

"Welcome, Jake," spoke a male voice. "And to you as well, Donah," it continued. "Good evening, Miss Ernst. Are you comfortable?"

As she was sure no one else had gotten into the ship with them, Eleanor blurted out in surprise, "Who is that?"

A smiling Jake offered, "Our ships possess artificial intelligence, or AI, with processors that function in the high teraflop per second speed realm. That's complimented by an extraordinary memory capacity approaching the same figures. Our AI teams have structured eight distinct personality types, and pilots can select the one they prefer, or one that's a combination of types. While amazingly lifelike, you won't find androids or robots from any TV series here.

"The ship itself is called a Transport Utility Grounder, or TUG for short. For some reason, one of the children took a liking to this one and named it 'Burt.' The name stuck. So say hello to Burt, Eleanor."

Looking around for something to address herself to, she spoke openly, "Hello, Burt, and yes, I'm quite comfortable, thank you. Please call me Eleanor; I'm not in the office anymore. How did you know who I am?"

"Your complete profile is accessible, and the mission parameters were entered prior to our journey here. I watched you approach through my external viewer and recognized you immediately," said Burt.

Jake pointed out the ship's AI used facial pattern and voice recognition algorithms, as well as retina scan and finger-palm biometrics to identify users. That's what she had seen him doing when they reached the ship; going through one of the recognition protocols. Additionally, it weighs occupants when they sit, and runs an electro-stimulus test when hands are placed on the armrests. Failure of a number of these protocols will result in the ship rejecting the applicant, so to speak. There were other safeguards as well, that Jake would go into later as time permitted.

"Suffice it to say it would be extremely difficult for an unauthorized individual to take one of our ships. Burt, initiate start sequence," he ordered. In response, padded inserts in the sides of Eleanor's seat moved forward, folding over her waist and chest area to embrace her firmly, yet left her lower arms and hands free.

She was startled as the entire front end of the ship disappeared! Everything forward and to the sides of Jake and Donah was gone, replaced with a three dimensional, one hundred eighty degree panorama of the top of the Danville building. This included the top and bottom of the seating area.

They appeared to be sitting in thin air!

As she turned her head, she could clearly see Hamilton and a number of other guards in the operations office on the roof, the helo pad lights, the city profile, and traffic on the streets twenty-five floors below... and a too infrequent beautiful night, cloudless with a bright half moon.

"This is absolutely stunning!" said Eleanor. "Fantastic wouldn't be strong enough to describe this. It seems I can reach out and touch anything I can see."

"Burt, please explain to Eleanor," requested a smiling Donah... remembering her first experience with such incredible technology.

Burt confirmed integrity of the ship has not been breached. Eleanor was viewing a high definition, or HD aspect of the forward exterior of the ship. While Earth based companies were still arguing intellectual rights, systems teams of Luna refined and expanded this technology years ago.

Some older style TV receivers used approximately two to three hundred scanning lines per second to display a picture. Earth's current HD technology, still in its infancy, was presenting up to one thousand eighty scanning lines. The display Eleanor was observing functioned at a scanning rate of three thousand two hundred and forty, or three times the ability of Earth systems.

Multicasting technology provided a three dimensional aspect and significantly sharp color definition being demonstrated.

"You're right. It can be thrilling to see this at first. You'll get used to it soon enough," added Jake. "We'll be leaving now."

As he said this, a curved instrument display magically appeared in front of both pilot seats, about waist high. It was tilted toward them, and

Donah pointed to several of the instruments. As she did so, Eleanor could hear sounds of activity within the ship, followed immediately by vibration.

"The control panels are holographic presentations and react to proximity. I'm not actually touching anything on the panel. As my finger approaches the item I've selected, it's registered by Burt, and the system is activated when my finger reaches an approach threshold."

Donah's right hand was resting on an indentation on the arm of her chair. As she moved her hand forward, the ship's vibrations increased, and they hovered about ten feet above the helo pad.

"We use vectored thrust, similar to your jump jet technology," she explained. "Our AIs provide balance by constantly monitoring and correcting for center of gravity. In atmosphere, we ride on a cushion of expanding gas, so use of actual wings and other such aerodynamic appendages is unnecessary. Altitude, pitch and yaw are controlled by exhaust ports located on the exterior of the TUG."

"Why aren't we making more noise than we are?" asked Eleanor.

Jake explained that today's methods of reducing noise in gas turbine engines generally consisted of muffler and baffle solutions. There were also attempts to mix incoming air with exhaust gas to slow down velocity, but none of those performed well. While their engines were not gas turbine, they did create hot gas. Use of a swirling technique created a phase inverted wave that interfered with the acoustic noise generated by their ship's engines.

"I think you would agree that it's remarkably effective," added Donah. "Burt, give us sixteen thousand positive Z and move away from the city. Enable Cordial protocol as soon as we're out of traffic," she requested.

"Thank you, Donah, Course enabled. I'll advise you when we have arrived," replied Burt.

Eleanor was thrilled to see the city below as its size shrunk with ever-increasing altitude. Three dimensional large screen theatre was one thing —but to seemingly be thrust into air with never before experienced movement and acceleration... all the while surrounded by such incredible visual stimulation was exhilarating! Her heartbeat increased with too-rare inspiration capturing her senses.

Regaining control after several slow, deep breaths, she wondered aloud,

"Why use electronics when it seems a window of some sort would be simpler. What would one do if this system died?"

"It's true that a clear viewing device would be easier, but that solution would introduce structural weakness where the window was installed," explained Jake. "Our HD system eliminates that problem. There are four backup systems, and in the extremely unlikely event that a full systems failure occurred, a fifth emergency system provides the command pilot with an isolated self-powered visor viewer that would allow for a safe descent and landing."

As they passed the Capital during their ship's climb, she could see aircraft surrounding the area. "Won't the airplanes at National be surprised to see us?" she asked.

"They won't see at all," replied Donah. "The TUG's exterior is designed to absorb light, similar to a solar cell, and stores the energy. Radar won't register us either. Burt can generate counter radar pulses that make the generating radar believe that nothing is there. Someone in an airplane or at a radar console would have to be actively looking for us, and we wouldn't show long enough for them to get any accurate information; we'd resemble background clutter if anything."

The TUG rotated to a forty-five degree angle and began accelerating rapidly. Eleanor was pushed back into her seat, and felt her breathing become labored. "Why are we speeding up like this? Where is Cordial anyway, in Wyoming?" she asked.

"I'm afraid not," said Donah. "Cordial is our major city on Luna."

"We're going to the moon?" she blurted in surprise. "Wait, damn it, I'm not an astronaut, is this safe? I thought I was wearing this suit for your protection."

"Yes, you're perfectly safe. The invitation was to see our neighborhood in Cordial. We have a lot to show you and I'm sure you'll enjoy meeting our friends," said Donah. "As I explained previously, we won't be stopping at Q, which is our normal procedure. Please don't worry."

Donah explained that Eleanor was experiencing the maximum amount of acceleration that would be felt during the trip. "Your shuttle's more like a delivery truck, and requires a significant fuel load and large engines to achieve low Earth orbit. It can only carry a limited amount of fuel to accomplish that, so it has to get there in the shortest time possible using higher acceleration as a result.

"We continue to make our own fuel as long as we're in atmosphere so don't have to travel as fast if we don't want to. Our trip will take about ten hours, and we'll use constant acceleration equal to one gravity until we reach our travel speed of about twenty-five thousand miles per hour."

"You still haven't answered my question as to why you call it 'Luna'," stated Eleanor.

Jake offered, "There are about forty-nine different languages being spoken on Earth at the moment, each with its own linguistic variations for describing the moon. It can be confusing. Actually, our children came up with it. With today's web-speak and shortcuts for everything, we found them referring to it as 'Luna', and it stuck. Keeps things simple, wouldn't you agree? It's been a long day for all of us. Why don't you try to get some rest? This is the dullest part of the trip anyway, and Burt will let us know if anything happens."

Darren Souser flinched inwardly at stiff reproach from his supervisor. "Damn it, Souser, you screwed the pooch on this one." Assigned to the new Home Land Defense Security Detail at the United Nations headquarters in New York, he was thinking he should have stayed with the FBI.

Christ, idiotic bunch of pinko fag bleeding hearts is all he saw coming in from Forty Second Street every day anyway. Hardly a decent white among the bunch. Probably get their jollies popping each other's back sides or whacking off when nobody's looking.

Although he had to admit he might allow one or two of the better looking third country hotties to get close to him, he much preferred the company of his own kind of full blooded all American white women.

"All I asked you to do was look into this report about a misplaced stereo in the Botswana delegate area, and you turn that simple job into an international incident!" snapped Chief Investigator Robert Heinkle. "Didn't you read the protocol handbook? I instructed Admin to ensure you received the orientation and protocol guides. These people get touchy when unmarried men are alone with their wives!"

"Look, Chief, I wrote it all up," Souser said in his own defense. "I identified myself and the reason for being there. What did they expect me to do, use x-ray vision to find their goddamn radio?"

Ignoring Souser's retort, Chief Investigator Heinkle fired right back, "You're off to a bad start here, Souser. You go back and re-read all that material you were given. Especially look at diplomacy, tact, and the section on how to approach nationals who have indigenous religious beliefs. After that, you'll write a formal apology and route it through here for delivery. Another screw up like this, and you'll be walking their dogs."

Souser left the Chief's office wanting to kick a few dogs of his own.

Son of a bitch. You'da thought I grabbed the ugly bitch's ass, way they were acting.

Returning to his cubicle, he sat down at his computer and prepared to write. As everyone else was engaged elsewhere, he reached into his inside jacket pocket and took a hit on the small ornate flask he kept there for just such emergencies.

Nothing like a little southern comfort to ease the day, thought Darren. Or the night.

Or any freaking time I feel like it, like right now.

Having started drinking at age twelve, he had a lifetime worth of experience in acting sober when he wasn't. His body wasn't showing the effects of alcohol poisoning at age forty-seven, but his habits were starting to catch up to him. While he might have lost the hard edge he used to maintain, it hadn't gone completely south either.

His pitted, rugged face, featureless eyes, and short, brown, thinning hair didn't put him on the top ten most attractive list; so he frequented the sleazier side of town for the excitement it offered, finding comfort where he could with an occasional hooker. He'd worked himself through enough school to get on the police force in his home town, and from there to a minor position at the Federal level with the FBI. Creation of the Home Land Security Cabinet resulted in so many rats jumping to the new ship that he slipped through the cracks in landing his new government job.

Navy Commander Benjamin Robinson sat six stories above the main deck of the nuclear powered aircraft carrier USS John C. Stennis. He surveyed his kingdom from within Primary Flight Control, bolstered by the comfort of a black lambskin covered captain's chair.

Not bad for forty-five. I sit higher than the old man with a better view to boot.

As Air Officer, or Air Boss, he owned the main deck, air operations, and five miles of sky around the ship. More from old habit than any operational necessity, he turned his head ninety degrees to the right for an exterior update, noting catapults one and two, numbered from starboard to port. Three and four were on the angle deck, which was used for aircraft recovery as well as launch.

From his lofty perch in Pri-Fly, he allowed his gaze to sweep the deck idly as new members of the arresting gear crew practiced seldom used aircraft training operations; in this instance setting the barricade used to snare aircraft in emergency situations. As no flight operations were scheduled, the deck was otherwise empty and shined with new paint and markings.

Focusing back inside his bit of heaven, he checked off the wind speed, direction and cross wind component on the instruments to his upper right, continuing to the gray and black phone handsets by his left knee. He finished the cross check with a glance at the large pilot information monitor above his left shoulder and two smaller video monitors below that.

Presently steaming about one hundred fifty miles off the San Diego coast on a short sea trial for refit equipment, the Stennis had been asked to serve as a convenient control element and emergency field for a joint test mission of a new air force fighter. Not requiring the services of his assistant Mini-Boss, or any of the other hands who would normally be present, Ben reveled in the luxury of having Pri-Fly all to himself for once.

Gave up golf on my free time for this. Must be slipping in my old age.

Bored, he contacted the carrier air traffic control center on the intership phone, hearing the familiar voice of his friend, Commander Charles Bosk, responding, "CAT-C, Bosk."

"Boski, any word from that Air Force jock we're supposed to be working with today?"

"Not yet. Nothing on the scopes except civilian traffic. I spoke with Thompson in the combat direction center a few minutes ago. He says CDC hasn't heard anything either. I've made contact with long range radar at San Nicolas and San Clemente. Someone will holler when he gets here."

"Well, hope this doesn't take long. I can still make tee time tomorrow morning if we can wrap this up today. Know anything about the jock?"

"Nope. Probably one of those airdale, nose-to-the-grindstone tight asses. Wait one, I've got an itinerary here some place; let's see if there's a name... yeah, it's E. S. Lewis, United States Air Force. Major type, one each."

"E. S. Lewis? That wouldn't be Edwina Lewis, would it? I know her! Met her at the joint training symposium at Edwards Air Force Base last year. Great attitude, lots of fun. Impressed the hell out of me with her knowledge of the new fighter. I'm glad she was picked for the test... she's one competent piece of business."

"Can't say, Ben, there's just the initials here; sounds like it'll be an interesting day."

"Well, I hope not too interesting. We'll maintain a ready deck until the pilot checks out of our area."

"The F22 Raptor air supremacy fighter is the most technologically advanced aircraft ever designed and built, with two Pratt & Whitney thunder sticks… the brain power of two, that's right cousins, players, and geeks of all ages count 'em and cryyyyy, TWO Cray supercomputers!" yelled the pilot with excited abandonment.

"You heard me right, I didn't stutter, there are three heads in this cockpit! And hold on, peanut gallery, Momma's little deuce coupe super-cruiser just punched the barrier at six hundred forty knots indicated and still accelerating—on cruise power and no burner… hot damn!

"There's only two of these stovepipes in existence, and SWEET POTATO, I'M FLYING ONE. WHAAAAAHOOOOOOO!" screamed a highly exuberant Air Force Major Edwina 'Showcase' Lewis to no one in particular, and to the whole world in general, yanking the F22 into a tight barrel roll with a pure adrenalin rush of exhilaration.

She noted the slight decrease in speed to push through the sound barrier which at sea level would be about six hundred sixty-two knots, understanding that the speed of sound varies with altitude and tempera-ture. At an altitude of just over forty-four thousand feet above the Pacific Ocean, Major Lewis was preparing to put the F22 prototype through its paces as part of the test program laid out by the combined team efforts of Messieurs Pratt & Whitney, Boeing and Lockheed Martin.

The F22 raptor was slated to take the place of outdated Air Force air-craft, becoming the new generation air dominance fighter. Its two Pratt & Whitney F119 PW 100 engines were capable of producing more thrust than any other fighter engine in existence. But where it came into its own was the fact that those same two engines could propel the F22 past the sound barrier without resorting to full military, or afterburner power. This ability was coined 'supercruise,' and resulted in significant fuel savings; giving it more time on station to stay in the fight.

The aircraft was technically capable of Mach 2 speed, and she intended to squeeze every drop of power out of those engines to see just how much of that plus fifteen hundred mile per hour target she could hit. There were also some weapons tests to be conducted, and she was eager to put the plane through those paces as well.

Recalling how her Dad used to brag about how cheap things were in his day, she thought, *this hot rod is the cheapest date on the block. Matter of fact, I'm gonna nickname it 'Stingy.' The tax payers are gonna love me!*

The Air Force had taken delivery of the two prototypes, and she had been selected from the available pool of test pilots to fly this one. After confirming her position, she keyed the mic and transmitted, "Stennis Control, this is Air Force Raptor one seven, over."

"Raptor one seven, Stennis Control... hey Showcase, how's it handling? This is Ben Robinson, long time, huh?"

"Ben, you old war dog! Last I heard you flunked Captain's Mast and had been scheduled for a keel haul. Good to be working with you!"

"Same here. We're looking forward to assisting your test program. Commander Bosk and the air operations team are all watching the show. When you screw up, try not to scratch the new paint on the main deck when we catch the pieces, the old man likes the pretty colors."

"Plow water, dolphin boy. You and your Poseidon pals ain't seen nothing yet! This is the greatest ride anyone could be on short of the space shuttle itself!" exclaimed Edwina.

"OK, but no hard feelings for us trying to put you through the ringer. We've got two Chukars coming your way, programmed to give you a real challenge," said Ben.

The BQM-74E 'Chukar' was a subsonic drone that could mimic antiship cruise missiles or enemy fighters. The Navy used the BQM-74E to provide their pilots a realistic, highly maneuverable threat simulation, in addition to testing new weapons. Today's program was a joint Air Force, Navy effort and had been blessed by the powers for the training opportunities it offered both services.

"You'll have to throttle back a bit, though," Ben stated. "Our baby's top speed is only a little over five hundred knots, topping out at about forty thousand feet. You'd have to come down to our level to play anyway, if that's where the action was in a real show. They should be in your area in about ten minutes, and we've factored in a max altitude of fifteen thousand feet."

Using vectors provided by the Stennis, Major Lewis reconfigured her fighter's course heading, speed, and altitude to intercept the two drones. She knew the F22's extremely powerful computers were teamed to advanced technology that permitted her to focus on the target while the computers worried about situational awareness; where the plane was in relation to the ground, the space it traveled through, and the distance to the target.

"Well, we'll loaf along in idle till I see 'em, then all I have to do is hunt and shoot. Let the plane fly itself," she said to herself. "We'll have a surprise or two for the squids before this day is over."

Edwina was soon to learn just how prophetic those words would turn out to be.

Wrapped up in smugness of the technological wonder she piloted, she was momentarily startled by the wake turbulence of something that flashed by... especially since her computer driven acquisition systems were indicating normal operation but failed to register the intruder with any type of warning. She had been reviewing the fighter's LCD multi-functional displays, and glanced up in time to see the back end of another craft moving away at a high rate of speed directly in front of her.

Brought to full alert, she blurted aloud, "Damn, don't tell me I've got bugs in this thing first day out!" She punched the self-diagnosis circuit to test the radars, and was puzzled to see the panel return a fully operational status. The fighter's electronic systems were capable of virtually one hundred percent accuracy in identifying a threat's aircraft type; otherwise the target is displayed as unknown. Her curiosity fired, she reviewed the secondary six point two five inch tactical display, mentally clicking off identifiers... friendlies were green circles, threats were red triangles, and unknowns were supposed to show as yellow squares. The displays were not showing any of those symbols.

Wonder what that's all about, she thought as she keyed the microphone.

"Aircraft approximately two hundred miles west of San Diego, flight level two one zero, heading one hundred ten degrees identify yourself."

With no response, she attempted twice more to contact the intruder, with no better results.

I'm not buying he doesn't know I'm talking to him... just who else is flying out here almost due east at twenty-one thousand feet?

She reasoned that if the intruder was here, it knew she would be here also, and that meant it had to be monitoring communications. She was torn between flying the mission test parameters or moving up to get a closer look at the damned thing.

"Stennis control, Raptor one seven, over."

"Raptor one seven, Stennis, go ahead," replied Ben.

"Commander Robinson, I know you said ten mics for time en route on those drones, so what just waxed my butt up here, over?"

Noting the tone of formality that had entered the Major's voice, Ben tightened up his banter to the straight and narrow. "Raptor one seven, Stennis. I've got our BQMs on the scope right now, Major Lewis. They're still about nine mics from your position according to our fix and their present air speed. That's confirmed with the GPS identifiers and your own IFF and transponder signals… and I've got you at Angels two one altitude. Whatever just went by is not from us. Did you get a visual?" asked Ben.

Major Lewis chewed that information over for a moment thinking, Global Positioning Satellites, Interrogative Friend or Foe ID protocols and transponder squawk have us all fixed on the map.

In like manner to the B2 Stealth bomber, she was aware that the Raptor was built with advanced composites and materials that effectively absorbed radar. Having weapons that were stored internally guaranteed her fighter's radar picture was minuscule next to most existing aircraft.

"Everyone can see me because I want to be seen, but I can't see you… what the hell are you made of, and why aren't you talking?" she wondered out loud to herself. She keyed the microphone again.

"Stennis, no joy on the visual, and I've got a bogey that's not registering on my systems. Can you see it there?" she asked.

"Raptor one seven, Stennis. Negative. All we see is you, Major Lewis. CDC's been in contact with the long range systems at San Nicolas and San Clemente islands. They're looking hard, but don't see anything other than you, either," Ben stated.

Damn! Someone's jerkin me around with a sneaky-pete to screw me over on test day.

Assigned to Edwards Air Force Base in the Mojave Desert, she contacted operations… wanting to hear from Air Force Ops and the F22 Program Manager himself.

It was a short conversation.

They did not send any covert mission to interfere with the planned tests today, and all F117 stealth aircraft were accounted for. They assured her that Vandenberg Air Force Base operations were reporting the same.

She was instructed to continue her mission, but attempt to get a better visual on the bogey if possible. Stennis was to stand by to scramble two flights based on her identification, in the event some discouragement was needed to ward off uninvited observers from some other government.

Acknowledging the transmission, she glanced again at her acquisition systems to scout for the bogey, and froze in mid glance. The image of a huge, dark-scaled reptile registered in her mind as the head of some insane monstrosity slowly became visible directly below her.

As if her feet were locked in a nightmare scene of being caught in the headlights of an oncoming locomotive, Edwina shivered; moaning involuntarily as the head of this impossible beast moved just forward of the nose of her aircraft and stopped there. She felt an electric sensation course up and down her legs as her buttocks involuntarily squeezed in response.

Suppressing another shutter of revulsion as her imagination gave way to a serpent crawling from between her legs, she violently checked her emotions and realized the bogey was keeping station with her Raptor. It was doing so at a distance that could be measured in inches below her aircraft!

Reacting instinctively, her right hand moved the side controller to climb away, but she was astounded to see the bogey move in precise formation with her. There was no perceptual lag in the movement either. It moved in exact synchronization, maintaining the same position and orientation.

"Stennis, Edwards, the bogey's right under me!" she yelled, simultaneously transmitting on both frequencies. "The damn thing's glued itself to my fighter!"

Edwards responded by directing her to switch all communication to Base Ops, while informing the Stennis to provide two flights of F-18 fighters to intercept the Raptor/bogey combination. Edwards went on further, advising her to maneuver in order to view and identify the bogey.

Stennis responded, but noted the additional time that would be required to scramble the fighters from Marine Corp Air Station Miramar as no planes were on board today.

Edwina moved her aircraft through common flight parameters in an effort to get a look at the whole bogey—being rewarded for her troubles by observing the thing precisely match each in turn. Rolls, turns, and both an inside and outside loop accomplished nothing to discourage her shadow, and its orientation to her Raptor never changed.

All she could see from her vantage point in the Raptor's cockpit was the top of the serpent's head and what appeared to be the beginnings of large intakes behind and to both sides of that appendage. From what could be discerned to the sides and rear, it was measurably wider than her aircraft.

Ok, let's see what you got, she thought, pushing the throttles to full military.

The Raptor's two dimensional thrust-vectoring engine nozzles and integrated flight propulsion controls responded instantly in carrying out her command, accelerating to its absolute rated power and speed settings. At over one thousand five hundred twenty-five miles per hour indicated and still accelerating, Edwina pulled the aircraft into an incredibly tight port side turn, bearing down on her abdominal muscles, flexing her legs, and grunting with the strain of maintaining consciousness under the crushing weight of gravity.

Putting her faith in the new Libelle liquid filled, full body anti-G suit she wore, Edwina trusted the Swiss company that developed it to know what they were doing. She was aware the Libelle used self-contained fluid that ran through expandable tubes, rather than compressed air as conventional G-suits did. Gravitational forces acting on the liquid produced counter pressure proportional to the force encountered, squeezing the suit fabric to constrict blood flow.

She had tested the suit in an Air Force centrifuge to over twelve Gs without ill effect, easily eclipsing the standard six to nine G test parameter. As the G-meter moved through twelve Gs her vision grayed, but the bogey maintaining its position directly beneath and in front of her caused her to push even harder. Even as the Combat Edge positive pressure breathing system helped her overcome the crushing weight bearing down on her lungs, every fiber of her body screamed with the effort.

With sight reduced to tunnel vision and at the point of losing consciousness, she admitted defeat and released both herself and the aircraft from further ordeal. Retarding the throttles coming out of the turn, she sucked in large amounts of oxygen to compensate for the deprivation and incredible strain her body had been subjected to; her heart pounding loudly in her ears from the effort. Fighting to regain breathing control, Edwina felt a moment of savage victory as she observed the bogey move away from her and take up a new position to starboard.

Suddenly, it darted toward her, reversing itself only at the point of seeming to collide with the Raptor!

Damn! What the hell are you doing now; her thoughts screamed in surprise!

She turned the Raptor to port and accelerated away from the bogey, observing as it rushed toward her that it seemed angled to pass beneath her aircraft.

With no understanding of its intentions, she was astonished as it hit her from below!

"**Edwards**, MAYDAY! The bogey just hit me; MIDAIR! The son of a bitch is trying to knock me out of the air!"

"Raptor one seven, this is Edwards Control, Brigadier General Abhram. You are armed and will immediately take all measures to protect yourself and your aircraft. Splash the bastard, Major Lewis. We'll have the Navy boys pick up the pieces for identification later."

On that order Edwina enabled all her weapons controls. The bogey had now repositioned itself approximately three hundred yards directly in front of her. She selected the M61A2 gun which had a six thousand round per minute gun firing rate at all flight loading conditions. A hydraulically controlled gun door, located in the wing root area, activated in milliseconds and opened ninety degrees. The gun's rate of fire, about one hundred rounds per second, gave her the shot density that would enable a kill when fired in one-second bursts. Loaded with armor piercing rounds, the cannon was for extremely short range use... within two thousand feet in an air-to-air encounter.

Although the acquisition radars refused to see anything in front of her, Edwina lined the aircraft up directly in line with the bogey's butt end. From this angle she could see that it was somewhat larger than her aircraft; big, black, and ugly. She gave up the idea of structure study in favor of weapons procedure. Standing on the trigger, she fired the full complement of four hundred and eighty rounds which left the gun in less than five seconds. To her consternation, the bogey appeared to lift its skirts and jink away at a speed measured in an eye blink!

"Dance your way outta this, bojangles." Edwina selected her Advanced Medium Range Air to Air, AMRAAM missile. The AMRAAM was a high-supersonic, day/night/all weather Beyond Visual Range (BVR), fire-and-forget air-to-air missile. While it relies on the Raptor's radar to track targets, it can do its own hunting, containing an independent radar system of its own. The AMRAAM contained a forty-pound high explosive warhead.

She carried two such missiles for testing today. The weapons bay door opened, and the mechanism carried the missiles outside the plane. After firing, the ejection system retracted into the weapons bay, allowing the bay door to close and preserve the Raptor's stealthiness.

Edwina watched fascinated as the AMRAAM's streaked on line directly to the bogey, then felt her mouth open in amazement as the bogey outraced the missiles! She could see the missiles' solid fuel motors run out of fuel, still attempting to acquire the bogey as they fell away. Even more amazing was the sight of the bogey turning toward the missiles, and observing pieces seeming to remove themselves and fall away separately, as if by their own design!

Disappearing behind her, Edwina turned to visually track the thing... hearing a voice in her headset as if someone where speaking through a tunnel! "Major Lewis, please slow your aircraft and initiate your ejection protocols."

"Hey—HEY, who in hell do you think you're talking to? Come back around here where I can get another shot at you, joker!" she yelled in frustration, maneuvering the Raptor left and right and she turned her head as far as she could in a vain attempt to locate the bogey.

That same voice now said, "Major Lewis, please observe your port wing tip."

As Edwina turned her head left to look at the wing, she saw in horror a portion of the wing's end suddenly disappear; sliced cleanly away by something she couldn't see! The voice now directed her to look starboard, and to her chagrin, the same damage was done to the right wing. The Raptor now encountered some vibration and turbulence due to the new drag induced from the wounds inflicted by the bogey.

The voice repeated, "Major Lewis, please slow your aircraft and initiate your ejection protocols, I have removed ten centimeters from your wings and stabilizers, and will continue to do so until you comply, or are no longer able to maintain stable flight."

The vibration and turbulence were now difficult to control, and master alarms were sounding on the systems panels. Edwina had enough presence of mind to understand how limited her options were. Before she could transmit her situation to Edwards' air ops, the Raptor began oscillating and pitching wildly.

She made a backhanded slap at the throttles while grabbing the center mounted ejection control located between her legs. The ACES II Advanced Concept Ejection Seat's electronic seat and aircraft sequencing system began timing the ejection events. An active limb restraint system simultaneously repositioned her arms and feet to eliminate flail that might have resulted in serious injuries during the ejection.

The three hundred and sixty-pound monolithic polycarbonate canopy with frame weighed slightly more on one side than the other, slicing almost ninety degrees to the right when jettisoned due to the designed weight differential. As she cleared the Raptor, The ACES II systems analog three-mode seat sequencer automatically sensed the seat speed and altitude, selecting the Mode Three high altitude settings for optimum seat performance. A mortar-deployed, fast-acting seat stabilization drogue parachute system located behind her head actuated to increase the seat's stability.

All of these events happened in seconds. Edwina was stunned by the most forceful kick in the butt she had ever experienced, and then slammed hard from an unbelievably absurd wind force encountered after exiting the aircraft. That double whammy buffeted her to the point of unconsciousness. The seat's automatic systems deployed her parachute once speed was reduced to safe parameters. As her senses slowly came back on line, she looked up to see the chute functioning properly, then realized that her seat had separated itself and was nowhere to be seen.

She was pleased to have survived the bailout with everything intact. The sound of air being provided by the auxiliary oxygen system was almost drowned out by the wild beating of her heart. As she became more fully alert she could see the bogey, and watched in dull comprehension as it slowly turned to come directly towards her!

With an adrenalin rush, Edwina recalled stories about pilots in prior wars being shot in their parachute harnesses by the enemy. Grabbing her service pistol, she resolved to defend herself in any way possible against that thing.

She could at least see it now and observed that its body resembled more a squid without tentacles than anything else. Its vertically elongated cockpit had no canopy as such to reveal exactly where the pilot was located. There was an appendage that ran back above and beyond the exhaust mechanism, with at least some semblance of a vertical and horizontal stabilizer, although it was remarkably small in relation to the size of the craft itself.

It was the deepest black that she had ever seen... so dark that purple and violet iridescence washed over it from reflected sunlight, and she couldn't see any control surfaces on the rudimentary wings. As it drew closer she could see the exhaust balancing the craft vertically and there appeared to be stabilizing and steering jets located along the body proper.

Edwina was surprised to see it match her descending speed exactly, then turn and present its starboard side. As it moved closer a small platform extended itself from the lower part of the bogey's head, accompanied by a vertical handhold extending in synchronization.

Drawing to within feet of her that same voice said, "Major Lewis, please step aboard."

Edwina did so now, grabbing the support and placing both feet on the platform. The bogey slowed to a stationary hover. As gravity caught up to her weight a wave of nausea coursed through her body with the rapidity of an electric charge. Gasping as her knees buckled slightly, she involuntarily tightened her grip on the handrail, not quite realizing the extent of exertion she had subjected her body to.

The bogey's stop resulted in Edwina's parachute collapsing over and behind her. Figuring this was it, she released the chute; pulling the shroud lines free and digging out from under the folding canopy before it yanked her from perilous footing thousands of feet above the Pacific Ocean. Free of the chute, she steadied herself in preparation for taking the pilot out as soon as she could figure how to open the door, assuming the damned thing had one.

As if in anticipation of her thoughts, the voice stated, "You won't need the weapon or your helmet gear, please let them go," emphasizing the request by retracting the platform about six inches.

Still somewhat dazed and now feeling like an idiot for releasing the chute, Edwina lifted her right arm up to shoulder level and opened her hand, allowing the handgun to fall. The helmet and breathing mask equipment fell away to join the ejection seat and parachute. An undetected panel suddenly opened vertically as an invitation to entry. Stepping into the darkened cockpit, the panel closed silently as she settled into the only open seat available. As expected from her initial exterior inspection, there were no windows, canopies, or any other device for seeing outside.

Turning to her left, she saw a pale humanoid figure sitting in a spherical aquarium! There appeared to be a rounded transparent partition separating the two of them. It was so incredibly clear that she ran a gloved hand over its surface to ensure it was solid. The framework securing it looked seamless; made of a substance appearing too lightweight for the job. The manner of attachment between the tank and craft flowed more like artwork than typical engineering, and she was able to determine it offered three hundred sixty degree structural integrity... looking as if elegant fingers of two alien hands had enfolded a crystal clear marble within its palms.

A harness apparatus similar to that which secured the humanoid now adjusted itself automatically, securing her firmly. Her body sank into the seat, forming its own personal indentation. Looking as closely as possible, she could see that the pilot was dressed in a tight fitting body stocking of some sort. There appeared to be tubes that somewhat resembled the high-G plumbing on her own flight suit. It was wearing a visor and mask more insectasoid than human, and she could vaguely make out tubing running towards its anal and genital areas. The helmet it wore was locked within a securing frame or device, allowing rotational movement as its head swiveled to the right to look at her. She noted similar framework along its arms and legs.

Uncertain as to origin of what she was encountering, her body stiffened. Worried apprehension now broadcast from her face as she blurted, "My God, what are you?"

"I assure you I'm as human as you are. My name is Alahn, Major Lewis. Please hold your questions for a moment, we haven't much time."

His fingers danced over illuminated light panels in close proximity to both hands, and the bogey jumped forward... causing Edwina to grab the seat's armrests in surprise and astonishment as the entire front of the craft suddenly disappeared!

Alahn briefly highlighted the HD and multicasting technology that permitted such visibility while drawing closer to Edwina's F-22 Raptor. She observed that it was still oscillating; the on-board systems having managed to capture some stability and continue flying. It looked sadly wounded without its canopy in place, lolling around in wide circular motions as if looking for a place to die.

Addressing himself to someone unseen, Alahn said "Horus, dissect the craft in fifty centimeter increments please," and his request was acknowledged by an unseen baritone voice.

Edwina felt a spreading sensation of numbness and dismay as large pieces of the Raptor mysteriously removed themselves in rapid succession, followed in turn by the fuel starved engines which plunged to the ocean surface far below.

"Where's the other pilot? How did you do that?" asked Edwina in rapid succession.

Alahn explained that the craft, referred to as a Starflyer, was controlled by an extremely powerful artificial intelligence which he had named after the Egyptian falcon god Horus. As the acceleration picked up, its angle of climb increased noticeably.

"When your Navy friends get here, there'll be nothing to see. The few items that will be salvaged from the water will only deepen the mystery, and at least for a while longer it'll simply be another swamp-gas fairy tale. When they find your helmet and parachute it will be assumed that you died after landing in the water and that your body was lost."

Edwina realized that only a few minutes had passed since the entire encounter had begun, such being the nature of high tech combat. "I don't get it," she said. "Why are you doing this? How is it that you seem to know so much about me? And while you're at it, how about explaining a little about yourself and this Starflyer of yours. Are you Russian or Chinese?"

Alahn smiled at the barrage of questions and then gave Edwina a run down on the holographic controls and AlSys system which powered the Starflyer; advising her he held no allegiance to any government here. He explained that a wealth of information was available to the pubic and it was of no consequence to look up what they needed to identity one of the top fighter pilots in the world with a certain set of characteristics. She had no immediate family, was strongly dedicated to the principles of peace and non-violent resolution, and willing to place herself in harm's way to ensure the safety of others.

"By the way," said Alahn. "I was very impressed with your ability to withstand so much gravitational force back there. Horus advised me you pulled almost eleven gravities in the course of your hard turn. He also told me the aircraft's rated to about nine gravities positive… even with an engineered safety margin you took quite a risk pushing it that hard."

"Well, a personal best," she replied, secretly pleased and smug in the knowledge that it was better than any other pilot in anybody's fighter program that she was aware of. Wrapped in the certainty of her accomplishment, she inquired, "How much can you do in this thing?"

"Eighty-one-G's," answered Alahn. "So far. And we've only started to scratch the surface." He turned his head to see Edwina looking straight at him with her mouth gaping wide open.

Composing herself, she responded, "There's nothing in my experience to understand how you can to that. How is that even possible?" she asked, eyes now wide with puzzled astonishment.

"While we can't repeal the laws of inertia, we can alter their effects on us to some extent. I'm sitting in a hermetically sealed environment containing an optically pure, high viscosity liquid fluorocarbon compound which assists in canceling out accelerative forces through counterbalancing pressure."

Alahn pointed out that his seat responded to changes in gravitational acceleration and would re-orient itself automatically to prevent blood pooling that causes unconsciousness. The articulated helmet harness controlled amount of travel for his head, and the same control was exerted by the other appendage frames she could see; preventing anything from breaking due to high-G maneuvering.

"The gas mixture I breathe is highly oxygenated. There is a tube entering my nose which contains a pressure sensor with three redundant backups terminating in my lungs. Under high-G situations, gas is introduced under a pressure system similar to yours, but without the need of an external containment vest. External sensors can interpret a change in gravity pressure, and working with the internal sensors, reduce the gas force in sufficient time to prevent any over-pressure situation.

"My vocal chords still vibrate, and a special throat microphone was developed to pick up those vibrations. Horus enhances the result so that you can understand my speech. The visor also contains two modified ear plugs that allow me to hear you. While we can't eliminate inertia's effects completely, the liquid immersion protocol slows them down significantly, allowing me to endure a much higher rate of accelerative gravity."

Alahn went on to explain that Dr. Wilbur R. Franks, a Canadian scientist who invented anti-g suits, experimented with mice. He built tiny anti-g suits using condoms filled with water, and was regularly able to achieve astonishing two hundred and forty-G runs with no harm to the mice. This research was renewed in developing the Libelle suit that he noted she was wearing. That same scientist also invented the centrifuge that administered her G-tests.

"I have to admit, you're remarkably well informed," she replied.

"Using your own test figure of nine as a factor against two hundred and forty gravities, you can easily calculate that twenty-seven-G's would be the equivalent of one-G to me. Therefore, at eighty-one-G's my body only feels three; about the same as an advanced roller coaster ride," he concluded.

"And let me try to put Horus's point of view into perspective concerning your aircraft's weapons. His electronic brain functions at trillions of calculations per second. He actively scanned your ship thousands of times per second, permitting him to calculate and adjust his position in relation to yours at a boringly slow rate for him. At his pace of processing data, each of your gun barrels seemed to require forever to move into firing position. As each round came into scan at the end of the barrel, he calculated speed and trajectory.

"He 'thinks' at the speed of light. Three highly refined laser devices, one on top and two on the sides of the Starflyer, provide Horus a pretty effective slice and dice capability. They're on articulated mounts, and can function in a three hundred sixty degree radius. He could simply have vaporized each round as it fired, or holed your canon so it wouldn't operate. We allowed you to fire as a demonstration of his capabilities."

Alahn then removed his visor. Edwina was startled to see that his eyes had been replaced with black circular disks, married to the visor with a network of small fibers. He explained that the disks were molded to fit over his eyes, and were composed of the same materials as the viewer that enabled her to see outside of the Starflyer, yet were connected to a vastly more complicated array of sensors. While she was treated to essentially a one hundred eighty degree panorama, his view was limitless; seeming to be pure thought hanging alone in space with no solidity around him.

"It takes some getting used to, I assure you," he said, "And you will be given the opportunity, if you want it. I've never personally flown an aircraft larger than a single engine two-seater, and have no training or skill in offensive fighters. Yet with Horus's assistance, your fighter was easily overcome. Someone with your skills could move our research forward into areas we have yet to achieve. As long as you're dead and seem to have some time on your hands, would you join me for dinner at our facility? It's called Quarantine or Q for short. We have an offer to discuss with you."

"**How** are we doing on arrival times for our guest?" Abigail asked as she stretched back in her seat, mouth opened for a yawn with arms spread wide. Monitoring AI identification protocols at Q was monotonous work, especially when you're young and would rather be playing wall tag in the Great Hall on Luna. The next supply shuttle wasn't due for several hours.

Glancing at the systems displays over her shoulder, Singe replied, "Fine. Alahn should arrive shortly. Waiting in low orbit for the approach window probably wasn't too much of a hassle for him, and I'll bet he enjoyed the time showing the sights to his fighter pilot."

Singe was fond of Abigail, rather like a favorite child. Although younger than he by almost fifty years, he enjoyed their times together. The intellectual discussions alone were stimulating, and joining in during physical activity time on Luna was always a treat. He was impressed when she decided to join the Council, and made it a point to ensure he attended the meetings.

The mountain and surrounding areas were uninhabited. Wind turbulence and outside temperatures were within expected parameters... deadly to anyone standing outside without protection at fifty degrees below zero Fahrenheit. At two fifteen a.m., accidental observation of approaching craft would be nonexistent. At over twenty-eight thousand feet, there would be little to see from the valley far below, even with a powerful telescope. The installation was sealed and pressurized.

The off-duty medical staff and personnel had already turned in for the night, leaving Abigail and Singe in charge of monitoring automated security systems, a mind numbing exercise even when something was actually going on. As everyone on Luna shared the monitoring duties equally, the burden wasn't overwhelming. It was becoming even less so as the population grew.

After completing her review of the installation security monitors, she got up and walked over to the main exterior view port. Composed of pressure-sealed quartz almost six inches thick, it rested behind an armored exterior shutter system camouflaged from the outside to resemble the mountain's topography; as was the entire installation. No sensation of the maelstrom occurring outside was transmitted to the sterility of Q's interior environment.

Crossing her arms, she calmly surveyed the exterior, impressed with the thunderous wind energy, bitter cold, and lack of breathable atmosphere. There was just enough moonlight for her to see the tops of lesser peaks protruding through silvery white cloud layers at lower altitudes, like fairyland castles reaching for the stars.

"Majestic, isn't it? Looking out and down truly makes me feel like I'm at the top of the world. I love Luna and everything it stands for Singe. But there are children who have been born there now who will have no knowledge or firsthand experience with the magnificence of Earth's natural beauty in full fury. They'll be so adjusted to low gravity that they'll never want to come here."

"Perhaps," he replied, strolling over to stand next to her. "But they'll have you and others like you who'll be there to teach them. There'll also be adventurers among them who will make the effort necessary to adjust to higher gravity situations and explore for themselves... here and elsewhere in the future. I wouldn't despair for the citizens of Luna just yet."

"It's incredible to think of what Jake, Alahn, and the engineering teams have accomplished, and in so short a time. This installation is a miracle of ingenuity and dedicated hard work. The teams had to use two TUGs working in tandem to lift some of the heavier hangar components into place. I heard there's a big event coming up. Do you know anything about it, Singe?

"Not really. I know that Jake and Donah left in one of the TUGs to pick someone up. I'm sure we'll hear all about it at the right time," he replied.

At that moment the station AI announced an incoming flight, identified as a Starflyer craft carrying Alahn and one passenger. Abigail and Singe returned to the station's system displays. She initiated Q's automated landing procedure, while Singe alerted the on-duty teams to prepare to receive a visitor. A section of the mountain face retracted into the station while simultaneously extending a landing platform. The Starflyer maneuvered expertly, hovering a moment then touching lightly onto the platform which quickly retracted into the station.

"What a ride! Sub-orbital weightlessness and one hell of a dynamite approach and landing," Edwina exclaimed excitedly. "I have to admit you're pretty good on the controls."

"I wish I could take the credit, but the AI does all the work much quicker and better than any human could do," responded Alahn nonchalantly. "Next comes the tricky part. I get pumped out while you'll be escorted by staff to a secure area after this bay is quickly re-pressurized... only takes seconds. I'll meet you there in a few minutes. I'm really looking forward to that dinner I promised." At that, the panel on Edwina's side opened. An older gentleman dressed in medical whites approached.

"Major Lewis, I'm Doctor Agave, Head of the Q medical department and staff, welcome aboard," he stated as he reached up to assist her in stepping out of the Starflyer. "Please come with me."

As Edwina followed, she noticed the Starflyer was in a room, or hangar, large enough to house a number of craft. There were organized items on pallets arranged around the periphery, and small vehicles recognizable as forklifts were parked adjacent to the pallets. It was pleasantly warm and extremely clean, with just a hint of ozone in the refreshingly brisk air she was breathing. She was impressed with the engineering effort it must have taken to build such a facility into the top of a mountain.

Stopping first at the infirmary, she was given a quick checkup by Dr. Agave and a female assistant, and didn't express any surprise that they seemed to have all of her medical information at hand. Once completed, her footsteps echoed from the walls as she moved through a number of corridors and was led into a small dining room.

"Alahn will be along in a few moments. Please make yourself comfortable. The duty staff has prepared a meal I'm sure you will enjoy, and

Alahn will brief you fully while the two of you enjoy dinner," he stated as he left.

She noted the room was sectioned by a glass window which partitioned the small dining table at its center, made to accommodate two guests. Taking a seat, she found the chair quite comfortable and saw that a dinner setting was placed at the end of both sides of the table. During the course of their flight to Q, Alahn had explained much of the history of Luna to Edwina. It was an incredible achievement for a private group to accomplish without government funding and she was as equally impressed with Q as well.

As promised, an individual opened the door on the opposite side of the window and entered the room. Edwina was pleasantly surprised to see that Alahn was in fact a very attractive human being. His tall muscular frame was topped with sandy blonde hair, and even through the glass she could see that his hazel eyes accompanied a ready smile and boyishly good looks. She didn't overlook his broad and well-defined shoulders, either.

"Sorry for the delay," he said. "The Starflyer's onboard systems maintain the environmental liquid at an acceptable temperature and drain the enclosure in seconds. Releasing harnesses and removing the personal systems takes more time, although that's reduced when assistants are available. It's still somewhat uncomfortable until you're completely dry and settled into loose clothing. It takes getting used to," he stated as he sat down.

Staff personnel brought dinner in to both of them, lighting candles on each side of the partition while reducing the ambient lighting. Edwina suddenly realized how hungry she was as she gazed at a fresh, crisp dinner salad. Filet mignon, baked potato and red wine completed the setting.

"I'm sure it does. Why are we separated like this?" she asked, taking her first bite of the meal and savoring an explosion of rich flavor bursting in her mouth. She suddenly realized how famished she was after the events of the day.

Alahn explained to Edwina that Q existed as a transition place for transfer to Luna, and noted that she had not appeared to be very surprised over the idea of colonists on the moon.

"Well, we've already been there. Not much of a leap to figure that in all this time someone else would have made the trip, although the reason why isn't readily apparent. Doesn't look like there's much to see there."

The corners of Alahn's mouth turned up in an enigmatic grin as he explained that Doctor Enrique Agave was a renowned South American biologist and infectious disease specialist, in addition to being a fine surgeon. Like all such scientists, he and those he worked with were hampered in their research by the constant battles for funding, facilities, and equipment. Q put an end to that battle. Doctor Agave and his teams had carte blanche to anything needed for their efforts.

They lived in a pure research environment without limitation, and had made discoveries in antibiotic application that promised to eliminate virtually all common infectious disease. An outcome of their research was inroads toward eliminating AIDS and cancer, although that was restricted for the time being to tightly controlled environments such as Q and Luna. A result of their research was a six-week program of environmental isolation and antibiotic drug application that removed all common infectious disease from one's body.

Included in the program was transition to E-suits and indoctrination to Luna's unique history and requirements. As Edwina hadn't entered the program yet, she would require isolation until Doctor Agave's teams certified her as medically acceptable. At that point, she would be free to travel there.

Lifting his glass for a sip of wine, Alahn asked, "How's your meal? I asked the staff for a quality wine, and I believe this is about a five year old cabernet sauvignon."

"It's excellent, Alahn. I haven't tasted steak this good in a very long time."

"Then you're going to be surprised to learn you aren't tasting it now. That's actually a synthetic, as is the butter on your potato. The steak is more mushroom than anything else. No fat or cholesterol. We've come a long way since the first days and can now provide one hundred percent of all our own nourishment from our lab and hydroponics processes. We still import a number of items, such as the wine, fruit and vegetables; but hope to be producing our own soon."

"This has been a day full of surprises for me," Edwina answered, slowly shaking her head as she sampled her own glass of wine. "This is wonderful. But research and facilities such as you have described, including where we're sitting at the moment, cost a great deal of money. Who's paying for all of this?"

"Please be patient with us. I promise that once you get to Luna, all questions will be answered to your satisfaction. My dad feels that guests will have a better understanding when they can actually see and touch the heart of our operation."

The balance of dinner was concluded with a general description of Q, its systems, personnel, and capabilities. The main course was then followed by vanilla bean ice cream topped with fresh raspberries and a splash of raspberry Chambord.

"The dessert is one of my father's favorites... he considers it his culinary gift to humanity."

"You must be very proud of your father. He's a great man to have accomplished all of this."

"Actually, he would argue that with you. My father is Jake, the founder of Luna. He's directly responsible for everything that has come to pass, including this facility, our vehicles; the colony.

"The first settlement was there over five years ago, and got off to a slow start until the engineering teams came up to speed... then everything really took off! He's dedicated to non-violence and doesn't feel there's anything special about him in particular. Frankly, you would be hard pressed to pick him out in a small crowd, he's that nondescript. If I were tasked to point out a specific talent in my father, it would be his ability to recognize genius in others. He and the original Council members have surrounded themselves with it. They seek out the best untainted minds with unlimited potential.

"You won't believe how young the people are who continuously push the envelope on our computer sciences, for example. They make Earth hackers look like amateurs playing with an abacus. If it's powered by electricity, they can access it. You're going to see advances that won't be seen on Earth for another 50 years or more. You will be privy to discoveries that are staggering in proportion. All of which brings me to the reason that you are here, Edwina."

Leaning forward in fascinated anticipation, she focused her full attention on Alahn.

"Our core philosophies deal with non-violence. We're aware that an increased level of exploration is contemplated by Earth's nations, and we have to face the eventuality that they may not all share our views. Frankly, we're sure quite a number of them will not be happy with the fact that we're there, and have been for some time. They may be... jealous... of some of the things we have discovered.

"Our Council and citizens agree that self-defense issues must be addressed. The question becomes one that given our philosophy, how do you defend yourself without harming that which seeks to harm you? The Starflyer you rode in is one approach. By the way, it's a prototype. We only have the one at the moment. It's actually a pure space vehicle that can incidentally move through atmosphere as well."

"Your Starflyer is one impressive piece of business. Whose idea was that fighter, anyway?" she asked.

"We prefer to think of it as a non-violent defensive solution, rather than an offensive weapon. There was a lot of discussion by the Council before approval was given to use it to recruit you. The fact that you just happened to be testing Earth's premier fighter when I came calling was coincidence. We will not use our science for violence that will lead to intentional harm of another human being. The primary purpose of the Starflyer program is scouting for exploration and mining operations."

He went on to explain it was the result of effort by their combined research teams. The systems being developed would be used for journeys to other planets, and more, if they were successful.

"That's where you come in, Edwina. We're offering you the role of our Master Starflyer Trainer. We have a fleet of Starflyers being constructed now. We'll need pilots; all personally selected by you from any Earth source you choose, regardless of nationality. You'll be able to pick the best, and train each one personally. I need to advise that you'll have to renounce your Earth citizenship and alliances."

Alahn paused and watched Edwina's face as she gently chewed one side of her lip in concentration.

"I didn't get up this morning with the idea that the most technically advanced aerial hot rod available on this planet would be shot out from under me; that I would captured by an alien, whisked off to the top of the world, and offered the most astounding job any pilot could ask for. I have to ask a very selfish question now. Why would I do any of this? Shouldn't you be speaking to astronauts?"

"We know your parents have passed on. You're unmarried and have no children, so there's no immediate family hold on you here. You're highly educated and even more highly skilled, and… most importantly, very open minded. I mentioned earlier that you're dedicated to the ideals of non-violence that we prize in all who come to us. We need people like you, Edwina, who can look at what we are achieving and commit themselves to our cause.

"I'm convinced you will find the social aspects of our culture enjoyable as well. You'll find no scarcity of eligible men who will gladly seek your company. We encourage family association and every goal we have is in furtherance of our children. I urge you to consider completing the Q protocols, and come to Luna. If you aren't convinced by what you see there, we'll allow you to return to Earth, asking only that you promise not to divulge to anyone here what you have seen."

"That's a lot to think about and digest. Let me sleep on it, Alahn, and give you my answer in the morning."

"Fine, that's what I'd do. I'll have a staff member escort you to your quarters. Our space is obviously limited, but I'm sure you'll find the accommodations acceptable."

Edwina was then escorted to a compartment and shown how to operate the door and personal facilities. Light was provided by panels placed throughout the rooms and was activated by waving a hand over a relay. The same action caused a comfortable looking bed to fold out of the wall, and the shower was automated also. The room was as sterile as everything she had seen in the facility so far.

Figures, no one stays long enough to hang a picture, she thought.

There was a well lit vanity stocked with personal items and a desk with speakerphone in the main area. She could access the computer network by simply speaking; results being displayed on a large flat screen monitor mounted flush within the wall facing the desk. Once alone, she tested the computer by asking it to bring up email access and was impressed when it instantly provided what appeared to be a link to every internet service provider available on the planet.

Realizing that checking her email would create a trail indicating that she was still alive, she opted to do nothing, and logged out of the computer. She showered and found a good assortment of one-piece jump suit garments to select from, including a number that were apparently for sleeping. After dressing she turned out the lights and lay down on the bed, staring up at the ceiling. Whispering in prayer she sighed, *"Dear Lord, have I got a lot to think about."*

"Yes, *you do."*

The voice purred as two arms came from seemingly nowhere to encircle him. "Ummm, you do smell good," Avia breathed in a husky whisper as she hugged her boyfriend, reaching to surround him from behind while pressing her breasts into his back. She moved her left hand down to claim again that which she most delighted in while the right hand rubbed his naked chest.

"Sure you have to go so soon?"

Robert put down the bottle of aftershave while turning to kiss her full sensuous lips. As they embraced, he slid the tip of his tongue down the side of her neck as she giggled in ecstasy. His hands acting to guide her in turning, he reached around her negligee to cup both breasts in his hands, allowing his index fingers to draw slow circles around her protruding nipples.

She leaned back against him, reached up and behind to hold the back of his head in both hands while relishing the luscious sensations he created.

"Woman, you are insatiable," he intoned in a low baritone voice just below her ear. "Two times since dinner last night! Is there no end to your appetites? And yes, I have to go. Performance reviews are due and I've got to do write ups on the new guys we have on board."

"Oh, I have something that might interest you. I pulled the psyche profile on your problem child, Souser."

"Souser," Robert repeated with a frown; the mood broken. "You get caught doing something like that, and you won't be working as Chief Nurse at Walter Reed or in anybody's hospital anymore." With a look of mischievousness in his eyes he asked, "What did it say, and did you make a copy?"

61

Avia straightened up as she turned to look into Robert's eyes with a look of concern on her face. "He's got some definite problems. According to the report, he was raised as an only child on a farm, which put him at a disadvantage in the social standings at the upper class school he was sent to… this apparently due to local busing and quota requirements. Being in a school district outside his own farming community left him self-conscious and isolated, with no interaction of anyone from a similar social grouping… somewhat of a fish out of water, so to speak." She walked out of the bathroom and retrieved her purse, sitting on the edge of the bed while searching through it for something.

"He was pretty detached to begin with, and one incident did a lot to push him over the edge. Taunting from other students was pretty rough, especially girls, but he was the favorite target of one clique in particular that made it their life's priority to single him out. Here's the copy, you can read the rest of it yourself."

The psychological evaluation depicted Darren Souser as a very troubled young man. He had run into a girl named Dagny Haynes and two of her friends while cutting across the neighboring fields on his way home from school one day. He referred to his antagonists as 'the three queen bees.'

"On second thought, make that the three queer bitches," Souser had told the doctor. "Got their noses stuck so freaking far in the air I couldn't see how they breathed. Think they're better than anyone else, just cause their folks got a little money."

Darren had tried to alter course that day to steer away from the inevitable, but they turned as one to follow and take special delight with their own brand of verbal recognition. They were merciless in taunting him… hurling cruel limericks about love affairs with his sheep and goats because a no-count white-trash farm boy couldn't get a real girl, and wouldn't know what to do with one if he had her.

Furious, he had chased them away, shouting that if he grabbed one of them they would get a ride they could brag about for the rest of their lives. To rid himself of anger and the self loathing he felt at times like that, he took particular delight in ridding the farm of pests in a creative way. Pulling the legs off insects grew to lizards, then frogs, after which he graduated to mice and the occasional rat. He would torture any hapless creature that had the misfortune of wandering his way, imagining the faces of his antagonists as he did so. Besides, he reasoned, his hobby was doing the planet a favor... getting rid of the excess nuisance population, or excess pets, or wherever the hapless victim of the day may have come from.

He especially liked the noises they made, vocalizing in the agony of their particular species as he carefully, and with cruel deliberate slowness, removed parts of their anatomy with his pocket knife. The doctor's notes were detailed in pointing out Souser's suppressed rage psychosis, and his concern about similar events setting Souser off in future.

Robert folded the report slowly and put it in his pocket. "I'm going to transfer Souser to night and swing shifts. That should keep him away from temptation until he gets tired of it and quits or moves on to become someone else's problem. While he's on the line right now, he hasn't actually done anything that I can fire him for... yet. How that idiot ever got a job with Homeland Security is beyond me."

He hugged Avia one final time and left to do battle with traffic on his way to another day in the paradise city of New York.

"How do you feel?" Donah asked Eleanor.

"Better, thank you. I must have dozed off. Where are we now?"

"We entered our braking orbit a short while ago. We're slowing down now for our approach and landing."

Eleanor took in the remarkable panorama spread out before her. The landscape was receding away from them, as the craft had positioned itself in reverse in order to decelerate. She tried to recall photos from the original landings so many years ago, but realized such memories paled when compared to actually looking at it from her present vantage point.

Studying the surface from a height of one hundred kilometers, she was impressed by the severity of all that she could see. A huge pizza crust with patches of orange peel wrinkles was her next thought.

Gray dust against solid blackness. Craters within craters. The place looks as if it's been groaning under the Sun's battering since time began. Such ugliness. Why would anyone want to come here?

"The bleakest desert I could imagine on Earth would have more to commend it than this,"

Without responding to her comment, Jake offered "We'll be on the ground in about ten minutes. Cordial is located on a boundary between Luna's near and far sides, about five hundred kilometers north of a prominent crater Earth calls Plato. Keeps us away from prying eyes."

The time remaining was taken up in landing procedure between Jake and Luna's control facility. The TUG had moved into a hangar seemingly carved out of the rock, just prior to settling down. Touchdown would have gone unnoticed if Burt hadn't announced it. Eleanor noted a number of other TUGs present in the hanger being offloaded by personnel. She was advised to be careful of her footing, as she only weighed about one sixth of her Earth weight.

She found the difference curious, and noted she hadn't experienced any of the fatigue she would normally encounter after waking up. She realized she hadn't noticed the weight of her suit at all.

After Jake and Donah put on their suits, all three left the TUG. There were a number of small vehicles lined up to one side resembling golf carts without wheels that Donah referred to as 'hoppers.'

"We'll all ride in this one," Jake said, as they climbed aboard. "It's just a short ride to the facility. They're equipped with AIs and totally automated systems."

He pointed to a display. "Just tap the up or down arrow to locate the intended destination, then touch 'Begin' to start your journey." Matching word to deed, the hopper rose silently and moved briskly toward a series of low rises in the distance.

"Why are we riding? Those hills look close enough to walk to," Eleanor stated.

Donah replied, "There's no atmosphere here. No familiar terrain or life forms such as trees for example, to assist in gauging distance. Such hyper-clarity creates difficulties with depth perception. That short walk you are referring to is eighteen kilometers from where we started."

The hopper slowed and descended into a shallow depression, settling on a pad located by a wall making up the left side of the hollow. Eleanor concluded she was looking at the front door, and confirmed this when Jake completed the recognition protocol and it opened.

As she looked around, her thoughts turned again to how stark and desolate her surroundings were. *This is the most inhospitable place I could ever imagine. My first impression was right... these people are all disturbed. No one in their right mind could truly want to live in a place like this.*

"This airlock is the primary entrance to Cordial. Initially, our settlement was here on the surface, but as we improved our living conditions we discovered areas that would allow us to transfer underground, so we removed everything that was up here."

As they stepped inside, Jake continued, "We'll descend on this elevator platform fifty meters underground, then enter the actual facility."

Once inside, Eleanor was introduced to Raul, a young member of the Council who escorted her to an area for E-suit removal. She was given a comfortable jump suit to wear. From there they went to a communal dining area where she was introduced to a few members of the Council by Jake. He made a point of including each member's nationality, impressing Eleanor with the group's diversity.

Maralah, the oldest female member of the Council, advised Eleanor they would meet later to discuss in detail the reason for her visit, but wanted her to see a few things first. She introduced her to Chateauleire and Iawy, who were to be guides during the time spent here. They wasted no time in hustling her off to breakfast.

"Cordial is our administrative facility," said Chateauleire, with a youthful yet delightfully refreshing French lilt. Getting to know each other during their meal, Eleanor learned that her nickname was 'Chat;' a bright eleven year old from French Canada. Soft freckles set off by close-trimmed, yielding black hair complemented her pert nose and deep blue eyes.

At completing her Master's degree in molecular sciences she had been recruited by Yoshko, an adult Council member, just after construction of Cordial was begun. She pitched in that their families had been invited to come as well, with her father receiving an invitation simultaneously to hers.

Iawy, a slim sixty-eight year old from Egypt, was the leading geologist specializing in heavy mineral geochemistry. He explained that each Council member brought a wealth of expertise to Luna in subjects dealing with the uniqueness of their environment, and were available to Luna citizens for any issue they might need assistance with.

After eating, the trio wandered throughout the facility, where the morning was taken up with Eleanor being introduced by an eager Chat, who by now had glued herself to the big sister she never had in her former life. Eleanor found herself taking an immediate liking to the quiet youngster, whose small child-like voice resonated feelings inside her that created an immediate attraction.

After viewing the gymnasium, medical and life support areas, they entered a much larger room and were joined by a seventeen year old former Briton named Walwyn, who led them into Operations; the nerve center of Luna. The first feature to catch her eye as she approached the entry was an impressive array of very large flush-mounted wall monitors. The next facet was a room full of hyperkinetically animated mannequins, seemingly energized in a St. Vitas dance of spasmodic pointing fingers and thrashing arms.

There were several dozen individuals of all ages, genders, and nationalities standing, sitting, or laying on comfortable looking lounges. Wearing helmet type units that enclosed their faces, each was gesturing in an irregular and unpredictable manner more reminiscent of storm whipped trees than computer science. Fingers and arms were encircled with sensors; wiring flowed up the length of both arms to connectors on the rear of the visor. A single umbilical ran toward the ceiling, terminating at the face of a panel located there.

"Our systems are more advanced than anything on Earth. Our people operate in a virtual computer world. In their minds, they see images larger than the wall units, and three dimensional holographic panels seem to float in front of each operator... it's like they're not even here," Walwyn said. "They're connected to every system there is.

"Discoveries in nanocomputer technology have resulted in real breakthroughs that permit our computers to operate at speeds and capacities never before realized. We're knocking on the door of quantum nanocomputer research, but haven't completely solved the energy state stability problems we've encountered. One real advantage we have is the ability to keep our processor modules and electronic support systems at shaded surface temperatures, usually around minus three hundred eighty degrees Fahrenheit. We've achieved unparalleled processor speeds and information transfer rates," he concluded... all of which went well over Eleanor's head. She freely admitted her own level of experience was limited to her laptop.

Walwyn shared that 'Prime' was the name given to the main computer AI that networked the entire systems of all three cities, including their contacts on Earth.

"I didn't notice any type of transmission towers when we were landing, Walwyn. How do your systems communicate? I know that we're a long way from Earth."

"We built antenna arrays disguised to resemble the surface features of

Luna. There are three of them located in the craters known as Plato, Copernicus, and Bullialdus. The smallest crater is sixty kilometers in width. Our antennas have an electronic diameter of fifty kilometers. They can be combined systemically to equal the equivalent of a single antenna one hundred fifty kilometers in diameter. It gives us a significant ability to see and hear anything that emanates from Earth or elsewhere. Our communications teams are doing the same thing to the far side of Luna."

As they walked through the room she moved to avoid contact with the more energetic of the operators, not sure if they were able to comprehend external stimuli and steer clear of visitors.

With a conspiratorial grin cracking both sides of his mouth, Walwyn offered softly, "I know it's called Ops, but we refer to this as the herky-jerk room."

Grinning with mirth at his revelation, Eleanor turned her gaze to see Chat raise both hands; covering her mouth to stifle laughter while her wide eyes berated Walwyn for exposing young secrets to the uninitiated.

"Don't worry," she said, reaching over to gently rub Chat's head. "I won't tell. Earth doesn't need another new dance craze at the moment. Thank you for the tour and introduction to your computer systems, Walwyn. It's a fascinating area."

Beaming at her complement, Walwyn added that all Luna vehicles from hoppers to TUGs and the Starflyer were controlled by Prime from here, and that each could be remotely piloted from this room if necessary. She was rescued from a dissertation on redundant systems, backups and nuclear firewalls by Iawy, who gently steered Walwyn back to operations while explaining they had much more ground to cover that day.

"We'll need our E-suits again," Iawy said, as they made their way back to the common dining area. "We'll be visiting Selene after lunch."

While eating, Eleanor asked where everyone lived, noting what she thought was an absence of living quarters during their tour.

Iawy explained that Luna was composed of three cities at the moment, each performing a unique function. Cordial was considered to be the capital city, due to its nature as the communications and medical center, including research in support systems; the accommodations being more apartment-like. Selene was the suburbs, major living center, and agricultural research area. Prexus was the manufacturing facility city where the engineering and geological teams worked and resided. Everyone was free to travel to and stay in any of the cities, and come and go as they please. The total populace was hovering around six thousand at the moment, infant mortality was zero, and resident growth was increasing at a satisfactory rate.

Manning of duty stations at any facility was done on a shift basis, with TUGs and hoppers performing public transportation service. He would explain the locations during the trip to each. After dressing, he and Eleanor took one hopper. Chat shared a second unit with Chidi, a thirteen year old young man of African Maasai tribal descent who had volunteered for the tour. Chidi advised Eleanor the hoppers were gyroscopically balanced, powered by AlSys hydroxy systems, and operated at an altitude of ten meters, sufficient to leave the dust over which they traveled undisturbed.

"Luna is six thousand eight hundred miles in circumference," Iawy said. "An interesting point is that traveling by motor car at about seventy-five miles per hour, one could drive completely around the equator in less than four days. The hoppers travel unimpeded by atmosphere. For safety reasons, we limit normal cruise to around five hundred kilometers per hour locally, but they are capable of much faster speeds when we travel between the cities. We're heading for an area south west of Cordial, that would appear in about the eleven o'clock position as viewed from Earth. They call it Sinus Iridum, but we have named our part of it Selene."

After a thirty minute ride Eleanor noted their approach to a large crater, and was surprised when the hopper climbed over its outer edge and dove towards the bottom. As they skimmed above the surface she could see the end of a massive semi-circle of rock towering above them, jutting almost a kilometer from the inner edge of the crater. It appeared to gradually slope downwards becoming flush with the surface once it reached the crater wall. Both hoppers slowed and terminated their journey at a sheltered opening containing more TUGs and hoppers.

Walking to the nearest side of the half circle rock in silence, the four travelers entered an airlock which terminated in a room set up for suit removal and storage. Once that was done, Chidi took Eleanor's hand and said, "We have a saying in my land… we will water the thorn for the sake of the rose. At the end of this corridor lies our rose. May you find it as comforting as we have."

They may be geniuses, thought Eleanor, but they're no different than any other child attempting to suppress excitement. She had seen the looks on both faces of Chat and Chidi, who looked as if a great secret was about to be revealed. She kept that observation to herself so as not to spoil whatever surprise they had in store for her. The corridor ended with a right turn into an auditorium capable of seating hundreds. It faced a large rectangular wall, easily several hundred feet wide and possibly a third of that in height. Stopping in the center, the group moved closer to the wall.

Gesturing to his right, Iawy stated, "This is our formal meeting area." Turning to his left, he said, "You might enjoy this."

The motion of his hand over a relay brought to life hidden equipment discernible through heavy vibrations reverberating through the floor. A horizontal crack split the full length of the wall; half silently rising into the ceiling while the lower part slid just as noiselessly into the floor. The articulated wall had concealed a window of equal size.

Eleanor gasped involuntarily, assaulted by a bright mosaic of riotous color exploding from every direction; stunned by the magnitude of a huge tunnel receding away from her as far as she could see. With the same feeling of awe that possesses a child at seeing a rainbow for the first time, she struggled to grasp the splendor that lay before her astonished eyes. Her mouth fell open and she stood in mute silence to wonder at the marvels of engineering that created a subterranean paradise in the center of Hell itself.

Reaching over to take her hand, Chat leaned against her side while Eleanor intuitively placed that arm around her young friend's shoulder.

"Oh Eleanor," she whispered with a sigh. "Is it not the most wonderful vista you have ever seen?"

There were white clouds against a light-blue sky, itself glowing with the brilliance of a sunlit day. There were plants and flowers everywhere. She thought she could recognize roses, orchids, lilies, and tulips. A small park spread out before her and a sea of rich green grass carpeted the landscape.

"My... God," she breathed softly. *Can that actually be a lake and waterfall?*

Sheets of slowly cascading water hung hazily suspended in the air, settling gently into the main body of the pool... itself a study in fluid slow motion as falling droplets created a never ending effervescence of dancing, crystal-like streamers bouncing on its surface. Individuals and families could be seen gathered around its periphery, enjoying both the serenity it offered and invigorating spray that settled kindly on upturned faces and purposely exposed limbs.

Eleanor could see people being transported swiftly on moving sidewalks. There were dwellings stretching everywhere into the distance and she could see children playing some sort of chasing game. With the bounding grace and beauty of nature's wild impala gazelles, they made huge arching leaps while running to touch each other.

"It can be breathtaking when seen for the first time," Iawy said. "Come, we mustn't stand here in idleness... there is much more to see."

Leaving the auditorium, they proceeded through another airlock and were met by a man introduced as Mr. Lloyd Boxe, a gray headed older gentleman with a kindly disposition. Jake had called ahead and asked that he meet Eleanor and the others and show them around. As they walked down the gently sloping path Lloyd told her this was referred to as the Great Hall. The air was brisk, fresh, and full of exotic aromas from the cornucopia of blossoms arranged along the pathway.

They stopped momentarily to watch more children at play. Eleanor smiled with delight at the gaiety and laughter that followed their spirited activity. At a query from Chidi, Iawy released him to join them. Chat continued to hold Eleanor's hand as they transited a short set of diagonally cascading moving sidewalks, each progressively faster than the one before it to reach the swiftest line.

"We call the main line 'zippers,' because they move so fast," said Chat. "Due to the lower gravity we have to speed up in smaller increments. That is why there are extra boarding walks."

Lloyd chimed in, "In the old days it was thought that the dark features on the surface were created by water or ocean activity, so they were named Mare, Latin for seas. There's a very prominent feature on the nearside called Mare Imbrium. The southeast edge has what appears to be a valley of some sort, about seventy-five miles in length and a mile wide, named the Hadley Rille.

"It's actually a lava channel, or tunnel, that was formed over three billion years ago. In time, the roof collapsed, leaving a valley-like indentation. You can find similar lava channels on Earth, especially in Hawaii. There are at least half a dozen of them here, known and mapped by Earth during the Apollo explorations, so it stands to reason we would find one or more intact. Selene is the biggest one we've discovered so far.

"Its length is ninety-three miles, more than six thousand feet in width at its widest point. The ceiling is over one thousand feet high in places, including where we're standing now. This tube runs deeper under the surface than the others, which accounts for why it hasn't fallen. We only had to seal off the one end that you came through; volcanic activity took care of the other end a long time ago. The metallic shields in the auditorium and second airlock were precautions, should anything happen to the front door, so to speak. We built the glass observation window in anticipation of visitors who may not have gone through the medical indoctrination, but wanted a glimpse of what we've accomplished."

"Lloyd, are you telling me this sky, the clouds, this incredible plant life… all of it extends for ninety-three miles?" asked Eleanor, with wonder in her voice.

"Well, I have to confess that we've only conquered the first eighteen of that, and the eighteenth mile isn't fully habitable yet. We've got the end of that mile closed off with a movable seal system, which is relocated as each section comes on line. The artificial grass is woven over impact matting, right here in one of our research facilities. We use it as a surface cover. If we had tried to pump out the dust, they would've seen the cloud all the way to Mars! The blue sky and clouds are simple holographic projection, but the sun was a neat trick.

"There are lamp bulbs on Earth that radiate light in frequencies similar to the sun, generally referred to as grow lights. Apartment dwellers and home types use them to grow plants indoors that would usually be outside, as do commercial green house operators. Some of our young geniuses have succeeded in marrying the best features of high intensity discharge, metal halide, and high pressure sodium grow light technology into an integrated panel system that we've installed along the ceiling using the hoppers. Synchronizing them to Earth's twenty-four hour system was easy, and you can see the results," Lloyd said, gesturing to the abundant growth around him. "The flowers are my own project."

As they continued their tour, he added, "You can eat breakfast at sunrise, and dinner at sunset. Auxiliary power and air come from AlSys systems. Our primary power source is photovoltaic... solar panels. We have huge arrays built on the boundary that provide virtually unlimited energy. Most people don't usually realize the back side of the moon gets as much sunlight as the front side. We have the Akamatsu manufacturing folks process, sterilize, and freeze hundreds of tons of water, which we bring here using TUGs. That accounts for the lake and waterfall, which is simply a surface display of our main water supply.

"There are quite a few high capacity water holding tanks buried under the surface in all three cities, capable of supporting a significantly higher population than we have at the moment. We're looking into constructing a misting system to mimic rain and morning dew, but that will have to wait... regardless of wishful thinking we've yet to find any significant water deposits here. The soil is absolutely pure and supports anything we grow in it so far. While we have hydroponics capability, you can see that flowers look better here than poking out of a tank.

"Every plant here is sixth generation... the first five iterations hydroponically grown in a sterile environment from a seed processed to the electron-microscopic level to ensure no bacteria or insect life came with it. In the labs, we've got experts looking at bees, hummingbirds, and any number of other life forms that can acclimate and add to the beauty here.

"We practice one hundred percent recycling, so very little liquid is lost regardless of source. We use the same portable severe habitat shelters here as we used on the surface, but they've been upgraded and modernized. You can hook them together and build yourself as big a house as you want. Each functions as originally intended in case anything were to cause depressurization. The people-moving sidewalks are knockoffs from commercial systems readily available on Earth, but we make them lighter and more energy efficient due to less gravity; they're faster too.

"What you haven't seen is the small maglev train that runs right down the center. It will eventually transit the full distance of Selene, running in both directions simultaneously. We gave the German manufacturer exclusive rights to research and development, including advertising on Earth in future."

Eleanor asked, "What's it all for? I don't see nearly enough people here to populate such a large area. I do notice quite a few older individuals."

In response, Iawy pointed out that every person whose services were needed, be they technician, engineer, scientist or otherwise, were permitted to be accompanied by those members of their families who were willing to make the same philosophical commitments to non-violence and renouncement of citizenship to Earth. Those that weren't were told their family member was being transferred to Asia for employment, and would be away for a long time. Frequent communication was encouraged via email, phone, or video conference, and generous allowances were forwarded to those that had stayed behind. The present population would grow in time, and there would be plenty of room for all.

"Jake wasn't very forthcoming about funding for this enterprise when I initially brought up the subject," Eleanor said.

Lloyd told her that many retirees possessed valuable skills and experience in a wealth of arenas, and being put out to pasture didn't sit well with any of them. Most had made fortunes during their lifetimes but were facing declining health and a growing feeling of uselessness.

"Jake and his people put an end to that," said Lloyd. "Emma and I converted everything we owned to cash and turned it all over to Jake. Every senior and senior couple you see here did the same thing initially, which is how all of this got moving. I'll let Jake tell you the rest. But consider this, Eleanor. I'm eighty-three years old and haven't stood this straight for the last fifteen years. And Emma's stoop is gone as well. Reducing the effects of full gravity, coupled with the medicinal advances made by Doctor Agave and his researchers, have added years... maybe another decade or so, to all of our lives.

"Look around, there's no stress, no violence, no pollution, no traffic;

no crime and no need of law enforcement or government intrusion. That's how we got most of this done in so short a time span. I'll also point out there's no exposure to sick people or any type of transmittable disease. There's no safer place to raise children and give them a fuller and longer life than anything they could expect on Earth, all dedicated to the furtherance of mankind. What possible use could a fortune be against the promise of what you're seeing, and the almost unlimited potential offered here?"

After a moment's reflection, Eleanor said, "You've made excellent points, Lloyd; certainly nothing that I could argue against. What you and Luna's engineers have accomplished here is miraculous and gives me that much more to think about."

Lloyd pointed out the air processing, pressurization and waste recycling facilities, speaking briefly with other inhabitants as they traveled on the moving sidewalks further into the depths of the Great Hall. As they viewed the protein synthesis and soil labs, Lloyd pointed out the carefully structured and well tended plots of plant growth, including his flower displays.

"And we're growing more than just flowers. We have viable wheat, oat, and other staples, very small scale. Each variety you see is actually a lab plot for that item, carefully studied and documented by researchers specializing in that field." He noted the only thing missing was real farmers, "But that will come in time."

"Will you contemplate our house for shelter tonight, Eleanor? You could meet my papa, and tomorrow we may travel to Prexus together," inquired Chat.

The look in her fresh eyes conveyed such longing for Eleanor's company that she couldn't refuse, buoying her new young friend's spirits considerably.

By now the group had worked its way to the end of the Hall and Iawy pointed out dinner time was approaching. Lloyd promised to advise Jake where Eleanor was staying for the night, and assured her she would be contacted tomorrow morning for the trip to Prexus. Holding her hand, Chat steered Eleanor to a zipper moving in the direction of her home, promising a wonderful meal followed by quality time between the two of them. The dwelling was located at about mile six; a short stroll from the sidewalk. Composed of six domed units arranged in a circle, each boasted a respectful sized view port.

Eleanor was pleasantly impressed entering the central area when "Dad, I'm home with company!" was thrown to the interior by Chat as "Le papa, je suis la maison avec la société!"

A tall, lean built gentleman with straight bearing strolled into the main room. Under a head of short gray hair, his masculine face displayed a mature and controlled disposition. Eleanor looked up into sparkling clear blue eyes and a vivid smile.

Extending his hand to grip hers warmly, he responded, "Le bon jour, la Madame, je suis Gautier Devereux. Bienvenu à notre maison."

Delighted with his kind welcome into their home, Eleanor's response drew an equally pleasing and just as surprised smile from Chat as she offered thanks, responding how happy she was to meet him, and enquiring as to whether he came from France; "Merci, Devereux de Monsieur, pour l'hospitalité de votre maison. Je suis heureux de vous rencontrer. Mon nom est Eleanor. Êtes-vous de la France?"

"Non, Eleanor," he replied with a small shake of his head. "Chateauleire et moi, nous sommes Canadiens."

Taking her hand and guiding her toward the dining area he complimented her French, "Comment charmant est votre Français. I can only hope my poor English may be understood half as well as your excellent French. The Council would have us all with one name, but this is difficult for the older ones who grew up with two or more. While there is no other named Gautier here, I am content to use the old way."

Smoothly moving into another subject, he continued, "I believe Maralah knows Chat better than I. She called earlier today to warn me that we would have a guest, so I've had time to prepare a meal. Please be seated.

Maralah also told me you are educated in law. The Council will have much to discuss with you about that, I'm sure."

Gautier turned to set dinner on the table, assisted by Chat.

"I'm eager to learn how I can be of assistance," Eleanor said. "Is Mrs. Devereux at home?" At this, an awkward silence stopped Chat in place as she stared blankly at her father.

"Come, Chateauleire, sit. We mustn't keep our guest waiting. My wife is dead, Eleanor, killed during a burglary after my daughter was born," he stated matter-of-factly as Chat placed the meal on the table.

"Small towns in Canada do not hide many secrets. In a moment of terrible passion I sought out the criminal and ended his life. Unfortunately, this occurred on the United States side of the border. Many felt I was justified, but I had usurped the authority of the State, so was sentenced to life in prison for my crime. My daughter was taken to be raised by others. Everything changed when I met Jake. Life was returned to me, along with my greatest treasure."

Saying this, Gautier leaned over to hug Chat; lightly brushing away the tears beginning to form in her eyes. "We have made a new and productive life for ourselves here on Luna. Chat and I work in Prexus, where I believe you will tour tomorrow."

Eleanor didn't respond right away. She was impressed with the straightforward honesty of Gautier, and his obvious emotional attachment and love for Chat. She felt strange not to be disturbed by his explanation as she might have been... but it helped her understand more about Chat's reaction to her.

"Thank you for sharing that with me, Gautier. You must be quite pleased with Chat's progress. Not many eleven year olds are knocking on the door of academia for Master's Degrees."

"We have her Aunt Victorie to thank for that. Chateauleire is naturally gifted with an enviable curiosity and high learning capacity. Victorie employed a robust home study program that placed Chat well beyond her peers. My only surprise was that she chose to study molecular science. She is a major contributor to the forming of new alloys, lighter and stronger than what has come before. Her specialty is application... design that flows as art, rather than bulk engineering. You can see the result in the Starflyer prototype. The pilot's environmental structure is a direct result of her work, and can withstand forces far beyond a comparable Earth vehicle."

"That's very impressive. Prexus is an odd name, what does it mean?"

"A rather loose acronym for 'Prisoner Exchange' and one of Jake's programs for recruiting the expertise needed here. It demonstrates his genius in obtaining loyal people to build his vision of the future. He has given new meaning to men and woman who had abandoned hope, and they are very grateful to him and the Council. My own work focuses on the Starflyer project. We are very happy with the results to date, and will be completing more soon. We are working on a larger edition to be used for exploration of our own solar system."

After a very pleasant dinner, Gautier suggested that Eleanor and Chat visit with each other. "I will bid you adieu for this day as I must spend some time reviewing our systems projects for tomorrow. Chat will show you to your room as well."

Gautier bowed politely, obviously pleased as she bid him good day, thanking him for the meal and excellent company, "Au revoir, Devereux de Monsieur. Merci pour le repas et la société excellente."

Taking Eleanor's hand Chat walked to her room; an open circular affair. Triggering a relay caused a couch bed to extend into the main area. Eleanor sat on the bed and was impressed with the room's neatness, noting the furnishings were more suited to an academic than what would normally be encountered in a typical young girl's room. One wall was sectioned with horizontal drawers and a vertical area for hanging the unisex coveralls worn by everyone here.

Chat picked an object off the desk and pretended to examine it closely as she walked over to sit next to Eleanor, drawing her legs up to sit facing her on the bed.

"How do you pass the time when you're not working, Chat?"

"Oh, with reading; there is access to internet and media which has been filtered for violent content. I enjoy greatly time spent with the other children playing wall tag in our Great Hall... it is quite merry. One can leap very high and run along some of the steeper inclines due to weak gravity, which also permits jumping up to high ledges and rocks. It is almost like flying. Papa says we resemble a primate grouping. Umm, what others might name a gathering of monkeys, yes?"

Eleanor smiled brightly at Chat's humorous description as she continued, "We have to be careful of some activities for that same reason. One may hurt another throwing an object; it would travel too fast and too far. Work is fun too, everyone is family. I like to collect rocks when I go exploring with some of the geologists."

Saying this, Chat shyly handed Eleanor the object she had been holding. "Merci de passer la journée avec moi et d'être mon amie. Ceci est pour vous," which Eleanor understood as "Thank you for spending a day with me and being my friend. This is for you."

"Je vous en prie, you're welcome, Chat. I promise that I've enjoyed this day as much as you have," Eleanor said, bending slightly to kiss her forehead; hugging her gently... a hug that was just as readily returned by Chat. "Thank you for being my friend and showing me this wonderful place where you live." Chat looked up into Eleanor's eyes with blatant adoration stamped in every feature of her face.

Eleanor examined the object that Chat had placed in her hand. Hexagonal in shape, it was rough with a deep red luster, about seven inches in length and half that in width.

"What is it?"

"One of the research geophysicists on Iawy's team tells me it is corundum. Most of it is clear, but this one has impurities that deliver the redness. It is ruby, I believe."

Interpreting Chat's comment as a color reference, Eleanor replied, "I never found time to enjoy many hobbies, including rock collecting. It's pretty, though. I think it would make a very curious paperweight for my desk, thank you."

"The geology teams found a place with much of that, and other corundum too, with a great variety of pretty colors. He says there are quite a few representations of the gem family. It comes from basalt, a volcanic rock. There are pretty ones called peridot that are my favorite, such as this one," showing Eleanor a fist size lime green gemstone. "They come from volcanoes... and trace elements have been found in meteorites too.

Think of it, Eleanor, this may have traveled the galaxy before being found here! One moment, I will bring my rock collection."

Springing from the bed, Chat opened a drawer from the wall array and carried a box back to Eleanor. As they examined its contents together, Eleanor reached for an irregular shaped stone about the size of a baseball.

"What an odd bit of glass. Is this the clear corundum you spoke of, or do the rock teams have another name for this one?"

"They say that one is a rather small example of crystallized carbon."

Turning it over and looking at it closely, a chill ran up and down her spine as recognition caused her head to snap up and look at Chat.

"Small? Are you saying this is a diamond?"

"Oui, I believe it is referred to by that name. Iawy tells me they found a volcanic pipe with a good deal of that also. I take pleasure in this one as well," she said, placing an object as large as a grapefruit into Eleanor's other palm. Even at one sixth gravity, her hand sagged as it took the full weight... which she estimated would weigh in at about thirty pounds on Earth. The familiar gleam was unmistakable.

"It is Au by atomic symbol... gold," said Chat. "They have found a quite large vein of it in some volcanic rocks he calls komatiites. There are many pebbles similar to that one just lying around as well. Iawy also said that all the gold and gems ever found by mankind on Earth wouldn't compare with the smallest part of what's here. Most of it was discovered immediately after the teams arrived in the first year, but they think there's more."

Eleanor's mind reeled with the implications of Chat's revelations. At the price per ounce she had earlier quoted Randolph, the 'pebble' she held would easily fetch high six figures within Earth's precious metals markets.

The glass stone in her other hand would shame the largest diamond ever found on Earth many times over... as would the ruby gift from her young friend.

Pebbles? The gold business card now made sense. The events of the last two days... Jake and Donah's words... her own unfortunate choice of words in describing what certain groups would do for their science alone,

much less the unimaginable resources just revealed to her by the innocence of youth.

Every Government… no… every human being who could muster the
power to get here would destroy these people just to get their hands on
such potential wealth. Mentally composing herself, Eleanor responded in
a soft and stable manner, "Well. Thank you for sharing your rock
collection with me. There certainly are some very unusual examples here,
Chat. Is it possible to use the phone? I need to contact my friends and let
them know I'm fine."

"Yes, do they have a videophone? That is what we use in the shelters."

Assuring Chat that they did, Eleanor provided the office phone
number. Chat verbally asked the computer to complete the call and turn
on the wall monitor. The secretary that answered was asked to have
Jennifer Long and Randolph Stein come to the conference room immediately, and turn on the video conference equipment. They were openly
relieved to find her in good health and spirits.

Eleanor introduced Chat and advised them her personal inspection of
the new client's facilities was progressing nicely and that she would be
returning in a few days.

Jennifer assured her all was status quo at the law firm, and while they
were looking forward to her return, "You deserve a few days off. Smell
the roses, we're doing fine." On that assurance the call was concluded.

The two new friends spent the next hours in girl talk, cementing a
friendship that held promise for a deeper union in future. Chat escorted
Eleanor to her room, showing her how to activate the bed and operate
the low-gravity shower and toilet. Mentally exhausted, Eleanor added to
the list of questions she had for Jake and the Council as she fell into a
troubled sleep.

The following morning found Eleanor, Chat, Iawy and Gautier embarking together; Eleanor being permitted to take the hopper controls for the first time. Gautier instructed her to select the manual setting on the destination screen so that a short side trip could be taken towards the southeast of Selene to an area known as Mare Imbrium. Stopping at its northwestern side, Iawy pointed out two volcanic domes.

"Let me say this before we continue. There are a number of theories as to how Luna came about. Some hold it condensed from the same gases that formed the sun and planets. Others will tell you it was captured intact as it is by gravity, eventually finding its way to where it orbits. Our generation has come to believe that a body, possibly the size of Mars, impacted Earth before it had completely solidified billions of years ago, and that Luna is a result of that collision when the debris eventually came together.

"However, that does not explain why the face of Luna has rocky plains, yet the back side contains mountains. A new theory is offered that another moon, perhaps a larger piece of the initial collision, was in the same orbital plane as Luna and collided on the near side. This companion moon may have actually flattened out and adhered, creating the differing landscapes.

"Precious metals and stones are products of high pressure, high temperature environments and found deep within a planet's core. Over time, volcanism causes these to be pushed toward the surface, so would have been present there on Earth where the initial impact occurred. We believe that the richest part of both wound up here. Come."

Iawy led them closer toward one of the domes, where ejecta could be seen lying at its base. Selecting a stone, he handed it to Eleanor. Approximately thirteen inches in diameter, Iawy advised her it was from the corundum family; a sapphire to be precise. They had recovered tons of such samples. This was repeated as they proceeded further, with Eleanor handling gem stones that would weigh thousands of carats on Earth.

"Corundum is aluminum oxide, and is second only to diamond in hardness. Impurities found within the stone give it color. Much of what you see here is not gem quality, but can be used as abrasives and polishing compounds. There are large dark areas on the near side of Luna easily seen with the naked eye from Earth, a result of volcanic activity. Luna's crust is thin there, so lava flowed from the planet's interior to fill lowlands in that area. It is reasonable to expect that one would find similar results to volcanic activity seen on Earth, and indeed, that is the case."

Eleanor could now appreciate Chat's 'small' remark as Iawy allowed her to handle samples of stones obscene in size. He went on to explain they had found deposits of crystallized carbon, Au, and other stones of gem quality.

"We form the natural gold material into ingots which are transported to our contacts at the Akamatsu Corporation, using as a cover story that it originates from Southeast Asia. It's sold openly for market price. Revenue from the stones and gold created all that you have seen these past three days. Of course, we carefully control the quantity of what is sent. It would be difficult to explain a three thousand carat diamond."

Concluding the field trip, they set off for the third city, a distance of about seven hundred and fifty miles northwest of Mare Imbrium.

"Prexus is more industrialized than our other cities," said Gautier. "Like Cordial, it too is located on the boundary between the two sides, lying almost due west of Cordial. It is a tunnel city based on engineering and manufacturing, so may not seem as appealing to the eye as Selene."

"Gautier, forgive me for changing the subject. I understand your reason for wanting to be here, but I find it difficult to believe that everyone else had circumstances similar to yours. I'm curious to know what motivates the others," said Eleanor.

"Luna has set us free from the need to pursue material possessions. There is no cost to any individual associated with anything here. Every need and want is satiated… family, housing, sustenance, medical care, travel and socialization with others. Consider; you must work for monetary gain on Earth to buy material things. Here, they are provided equally to all in exchange for that which each individual chooses to do freely and naturally... in an incredibly unique environment free from the stress of deadlines, or any stress for that matter."

Gautier explained that simply being here provided a level of mental stimulation unachievable anywhere else. On Earth, a young computer engineer is stifled by need to compete with hundreds of others for a lucrative position in order to survive in a universe of materialism. Here, the intellect is set free to explore as far as possible, unfettered by restrictions of any kind; the best and most modern equipment provided for every endeavor.

"Kelly, as Administrator, meets with representatives from each city daily reviewing systems operations, ongoing and new equipment requirements. She is assisted in this by Donah Morning. While scientific research is not Donah's forte, she is an extraordinarily competent manager, coordinating the administrative affairs of exchange between Luna and our interests on Earth... which is to say she runs the checkbook on a planetary scale.

"She would never have had such an opportunity anywhere else in her lifetime. Jake and Alahn act to recruit and build our population based on the common goals of everyone here... the betterment of Luna, true scientific research, and the most secure place in our known solar system to raise a family. Every human being here is an explorer, confident that we will see the planets and possibly more in our time. It took a man of vision, Jake Starnes to be precise, to bring about all that you have seen."

Arrival at Prexus was a repeat of the first two visits. After leaving the suit room, it was a short zipper trip to the main facility. Eleanor found Prexus to be in tune with most of the industrial parks she was familiar with on Earth, but much grander in scale. Like Selene, it boasted similar ground cover and sky effects. As the entire facility was protected underground, everything was done in the open. TUGs, hoppers, and a number of other ships could be seen in various states of construction.

"AI computer controlled industrial robots are used for the more complicated tasks, including installation of the heavier pieces, many of which were initially constructed on Earth and transported here," explained Gautier. "Technicians focus on critical items, such as each craft's AI and related computer controlled elements. You can see the new Starflyers taking shape there," pointing to a number of craft in varying stages of assembly.

He explained that Luna was producing more of its own parts now, and would soon be completely self-sufficient. "But come, look at this," he said, leading the small group into another hangar type area. At its center was a very large ship under construction, hundreds of feet in height and width. "It will measure approximately three fourths of a mile in length when completed. At that point it will be disassembled and put back together in orbit on the farside."

"What's the purpose of this ship, Gautier?" asked Eleanor.

"It can transport TUGs and Starflyers, as well as provide a research and lab environment for hundreds of scientists and their families," he responded. "While TUGs are configured as landing craft, the primary function of the Starflyer is to act as scout, seeking out new areas for exploration and mining in advance of the main group. It has been equipped with cutting lasers for that purpose.

"The carrier ship will give us the ability to completely explore our own solar system. It can provide the same accelerative protections as the Starflyer; meaning that trips to the outer planets can be accomplished in months instead of years. We held a contest with the school children. 'New Hope' is the named it was given."

Next on the agenda was a visit to the metallurgy laboratories, where Chat assisted with alloy research. She explained how challenging it was to find new combinations of alloys that would outperform heavier solutions used in past, and how thrilled she was when her design was selected for the Starflyer pilot environment. Alloy models constructed in a computer had samples run off in an automated lab for real time results.

"I above all delight in forming the actual framework. I find that curves are much more aesthetic than straight angles, and Jake's son Alahn told me he was very pleased with the result. He is the test pilot for the prototype."

"Oh, and do you like Alahn?" asked Eleanor.

Chat stood pigeon toed with the tip of one foot idly scraping the floor and head bowed slightly. With both hands clasped before her and shoulders shrugging up a bit, she blushed.

"Everyone likes Alahn… he is pretty."

Her response drew a knowing smile from Eleanor and chuckles from the others. She hugged Chat to cover her embarrassment as the small group continued their tour. After a stop for lunch, Gautier left the group to join his research teams, leaving Iawy to escort Eleanor and Chat back to Cordial.

Maralah met the trio, informing them a meeting with the full Council was underway and they were eagerly looking forward to discussing the reasons for Eleanor's visit. Entering the Council's meeting room, Jake asked everyone to make themselves comfortable.

Handing Eleanor a list of the Council members, he introduced each in turn. Apologizing, he explained that Alahn was still occupied at Q and that Kelly would act in his stead during the meeting.

As she reviewed the list, Jake addressed a previous discussion.

"In your office, you interpreted our use of the term 'elite' in the negative sense. I alluded to the diversity in our society once before. That list demonstrates twelve cultural nationalities within our Council alone, and you would find many more were you to poll all of our citizens. I also want to point out that we permit no bigotry toward any person or group based on belief, gender, or association. The heart of our nonviolence philosophy binds us all."

Somewhat taken aback by Jake's openness, she responded, "Thank you, Jake. This list will make it easier for me to learn everyone's name."

After a moment of reflection, she added, "In retrospect, I was wrong. My rush to judgment was improper, leading me to voice too strong an opinion. I apologize for what I said when we talked in my office. You were correct that I needed to see this first hand. I'm very impressed with the diversity seen here… the love of family that permeates Luna.

Everyone I've met is genuinely dedicated to the goals and vision you shared with me. I'm eager to hear how I can be a part of this."

The Council members looked at Eleanor as Kelly interjected, "We want to hire your law firm, in its entirety, to focus on one issue. We are declaring Luna to be a sovereign planet… closed to colonization."

Eleanor sat in mute silence, the enormity of Kelly's words causing her to stare impassively at them all while an absurd picture of the old man on the wall leaped into her mind; seemingly advising her that right now would be a very good time to keep both ears wide open.

After a moment's reflection, she replied, "There's nothing in my experience… legal background or otherwise, that would allow me to consider how we could possibly accomplish that for you."

"We took a look at it from the layman's perspective. Earth has centuries of law to draw on. Simple possession still seems to be nine tenths of the law, at least according to history. By your own observation, we are the only tenants in possession of Luna."

"That's true for the time being, Kelly. But who possesses this place can change in the time it takes an Earth government to come here and root you out."

"Point taken and we've been preparing ourselves to face that reality. We're also comfortable that a claim based on squatter's rights would be viable."

"Our firm has adjudicated cases in the past based on that claim. An issue of adverse possession comes into play. Generally speaking, you can claim land only as long as you are there openly, adverse or notorious meaning that anyone can see that you are in possession. By your own admission and practices, you're not in anyone's view, and have taken positive steps to hide your presence for the entire period you've been here. It would be difficult to assert ownership under that condition."

"Be that as it may, we all understand we're talking incredible legal precedence here. We strongly feel we can persevere under a claim of right. We've been here for more than five years, accomplishing what no others could. We've made improvements; no one can claim that we aren't good stewards of the land," said Kelly.

"Possibly, but that would be for the court to decide. I feel you've satisfied some aspects of your claim. You've been here continuously over a significant time period, and there aren't enough creative clichés to adequately describe your miraculous achievements. It's the undisguised and conspicuous part of it that creates doubt."

Handing her a large envelope, Jake continued, "We're confident that you will find the solution. I suggest you seek it in simplicity rather than complication. In this packet is a contract and retainer for thirty million dollars. You can use the enclosed card to draw against that amount on an international account in Hong Kong. It will be replenished as needed. It's our desire that you immediately close the caseloads of all one hundred and thirty-two of your employees, settling any claims out of that while referring your customers to other law practices.

"We want the full attention of your entire law firm focused on our issue only. Once you have arrived at a solution acceptable to us, you will file the legal action through the United Nations and World Court.

He went on to instruct that in this one instance only, and simultaneous with that filing, members of Eleanor's firm will travel to the respective countries and present a copy of the brief to representatives of the G8 governments—presently Canada, the Republics of France, Germany, and Italy; the countries of Japan, Russia, the United Kingdom, United States and the European Union.

"We're including China as well. After that, we will not contract with any individual nation on the planet Earth, but will restrict our dealings to the UN only. While we have agreed in principle to accept the decision of the World Court in this matter, our expectation is that it will be in our favor. In the interim, we expect an international restraining order from that Court effectively closing Luna to attempts by any individual or government to come here. Any violation of that provision will be interpreted by us as hostile intent, and they will be turned back, regardless of the Court's stance.

"Everything in the packet is on CD, but you'll also find hardcopy pictures of our daily activities here sufficient to support our claims for what's been accomplished."

As she reviewed some the packet's contents, Eleanor smiled despite herself at one picture taken of Gautier, Chat, and others standing next to a large sign proclaiming *'No Trespassing,'* with the background of Selene stretching into the distance behind them. There was a second picture of them both in E-suits on the surface, posing with the same message against the backdrop of Luna.

Kelly spoke up, "We felt it was important that you see us openly, with nothing hidden. I'm confident you are convinced we are without guile, and true to our vision. The packet contains a non-disclosure agreement. Your employees must agree to sign it before you brief them. Any one that doesn't will be offered an opportunity to go elsewhere with a generous severance. Dedication and focus to our issue must be paramount, to the exclusion of all other factors except family.

"You are free to speak of what you've seen here, including our trans-ports... but not in detail. The Starflyer and New Hope must not be discussed with anyone on Earth before we are ready to reveal them. We expect you to be discreet in discussing aspects of our science, and extent of mineral wealth as well.

"Please do not mention Q or the Akamatsu Corporation. We are granting you citizenship of Luna with full privileges, but will not require you to relinquish your Earth citizenship. This will permit you to operate openly and legally in both societies. The Council has also agreed that your firm will have exclusive rights to represent Luna in all legal matters. You are free to hang your shingle here, Eleanor, as the only legal repre-sentative of our planet.

"Welcome aboard."

At this point, Walwyn walked over and handed Eleanor a number of objects. "The cell phone looks common, but you can call us direct here by simply selecting the name you wish to reach. It has a biometric recog-nition circuit that will read your thumb print as you hold the phone, and will complete a voice analysis as you speak. Anyone attempting to use it other than you will cause the phone's battery to overload and melt the internals.

"The earrings are the same, but respond to verbal input; one is the microphone, the other the ear set. Touch the left one for recognition. Both systems require a password. The ring is an emergency signaler. Turn the stone to the left, press down, and then back to the right; we'll get in touch. I'll let Jake explain the disk."

"Every citizen of Luna has one of those, Eleanor," said Jake. "It's coded to the user and contains a GPS locator and medical telemetry capability. We insert it under the skin of the left arm, with no scarring. It's very effective in knowing where our people are when they visit Earth, and their state of health. We're asking that you come to see us bimonthly with an update on your progress. We have a TUG assigned to you exclusively. Given the number of experts focused on one issue, we're hoping you can be ready to proceed within the next sixty days. Dr. Agave is expecting you after the meeting."

After discussing a few details, Eleanor was advised she was free to return to Earth, and that Gautier and Chat would be allowed to accompany her if she desired. After they had left the room, Jake turned to the Council members.

"We're on schedule with the Starflyers. Alahn called and told me that Major Lewis has accepted our offer and entered into the Q program. She'll be here in five weeks, and he's returning today."

"Gautier says we'll be able to produce two Starflyers per week soon," piped up Chaylen. "We have eight on the floor waiting for finishing touches, and should be able to reach our first goal of twenty-five by the time Eleanor comes back with her finished report."

"Jake, are you certain about this?" Anoki asked worriedly. "I'm not comfortable with diverting a pure research vehicle to some other use."

"It's not in my nature to stifle creative debate, especially within the Council," responded Jake. "We've been over this and everyone understands the necessity. I assure you there will no deviation from our core values. We've mapped out our plans and strategy, and will operate in a purely self-defense mode."

"How will we pilot the new craft?" asked Natalya. "Beyond Alahn, we have only your Lewis, and she's not trained yet."

"You're well aware that Prime can operate every Starflyer we have. Look at how little training Alahn had. I believe, and you have all concurred, that having a human intelligence in each ship is preferable. It won't take long to bring the new pilots up to speed. Alahn has advised me that Lewis has already initiated a long list of candidates. Those will have to be screened for acceptance, and each one accepted will have more recommendations to make. We won't have the luxury of time that he had to single out one individual so I suggest we bring all of the selectees to a common meeting and recruit them as I did the original Prexus makeup. If that's agreeable, then Alahn and I, accompanied by at least two members from each group of the Council should meet with them for the effort."

A vote of the Council generated full consensus, with the balance of the meeting dealing with details of contacting the pilots and setting up the recruitment effort.

Eleanor's trip back to Earth provided quality time with the Devereux family. Gautier seemed unlike others who oftentimes appeared more interested in her social and financial standing than any type of emotional relationship. She found this appealing and conceded that her feelings for both were growing stronger with each day.

She felt strangely alone after returning to the Danville... missing Chat's closeness, her smile and youthful demeanor. Throwing herself into the business at hand allowed her to put those feelings aside for the time being. She announced a mandatory general business meeting to be held in emergency session the following day. Pleased with the full turnout, she wasn't surprised to see that every one of the employees of E, L & S stayed with the ship.

"Are you kidding?" said Jennifer. "No way am I going to miss the biggest thing to come along in law since the dawn of mankind. It's obvious no one else is going to miss out either. My God, Eleanor, we'll be the most famous law firm ever in history!"

"We'll be the biggest goats in history if we blow this one, Jenny, and every big-gun law firm on the planet will be pestering me to accept their assistance. I'll decline them all, so you can be sure they'll be watching us like hawks.

"Get the firm started on every precedent available on squatter's rights, claim of right, and other legal basis having to do with possession of land, owned or otherwise. Look for creative interpretations... wait! On second thought, include our younger hotdogs on that 'creative' one. Sometimes their approach puts new eyes on old standbys that might add a welcome twist. Randolph, look at government and international examples, perhaps dealing with claiming new volcanic land mass or islands. My concern from the onset is that existing laws deal with land owned by someone else, with a third party making a claim against some portion of that.

"As Luna isn't technically owned by anyone, complications are sure to arise... but, that same point means the field is wide open. Forget about hierarchy. Every member of the firm is a full partner as of this moment. I'm borrowing a page from Jake's book. We're doing this as a full team press. We'll sure as hell all sink together if we fail, so the stakes are the same for everyone. We've got less than sixty days now, so get busy. There's carte blanche on overtime and weekends. Everyone's on double pay effective immediately, and triple pay for anything past eight hours, including weekends."

Jake's pilot arrived on schedule, insisting on piloting the TUG herself. Edwina was eager to get started, having been assured by the Council that her first batch of trainees would be arriving as quickly as they completed the Q protocols; time enough for her to come up to speed in the Starflyer prototype. She was given a full tour of the cities, preferring to remain at Prexus and monitor production of the new ships when she wasn't occupied in the gymnasium at Cordial.

Due to the unique gravity conditions on Luna, Edwina asked the physical therapists to put together a rigorous program that would keep the pilots in top condition, including herself. She selected a combination personality AI to run the Starflyer she chose as her personal vehicle.

"Are you sure you want that?" asked Walwyn, looking up from his computer terminal. "We've found some of the combos are demonstrating characteristics that could be interpreted as, uh… creative!"

"Oh, define 'creative' please," said Edwina, smiling with both hands on her hips.

"We've been experimenting with abstract thought algorhythms, approaching emotive capability. The one you've selected has demonstrated a tendency toward humor."

"Good, then I'll never be bored," Edwina replied with a chuckle. "Name him Sidney and make sure his repertoire is as creative as you say."

Working closely with Edwina, the production teams had her ship ready to go in two days.

"The AI is programmed for all navigation within our solar system, with applicable star charts and standard Earth routes as well, so you don't need to concern yourself with situational awareness… just tell it where you want to go," instructed Gautier. "Please confine your training area to the farside. Go as far and fast as fuel will allow, but keep Luna between you and the Earth. We're not ready for them to know our capabilities just yet."

"I intend to start with acceleration protocols. I want to push the envelope and see how much I can wring out of a Starflyer!"

"Edwina, let us speak a moment," said Gautier, pulling her aside. "While I of course applaud your desire to explore the limits of your ship's capability, I believe it would be prudent to go easy at first. Remember, this is primarily a vehicle for exploring space, with a structure reinforced for careful exploration of dangerously extreme environments such as may be found on Venus. Flying through atmosphere is a secondary function."

He advised her to never forget its true purpose... the acceleration capability was designed for swift travel between planets, not aerial combat. His concern was that her fighter pilot instincts may act against her in the event she was faced with perilous conflict. Earth's pilots had been superbly trained. While Starflyers were well designed and well built, they are neither armored nor bullet proof.

"Always keep that in mind. Also, we have attempted to take into consideration as many different aspects of body orientation, inertia, and gravity forces as possible, but can't predict every possible contingency. You may find yourself in a situation requiring an application of acceleration that while within the ship's capabilities, would exceed the fluoro-carbon environment's ability to protect you. If that were to happen, we would find ourselves pumping you out with the liquid. Please be careful."

Edwina added Gautier's advice and warnings to her list of important things to make note of, promising herself to complete a thorough study for inclusion in her training manual. Assistants helped her into a body suit, waste recovery and breathing system. She donned the helmet and inserted the HD contacts herself; surprised at how comfortable they were given she always had an aversion to putting anything into her eyes. The visor provided only limited viewing at this point; the full system would come on line once she was plugged into the ship.

Taken to the transition hangar, she positioned herself within the Starflyer's pilot enclosure and found the articulated helmet and limb harnesses to be intuitive—especially as the ship's AI activated and secured each as she placed the appropriate limb within its vicinity. Just as surprising was how quickly the compartment filled itself with pleasantly warmed fluorocarbon. While she knew the liquid was there, the visor displayed the ship's interior as if it wasn't.

"OK, Sidney, I'm ready, light it up." In response, the ship disappeared and Edwina found herself sitting on absolutely nothing, approximately three feet off the deck.

Damn! Alahn was right. This will take getting used too! But ooh-wee, what a view!

Three dimensional full color holographic semi-circular instrument panels appeared within easy reach of both hands, accompanied by a three hundred sixty degree compass rose the same size as the full pilot compartment. The compass depiction provided orientation gradients in all aspects of vertical and horizontal direction. In anticipation of flight, her pilot seat repositioned itself, reclining backwards into a slightly more horizontal plane.

"Stunning accoutrements... perfectly suited for a warrior Queen. My compliments to your tailor. Would you prefer to be addressed as Commander, or Your Highness?" queried the AI.

"I'll leave the titles up to you, just make sure everything works. Open the doors, Sidney, and let's do a shake down."

On that order the hangar was depressurized. Due to the dampening effect of the fluorocarbon environment, she felt and heard nothing.

"You may control the ship manually using the representations I have provided, or simply state the desired result and I will accomplish it for you."

"Fair enough—turn it all off. Let's do this first trip naked, I want to see the stars through your eyes without all the panel whitewash." The input panels and compass rose instantly vanished, leaving Edwina with the feeling she was literally floating out of the hangar on an invisible flying carpet.

"Where to, Heavenly Duchess?"

"Take me to the boundary, Sidney; I want to look around." She very quickly found herself in a stationary hover taking in the grandeur of Earth, seen with a clarity she had never imagined possible. Turning her head, the sky filled with stars usually eclipsed by the moon's brilliance, but now laid bare by Luna's science.

I was born for this. I am truly a child of the stars.

Looking deep inside in a more introspective manner, she thought about the incredible circumstances that brought her to this point. She had declared loyalty to governments in the past, but now swore an unbreakable oath to herself this day.

Call it karma, destiny, or fate, but by whatever path... thank you God for the miracle you provided that put me here. Thank you for these people and their science. I am to be their defender and pledge my life to that responsibility... I won't waver in the duty you've placed in my hands.

After a few moments of contemplative silence, Edwina asked Sidney to project a course to Earth. A line magically appeared at the center of her chest and stretched itself in a parabolic curve to demonstrate where the Starflyer would intercept the planet. It continued around the targeted globe, depicting an orbital plane. She had the AI display all control inputs and instrument capability for familiarity, then spent the remainder of her training time exploring the acceleration capabilities of the ship.

Edwina did not push far beyond the limits revealed to her by Alahn; keeping in mind the three gravities she experienced in her internally protected environment exceeded eighty gravities externally. It was sobering to grasp how far beyond present Earth aeronautical science this ship was. Simply stepping on the gas translated into an accelerative force sufficient to destroy any aircraft she was aware of and killing an unprotected pilot in the process!

And most of the damned thing was designed by children with savant genius!

She instructed Sidney to return to Prexus; she wanted to begin work on a training syllabus for the new pilots that would be arriving soon.

"OK, Souser, I figure you've probably already heard this on days, but let's go over it one more time. The United Nations plaza is composed of four buildings located just off New York City's East River. At over five hundred feet, the thirty-nine story Secretariat Building is the tallest. The General Assembly Building is north, with the Conference Building east by the river. The Library is on the southwest corner.

"Equipment on the Secretariat's roof is concealed by an aluminum grill. The eighteen acre site was officially converted to international territory so it doesn't belong to the United States anymore. There's a small public park immediately north of the General Assembly Building, and an open grassy area across First Avenue facing the complex. The park has a left-over helicopter landing pad that we keep an eye on. It's a little unusual as they built it up off the ground to keep clear of pedestrian traffic. The water behind us is more cesspool than river, in my opinion," intoned his shift buddy for the night, George Bowling, matter-of-factly.

Souser was livid when told he was transferred to swing shifts but didn't have enough seniority to protest the assignment.

"You might want to keep in mind that regardless of who we're working for, these Internationals don't see us as much more that glorified rent-a-cops. Let's get going. We've got a lot of ground to cover before our first break," said George. Patrolling the complex required timed observation between check-in stations. Sullen and moody, Darren followed George as they began the first set of rounds, glad that he'd at least had a chance to fortify himself against the elements before the shift started.

"What'd you do to your face," asked George. "Get into a pissing contest with your cat, or some other brand of feline?" he chuckled.

"Nah, musta chewed it up shavin," Darren lied. Truth was he'd been with one of his hookers earlier that day. He'd gotten a little rough and she had repaid him in kind. He got an adrenalin rush manhandling the whores he bought.

I paid for the slut; I can get off any way I want. They don't like it, they can quit the business.

A number of his trysts wound up requiring medical attention after one of his friendly visits, and he felt the same way about them as his little fancies with the animals he had caught on the farm. He figured the shift change was retribution, but couldn't put his finger on anything he'd done lately to deserve the switch. He bounced between filing a formal protest to just cooling his heels for awhile until he could bid for a better time slot.

For the moment, he put it aside as he marched forlornly through the endless repetition of strolling the UN headquarters complex, vigilant against nothing except his own perception of being endlessly victimized by those in power... building resentment against the day that payback would be in his hands.

Taking a deep breath to calm herself, Eleanor declared, "We feel we're as ready to proceed with this as we can be," addressing the full Council, entire population of Luna, and complete employee base of Ernst, Long & Stein from the dais in the formal meeting auditorium of Selene. The room could house hundreds, and she had been informed by Jake that everyone would be watching her presentation today. The meeting was being video-cast to anyone not physically present in the room. Returning periodically as requested, she had kept the Council abreast of progress; her firm not requiring the full sixty days to prepare. She beamed a reassuring smile to Chat and Gautier... seated in the first row among the other Council members and was gladdened by the response from both. Glancing at her notes, she began by advising how their law firm expected to approach the issue at hand.

E, L & S would engage in an extraordinary action to establish legal precedence in an area never before addressed or argued in law in the history of mankind. The combined expertise and efforts of every member of their firm were fruitless in locating any previous example to build on.

The absence of existing law required that they reexamine concepts of ownership established by explorers throughout mankind's history, so that they may present before the World Court an argument in support of the Council's claim based on reason, common sense, and rule of law.

Key to that research was the concept that such exploration land claims made in past were in the name of governments and rulers existing at the time. In like manner, the Luna Council was able to demonstrate an existing government claiming possession.

In nineteen seventy-nine, an attempt was made to initiate an international Moon Treaty, known as the "Agreement Governing the Activities of States on the Moon and Other Celestial Bodies." Couched in language that appeared beneficial to mankind, it was nonetheless perceived to be a shallow attempt to outlaw property rights and stop settlement of space by creating a common heritage quagmire. The treaty was never ratified.

Numerous other attempts had been made addressing different aspects of the issue, including fringe elements claiming everything in space and wanting to sell land to anyone gullible enough to hand over money. Such issues would not be enumerated here. While some of the attempts were laudatory, no one had actually settled on another planet prior to Luna citizen's occupancy and no test of law existed as precedent. A review of the issue of claiming land was undertaken.

From a layman's perspective, it may seem reasonable to stake a claim based on squatter's rights, an ancient and simplistic doctrine used in claiming title to land owned by another. Much historical law and precedent exists to define and support this long held standard. However, squatter's rights assumes another party already has title to the land in question, and that the claimant has been in open, or adverse possession of some portion of that land for a long period of time… usually amounting to decades under present Earth law. As no legally recognized owner of Luna exists, this point became moot.

Moreover, the habitation of Luna could not meet an adverse or notorious standard. Their presence on Luna had not been open, and in fact, no one beyond their representatives on Earth knew of their existence at this moment. Having pointed that out, it was felt that some portions of the law in this arena may be successfully argued. E, L & S intended to demonstrate prescriptive easement, a doctrine based on the idea that as Luna's citizens have used the property without protest, it belongs to them. It can also be shown those citizens had been in exclusive and continuous possession.

Due to the distinctive nature of their claim, the Court would be requested to stipulate that in this instance, continuous possession exceeding five years was enough to satisfy residency time requirements. They intended to also argue that a claim of right exists. That is, the citizenry of Luna will claim ownership by possession as they believe they are the rightful owners.

Demonstration of accomplishment achieved on Luna would act to bolster that point; they would tie in international doctrine established in the early seventies based on land-to-the-tiller. This concept of land reform resulted in legal title to land being given to over one million Southeast Asian farmers. Simply put, Luna's citizens were and have been the only tillers of the land in question.

E, L & S will hold that a right of pre-emption exits to all other claims. In effect, in the absence of any other holder of the land, the citizens of Luna are entitled to acquisition of the property they've enjoyed as their permanent home. They'll be able to demonstrate a stable government and an ability to travel freely between Earth and Luna, establishing trade and other relationships beneficial to both planets.

"Finally, we intend to argue before the World Court that the rare circumstances of our claim require a broad interpretation, beyond the confining scope of present Earth law dealing with similar issues. Prior to these issues being weighed in jurisprudence, we will file a motion requesting that an international restraining order be issued, and remain in effect until the Court has reached a decision."

Eleanor answered questions for several hours, ending her presentation to meet with the full Council in closed session. As she moved to sit next to Gautier, Chat sat on her lap and embraced her with a hug. Eleanor returned the affection with a kiss and hugged her warmly. Maralah thanked Eleanor for the efforts of her firm and asked if there were more legal areas that could be explored.

"The presentation was meant to convey only high points, or executive level of the path we intend to pursue, eliminating the minute details of the course that will be followed in presenting your case. I assure you all that every employee of the firm of Ernst, Long and Stein is prepared to go the distance in establishing new law."

Noticing her tired appearance, Singe offered, "You appear pensive, Eleanor."

"I would be lying if I told you that I'm not apprehensive about this. What you have here is precious beyond measure. I've come to realize that you have truly moved above the struggle that Earth seems doomed to deal with in perpetuity. Your potential is unimaginable. I fear for the safety of your people when Earth finds out about you. Your secrets won't remain so forever. As written in the course of human history, there are powerful people who will turn a conqueror's eye toward this place, seeking only its treasures and with no concern about the lives of its people."

Glancing at Chat and Gautier, she sighed in a subdued tone, "I now have my own selfish reasons for feeling this way."

Hugging Eleanor tightly; her small voice plainly heard by all, Chat said, "Je vous aime, Eleanor. You're part of our family now."

"The rest of us echo Chateauleire's sentiments," offered Jake. "You're respected by all here, and are now a part of our rather large family. You mustn't concern yourself with those issues Eleanor; we've been planning this moment for years. The Council and just about every citizen of our community have been discussing just the possibilities you have raised; we have plans in place to prevent those events from happening. I also want to assure you that no one will come to harm as a result. More will be revealed to you in future, depending on the way things progress. Until something happens to require a response, I suggest you don't worry."

As the car approached the Peace Palace at The Hague, Netherlands, Randolph asked Eleanor what she knew about the Court itself.

"It's actually called the International Court of Justice and was formed in 1946 as a replacement for the Permanent Court of International Justice. It's considered to be the United Nations' primary judicial body," she replied. "It acts to settle disputes between members of the UN and also provides advisory opinions on legal questions."

"Well, that's reassuring," he replied. "A bunch of old goats on the retirement list regurgitating former glory. Do we have any friends there?"

"We can't apply home turf standards here, Randolph. There are fifteen sitting judges, representing quite a diverse international community. I'm confident they'll give us full measure, especially when they see the list we're providing of our citizen base broken out by nationality."

Jennifer added, "Luna isn't a member of the UN or a recognized state. But remember that we're going to ask for the same consideration that's given to Switzerland, which is also not a member. A factor in our favor is that the Court decides for itself whether or not it has jurisdiction. We turn in our written case and then go through public oral arguments before the Court. The Court then deliberates and its judgment is presented at another public hearing."

"Interesting," replied Randolph. "I also understand the only appeal process is through the UN Security Council. Hmmm, get it right the first time or fall on the sword of justice, huh?"

"Don't be so negative. If you had read the fine print in that brochure I gave you, you would have noticed the Court has heard cases dealing with land frontiers, territorial sovereignty and nationality, for example."

Holding the brochure up and reading from it, Jennifer intoned, "Sources of applicable law. The Court decides in accordance with international treaties and conventions in force, international custom, the general principles of law and, as subsidiary means, judicial decisions and the teachings of the most highly qualified publicists."

"I submit for the sake of our discussion that the Court can as easily deal with the issue of Luna."

With enviable punctuality on that Monday morning, Eleanor Ernst, Jennifer Long, and Randolph Stein filed their case through the Clerk of the World Court's staff. Given the difference in time zones, it required that day and one more for associates of E, L & S to present the same case to applicable offices of the G8 Nations, China, and United Nations, but presented they were.

Chaotic response from the world's media made a shark's feeding frenzy pale in comparison.

The Danville Building's automated switchboard system was overwhelmed by domestic and international phone traffic; the sheer volume acting to shut down service to the entire building and threatening to engulf the regional phone system switching mechanisms as well. It seemed every press organization on the planet was demanding appointments and interviews with representatives of E, L & S concerning the usurpers on the moon.

Having anticipated exactly that reaction, Danville management had additional trunk lines installed to relieve the building's normal phone traffic and hired extra security guards to manage the crush of unwanted visitors. A special office had been set up with carefully scripted announcements released daily. A week passed by with no let-up in sight.

"Miss Bea, this is Cindy, the Danville Receptionist. There's a gentleman here to see you. He has two associates with him."

"Cindy, I simply don't have time to squander on frivolous interviews. Please hand them the prepared statement and advise them we aren't granting interviews, public or private."

"I already did that, Miss Bea, but this gentleman insists it's very important that he speak to you."

With a short sigh of resignation she asked, "Did he give a name?"

"He says he's Mr. Baruti Harakhty, Secretary-General of the United Nations. His associates are the Deputy Secretary-General and his Aide."

Instantly alert, Eleanor muttered, "Damn!"

Recovering, she asked Cindy to call Security. "Have them escorted with all honors to the executive conference room. We'll meet them there," she stated hurriedly, punching the intercom and telling Jennifer and Randolph to drop everything and get to the Exec conference room immediately. She ordered refreshments and then rushed to greet her unexpected guests.

After introductions, Eleanor stated, "I'm sorry for any wait you encountered, Mr. Harakhty. We weren't expecting such distinguished visitors."

The older gentleman bowed courteously, and with gracious good manners replied, "It is for me to apologize, Miss Ernst. My callous disregard for protocol in dropping in unannounced has taken you away from your monumental task of petitioning on behalf of the good people of... is it 'Luna' in the singular?"

Impressed with Mr. Harakhty's gentle nature and open sincerity, Eleanor replied, "Yes, just Luna. Please, sit and let's have coffee."

After refreshments and some small talk, she inquired politely, "What brings you to our door today, Mr. Harakhty?"

"Under the circumstances, I would ask that you please call me Baruti. I am imposing on your good graces and precious time, and would feel more comfortable with less formality. Your announcement and written plea for your clients has fired the imagination of everyone on this planet. Who among us has not longed to explore the unknown; to see our world from another vantage point?"

Astutely, Eleanor gleaned the purpose of today's meeting. "Would you and a number of your associates like to form a delegation and visit Luna, Baruti?"

"Ah, such insight. Yes," he sighed, eyes alight with excitement. "The writ we received does mention significant accomplishment. It is felt that to see such work first hand would go a long way in winning others to your cause." Smiling, he added, "I believe there is a saying in America that... to see a thing is to believe it?"

Grinning at his simple adage, Eleanor responded, "That's correct, Baruti. If you'll excuse me for a moment, I'll step out to make the arrangements." Moving into an empty office adjacent to the conference room, Eleanor took out the special cell phone given to her by Walwyn and punched in Jake. It only required a moment to obtain permission for the plan, and Jake assured her the Council would eagerly approve her suggestion. A TUG would be dispatched and scheduled to arrive at the UN the following Wednesday by about ten p.m.

The Delegation should plan on boarding and takeoff by midnight. The interim time would permit the TUG's AI to top off fuel tanks for the additional weight.

Returning to the conference room, Eleanor advised everyone of the plan, suggesting that Baruti was welcome to invite eight other members to form his Delegation.

"Wonderful," replied Baruti. "Thank you, Eleanor. We will all look forward to next week's adventure with joyous anticipation." So saying, the meeting adjourned, leaving Jennifer and Randolph to discuss details with Eleanor.

Leaning forward over the table and speaking in somewhat of a con-spiratorial tone, Eleanor offered, "The TUG can take twelve passengers, so Baruti can put together quite a powerful international group for this visit. They won't need E-suits; the pilots will wear theirs. Providing them with the antibody booster I was given should be sufficient to allow limited free association."

With a puzzled look, Jennifer asked, "Last time I added them up, eight plus one equaled nine. Where are the other three coming from?"

"I'm going along and bringing you two with me. It's time you met your clients.

Reaching over to grasp her hand, Jennifer beamed with enthusiasm, "Oh, that's wonderful! How exciting, Eleanor! Thank you, thank you." In a more somber tone she added, "Will I get to wear one of those pretty suits like they gave you?"

Jennifer's exuberance drew laughter from the other two, and they all shared a rare moment of jollity together. "Yes, Jenny. The two of you may have your choice of the pretty suit or a more subdued gray one, if you like. We'll offload the Delegation in the pressurized hangar at Cordial, and make arrangements for a tour there by isolating selected areas from Luna's citizens. We'll use a TUG to get around elsewhere.

"They can view the entrance to Selene from the visitor's auditorium. I'll talk to Mr. Boxe to determine the feasibility of an interior inspection for a short distance inside that city. They don't need to know about Prexus just now. We'll put together a carefully crafted visit to keep them away from other sensitive places. And I'm sorry, you two. You're my closest friends, but there are some aspects of Luna that I'm not free to reveal right now. I'll fill you in completely when the time is right."

Randolph was equally pleased and pitched in, "This is only the beginning. We can offer the same opportunity to members of the World Court, and any other influential organization that will assist in our cause."

"OK. You two can start putting together suggestions for tour participants, starting with a formal invitation to members of the Court. We can build on that and take it from there, but remember that the Council will be the approving authority," said Eleanor.

"**I** want an immediate meeting set up with the full Presidential Staff, Joint Chiefs of Staff, Central Intelligence Agency, Federal Bureau of Investigation, Home Land Security and anyone else I left off the list. I want to know who we're dealing with, how we missed this, and what sort of danger this group represents."

"Yes Sir, Mr. President," his aide responded, turning to move quickly from the Oval Office.

"Wait. Set up another meeting with the heads of the G8 nations. We're all on the list so I suppose we should get together."

"Shall I include the U.N.?"

"No. That's about the most worthless bunch of do-nothings I know of. Once I decide what we're going to do about this, I'll get the other Governments to climb on board. We'll let the U.N. know so they can go along like good little boys and girls."

President Stewart Talefer Caneman III didn't like surprises. He especially didn't like the idea of someone claiming territory that by right belonged to the United States.

We got there first. Doesn't matter that the place is worthless, goddamnit, it's ours. Put a base there and we'd control this planet into the next millennium. Damn! That would be one for the history books, with my name splattered all over it.

Regardless of who was there now or how they got there, he was going to ensure things got set right, and if there was going to be anyone inhabiting the moon, it would be the United States Air Force Space Command waving the flag.

"And before you leave, get NASA in here. I want to talk to them about upgrading the space shuttle."

"Yes Sir."

Cutting off the vid phone connection, Chat leaped with elation on the news from Maralah that she and Iawy had been selected to pilot the TUG that was to pick up the UN delegation. She planned to arrange a special visit during the few hours of down time that would be available.

Running into the main room, she excitedly shared the news with Gautier. "Oh, Papa, I will see Eleanor again. Won't she be surprised! I have missed her so these past weeks."

"You really love Eleanor, don't you?"

"Yes, we are common in many things together. I have promised to show her how to play wall tag when next she comes. Speaking on the vid phone is not as fulfilling as walking side by side." With a tilt of her head and an inquisitive look, she asked, "I think you like her very much as well, Oui, Papa?"

"Your observation is correct. I have grown quite fond of Eleanor in the time since we first met. I will admit that I too am looking forward to her next visit. Like you, I find that I prefer communicating in person; like this!"

With a mischievous gleam in his eye, Gautier grabbed Chat from behind and swung her in a wide arc circle as she squealed with glee; arms spread wide and legs wind-milling in the air! Even eleven year old geniuses still delighted in such personal attention from their fathers.

Setting her down, they rolled on the floor together. He tickled her sides as they both erupted with laughter and glee. Once their combined hilarity had subsided, they rose kneeling to face each other. Gautier hugged her closely; kissing her cheek and nuzzling one side of her neck.

Leaning slightly back to glaze full into her eyes, he softly caressed her hair and offered, "Perhaps a day will come when our family will be complete again, yes?"

"It is the greatest wish of my heart, Papa," said Chat, returning his hug just as tightly.

Releasing his daughter, Gautier led her happily into the dining room for an undisturbed dinner and discussion of the day's events.

The week flew by quickly. The trip to Earth was uneventful, dull, and boring. Chat was barely able to contain her excitement at the idea of surprising Eleanor by dropping in unexpectedly. Calling ahead had confirmed that she was indeed working late and would be at the Danville when the TUG arrived.

Approaching slowly from the south, the TUG maneuvered in low over New York's East River and made a descending turn toward the public park located on the north side of the complex. Settling gently onto the helicopter landing platform, Iawy instructed the AI to commence shut down procedure, using AlSys to refuel for the return journey and take into consideration the addition of twelve passengers and gear. Chat leaped out of her restraining harness and moved toward the exit portal.

"Chateauleire, wait," called out Iawy. "I'll only be another moment."

Filled with youthful impatience, Chat told the AI to open up and rushed through the upwardly sliding portal. Her hopes to be greeted by the driver of a vehicle hired to carry her to the Danville were crushed by a huge hand that clamped her throat, lifted her bodily off the ground and slammed her into the side of the TUG. Stunned and gasping for air, she grabbed that hand with both of hers and kicked out as hard as she could.

A male voice quivering with excitement exclaimed, "Well, whadda we got here? A little moon princess!"

Another hand roughly explored her chest, then just as rudely probed between her legs; pinching and squeezing her buttocks. "I've got time to show you a few tricks before I turn you in, moon pie. I know you're gonna like it!"

Choking for air, Chat was trying to comprehend what was happening as she was being cruelly brutalized.

Darren Souser just happened to be making his patrol rounds on the north side of the UN complex when the TUG made its landing approach. There could not have been a single person on planet Earth who didn't know about the moon base and the usurpers claims for sovereignty.

That particular news story had consumed every form of media available for weeks. As his eyesight took in the approaching TUG, Souser was instantly overwhelmed with one all-consuming goal; a plan that in his warped mind that would vindicate his past and make him a national hero... both in one stroke.

He would capture the vehicle's occupants and turn them over for prosecution.

Bunch of rocket fuel snort'n idiot pinko freaks. Where do they get off claiming our moon? It belongs to us, not them. I'll be famous... maybe get a promotion out of this... transfer to some soft indoor job. I'll be on every talk show in the nation. I'm rich! I'll be able to buy moon pie three times a day.

Distracted in idly rubbing the body he held before him and just as impervious to the harm he was causing, Souser glazed off into the night in further contemplation of his fantasy rise to fame and glory.

His sudden return to reality was crudely accomplished by a heavy thud associated with an unexpected bright light and explosion of pain behind his eyes. He was momentarily staggered by the force of the blow that hit him. Although approaching seventy years of age, Iawy had a wiry musculature; excelling in sports as a young man in Egypt. While compact and small he was solidly built; staying toned with a rigorous fitness program on Luna.

His lifelong philosophy of non-violence was not at odds with an equally viable belief in preserving another's life in self-defense. Exiting the ship found him at Souser's back, ignited with adrenalin from witnessing the battering on his young charge. Seemingly unimpeded by the E-suit's weight or increased gravity, Iawy had shaped his focus and executed a perfect spin kick that connected with the left temple of his target's head.

Darren Souser forgot that the first rule in fighting is to never lose your temper. With a bellow of rage, he threw aside his temporary distraction and turned to face his assailant.

Chateauleire Devereux had been surrounded by loving family during her almost twelve years of life. After the death of her mother, regaining the presence and love of her father acted to block out emotional difficulties faced during his absence. Physical pain was limited to occasional scrapes or bruises suffered by all children at that age.

As her body hit the edge of the landing platform, several ribs broke, one of which speared her left lung. Already stunned by the mauling received at Souser's hand, and with no frame of reference for dealing with such an enormous shock overload to her nervous system, she mercifully lost consciousness.

Falling fifteen feet to the pavement below resulted in striking head first. Her E-suit's helmet absorbed much of the shock, but not enough.

Chat's neck broke and she lay crumpled in a lifeless sprawl.

Iawy calmly side-stepped Souser's initial bull charge, bringing the heel of his left palm up. The forward moving hand combined with Souser's momentum to smash his nose as he passed by. With blood splattering everywhere, Souser turned to seize his opponent, screaming in fury. Given little room to maneuver on the helipad's deck, Iawy could not hope to long avoid personal contact with the madman confronting him.

Life fluid splattering onto the arms of Iawy's suit made it difficult for Souser to arrive at a firm purchase as they wrestled. Iawy slipped free, delivering another spin kick to his foe's right knee. A dull groan escaped Souser's lips as a blast of fire shot up his leg. A vicious backhand by Souser snapped Iawy's helmet back, allowing Souser to lunge out and encircle him in a bear hug. While struggling, their positions reversed and they stumbled into the TUG's entryway.

Sensing the proximity of occupants, the AI had kept the portal opened. It could not comprehend the actions taking place before its sensors, and was receiving no response from either pilot. Comparing Souser's bloodied face to algorithmic representations of Luna's full population did not produce a match. The AI then queried Prime on Luna for an appropriate response.

Iawy again kicked out at Souser, connecting with his testicles and forcing him to back away into the TUG grunting with pain. Thrown off balance by the move and with his back to the open portal, Iawy reached out sideways and grabbed both sides for stability.

Even pain maddened bulls enraged by the Matador's barbed dart banderilla can see with clarity at times.

Ignoring his injuries, Souser leaned back and lashed out with one foot encased in a large military style boot to strike the center of his enemy's chest. The blow crushed Iawy's sternum and propelled him up and out of the airlock. Unlike Chat, he missed the edge of the platform and fell to the pavement in an arching trajectory. His body joined that of his traveling companion in a deathly imitation of broken dolls left for rubbish.

The TUG's AI continued to query Prime, recording everything that occurred; audio and video sensors fully engaged. "Please identify yourself," it demanded.

"Up yours," spat Souser, as he sat down in one of the pilot's chairs in an attempt to relieve his pain. Pinching his nostrils shut while tilting his head back allowed him to swallow the excess blood flow from his broken nose until it subsided.

He massaged his crotch and knee in agony.

Son of a bitch! How could a skinny bastard like that hit so hard?

Placing one hand on the arm of the seat, he adjusted himself in the most comfortable manner possible. The pain in his groin and head commanded so much of his attention that he did not notice the slight electrical tingling coursing through his hand.

As the interloper had failed every biometric identification test available to the TUG's AI, including voice and retinal recognition, it broadcast an Intruder Alert to Prime. Continuing to receive no response to its queries from either of the legitimate pilots, and unable to separate or identify them from the group of people now seen running toward the helipad, it was also unable to decipher the heated exchange of words taking place below the platform. Prime ordered the TUG to secure the lone occupant and return to Luna.

With no understanding or comprehension of exactly what he was sitting in, Souser was taken by surprise when the ship's restraining system locked him into the seat. Strong as he was, his efforts were for naught in attempting to wiggle out of the harness. Senses suddenly alert, he was brought to a high level of apprehension when the TUG initiated its start sequence; momentarily sending strange thumps, clangs, and pumping sounds reverberating throughout the craft's structure as systems were energized and brought up to operating pressures.

He forgot his pain and let out a cry of startled alarm when the three dimensional HD multicasting unit took away the front of the TUG. As it lifted off and accelerated into the night sky at a forty-five degree angle, Darren Souser wet his pants.

President Caneman's staff wasted no time in exploiting the conditions of the report forwarded through the Department of Homeland Security channels.

A clear television feed had been established to every major news organization, opening with, "Good morning from WNN News; Betty Newcastle here with an exclusive report on a breaking story. In just a moment, we'll transfer to the White House where a special conference has been set up by the President's Press Secretary, Ralph Dominic. Stay tuned after the Presidential broadcast, so our analysts can explain it to you. We take you now to the White House."

The picture in every household blinked to the conference room, where the Press Secretary could be seen standing behind the Presidential podium, appearing as officiously rigid as the Presidential Seal adorning its face. He was fronted by a large group of media representatives all clamoring for recognition.

Appearing stern, Mr. Dominic called the room to order, beginning, "Ladies and Gentlemen, last night a Special Agent of the Homeland Defense Security Detail of the United Nations was gravely injured in an unprovoked attack. We have actual footage taken from surveillance cameras."

Mr. Dominic's visage was replaced by video of Iawy and Souser, taken from an angle that eliminated any view of Chat. For that matter, all content that led up to Iawy's intervention had been edited out. The viewing audience could only see Iawy's first kick at Souser, leaving no room to interpret events otherwise. It ended with Iawy's plunge off the platform, and the liftoff of the TUG shortly thereafter.

"As you can see, our Agent was then abducted by unknown individuals thought to represent moon factions seeking unprecedented recognition of

115

illegal claims to territory first explored by our people. President Caneman has expressed grave concern over this egregious turn of events, and promises you that the government of this country will bring all remedies to bear in obtaining the safe return of our Agent, and prosecution of the two perpetrators now in Federal custody."

President Caneman watched the news presentation from the Oval Office with members of his senior staff. As Mr. Dominic opened the floor to questions, the President dismissed everyone but indicated to the Attorney General that he should stay; there was a small matter he wanted to discuss with him dealing with the Supreme Court.

While we're at it, I think we'll have a talk with those two in the hospital, he thought with egotistical smugness.

The WNN broadcast shifted back to Ms. Newcastle in the WNN newsroom. "Stay with us now, ladies and gentlemen, as we take you through a slow motion presentation of the attack that occurred on one of our elite Federal Agents. We'll explain everything to you so you can understand the significance of these actions."

"Off," said Jake to the monitor, which instantly complied. Turning to Gautier with a look of disgust on his face he said, "I'm as concerned about Chat and Iawy as you are. Thank God they're both still alive. We've pinpointed them at Walter Reed Army Medical Center, on Georgia Avenue in Washington, D.C. Their life signs are low but stable. Beyond that, we don't know what their exact conditions are.

"Eleanor's people were able to tell us they're under heavy guard in the intensive care ward with no visitors allowed. We'll know more when Ops has hacked into their systems, assuming medical information on the two is being entered into the hospital's computer system."

With anguish spread over every feature of his face and hands shaking with fury, Gautier implored, "Jake, mon bon ami. I beg you from the depths of my being; give me but one moment unattended with the monster that has done this. There will be no need to further burden the legal systems of either planet."

"If it were only in my power to do so, my good friend. I remind you of your vow of non-violence. The Council is unanimous in their decision; you're to remain here in Prexus. Your security access to transportation devices has been revoked. You can continue to work, or stay in your quarters if you like, but you are prohibited from coming to Cordial. Be patient with us; there will be sterner work for you ahead."

Reaching up to place a reassuring hand on Gautier's shoulder, Jake continued, "Please stay in touch with Eleanor. I'm aware she is as devastated by this as you. She needs your strength now, Gautier, not violent passion. I have an appointment I must keep with Emma Boxe. You'll be the first to know of new developments, I promise you."

Regaining his composure somewhat, Gautier nodded his head in reply. "Will you allow me to organize a rescue effort immediately?"

"Not now, Gautier. They're safe for the time being; in this case the fact that they're being guarded works in our favor. We'll address their return soon enough. I must leave now."

A father himself, Jake was as heartbroken as Gautier; sharing his torment and sense of helplessness over the plight of Chat and Iawy. Walwyn had contacted him as soon as Prime had received the TUG's intruder alert. It wasn't difficult to locate them with their identifier disks, but the medical telemetry was too basic to determine the extent of their injuries. Once the TUG had returned to Luna, it was directed to a quiet corner in the main hangar on Cordial. A combative and unrepentant Souser was taken into custody with little effort by the brothers Zieng and Wiang. After being examined and treated by E-suited medical staff, he was secured in an isolated habitat.

"Excuse Sir, with pleases, this rude interruption to your privacy, Honorable Secretary-General; it is imperative for you to come quickly. An urgent request for your presence in the General Assembly Building is being received," implored the Aide. A trustworthy assistant from East India stood in the doorway while rubbing his hands and bowing nervously.

"What is so important at this moment?" Baruti snapped in exasperation. "Can't you see that I must complete this witness report on the assault proceedings? Much is at stake in the lives of two innocents; I must work undisturbed."

"That is why immediately you must come, Sir. The Government of the moon peoples is on the main video monitors for conferencing. They have demanded an audience with you and the full United Nations membership."

At hearing this, Secretary-General Harakhty dropped everything and rushed to join the swarm of U.N. members heading for the General Assembly Hall.

Two huge video monitor screens faced the audience, located about twenty-five feet above the floor on either side of a dark cream colored center stage obelisk bearing the United Nations symbol. Displayed on both was a group of rather ordinary appearing people standing in a semi-circle around two men and two women. All were dressed in matching jump suits of the same color.

"Good day, Secretary-General Harakhty. I am Jake, Council Leader of Luna. I apologize for the short notice; we'll have CDs available for everyone not in attendance. I had hoped that a more precipitous occasion could have brought us together, but we must deal with events at hand. Allow me to introduce Alahn, Assistant Council Leader... our Administrator, Kelly, and Assistant Administrator, Donah." Kelly then introduced the other members of Luna's Council.

Secretary-General Harakhty nodded in response to each introduction, and offered his condolences that their first meeting had to be under such strained circumstances.

"On behalf of the full Council of Luna, I want to thank you and the members of your delegation personally for attempting to come to the aid of our people. It would comfort their families if you would provide us with a detailed report of their injuries," said Jake.

"You are most welcome, Mr. Jake," returned Baruti with humility. "We did only what any person of good conscience would do under such circumstances. It is regrettable that we were unable to do more. Unfortunately, our inquires to date have fallen on deaf ears. While we will continue in our efforts there, I fear we are seen as outsiders. The local Government sees this as an internal affair, and we are politely but firmly told to mind our own business."

At those words, a sobering change seemed to sweep over the Council members, young and old alike. Rising to his full height, Jake took one step forward of the others.

Gazing with cold, unwavering directness at the camera, he spoke slowly with firm conviction and strong voice, "You are going to find in the near term, Mr. Harakhty, that being the Secretary-General of the *United Nations* is going to take on an entirely new meaning." Jake had purposely emphasized the title, continuing, "You, and the combined U.N. Assembly, are going to be moving into a new era of leadership. I suggest you prepare yourselves. As an initial duty under that new role, this Council is demanding from you the return of our citizens.

"The criminal Souser will be transferred to you unharmed for prosecution by the American government. We'll stay in touch to arrange the transfer. Methods to contact us and the communication tools to do so will be forwarded to you shortly by our representatives there on Earth. Be advised that from this point forward, the Council of Luna will deal only through the United Nations, as spelled out in the writ provided. We will not deal with any individual government on your planet. I apologize that we have to delay your trip for a while. Good day, Sir."

With that, the screens went blank, leaving the Honorable Secretary-General of the United Nations and hundreds of members with an equally blank look on all their faces.

In the days that followed, the Secretary-General received a package sent by the law firm of Ernst, Long and Stein. It contained a pre-programmed cell phone for him and the Deputy Secretary-General. A vehicle from Luna arrived as prearranged and delivered Agent Darren Souser into custody of U.N. Security, then left just as quickly.

Alone in his Cordial quarters, Jake was reviewing project progress reports. His solitude was interrupted by a visit from Kelly and Maralah.

"Turn on your vidphone; we've just received an urgent call. Walwyn's people were going to terminate it and erase any connection record, but checked with us first. We felt it was important enough to see you personally," said Kelly.

As the unit sprang to life, Jake found himself looking at a young man who was trembling and visibly shaken. "What seems to be the problem?" he asked.

"Mr. Jake, sir, I'm Levi Weizman, a high school intern at Ernst, Long and Stein. I tried to use Miss Bea's new cell phone, but it started smoking.

The conference room video phone caller identification had an odd number on it, so I assumed it would connect me to someone there. It's nine o'clock here. Strange people identifying themselves as Secret Service agents came into the company a few minutes ago... "

At this young Levi buried his face in his hands and began crying uncontrollably.

Jake allowed him a moment, then spoke softly, "Levi, please share with me what has upset you so. Events that transpire there affect me as well."

Wiping tears from his eyes with the back of his hand, Levi stammered, "They put Miss Bea, Miss Long, and Mr. Stein in handcuffs and leg chains. There were ugly men taking pictures of them as they were led out. They wouldn't tell us where they were going or where they were taking them... Oh, oh," cried Levi, as his composure failed him again.

"That is startling news, Levi. I admit it upsets me as well."

Levi continued through his grief, "My grandparents were taken at night during the last great war, Mr. Jake, never to be heard from again. My parents barely escaped with their lives. Are these men coming to take us all?"

Heartbroken and moved by the young man's distress, Jake assured him that he would do everything in his power to ensure that wouldn't happen. Levi was to stay in contact with Kelly or Maralah and keep them updated on events. Jake promised he would attempt to determine their whereabouts and pass that information on to Levi, severing the connection as he bid him good night.

"Maralah, go to Prexus and see Gautier personally. He'll need a strong shoulder. Kelly, come with me. I'm going to Walwyn and his people and see what they can do to locate our three friends."

In silence, the Agent placed his hand on top of Eleanor's head as she bent down to enter the dark unmarked cruiser. Off balance, she stumbled into the rear seat, hindered by handcuffs and leg chains encircling both ankles.

"Where are you taking us? What have you done with my friends? I demand to know the meaning of this!"

Her protests went unanswered and she felt foolish for having left the special cell phone on her desk as the car sped off into the night. With presence of mind and pressing her hands together, Eleanor managed to get to Walwyn's ring. After a moment of finger gymnastics, she pushed the stone down and turned it. With some confidence returning, she knew that eventually someone would be removing the handcuffs, at which point she would attempt to use the earring system to contact Jake or another Council member for assistance.

After hours of driving, the car exited the turnpike, continuing along a two way municipal road. A few more turns and she could vaguely make out an off-white, nondescript building that seemed to blend into its surroundings. A wooded area could be seen behind and extending to both sides. A large grass field on the west side was severed by a security fence which enclosed acres of open area illuminated by security lighting.

Noting a red-capped stone mounted in front of the facility, Eleanor attempted to crane her neck around and take in the complete display but was only partially successful. She was dismayed to catch "County Prison" in her field of vision, and her sense of apprehension increased as she noticed formal yellow framework encompassing both the windows and entrance doors.

Where have they brought me?

The car turned left passing through an outer fence, then left again through an inner sally port. She was removed from the car and turned over to an officer identifying herself as Corporal Bennington.

As if by rote she intoned, "This is the intake area. You'll be held in a classification unit for a few days. We'll check your personal needs, medical and mental health. Once that's sorted out, you'll be assigned a cell in the female general population. We have nurses on two shifts, and a doctor on call."

"Can you tell me anything about why I'm here?" asked Eleanor pensively.

"The booking sheet only tells me we're holding you for awhile. If it's worth anything to you, my experience tells me we see that kind of entry when it concerns the Feds. Beyond that, I have no idea."

So saying, Corporal Bennington removed the handcuffs. As she kneeled down to remove the leg chains, Eleanor touched her left earring, softly saying "Jake."

Startled, Bennington looked up and demanded, "You say something to me?"

"No, sorry. Just... just thinking out loud."

Putting the chains and cuffs aside, she stood up and removed Eleanor's earrings and other jewelry.

Hope the line stays open long enough for Walwyn to get some idea where I am.

Asked to remove her clothing, Bennington performed a strip search, a procedure that deeply humiliated Eleanor. She was then handed a reddish pink shirt and pant uniform in exchange, and given a pair of shower shoes for her feet. Bed linens and a pillow were placed in her arms with soap, toothbrush, and toothpaste being added to the lot.

Corporal Bennington escorted Eleanor to a dual door cage which separated them from the prison depths. Motioning to a security room guard sitting behind bullet proof glass caused the nearer steel barred door to slide open. After entering, this door slammed behind them with a resounding clang... as if to announce to anyone within hearing the pending arrival of humankind's latest societal failure. At locking, a second door opened and regurgitated Eleanor into the interior hallway.

Apprehensive, not knowing what to expect, she noted the high luster shine on the floors; how clean the facility appeared. That same observation took in security cameras and numerous monitors inside the security room. Rooms aligned along the corridor appeared to be used for teaching, if blackboards were any clue. She was even more impressed as they passed a gymnasium on the opposite side of the hall.

I've been watching too many late night gangster movies.

Stopping at another sealed security room, they were buzzed through the door. While Corporal Bennington paused momentarily to speak with the guard, Eleanor noted they were in a large open day room, composed of a two story cell block unit against the far wall and two tables with integrated seats bolted to the floor in the center. Although it was dark, she could make out that a number of the cells were occupied. On her right was a visitation room with a large window for observation by the guard. There were several phones on the outside wall.

I'll call the Firm, someone there will get me out of this. One step at a time, Eleanor.

Bennington grabbed Eleanor by the elbow and walked her to an open cell at the end of the ground level cell block. "You can make the bed and set your personal items on the shelf there." Motioning to the guard resulted in movement of a green painted cell door. The hard mechanical locking mechanism slammed home—sending a hard, cold echo throughout the day room... signaling a degree of finality to Eleanor's journey that sent a chill through her body.

Don't leave me here.

The process of incarceration can be a bewildering experience; especially to a law abiding citizen who has never seen the intimate details of a prison. It was after nine p.m. when Eleanor and her friends were removed from the Danville, and she had been hard at work since four a.m. that morning. Now one a.m. the following day, she was exhausted, both physically and mentally. The physiological impact of this evening's events piled up, creating a higher level of apprehension.

"Corporal Bennington, wait a moment, please," she implored. "I don't know what any of this is about. I was taken from my office by people I don't know and who have refused to answer my questions or even speak to me."

Laying the linens and other items on the upper bunk, she turned back to the cell door and continued, "Constitutional laws dealing with habeas corpus require that I can't be held without being charged with something. Why haven't I been offered an opportunity to call for legal assistance? What about arraignment? What are the charges against me? Why am I here?"

Bennington looked through the cell door with doubt written on her face.

"Look, you don't seem like the type we normally get in here," she said somewhat apologetically. "The Warden will be in first thing in the morning, and I'm sure he'll come in to talk to you. Why don't you make up your bunk there and try to get some sleep. Breakfast will be brought to you at six-thirty in the morning, lunch at ten-thirty, and dinner comes around four-thirty. Cells are opened at seven a.m. daily and lockup is at eleven p.m.

"You'll only be in this unit until you're classified. Once you're moved into the general female population, you'll stay in your housing unit and interact with others there during the day... unless you get involved in education or some other such program. There's a television set in each housing unit also, and you'll have access to a library, but no computers or internet. I'm sorry, but that's all the information I have for you at the moment."

Turning, she walked away, leaving Eleanor to contemplate her circumstances as Bennington's footsteps echoed off the cell block's walls. Looking around the enclosure, she figured the cell measured about ten feet in length and fifteen feet in width.

My closets are bigger than this.

Two metal bunks were topped with four inch thick black striped mattresses; the one on the lower bunk being torn and both sporting what appeared to be water stains.

Guess the previous tenants needed diapers.

The dun colored shelf that Corporal Bennington referred to earlier was actually a smooth, waist high concrete block protruding from one wall, and she placed the toiletry items there. To the left of the shelf was a window about four feet tall and perhaps one foot wide, with a yellow solid steel bar covering the full vertical length of a wire-glass insert.

At least there's something to look out of.

Interior decoration consisted of the last resident's scribbled calendar of descending days to mark time, accented by graffiti covering the wall opposite the window. A stainless steel arrangement consolidated a sink and integral toilet mounted about eighteen inches off the floor. There were no electrical outlets to be seen.

Tired and depressed, Eleanor walked over to the cell door. Resting her head against the center, she reached up to grasp bars with both hands. Cool steel touching her forehead offered little distraction to an increasingly descending mood. Coupled with a surreal image of barred shadows created by reduced lighting in the day room, the prison's inhospitable sterility succeeded in generating a frightening melancholy.

Oh God. What have I done? What am I doing here? I'm a distinguished graduate of one of the greatest institutes of legal learning on this planet. I've never had a parking ticket. Will anyone tell my family where I am? Is Jake's science good enough to find me? And then what? How can this be happening to me? To anyone? What's happened to Jenny and Randolph? Has the world gone mad? Oh Chat!... Gautier!

A heightened need to urinate brought Eleanor's thoughts around to practical matters. Sliding down her pants, she stooped uncomfortably low to sit on the lidless metal toilet. Cold shock punching through buttocks and thighs sent an insulting shiver racing up her spine; blocking her water. The totality of this day's events claimed her and another dam broke instead.

Staring down at prison issued flip-flops pasted to the bottom of her feet; the horrible absurdity of her situation came as a slap to the face. Eleanor's world suddenly shrank to eighteen inches above an impersonal concrete floor as she lost the fight to control her emotions, shaking and crying uncontrollably into her hands as anxiety, apprehension and depression overwhelmed the last bit of mental strength she possessed.

"Miss Ernst, I'm Zachary Framer," stated the Warden, taking a seat opposite her at the table. Eleanor had been told to expect him after breakfast the following day. Brushing hair from her face, she attempted to straighten her prison blouse, more from habit than necessity in this place. She had been successful in removing most of her ruined makeup with lukewarm water from the sink; wanting to make the best impression possible.

With as much grace and formal bearing as she could muster, she looked directly into the Warden's eyes, saying, "Good morning, Mr. Framer. Why am I here? Did someone suspend constitutional guarantees without notifying the public?"

"Can't say. I received a call from the office of the Attorney General in Washington, D.C. Apparently, they have you connected in some way with the moon issue."

"It doesn't surprise me that the only people on this planet who wouldn't know that would be employed there."

"Be that as it may, the caller said something about plotting sedition and treason against the government of the United States. Given the state of world affairs at the moment, the President has suspended normal legal protections... something about your citizenship being questionable. Your two friends are here as well, and we've been ordered to hold all of you indefinitely. We've also been ordered to keep you separate from each other."

"Warden Framer, how can you do this? You took an oath to upload the legal protections of this country. In your role, you are the first defender of those rights to the people in your charge. I demand you put an end to this. I want to call my law firm and place into motion challenges to everything that's happened, starting with a writ of habeas corpus to release me from here immediately."

"I'm sorry, Miss Ernst. I'm a prison warden, not an expert at law; constitutional or otherwise. I've been ordered to hold you incommunicado. You won't be permitted to contact anyone. Personally, I'm sorry for whatever state of affairs has brought you to me, but I have to take orders just like anyone else. I'll keep you posted on any changes that come to my attention."

Eleanor stared at Warden Framer's back as he left the visitor's room; incomprehension written on every feature of her face.

"**Mr**. Jake, you must forgive this unfortunate intrusion, but we have grave news from the government of the United States," said Secretary-General Harakhty, addressing the full Luna Council.

"President Caneman would not speak directly with us. Our information comes from the Secretary of State's office."

Mr. Harakhty could be seen at the dais before a packed room in the UN General Assembly Hall, with an overflow crowd in the isles around the room's periphery. He possessed a most unhappy look, and worry could be seen in his eyes as he picked up and read from a document. Jake was observed standing attentively in front of the Council members.

"The statement in my hand is from the Clerk of the Supreme Court of the United States. The President ordered an extraordinary session of the Court to decide an issue dealing with constitutional protections; specifically, the granting of rights and legal status. The Court has sided with the President in ruling that you and your people are not citizens of Earth, and have no rights under the constitution of the United States, or any other country on this planet. In addition, it has been ruled that such protections were lost when you left over five years ago.

"Given that, the Court rules that no crime has been committed against your people under the laws in effect here, and no prosecution of the injured Special Agent will take place."

Secretary-General Harakhty looked up at the monitor screens; shoulders slumped by the weight of his announcements and appearing much older than his years would have him. He found no friendly faces among the Council members looking back, and only stony silence greeted him from Jake.

"I am terribly sorry, but there is more for you to hear. The Agent in question has been promoted and is being feted for his heroic actions against insurgents who would upset the peaceful order of Earth's communities and citizens. Your two people, the beautiful young girl and her protector, will be prosecuted to the full extent of existing law when released by competent medical authority.

"Your representatives, specifically those employed by the firm of Ernst, Long, and Stein, have been taken into custody and will be tried for crimes of sedition and treason against the lawful government. More arrests are contemplated as additional details are gathered from those involved, where ever they may be found on this world."

Baruti Harakhty was devastated by the duty placed on him. He and his associates had been stifled at every turn in attempting to arrive at some compromise that might turn this fiasco into a positive understanding between the societies of two worlds. He placed both hands on the dais before him and bowed his head in defeat.

Motioning to an assistant, Jake spoke levelly, "I am directing that all communication systems transmit our response worldwide, as what is about to be said will affect all there." After a short pause for confirmation, he introduced himself and the Council to the people of Earth, briefly outlining the events that had transpired up to this moment.

"Societies do not spring up intact overnight," he stated. "Like-minded individuals and small groups come together for their common good; guided by principles that offer protection, growth, and safety for the whole. The promise of a bright future fuels their synergy, and love for their children ensures that future goals will be accomplished. The role of their leaders is to guarantee that a nurturing, safe and non-violent environment conducive to those goals is established and maintained.

"You once possessed those same goals and principles; but have allowed them, by indifference, to erode away. When you even deign to become involved in your political processes, you choose leadership by default, not by demonstrated ability to steer you into a worthy future for generations to come. You have lost your courage and your way."

Jake paused a moment to allow his words to be translated and assimilated by the people of Earth. "There was a time in all of your societies that to harm one individual was to harm all. As you have multiplied, you now seem moved to action only when thousands come to harm. Indeed

... millions have died, slaughtered by the greed of rogue alliances and you do nothing. You are a world ruled by intimidation and controlled by violence; eventually doomed by your indifference to it, in our opinion.

"On the other hand, our new world has been formed by, and holds to, the standards you have so callously discarded. In peace and out of respect for the laws of your land, we proceeded in a cautious and open manner to seek and obtain recognition through your highest court; the type of recognition that would have profited all of your societies immensely. We anticipated that our efforts would be seen with suspicion and fear, but hoped that they would be viewed in the light of calm reason.

"We were wrong."

"Concerning our citizens and friends... abduction at night by faceless government officials was not unexpected. Those officials, which you elected by the way, have reverted to type as chronicled throughout the history of mankind. Their immature attempt to paint us as perpetrators has revealed the corruption that fills your government. Their failure to return our harmless citizens to us leaves only one option."

Raising his arm up, Jake glanced at and read from a document held in his hand. "It is the decision of the leadership of Luna, with the concurrence and support of our population and the full Council that as of this moment a state of interplanetary conflict exists between our two peoples."

The monitor screens went dark. Jake's announcement stunned the Assembly Hall's occupants into silence, as each in turn contemplated what fate would befall the world as they knew it today.

The Nearside Lounge door pinged for the fourth time before Jake responded, "Open."

The young woman entered the observation room to find him standing alone, staring through the quartz window at a deep azure and soft white pastel covered Earth; war declaration crushed in hands folded behind his back.

Noticing her reflection, he offered without turning, "Come in, Chaylen."

Her voice quavering, she said, "We all missed you. I knew you liked to come here, but when you didn't answer I was about to ask Walwyn to override security access to see if you were all right."

"Thank you, I'm fine." Jake said, altering his initial curt response to a moderate level in deference to her youth as he motioned toward a vacant settee.

Sitting down, she looked at him with fearful eyes and blurted, "Jake, I'm scared. A lot of the others are frightened too. Earth is so much bigger than we are, and unlike the other children, I was born and lived there. I know how hateful and ugly those people can be when they get mad."

Without turning around he responded levelly, "You've attended the planning conferences and meetings. I don't expect you to understand the full depth of tactics we're proposing, but you're aware we're not meeting any of the Earth's militaries on their terms."

Jake took in a troubled breath. Exhaling with a sigh, he walked to where she was seated and sat next to her. Glazing fully into her eyes, he remarked, "Chaylen, you've performed brilliantly for someone your age, both as a Council member and in representing the interests of Prexus engineers working on the Starflyer and New Hope projects. I need you to be strong and reassure the others that everything will work out fine. You'll be kept informed of developments as they happen. I expect you to ensure that everyone you talk to is up to date as events unfold. You'll need to be at the forefront in supporting our pilots in the upcoming conflicts, when they leave and especially when they return."

As if coming to a decision, he then said, "Come with me."

Taking her by the hand, they left the lounge and headed toward Operations. Walwyn met them and Jake asked to see Prime, explaining to Chaylen that it was time she met him.

"Him? I don't understand. I thought Prime was simply a name for the main computer," Chaylen said.

"Please be patient for a few moments more," replied Jake. Walwyn led them to a large vault type door and completed a full series of biometric recognition protocols, including retinal and palm print scans. Once approved, it was necessary to enter a numeric identifier and password code. Jake and Chaylen were required to be identified as well. Satisfied, the vault security system then permitted Walwyn to activate the massive locking mechanism and release the door.

As they entered a room with subdued lighting, the vault door closed silently behind them. Chaylen could see a young boy perhaps six or seven years old, standing on a circular platform that was raised several inches above floor level. Soft illumination to another area just beyond and to the right of that could be seen, but appeared to be discreetly blocked. The platform was fronted by a row of comfortable lounge seats, and Jake motioned for the two of them to be seated as he moved to join the child.

"Good day, Ahmose. How are you?" asked Jake as he knelt to face the boy.

Chaylen leaned toward Walwyn and whispered, "Did he call him Amos?"

"No," he whispered in return. "His name is KhenemetAhmose. It's Egyptian. It translates somewhat into 'the one joined with the moon is born.' Pay attention. You'll learn more that way."

"I'm well, Jake, thank you." Turning toward the other visitors, he continued, "Good day Walwyn. And good day to you, Chaylen. I've been looking forward to meeting you and other members of the Council in person."

So saying, the child walked smoothly toward Chaylen, stepping flawlessly from the platform to the floor with hand extended to take hers. She noted the firm grip and warmth of his hand; how smooth the skin was. His short dark hair was neatly trimmed and combed with a part on one side. Light speckled brown eyes looked directly into hers as the face opened into a rather friendly smile, eliciting one in return from Chaylen. His large pupil eyes blinked with liquidity as he released her hand.

Chaylen noticed a cable trailing from Ahmose's left heel back across the platform. "Are you plugged into something? The herky-jerks have lots of cables hanging around when they're interacting with systems."

Bending down, Ahmose twisted and unhooked the cable where it met his heel; laying the free end on the platform. "In a sense, yes," he responded. "My cognitive functions exist in a protected environment elsewhere. The part of me that stands before you gives me freedom of motion… the result of a marriage of audio-animatronic software, anthropomorphic and bipedal research on loan from a very wonderful Asian corporation. I'm capable of functioning autonomously in this fashion for several days using internal energy alone."

Chaylen realized that what stood before her was not human, not alive. It was a personification of the computer intellect known as Prime.

"Ohhh," was all she could manage in return while unconsciously crossing her arms in puzzlement—mouth open in astonishment and staring dumbly at the boy computer with wonder written all over her face. Composing her thoughts, she turned to Jake and asked, "Why would we want the most sophisticated computer system ever assembled to be represented as a child?"

"Ahmose is six years old," he stated. "You might say he was born when we first arrived here. He's learning daily, just as any normal child would do. We decided to start in this manner, aging him physically as he learns to explore his world in a tactile sense. We learn how to expand our knowledge in robotic articulation while Ahmose learns to grow into adulthood. He has quite a number of caring tutors to learn from, *and one very uniquely special parent.*" Having carefully emphasized that last, Jake quickly moved on.

"It's an extremely rare opportunity to mature together. Our eventual goal is for Ahmose to explore those areas where we can't go ourselves. He's capable now of taking a walk on any part of the surface."

"Some children are mean. Can Ahmose hurt anyone?" she asked.

Responding evenly, Jake added, "No, Chaylen, he can't. Over millennia, humankind eliminated anything that tried to prey on us while we grew as a species. In that sense, you could say that our violent nature got us where we are today. But we'll never grow beyond what we are until we do a better job of controlling that particular flaw in our common psyches. We have to take the next step in evolving out of our beginnings.

"A very wise writer, Mr. Issac Asimov, once wrote about ethics dealing with laws of robotics. We have followed Mr. Asimov's philosophy in teaching Ahmose that first, he must not harm a person, or allow a person to be harmed through inaction. Second, he must obey orders given to him by people, except if such orders were to be in conflict with the first requirement. And third, he may protect himself, unless that would conflict with the first or second requirement.

"Neither he nor his external presentation have the ability to feel sensation, so can't be harmed physically. We're working on that, as well as meaningful programming concerning self-worth, preservation, and emotion. We have purposely limited Ahmose's exposure to others until he reaches a point of maturity and experience that will provide judgment and people skills, just as any child does as they grow into adulthood. It's a complex business, and will require years for even our own computer geniuses to master, but we are all of us excited about a potential outcome which may lead to an unprecedented level of artificial sentience if we are successful."

Addressing himself to the boy, Jake asked, "Ahmose, can you provide an update on the status of our missing people?"

"Yes," he replied, walking back to join Jake on the platform. "There has been no change in the location or medical condition of Chateauleire or Iawy. A synopsis of their injuries has been obtained and is being studied by Dr. Agave and his staff. The three legal representatives have been relocated to a county prison located approximately ten miles west of the town of Mechanicsburg, Pennsylvania, in an apparent attempt to sequester them from discovery. The primary liaison, Miss Eleanor Ernst, was initially acquired through her wrist locator. She was subsequently able to initiate contact through her adornment communicators sufficient for me to confirm the location of their confinement facility. I accessed the prison's computer system and note they are being held in different areas of the facility. Their medical conditions appear normal.

"Her law firm is barraging the United States government with legal challenges to their actions, but are being shut out with endless counter-claims and motions designed to wear them down. Otherwise, there has been no change, and all are safe for now," he concluded. "Do you wish to have them returned to Luna?"

"Thank you, Ahmose, but not at this time. The critical care unit at the hospital is relatively germ free and heavily guarded, as is the prison. We'll leave our people there for a short while longer to keep them out of harm's way. Please provide Edwina with current flight schedules of all civil aviation for the G8 and other nations we identified on Earth, along with their scheduled crews and routes of flight. Be prepared to initiate Operation High Ground in five days as planned."

"Yes, Jake."

As simply stated as that, the war began.

ELEVATION

"**Good** day. I'm Jake, Council Leader of Luna." Telecommunications across the globe were suddenly interrupted by his now recognizable visage. "We have arranged for portions of this broadcast to be sent simultaneously through all available satellite transmitters. Virtually every citizen of your world and ours has the ability to see what we will now present, with appropriate subtitles for all languages," he said, signaling to someone not on camera.

The scene shifted to mid-morning sun filtered through dancing tree leaves, which cast shadowed patterns onto a wide walkway leading into a single-level block building. An aged brick monument stone bearing the legend "Tern County High School" stood silent vigil next to two youngsters; each clutching a microphone in one hand and notes in the other.

Emma Boxe had recommended to Jake two very talented and promising students from her old school district. They introduced themselves with youthful enthusiasm.

"Hello. My name is Bobby Reynolds!"

"And I'm Adelaide Matthews!"

Pumping their hands in the air with vigor, they chanted, "We're the Fighting Bear Kats from Tern County High School!"

Composing herself, Adelaide continued, "We're with Mr. Worth's tenth grade journalism class, and today we're featuring an exposé of corruption within the Government."

"That's correct, Adelaide," piped in Bobby. "Several weeks ago, members of President Caneman's staff presented a false version of events that occurred at the United Nations complex in New York. Let's take another look at the video presented to the public at that time." The scene shifted to the images that had aired previously.

Adelaide said, "What you witnessed were scenes taken from an isolated camera located west of the helicopter landing pad. Those scenes were purposely edited to eliminate what we will show you now. We have footage taken from seventy-nine surveillance cameras located within and around the UN complex itself. We want to warn you that what you are about to see is violently graphic in nature. Sensitive adults and children should not watch."

On those words, the next minutes were filled with the actual assault that took place. Camera angles were presented to demonstrate beyond question who initiated the attack. Audio digitally recorded by the TUG had been carefully synchronized. Every word uttered by Souser was crystal clear. The audience was also made privy to the actions that happened out of the TUG's range of video sensors.

Alerted to Souser grappling with Iawy, several of the other U.N. Security Guards had come running. With no thought given to ascertaining situation or injuries, they roughly and callously bound Chat and Iawy's hands and legs, further exacerbating their wounds. Secretary-General Harakhty could be plainly seen with his Delegation, taking the security detail to task for their actions as the TUG flew away into the night; ordering one of his own people to call for medical assistance.

"The images just presented speak for themselves," said Adelaide. "We are asking the viewing audience to contract your congressional representatives to request a detailed investigation into this fiasco, and prosecution of the man responsible for the crimes against two innocent visitors that you've witnessed. Presidential staff members and WNN employees responsible for the blatant distortions aired previously should be removed from their positions and brought to justice," concluded Bobby.

"For Tern County High School journalism, this is Adelaide."

"And Bobby, saying good day."

"I've never seen anything so miserable in all my life!" thundered President Caneman in volcanic fury the following day. "Who's responsible for this debacle? Where's that idiot Press Secretary Dominic? It'll be curtains for his butt if he did this," he yelled.

The meeting consisted of Presidential Staff, Department Heads for the Central Intelligence Agency, Federal Bureau of Investigation, and military Joint Chiefs of Staff. The Head of Home Land Security was in the hot seat at the moment.

"Every Government on this planet, Congress and Representatives from all fifty states are trying to get through to the White House," spat the President. "They're demanding an Independent Investigator be named, along with investigations by the Attorney General, Inspector General and every other idiot with an investigator's license, for crying out loud!"

Calmly deflecting attention away from the others, four-star Army General Johnson McMinn, Chairman of the Joint Chiefs of Staff, interjected, "Mr. President, the video report was factual, as far as it goes. Working with the other agencies, we've determined the tape was taken from a surveillance camera across the street from the helicopter platform by an off-campus security guard employed by a private concern.

"He sold it to WNN for a quick buck. It was first sent to Home Land Security and forwarded to Mr. Dominic's office from there. I believe he had nothing to do with it. Some CEO wag at WNN will claim source privilege and that will be the end of it. Investigations won't find a smoking gun here. We can throw them the agent who molested the girl and old man. What's more important at the moment is determining how those people grabbed our satellite communication systems and knocked everyone else off line. All of the major news organizations are screaming for heads and threatening suit. In the interim, I have people looking into the satellite issue, as well as how they came into possession of video from all those other surveillance cameras."

"Jesus, scooped by two school kids! That's rubbing their media noses in the dirt. I don't give a tinker's damn about any of them," retorted the President. "You just make gosh-damned sure nobody even thinks about touching those kids. Leave them and their families alone. Find out what you can otherwise," he directed. In a softer tone, he added, "The Secretary-General of the UN relayed the demands from the moon group leadership. Has anyone determined exactly who and what we're dealing with here?"

General McMinn spoke up, "Sir, allow me to introduce Lieutenant General Florica Ramsu, head of Army Joint Intelligence, who will brief you on what we have so far."

Standing up, she passed printed copies of her brief to everyone as a computer generated image was projected to a screen at the end of the room.

"The image you see was taken from a CD given to members of the UN after their last public announcement. We've identified their Council Leader as Jacob 'Jake' Starnes."

After a short pause to study the picture, President Caneman snorted, "He doesn't look particularly imposing. What is he, another one of those Raelian nuts who want to clone everything?"

"It's far worse than that, Mr. President," she responded. "He's Colonel Jake Starnes, United States Army... a highly decorated combat veteran of just about every conflict that's come down the road in the last thirty-five years. He's one of us. A highly respected graduate of every class of warfare taught in this country, including the Army, Air Force, and Naval War Colleges. Academically, he scored in the top one percent of them all.

"A number of the young individuals seen with him have been positively identified as incredibly talented students with IQ's approaching savant genius levels, who were either in the process of Doctorate level computer and technology studies or had completed them. Without notice, they suddenly dropped out of school or left their neighborhoods, and most of their families disappeared with them. He has come into possession of some remarkable technology, although we haven't discovered his funding source yet, or how they've produced any of their hardware.

"Initial analysis seems to indicate his people possess stealth ability far beyond what we have. They've demonstrated the ability to control our own satellite communication systems at will, and it's a given they have vehicles that can rapidly transit the distance between the earth and moon. They haven't made any move yet that we're aware of, but I remind you they have declared war on us."

"Well, what the hell does anyone expect me to do?" he fumed. "Throw rocks at them? Have we got anything we can use in self-defense? Can we go there and take them out? Is there anybody in this room with ideas about what they're capable of?"

A wave of murmuring swept through the assembled leadership, but no one else volunteered to add to Lieutenant General Ramsu's assessment.

Continuing despite his rudeness she offered, "No Sir, not yet... this situation is young and it's too early to determine how to proceed. We can't see any development on the face of the moon, so we don't know exactly where they are. Our best guess is that they've settled somewhere on the boundary between the near and far side. We're still trying to run that one to ground. We have no figures on population, war fighting strength or weapons. Also, let me remind you that since the close of the Apollo programs, we do not have any ability to take the fight to them.

"Marine General Burrister and I agree it would require about five years to prepare vehicles and an expeditionary force capable of fighting in that environment, and we're talking about a very limited effort... essentially a one-shot attempt requiring our team to take everything along on one hop. We would have only limited resupply ability. The taxpayer cost would be staggering, and not something I would be willing to shoulder during an election year. The best and only course of action left to us at the moment is to be very alert and let them make the first move, then take it from there.

"I would like to point out the focus of Colonel Starnes' public announcements appears to be a platform of non-violence, so that should make for interesting warfare. Also, we've attempted to interview the young girl and older gentleman with her at Walter Reed Medical Center. Neither of them will respond to our questions. The three representatives from the law firm are just as reticent."

Looking straight at the President, she added, "I hope the barristers you're trusting know what they're doing. The Judge Advocate people on our staff are vehemently opposed to the course of action that's been taken to imprison these people. They assure me we are in violation of every Constitutional protection there is, regardless of the flimsy legal opinion given by the Supreme Court."

"What they think is meaningless," President Caneman ejected. "Right now those prisoners are trump cards and will stay right where they are until I decide otherwise. General Burrister, I want the highest priority given to that Marine Expeditionary force spoken of, and you can forget five years... you'll be there in six months if I have anything to do with it. You get in touch with the Air Force and space boys at the National Aeronautics and Space Administration right now, and I want a plan on my desk by week's end. You'll work their asses twenty-four by seven to pull this off if you have to. OK, we wait and see what they're up to. The meeting's over. All of you get on top of this, and I want full reports by tomorrow's meeting."

"**The** New Hope will ferry twenty-eight Starflyers. Those will be broken into ten teams of two, with four teams as standbys. The standby teams will be rotated within the active component, so all pilots will receive engagement opportunities. Ten TUGS will accompany for back-up or recovery purposes," said Edwina to the assembled pilots, Council Members, and others who had taken time from other duties to attend this final briefing.

The New Hope's Operations room rotated around its axis, using centrifugal force to generate normal gravity. "You've all been trained and briefed on Operation Elevation. After orbital rendezvous, you'll proceed to the country of assignment. All civil aviation operations have been uploaded into Prime, so you'll be directed to your targets in Canada, China, France, Germany, Italy, Japan, Russia, the European Union countries, United Kingdom and United States."

A hand shot up. "Yes, please," said Jake, pointing to a pilot in the second row. "Colonel... oh, um, sorry. Mr. Jake, sir. I'm comfortable with the auto-refuel aspects of the Starflyer design, but every contingency can't be planned for. Do we need to have any concerns about fuel?" It was difficult for some of the ex-military pilots to drop old habits.

"No, none at all. All Starflyers will leave here and arrive fully fueled. Additionally, the New Hope will be towing a low profile iceberg. We've frozen several hundred tons of water, simply as a precaution. We'll park it behind one of the larger communication satellites in synchronous orbit about twenty-two thousand miles above the Earth, and reposition the New Hope as required to avoid detection. The AlSys in each of your craft will continuously refuel as you move through atmosphere, so you shouldn't worry needlessly about that."

Stepping to the front of the room, Kelly addressed everyone. "Under

Edwina's tutelage, each of you has satisfactorily demonstrated your functionality in the Starflyer to the members of the Council. You are superb pilots, and your craft are decades ahead of anything flying on Earth at this time. You all understand the purpose of what we're doing and what is to be achieved with this mission. We would not be here if there was any other way to accomplish what needs to be done."

Jake spoke up, "I want to reiterate that you can simply jump away from and outrun anything that can be fired at you, and we are not doing this to posture or cause needless harm. Stealth must be maintained at all times and needless exposure is to be avoided, except to your targeted aircraft. In the extremely unlikely event that you find yourself unable to return to the New Hope, remember that Q is a safe haven in the event of emergency. Your initial approaches through atmosphere must be made slow enough to avoid friction related visibility. Unless there are any last minute issues we need to discuss, I suggest you all spend some time now with your families, then head for Prexus. You'll be ferried up to the New Hope from there. Check out your individual ships and try to get some rest during the journey to Earth. You leave in three hours."

On arrival into orbit Edwina teamed up with Alahn. The others more or less decided among themselves who they wanted to fly with. Those with language experience were directed to specific countries; otherwise the speaking chores were left to the Starflyer's AI.

As they slowly maneuvered their way through the atmosphere, Alahn inquired over his ship-to-ship communicator, "Edwina, please tell me one more time how we're going to ground commercial airliners without harming anyone"

"OK, I realize your aviation experience is limited. Airplane wings generate spinning vortices at the wingtip as the wing is moved through air. Were they visible, they'd resemble funnels trailing off and behind the end of each wing," she explained.

"It's an interesting phenomenon. If you happen to be watching the wing tips on a high humidity day, you may see them begin to form. These vortices are caused by pressure differences between the lower and upper surfaces of the wing and can literally flip over another airplane following too closely behind, both on takeoff and in the air. Unfortunately, this had to actually happen before studies were initiated to understand the problem. As a result, most commercial airports require a time interval between takeoffs in order to allow those vortices to dissipate, especially for the big and heavies.

"It was discovered that addition of a winglet, that vertical looking extension at the end of a wing, resulted in a number of positive improvements. Those winglets significantly reduce both wingtip vortices and drag while creating a real savings in fuel and operating costs in the process. Most commercial airliners are now being produced with winglets right out of the factory, and older models are being retrofitted. The point is that pilots like to land with everything they had when they took off. When pieces go missing it makes them nervous, especially if those missing pieces are six or seven feet of winglet. If those same missing pieces cause a little wiggling or a bit of shake, they'll want to land in a hurry. Fact is, the plane can fly just about as good without the winglets as with them. Our intent is to make them anxious."

"OK, that makes sense. According to Horus, we're approaching our first victim… looks like a three hundred series Airbus, maybe an A340."

"Right, Sidney confirms. I'll reposition about twenty-five kilometers forward, and you take the first kill."

Captain Neet Edwards and First Officer Michael Richardson, flying for Charter Airway out of New York, were enroute to San Francisco with a stopover in Houston, Texas. There were two hundred and four passengers plus five crew members on board. At eight twenty-two p.m., the aircraft leveled out at a cruising altitude of thirty-five thousand feet at five hundred forty miles per hour. Captain Edwards announced smooth air all the way and turned off the seat belt sign, signaling the start of beverage service in the passenger cabin.

"What a way to earn a living," yawned First Officer Richardson as he settled back into his seat for a relaxing flight. Crossing both hands behind his head and stretching, he added, "Doing what you love to do and getting paid for it." He finished the stretch with a large grin and smile.

As he leaned over the center console to check equipment status the Captain beamed, "You're right, Mike. With all these electronics, we're more computer than anything else. Screens instead of manual instruments, and fly-by-wire rather than mechanical linkage. We've jumped from a Model A to a Cadillac; this should be a milk run."

He was brought up in his seat, startled to hear a strange voice speaking in his headset. "Captain Edwards, reduce power and land at the nearest facility capable of handling an aircraft your size."

Not intimidated, the Captain fired back, "This is Charter Airway flight AB165. Who are you and what are you doing on our operations frequency, over?"

The same demand was repeated.

Puzzled, Captain Edwards turned and said, "Mike, I'm going to push a little right rudder, look out the window and see if you can spot anything out there."

With both hands cupped around his eyes and face pressed hard against the window, First Officer Richardson strained to see through the darkness and muttered, "I can't see a damned thing, Captain. Try your side."

"No good here, either."

"Captain Edwards, please observe your N2 console monitor, and look at the portside wing." As it was difficult to view the wing ends from the airplane's cockpit, a camera was installed in the tail to permit taxiing and viewing forward. Captain Edwards glanced at his inboard monitor and was astonished to see the left winglet disappear... apparently sheared off at the wing's surface!

"Jesus, Mike, we've just lost the port winglet," he said, tension rising in his voice.

"This side just vanished, too!" yelled Mike in return. "Damn, Captain, What's going on?"

Captain Edwards could now discern slight vibrations through his hand grasping the side stick controller, which had replaced the more traditional yoke. The vibrations were being transmitted through the structure of the aircraft; generated by unstable air flowing over the fresh wounds inflicted by Alahn's Starflyer.

"Captain Edwards, this is your final warning. Reduce power and land at the nearest facility capable of an aircraft your size. I have removed your winglets and five centimeters of your horizontal and vertical tail surfaces and will continue to do so until you comply." This statement was verified by an increase in the amount of vibration.

Without warning the entire airplane was now buffeted by strong turbulence. Captain Edwards turned on the seat belt sign, ordering all passengers back into their seats and cabin crew to immediately terminate service and return to their seats as well.

"Edwina, I'm moving into the hi-vis aspect of the mission now," reported Alahn, as he moved the Starflyer to the left side of Charter Airway flight AB165.

He allowed his craft to move perilously close, so close in fact that he could make out individual faces of passengers gawking back at his ship with looks ranging from amazement to outright fear; many of them pointing and gesturing towards his craft while alerting others. One or two of the clearer heads could be seen actually taking pictures. The Starflyer then moved over the Airbus fuselage to its right side for a repeat performance. The results were just as gratifying, but not to the two pilots trying to maintain control. The buffeting increased, and both flight deck officers could plainly hear cries of alarm from their passengers.

"Reduce thrust to maneuvering power," he ordered. Flight Officer Richardson immediately complied, slowing the aircraft to best speed for penetrating turbulent air.

"How does it look back there, Alahn?" asked Edwina. She and Sidney were the cause of Charter Airway AB165's flight problems; tearing up the air in front of the airliner with power thrusts and severe maneuvering specifically designed to create unstable air.

"Pretty good from here," he answered back. "We've pulled back a ways to watch… looks like they're taking a pounding. The Captain has reduced speed, and he's started a descent. He's yelling for assistance from just about every agency on the air right now, so I guess we've shaken them up enough for one evening. It's still strange for me to hear the flight following center telling the Captain they can only see him on their radars, and nothing else."

"We'll pass that on to the engineers at Prexus. They'll be happy to hear the results of their efforts," replied Edwina. "We'll follow them down far enough to confirm they're putting it on the ground, and then it's off to pick on our second and final victim for the night. After that we'll head back to the New Hope."

"It's your turn, Edwina, so lead on," goaded Alahn.

As word of Charter Airway's incident was being spread through the civil aviation flight control infrastructure, Edwina's selected victim was more quickly persuaded to head for cover than his predecessor. She and Alahn returned to the New Hope sooner than initially anticipated. As quickly as Edwina had completed her debriefing of all the pilots, she and Alahn went to see Jake.

"It went as easily as we had anticipated," she advised. "All Starflyer pilots have returned and reported in. On this evening twenty commercial aviation aircraft flying in the airspace of ten different countries, along with passengers and crew, prematurely terminated their intended routes of flight and landed safely at the closest airfield capable of handling their aircraft."

"There were no complications or losses," added Alahn. "Reaction of the civilian pilots was exactly as you predicted. The entire operation was very anticlimactic."

"Which is as it should be, Alahn," returned Jake. "There are worse conditions in war than being frightened a little. Let's continue to ensure that nothing happens beyond that. Edwina, please pass on my personal thanks to the pilots for a job well done, and continue the daily reports after everyone has returned."

Tens of thousands of flight reservations world-wide were cancelled the following day on news of the attacks. Published photos of the strange craft did as much to derail airline management's attempts to comfort the flying public as the incidents themselves. In the days that followed, fewer civilian aircraft were encountered.

After bouncing an airliner, Edwina decided to fall back behind Alahn and watch the show from his vantage point.

"I really don't want to rain on your parade, Highness of the Night Sky, but I've detected a party crasher," broke in Sidney.

"Where away?" queried Edwina to her jesterized silicon companion.

"Coming up quite fast for standard fighter fare. Speed just over Mach two, your four o'clock low position."

Edwina now saw the bogey approaching. Before she could recommend a firing solution, Sidney shoved the Starflyer to port with a hard burst of acceleration as a stream of tracer fire streaked harmlessly past. The pilot may not have been able to see the Starflyers on his systems screens, but those systems could see the commercial airliner and there was nothing wrong with his eyes or night vision acuity.

Broadcasting on an open frequency, the AI greeted their visitor with effeminate grace.

"Well, and hello to you as well. Aren't we impatient? Allow me to introduce myself, I'm AI Sidney, and you are?"

This salutation was answered with a brace of supersonic missiles that to the consternation of the fighter pilot seemed to come apart long before reaching their intended target.

"Oh my, how terrible! Tsk, tsk, such shoddy workmanship. Who can you trust nowadays? I have some sticky tape. Perhaps we can put them back together? Was there warranty? Give me your address and I can have the pieces delivered to you. No? Well, I tried."

Edwina listened as the fighter pilot scorched the airways with some of the most creative profanity she had been privy to while Sidney dismantled his aircraft. She hung around long enough to ensure the pilot's chute opened properly, then rejoined Alahn.

Reports started to come in that more flights were being escorted by military fighters. The standby teams were assigned to those areas, following the primary Starflyers at long range. As soon as the fighters moved to engage they were acquired and quickly put out of action, finding their weapons suddenly full of holes and incapable of firing, flying, or doing anything other than hanging inertly on their wing mounting points; guns and canons included! And the assailant was never seen!

It was embarrassing for hardcore fighter pilots to return to base in their country's most expensive flying platform, having demonstrated that the only expertise they commanded was in going up and down. The press was merciless in naming these yo-yo flights, and volunteers suddenly became hard to come by. Governments not eager to lose billions in military aviation hardware had only one option available.

Civil aviation came to a halt.

"We haven't had a report of anything flying passenger service for almost two weeks now," said one of the Starflyer pilots during the daily briefing on the New Hope.

"Good, let's keep it that way," returned Edwina. "I want the patrols to continue. In the interim, stay up on current events. If you've been watching, they're reporting that travelers have switched to rail and bus systems for transport, and even more private vehicles are on the road now than ever before. The threat to civil aviation is costing the affected economies billions of dollars each month."

"Why haven't we gone after general aviation?" another asked. "They've got some pretty big corporate jets in the air nowadays."

"Which for the most part are privately owned and funded," Edwina answered. "We're after the big boys, the Governments and large corporate entities, not mom and pop. If you took a look at the percentages, all the corporate planes available couldn't handle the smallest part of the general flying population. Most of them have voluntarily grounded their fleets anyway; keeping an eye on which way the aviation political wind blows. We'll now discuss the next phase of our operations."

High humidity, muggy nights are common along the California coast. The security guard removed his hat and wiped perspiration from his forehead, ignoring the irritating sweat-soaked undershirt that clung to his skin while wiping down the back of his neck.

Hell of a crummy job, he thought. *Stand and sweat, stand and sweat. Shoulda stayed on as a life guard; at least I could watch the babes. And these people lean on me, like it's my fault the bridge has to be closed for a while! Cheese, gotta have a hole in my head.*

The Vincent Thomas Suspension Bridge, located in Los Angeles, California, opened in 1963 and provided vehicular access between Terminal Island and San Pedro. Considering the amount of future traffic flow, City Fathers had wisely opted for a four-lane bridge rather than a two-lane tube tunnel. With a length of slightly over one mile, its main suspension span was fifteen hundred feet long, with two towers climbing three hundred and sixty-five feet into the air.

Containing over one hundred and twenty thousand tons of concrete, cement, steel, and suspension cable, it was designed to withstand ninety mile per hour winds.

It was not designed to withstand creative warfare.

At approximately ten pm, traffic was halted in both directions by security agents from a private company, who then cleared the full bridge of all traffic.

"Hey, what's up?" came from the first semi-truck driver in line, yelling to be heard over the cacophony of horns blaring in protest. "I've got a load of perishables due for delivery in forty-five minutes. Why've you closed the bridge?"

Stepping from behind a barricade, the obviously uncomfortable security guard advised, "There's a problem with the center span. We're told to hold traffic for about an hour. You'll be a little late, but I don't think you'll lose your load or your job over it. Relax. We'll open up as soon as we get the all-clear."

Traffic jams and mile-long backups were old hat for seasoned Los Angeles veterans, so most simply hunkered down to wait it out. They didn't wait long.

Thousands of citizens stared in fascination as a number of very strange looking aircraft made strafing runs across the length of the Vincent Thomas Bridge, slowly maneuvering around the bridge spans. Only it wasn't ordnance they were dropping, it was oil!

Or more to the point, an environmentally friendly, biodegradable synthetic friction reducing compound... specifically engineered to require approximately two months to completely dissipate. It would be quite a while before the tires of any vehicle would be able to gain firm purchase in order to cross the bridge.

Doctor Robert St. Michael, Professor Emeritus of Astronomy at George Washington University, enjoyed spending time with his son Eddie in searching the skies. He was secretly pleased that his choice of careers had generated an interest in his young son for amateur star gazing. As a tenured instructor at GWU, he was granted access to any number of optical devices for personal use.

Cloudless with a light breeze, the gorgeous spring night was filled with a promise of discovery. As Robert finished attaching a new video camera to their borrowed ten inch reflector telescope, it was hoped that between the two of them something of note might be captured for Eddie's upcoming science report. Aerial phenomena were always good for school credit and of special interest was the fact that increased meteor showers had been predicted for that evening.

Suddenly leaping with excited joy, Eddie shouted, "Dad, dad, look, there's one, there's one," as he pointed toward the eastern sky.

Indeed, there was one, exactly as Eddie said; quite a big one, in fact; observably larger than the average space pebble or fist size rock capable of drawing attention. In this case, a significant body of some composition had entered the Earth's atmosphere and was now heating to the point of incandescence. A long, fiery tail marked its passage at the edge of space as the voyager majestically traversed the heavens.

Robert started the camera, easily following the bright object as it moved westerly along its course. Initially distracted by Eddie's excitement, he now focused more intently on the meteor, noting that it seemed to be changing its trajectory somewhat. Most meteorites entered the Earth's atmosphere at rather shallow angles, perhaps fifteen to seventeen degrees on average. The object in his camera's view finder was noticeably altering its angle of descent, which Professor St. Michael now estimated was closer to forty-five degrees from the horizontal and getting steeper.

"Dad, is it supposed to do that?" asked Eddie. "It looks like it might want to come straight down. I thought it skipped on the air for a while before it fell."

"You're right, son. There's definitely something odd about this one. We'll be able to study it at leisure tomorrow; I'm getting all of it on our new camera." His sense of unease grew as he observed that the meteor had by now completely reversed its course while descending, and appeared to be heading in their vicinity. He comforted himself with the knowledge that very few human beings had ever been hit or injured by such activity since the dawn of recorded history... even as he took note of the sonic boom that now reached their ears.

That sense of comfort evaporated when it became abundantly clear that the space traveler was headed their way at tremendous speed. It passed overhead in a heartbeat, impacting the ground about one half mile east of their position. They both heard a heavy thud and were able to see a significant debris cloud rising from the impact sight. Yanking the camera off the telescope, Robert grabbed Eddie.

"Come on, son, let's go see where it hit the ground! I feel certain I can guarantee that one ninth grade science student has just nailed an A-Plus to his score card for this semester."

"**General** McMinn, there's a goddamned hole in my front yard today Sir. Would you or your staff want to explain to me how in hell that got there?" spat President Caneman.

"One moment, Sir," responded the General. "Allow me to introduce Doctor Robert St. Michael from George Washington University. We were contacted by the school and advised that he and his son taped the episode. We're also fortunate that the Professor happens to be an expert in astronomy."

He explained there were no injuries due to the fact that someone apparently hired a private security company to move everyone out of the Ellipse area, explaining that an impromptu fireworks display was going to be held. The irony of that statement raised eyebrows among all of the meeting's participants.

"Please tell us what you have discovered at this point, Doctor St. Michael."

"Thank you, General McMinn, Mr. President, ladies and gentlemen." Putting on his best lecturing persona, he began, "Please, begin the presentation."

Eddie St. Michael's video got much more attention than he could ever have imagined as the President, his staff and the various Department Heads were treated to events of the previous evening. As the audience watched, Doctor St. Michael explained what occurred.

"It's obvious the object was being guided in some manner, perhaps with rudimentary stabilizers similar to a standard military smart bomb. However, the friction phase of descent would have made radio control very difficult, if not outright impossible. I suggest that a computerized low level artificial intelligence installed on or inside the thing could as

156

easily have done the job. Also obvious was the intended target; the Ellipse area fronting the White House."

Offering that after careful measurement, he and his staff agreed that it was approximately two feet in diameter and estimated it traveled at a velocity of seventeen kilometers per second. Based on initial analysis of particulate material and ejecta found at the crater, they concluded it was composed of solid material. The final impact angle, about sixty degrees, resulted in a crater diameter of two hundred thirteen feet. Instruments at GWU registered the impact at one point three on the Richter scale, generating a wind velocity of approximately twenty-five miles per hour with a sound intensity of seventy-five decibels; about what one would expect from heavy traffic.

"It has come to our attention that similar events have transpired at other locations worldwide, with holes appearing before Buckingham Palace, Moscow's Red Square, The Arc de Triomphe in Paris, and so on... essentially all of the major Nation countries. In an astronomical scheme of things, the totality equates to a non-event. However, in the context of our present conflict situation, I suggest someone just demonstrated a convincing ability to bomb us with accuracy far beyond what our own military could ever hope to accomplish under similar circumstances."

"Well, that's just terrific," retorted the President. "The other rocks, the one they dropped on a water treatment plant sometime later, and that last report, what? Two more on some island in California. Was that intentional or did they miss something else? I don't see any military value in what they did there."

President Caneman's Secretary of Staff introduced Mr. Carlton Hines, Director of the District of Columbia Water and Sewer Authority. After introductions, Mr. Hines stated the missile that hit their treatment plant was intentionally placed, and apologized that some detail would be necessary to explain the consequences of that act.

Not much attention was given to events that transpire after a toilet was flushed or dishwater allowed to drain. Millions of gallons of water were used daily by communities in moving human waste. Water action combined with gravity washed the waste products into progressively larger pipes. Depending on the system layout, grinder pumps or lifting stations may be needed to assist in moving it over higher elevations until reaching a wastewater treatment plant.

There, wastewater went through a series of processes that culled out solids for landfill disposal or incineration while providing for bacterial activity and settling. Those steps accounted for removal of up to ninety percent of organic materials and solids.

Chemicals may be used for a final treatment stage to eliminate nitrogen and phosphorous, with chlorine being added to remove residual bacteria prior to returning the treated water to rivers, reservoirs, oceans and streams, or reused for landscaping and irrigation. Waste-water treatment plants use very large, open, water tanks or ponds that can be easily seen from the air. Too easily, perhaps, as everyone was now painfully aware. Washington D.C.'s Blue Plains Wastewater Treatment Plant, located immediately off the Potomac River, processed almost four hundred million gallons of wastewater a day on average; topping out at a little over one billion gallons daily at full capacity. It was spread out over one hundred and fifty acres and treated water was returned to the river.

"While the primary source is wastewater, we have to contend with storm water drainage on occasion. A combination of the two easily over-whelms rated capacity, resulting in what we call a combined sewer overflow, or CSO. In an example of this type, the environmental impact is lessened somewhat by the dilution of the waste by storm water. While having a CSO event flow back into the river can be managed in the short term, anything more than that would be an environmental disaster.

"The immediate problem is that our holding tanks and ponds have been cratered and holed, resulting in a significant escape of effluent in various stages of treatment flowing everywhere except the river. We have to turn the pumping systems off to complete repairs, estimated to require about three weeks. Leaving them on simply pumps more effluent into the affected areas. My higher concern is the pumping stations, grinder pumps and lifting stations.

"Those moon people knew exactly what to break to inconvenience the wastewater plant. If they interrupt the pumps I spoke of, untreated waste will back up throughout the system, resulting in the entire Washington metro area becoming a cesspool."

"Thank you, Mr. Hines, I understand we'll have to put up with disagreeable odors for a while," said the President. "Can we hire portable toilets and set them up for public use?"

"No Sir," answered General McMinn. "We've discovered that over the last few months a private company has been discreetly contracting every porta-potty and portable toilet facility rental company in a four state area, sending the units on one way trips to the central United States. You can't rent or purchase a single unit at the moment.

"They've done an excellent job of coordinating this little campaign. We're putting in a slit trench arrangement behind the White House until some of our more talented soldiers can manually construct restroom facilities. The Washington D.C. area will have to be placed on alert and go into water rationing today. We're contacting every company in the porta-john industry nationwide, and we'll truck, rail, and fly in what we can.

"However, best estimates say the wastewater plant would be back in operation before we could have enough units set up to handle the current population. I'd like to point out there's nothing preventing them from simply dropping another rock on the repairs as soon as they're completed. No pun intended, Sir, but taking out the wastewater plant places us in one big stink of a mess. You might want to think about the impact on the country as a whole if they were to take out those systems in all of the major cities."

"Wonderful," sighed the President, with consternation written all over his face. "All right, help me understand the bridge and island thing," said the President.

Lieutenant General Ramsu pointed out the Vincent Thomas Bridge was the only vehicular link between the city of San Pedro, California, and Terminal Island. The island was man-made and housed a naval base, some canneries, shipyards and a Federal medium security prison for men.

That bridge, and the rail line located on the east side, were the only two land access routes onto the island. A significant flow of containerized bulk foodstuffs and material crossed both for loading onto container ships bound for overseas destinations. Of particular concern was its designation as the primary loading terminal for the island of Hawaii… which for all practical purposes had been brought to a halt. No vehicles could transit the bridge until the roadbed was cleaned. An anti-friction compound dumped on it had been absorbed into the surface and would require weeks, if not a month or more, to remove. The rail line had been holed on both sides of its bridge crossing onto the island, and would need even more time to repair.

After a moment of reflection, he asked, "Can't we fly the stuff over?"

"No Sir. All the planes we have couldn't handle the sheer bulk that's transported via cargo container ships. The Hawaiian Island chains are on ten days of supplies right now, and the Governor has been asked to institute strict rationing until we can resolve the flow situation from our side of the fence. As the other port loading facilities are fully engaged for cargo earmarked for other markets, we have to be very selective in squeezing in Hawaii bound shipments. Those will have to be restricted to essential items only until the bridge situation is resolved.

"Tourists and Cruise ships enroute will have to be turned back. It goes without saying that financial losses to the tourism industry there will be significant. As explained earlier in the briefing, private security firms were hired to ensure no one was in the immediate vicinity of the bridge or the rail access points. Analysis indicates our rail assembly areas are extremely vulnerable to this type of interdiction. It doesn't take much to imagine what the impact would be if these people decide to focus their attentions there," she concluded.

"OK, I get the picture. The score is one hundred percent for them and zero for us. Can we increase security throughout the rail system?"

General McMinn responded, "There aren't enough security troops in the entire United States military to secure all the areas that could be attacked. They could drop a rock anywhere on the map and stop the flow of rail traffic nationwide instantly. Our systems were never built or designed to withstand this sort of tactic. The national defense strategy has been based on conventional warfare, with a missile shield defense system at its heart. The moon leadership has stopped our civil air industry, and now they're aiming at our national rail infrastructure. I would also like to point out the same thing is happening to the European countries, who rely more heavily on rail transportation for moving personnel than we do. Their citizenry are going to be raising hell before this is over"

Looking around the room, the President stated, "I agree they seem to be remarkably accurate in accomplishing their objectives. What would happen if we turned off the global positioning and communication systems to prevent their use and conversion by these people?"

The Secretary of Defense spoke up, "We've already tried to regain control or turn them off. They've taken over every satellite we've got. The Air Force teams have informed me they're powerless to do anything with them."

"How could that happen? I thought we had software safeguards in place?"

Air Force Lieutenant General Susan Collings interjected, "Mr. President. Our communication system is a relatively low end 'receive, boost, and re-send' arrangement. Satellites receive carrier signals beamed up from Earth. Due to the distance traveled, those signals have relatively little power by the time they get there. The satellites then use sets of high power amplifiers to boost the power levels and re-transmit those signals back to earth. The equipment that amplifies those carriers within a frequency range is generally known as a transponder.

"We believe the moon people have simply parked their own transponder devices adjacent to our satellites. When they want to transmit, they just overpower our weak incoming signals. Simple, if you're able to move around up there as easily as they appear to do. It's also readily apparent they have the ability to crack just about every software firewall and encryption code we have in the inventory. I refer to a previous briefing by Army Lieutenant General Ramsu.

"We've been able to determine that some of the missing students she spoke of were considered to be savant geniuses in every math discipline available today. Their college tutors and professors advise us that mentally completing mathematical long-string algorhythms, without the use of a computer, I would add, is child's play to them. Add high-level computing power to that kind of natural intuition, and our best teams backed by Cray super systems would be hard pressed just to keep up, much less think of beating such opponents."

"More wonderful news. Thank you. I've been working with some of our special ops people. I think we may have a surprise or two for our friends up there. I'll let you know when we're ready to proceed." Having made that statement, President Caneman dismissed the assembly.

The city of Oakland is located somewhat east of San Francisco, California, and boasts a significant containerized shipping industry. Huge container cranes work day and night to load and offload material vital to the economy of the United States, as well as those member nations that thrive on the import and export business taking place there. Local and national overland shipping companies transport thousands of containers within the state and across the nation using semi-trailer big rigs to move them.

Not much attention is paid to the fact that rail traffic accounts for an even bigger part in moving those materials. Most interaction with the public is usually restricted to children counting rail cars when a train is spotted as the family enjoys a drive through the countryside. Located in Oakland is a robust rail yard composed of numerous rows of tracks running parallel to each other. It's here that freight cars are coupled together as newly configured 'consists' using switcher engines. The completed consists are then mated to an engine team powerful enough to move that particular tonnage.

All those parallel tracks eventually narrow to just one or two sets at both ends of the yard, permitting a completed train to begin or end its journey. Many port cities located across the United States have similar arrangements in place to accomplish the same goal of moving those items required by a supply and demand oriented capitalist economy. At about eleven p.m. that evening, both ends of the Oakland rail yard were holed by rocks from a celestial source. All rail traffic coming and going in Oakland was instantly stopped.

There was one casualty… a transient visitor who had the misfortune to fall asleep out of sight of the private security company that was hired to scour the rail yard approaches for a mile in both directions. Fully engaged in his cups and fortified against the elements by his favorite nectar, he felt no distress when the shock wave re-deposited him thirty feet from his original position. His fifteen minutes of fame came at the hospital emergency room the following morning, as he described his harrowing escape from death or worse to the fascinated TV news crew that crowded around him. They didn't seem particularly interested in the fact that he was unmarked and uninjured. So far, he was the closest thing to an actual victim they had been able to locate since the beginning of hostilities.

The citizens of planet Earth were not significantly jaded by the so-called conflict to ignore moon oriented transmissions. Most were fascinated to find their television programming switched to what appeared to be a classroom of sorts, although it was somewhat disconcerting to see children moving easily about in weightlessness as if born to it.

A happy "Good morning, children!" was answered by a polyphonic chorus of "Good morning, Mrs. Boxe."

A fully briefed and quite aware Emma Boxe was onboard a TUG being controlled by Prime. She and thirteen of her grade school students were presently in close Earth orbit.

"Let's say good morning to our TUG's artificial intelligence, or AI, which the children have named Button."

A monotone male voice responded, "Good morning, all."

"And good morning to children everywhere!" enthused a radiant Emma Boxe, as everyone turned to face the camera and wave to the electronic audience. "Welcome to Luna's first ever third-grade field trip. Before we begin, let's take a look at the wonderful satellites that permit us to visit you at home."

For the next couple of minutes the picture switched to a multi-screen presentation. Displayed was a progression of satellites in various configurations and orbits above Earth, and lingered on a select number somewhat longer than the others. On ending, the view returned to Mrs. Boxe and her class.

"Today we're examining a visitor headed our way, and felt it might be of some interest to include Earth's children in our exploration. Come with us as we explore together in our exciting classroom in space! Now, what can someone tell us about our visitor? Yes, Andre?"

Eight year old Andre pushed away from his security harness to position himself close to the high definition screen at the front of the TUG. Pointing to an object on the screen, he recited, "We saw this yesterday as it left Earth. It seems to be coming our way. We're trying to find out what it is."

"Excellent, Andre. Juniata, can you add to Andre's observation?"

"Mrs. Boxe, can Button make the visitor so we can see it better?" she asked.

"Yes, I believe so. Button, please enlarge the object for Juniata."

The screen now displayed a greatly expanded picture of the object. "Is magnification factor four satisfactory?" asked the AI.

"Thank you, Button," said Juniata. After a moment scrutinizing the larger image, she offered thoughtfully, "The visitor appears to be a common Delta II launch vehicle configuration, Mrs. Boxe. While this is normally manufactured by the American Boeing Company, it's peculiar that symbols or identifying marks are absent."

"Yes, that is odd, Juniata," replied Mrs. Boxe. "Can someone tell us more?"

A hand shot up toward the back of the TUG's compartment, with an excited "Me! Me!" plainly heard by all.

"Samuel," acknowledged Mrs. Boxe. "What would you like to share with us?"

"Mrs. Boxe," he answered. "The Delta II's main engine is an RS-27A built by Boeing Rocketdyne. For bigger payloads, up to nine solid fuel graphite-epoxy motors can be added, and our visitor has all nine." Pointing gleefully toward the missile's base, he exclaimed, "See! You can count them yourself! It would have plenty of boost to come and visit us," he ended smugly... the excitement of discovery in his voice.

"Oh, you've got it all wrong, again!" countered Angela. "The extra rockets are for low Earth orbit; for really heavy loads. The Delta II can have two or three stages. If it has all of the booster rockets still attached, how can it be coming all the way to Luna to visit us?"

"That's a really good question, Angela. Can anyone answer?" asked Mrs. Boxe.

Thomas pitched in, "I believe it hasn't reached the point where the stages would separate yet, and seems to be carrying an unusually heavy cargo, hence the need for additional thrust. It's probably been in low Earth orbit until a proper launch angle is obtained." As if to illustrate his point, the lower portion of the visitor now detached itself and the second stage ignited. The class's TUG had no difficulty in keeping up.

Emma watched with interest as several of the students hovered around a display.

"I see another hand... Yes, Francois?"

"There's a really strong radiation signature coming from the visitor, Mrs. Boxe," he replied. "We checked with Button, and he agrees that it's consistent with beryllium reflected plutonium that's been boosted with deuterium-tritium."

Scanning the colorful holographic generated console magically floating before him, he continued as his finger moved to follow his reading. "It shows here there's also some aluminum and uranium, along with oralloy. We also see that the plutonium appears to have been enriched with deuteride fusion fuel... possibly ninety-five percent lithium-six."

"Francois, that's amazing. Thank you for contributing such detail to our study of the visitor," said Mrs. Boxe. "So, class, let's review quickly. Our visitor has been launched from Earth and is coming toward Luna. We see there's evidence of energy."

With elbow resting in the palm of her left hand and right index finger tapping against the side of her face as if in deep thought, she looked up over her glasses, smiling. Moving to grasp both hands together at chin level, she exclaimed, "Oh, how wonderful! Our Earth friends have decided to provide us with a power source that will last for a long, long time!

"But Mrs. Boxe," blurted out Halima in contradiction, both hands waving in the air, "I'm on Luna's Energy Council, and we have enough power reserve to last for th..." was quickly overridden by Emma's, "I understand such vehicles are fairly common. This one could have come from a number of places. Can anyone tell us more about where our visitor originated?

"Yes Mam," said Hoshiko, surrounded by several of the students. "We've downloaded the visitor's redundant inertial flight control guidance system's software programming. The visitor is headed for a point near to one of our cities, but not too close... we assume as a result of pretty good guesswork. We have noted that the program has a standard author's identification line which indicates this particular one was written by Professor Anaeli Hodges-Smythe, a well known published researcher employed at the Los Alamos Scientific Laboratory. That Lab is operated by the University of California, for the American National Nuclear Security Administration, and is located in Los Alamos, New Mexico... the United States."

"Thank you, Hoshiko, for that insightful analysis. Well, children. It seems we're not in need of any additional energy at the moment. I believe the gift being sent to us cost a great deal of money to manufacture. I suggest we return it to our friends in the United States. What do you think?"

The reaction that followed Emma Boxe's question was dramatic, as the students looked from one to the other searching for understanding.

Those same feelings were echoed in President Caneman's staff meeting, which had been watching the classroom presentation, albeit with greater apprehension than the rest of planet Earth.

"Dear God," muttered Lieutenant General Ramsu in a soto voce stage whisper, "What bone-head authorized this?"

General McMinn didn't display any qualms about speaking up for all to hear, "That radiation signature just described by a third grade student exactly matches the specifications of a strategic thermonuclear weapon... and a really big one at that."

Looking straight at the President with narrowed eyes, he added in disgust, "So, you had your skunk works boys tinker up a little welcome package. Filed off all the serial numbers and brand names, and launched it from somewhere in South America, no doubt. But nowhere in that entire intellectual madhouse you pay billions to support can be found one genius with enough brain power to delete a common author's note heading up the guidance program. You may as well have signed the damned thing yourself!"

Sitting straight up in his chair, his voice conveyed loathing as he continued, "I suggest, Mr. President, that you get busy with your news people. You'll need every favor you've got coming to spin your way out of this, and I wouldn't bet three cents on your re-election chances at this moment, if you aren't impeached first."

"You're out of line, General," retorted President Caneman in cold fury, his face an open scowl. "Another crack like that and you'll spend the balance of your tour heading up the Unknown Soldier detail. I took action against a declared enemy."

Shaking his finger directly at General McMinn, he shouted, "And I haven't seen any bright ideas come across my desk from you or any of your other military cronies since this started."

Slamming his closed fist on the table top for emphasis, General McMinn roared back in equal measure, "Let me point out that it was your empty headed security people who screwed this up from the beginning, *MISTER PRESIDENT!*

"Numerous opportunities for diplomacy have been available, and you've ignored them all... and now your little three hundred kiloton *present* is on its way back to haunt you."

Everyone in the room stared speechless at the lambasting being administered to President Caneman by the General. With sarcasm dripping from each word, he growled, "Care to let us know which city in which country can expect the return of your thoughtful little gift? You haven't displayed any sign that you understand just exactly who and what you're up against."

Johnson McMinn pushed forward to emphasize his next point. "Did the fact that you just saw every one of our communication and military satellites simultaneously, live and in color, mean anything to you? If you had looked hard enough, you would have recognized a number of them that no one is supposed to know anything about!"

Relaxing somewhat while drawing a deep breath and in somewhat a more somber tone; he leaned back in his chair and added, "Christ, man... they've got one of those stealth ships of theirs sitting next to each one, taking pictures for every school kid and unfriendly government on this planet. That fact alone gives you a minimum starting point on how many of those ships they've got. And did you happen to note they only showed ours! I don't have any doubt they know exactly what's up there and who owns it.

"Colonel Starnes just sent one hell of a message to planet Earth. And that student's crack about guesswork... that's all you'll have from this point forward about where their cities may be because you won't be getting any more intelligence from space telescopes either. We've determined his people have parked large controllable disks in front of each one, apparently oriented to the observation end of the scopes. You can use them to look at anything you want, except the moon. You should have talked to us first before you took this action. Your one-man show is starting to wear awfully thin with the people of this country, and the rest of the world is watching, I might add."

Their argument was interrupted when one of Mrs. Boxe's students began to speak. The room fell silent as all attention was refocused back on the video monitors. Yahto spoke softly yet clearly to answer Emma's query.

"But Mrs. Boxe. If we send the visitor back to Earth, won't someone get hurt?"

"Why, yes, Yahto, that observation is correct. It may be difficult to ensure it lands exactly where we would want it. Hmmm, well, I see there aren't many options available. How many of you feel we should just send it into the sun?"

Thirteen arms shot into the air to register a unanimous vote to sweep the visitor into the solar system's garbage can.

"Well, that concludes our class for today, boys and girls," ended Mrs. Boxe in full grandmotherly fashion. "We'll let Button work out the details and push our visitor in the right direction towards the sun. We hope you have enjoyed our field trip as much as we have. Good Day."

The United States has over one hundred atom fueled power facilities. Of the ten power generating stations in the state of Arizona, one is nuclear. Tonopah, Arizona, about fifty miles west of Phoenix, is home to the Palo Verde Nuclear Generating Station. It produces just over three gigawatts of electricity annually without the use of fossil fuels or any type of emissions. Another interesting fact is that treated sewage effluent is used for cooling water; about twenty billion gallons of it each year.

Like most electrical generating plants, a power distribution system is located adjacent to the main production facility. Electrical energy is transmitted along five hundred thousand volt lines to service millions of customers in cities located within Arizona, California, and Texas. Local high voltage substations direct the current into distribution hubs, which eventually power businesses, homes, and other every-day users.

All of the power generating systems within the United States are hooked into a national grid system, so loss of just one would not necessarily disable the whole... but would act to slow it down a little. Not many would enjoy brownouts and scheduled power outages for the weeks it may take to replace or repair some major component.

It only required one rock to disable the Palo Verde power distribution system.

Even though it's normally unmanned, an urgent email message had come into the plant's control room, seemingly from senior management, to have everyone assemble for an emergency meeting at one a.m. The plant's entire second shift was dutifully present and one hundred percent accounted for when the distribution system ceased to be, leaving the Palo Verde nuclear power facility all dressed up with nowhere to go.

The International Space Station, or ISS, orbits the Earth at an altitude of about two hundred and fifty miles. Commanded by Colonel Sage Appleby, she was accompanied on this particular tour by Professors

Hideo Ishikawa of Japan, Petr and Darya Alexandrovna from Russia, and two Cosmonauts forming the balance of her crew.

One of those crew members, Kisa Popova, had just relieved Vladilen Koslova from his twelve hour systems watch. "What news to report, Vladilen?" she asked.

"All systems are nominal. Keep an eye on the forward solar panel array. I noticed slight variation in power approximately one hour ago… likely due to increased ion activity from the solar flare that was reported yesterday. Otherwise, all is well." Having completed his turnover report, Vladilen left for the habitation module and rendezvous with his sleeping harness.

After reviewing the systems monitor for updates, Kisa began an inspection of the six laboratory modules that made up the research area of the ISS. Stopping at lab two she smiled, enjoying a stunningly crystal clear view of Earth… a perfect sphere swept by wispy tendrils of lacey bright cloud. She could make out the South American continent, visible as verdant greens surrounded by a carpet of aqua blue sea encapsulating a tan leather land mass.

The planet hung suspended against a backdrop of profound darkness… bringing wonder to her mind that over millennia mankind had somehow actually reached space. While she seldom wasted time in idle review and never imagined herself a daydreamer, she couldn't deny the appeal of allowing her thoughts to drift in contemplation for a moment.

I will never believe that what I'm seeing was an accident of universal fate. Only a divine hand could have created such beauty. Surely, God must have shed a tear and here it is before me.

The emotional part of her mind wondered if we were truly alone. That thought was as quickly vanquished as her logical processes assured her that billions of stars and planetary systems must have birthed similar beings with the same desire for exploration.

All guided by the same divine hand. Given enough time, we are bound to meet someone.

Refocusing her attention inside the lab, she continued her inspection duties. As the window was built with both a primary and redundant pane, there were no apprehensions concerning possible pressure loss as she was aware that a specially designed debris panel was included in the construction to protect against impacts from meteorites. When unused, most of the observation ports were shielded using blankets and shutters.

Safety from debris is one thing; protection from surprises in space—something else altogether. Even for an astronaut trained to be composed under stress, the sight that greeted her from the portal in module four jolted her into thinking that something or someone had come calling well before anyone was ready.

"Commander Appleby, everyone, emergency! Come to module four now!" was sent out on the ISS interphone. The urgency conveyed by her voice motivated the others to move quickly; several dressed only in sleep-ing shorts and t-shirts.

"What is it, Kisa?" asked Sage as she hastily floated into the lab. The window wasn't large enough for six bodies to crowd around at once, but even glimpses were enough to leave faces curious with astonishment.

Moving to see what Kisa was indicating through the view port, she stopped wide eyed and muttered "What in the name of creation can that be?"

A huge apparition had stationed itself within close proximity of the ISS. With no apparent order to its makeup, it appeared to be a mishmash of every child's nightmare of tinker toy construction. Neither the whole nor any part of the mystery was immediately recognizable as a type of space vehicle familiar to any of the ISS inhabitants.

A sharp intake of breath forced Sage to turn and face the issuer. "What do you make of this, Hideo? Did you see something?"

"Yes, Commander. Observe the lower right corner; below the item which may be an antenna of some kind. Is that not an American flag representation?"

"Yes, I see it. You're correct. Over there! That's the lunar landing mod-ule from Apollo Eleven! Look carefully and you can make out the complete outline!

"To the left of the mass!" exclaimed Petr, pointing. "A lunar rover vehicle, and beside it... can that be one of the seismic devices left behind for research?"

Comprehension suddenly dawned in the mind of Commander Appleby. Every piece of equipment brought to the moon by any means, whether from unmanned exploration or the Apollo mission series, had without warning found itself relocated and parked on the doorstep of the ISS.

"There are other flags positioned as well," said Vladilen, indicating their location. All could now see the red, white and blue emblems... six in total; one for each of the Apollo moon landings. Bundled together at what was obviously meant to be the top of the pile, they crowned a plaque on which had been inscribed, "*NO LITTERING.*"

"Darya," said Sage to the communications specialist, tight lipped. "Please contact Houston, and have Flight get in touch with the White House. Hideo, set up a camera."

Jake's planning discussion with a number of the Council members was taking place in the open common area over coffee. He was quietly interrupted by Walwyn with, "There's a caller asking to speak with you, Jake. It's the young intern at E, L & S."

"Did he say what it's about?"

"No sir; just that it's quite important and he's certain you'll want to respond. He's asking that you use a private area."

After excusing himself and returning to the Council's private conference room, Jake asked the computer to transfer the call there. Slightly surprised at finding himself facing a concerned Levi Weizman in the E, L & S conference room, he spoke in a kindly manner, "Levi, you've interrupted a very important meeting. Is the reason for your call something that needs to be discussed at just this moment?"

"Mr. Jake, Sir, I'm sorry for intruding, but there's a gentleman here who insists it's vital that he speak with you. His credentials are very impressive. The senior partners who are filling in for Ms. Bea and the others interviewed him before coming to me." Looking embarrassed, he added, "They all seem to think I should continue to be the contact person, especially since you sent me that special phone."

"Yes, Levi, it's acceptable to me that you continue that function. Now, where is your visitor?"

"Right here," answered a gruff voice off-camera.

The TV mounted VOX camera rotated around to focus on the speaker... a tall, dark-toned and powerfully built, but casually dressed man with close-cropped, gray streaked hair and grizzled features.

Jake's composure shielded his surprise at recognizing Levi's guest; not wavering as he stated, "Levi, say nothing. Please leave the room and close the door behind you. Wait there and ensure we're not interrupted."

"Yes, Mr. Jake," replied Levi, quietly pulling the door after him as he exited.

The two men looked at each other in silence for a moment. "Taking quite a risk, aren't you, General McMinn?"

"Perhaps. But that's my worry, not yours."

"How are Samantha and the kids?"

"Fine, fine, couldn't be better. Martha and Frank just had a new baby girl. I'm a grandfather now."

The significance of Johnson's presence was not lost on Jake, so he cut straight to the chase. "What are you doing here, Johnson? You and I haven't talked since Natalia..." his voice tapered off. "I figured that under the present circumstances all ties had been severed."

"There's not a one of us that doesn't miss Nat as much as you do Jake; she was one great lady. We were all upset to hear about the marketplace bombing. It was your disappearance right after that surprised hell out of everybody. We didn't understand why you weren't around to help us put an end to that mess."

With a brief pause to lay coat and hat on the meeting room's table, he continued with some frustration, "Next thing I know you're Emperor of the moon or something."

"Johnson, I know you didn't put your career on the line for a stint in prison to talk about family and old times. Why are you here?"

Throwing his arms wide in exasperation he replied, "That idiot Caneman. He's the south end of a north bound horse. Jake, I can't figure

him. That arrogant son of a bitch has his hand in something. The other
Chiefs of Staff and I have gone over every angle. We can't figure why he's
got his sights set so hard on your ground. He's ordered a full court press
putting together an expeditionary force to take you out, and pushing
every button there is to speed it up."

"Let him, Johnson," Jake remarked casually. "His efforts won't achieve
anything."

Frazzled from that day's effortless attempts combined with fruitless
political confrontation, McMinn replied in exasperation.

"Damn it Jake, we've known each other for almost forty years. I don't
care how good your technology is or how many of those dark ships
you've got. I know you've got a pocket full of smart people but after
reviewing who's missing lately and your broadcasts, I haven't recognized
any tacticians in the lot. Caneman's a crazy man. He'll clear a path to
your front door with tactical nuclear weapons and he's got enough of
them to do it."

Rubbing both temples to relieve his stress and shaking his finger for
emphasis, he followed with, "Regardless of his faults he's one savvy
political bastard with friends in the Supreme Court who'll give him the
justification, and more political ass-kissers than you have ever seen in
your life promising him everything he needs. You should see those staff
politicals he's surrounded himself with... they don't have enough
backbone combined to stand up to a three-year old. They sit during the
briefings and meetings, nodding their heads and doing nothing except
saying "Yes, President Caneman—whatever you say, Mr. President." It
makes me sick to watch it. We're looking into how we can keep the
military out of this legally, but it doesn't look good."

With no response forthcoming from Jake, Johnson McMinn paced the
floor before continuing, "We've also interviewed all living astronauts
from the Apollo missions, and poured over every bit of data recorded on
those trips. There's nothing there, nothing. Caneman's efforts simply
don't reflect an ego pissed off over who possesses barren territory. This
can't be about having a base there... no one else on this planet has shown
any interest in having one. Before this, he would have paid as much

attention to you as he would sidewalk vendors in Berkeley camped out on a hilltop."

Jake stood silently, observing passively as his old friend walked through everything that had happened up to that point. He showed no surprise at Johnson's next comments.

Turning to look straight into the camera, Johnson stated, "You found something, didn't you Jake?" Pausing, he then said, "You don't have to tell me. My only interest at this point is how Caneman found out." Revelation drained the blood from Johnson's face as he exclaimed, "The two captives at Walter Reed; he got to them somehow! That's got to be the answer. Your people in the prison would be too difficult to approach; too open with too many witnesses. The girl and old man have been isolated all along."

"You're slowing down. The Johnson McMinn I used to know would have solved that one before breakfast. We have the ability to monitor those two, and have been disturbed by changes in Iawy's life signs. Chateauleire has remained stable, so my guess is that your President sent a caller to see him."

After a moment of reflection, Jake asked Johnson to signal Levi to return to the room. "Levi, I know that you've probably already had a long day. What I'm about to require of you might seem unusual, so I'm going to ask that you trust my judgment."

"Sure, Mr. Jake, what can I do for you?"

He was advised that at approximately eleven p.m. there would be a shift change of Danville security personnel. A memorandum would arrive prior to that announcing a mandatory meeting of all security personnel to take place in the main conference room. Levi was to arrange for refreshments... a lot of them. That should give him about twenty minutes before anyone would become suspicious. As quickly as he confirmed one hundred percent accountability, he was to go to the rooftop helipad area and enter the security office, then locate a manual power switch on the far back wall.

"It's left over from the original construction and no one took the time to upgrade it to function electronically. At exactly ten minutes after eleven, pull the handle. That will disable the security systems and lights at the helipad. At eleven fifteen, I want you to restore the power and return to the conference room. Do you understand?"

"Yes Sir, Mr. Jake."

"Good, Levi. If anyone asks you about any of this just say you don't know; you shouldn't be bothered otherwise. I also want to ask a personal favor. Please do not mention anything of our guest to anyone. Also, pass on that request to the partners who spoke to him earlier. You better go now and prepare for the meeting."

Once Levi had left, Jake addressed Johnson. "Turn left when you leave the conference room. End of the hall is Eleanor Ernst's office. Use her phone to call your team and take a week off. I'll arrange for the call to be secure and untraceable. Stay there until ten minutes after eleven. Take her private elevator to the roof and head to the helipad... one of our vehicles will wait there for exactly three minutes. No time for explanations now. If there's still trust between us, be on that ship."

Midnight on Sunday doesn't usually find too many stirring in Washington. Late nighters were startled to hear an obviously computer generated voice issuing from TV sets and radios... on every channel. "WARNING, Washington, D.C. Detonation in one hundred and twenty hours. WARNING, Washington, D.C. Detonation in one hundred nineteen hours, fifty-nine minutes. WARNING..." over and over the same message droning out of every device capable of reproducing sound; driving its insidious countdown into the minds of the citizenry of Washington, D.C. That same warning was simultaneously being transmitted over every computer network, overpowering any other display to obnoxiously flash itself into the user's consciousness. It didn't take genius to figure out that something was going to explode at midnight the following Friday in Washington, D.C. No one stuck around to turn the lights off.

"**You** *have to go, Mr. President,*" ordered the Vice President. "Everyone's being evacuated to the NORAD facility at Cheyenne Mountain in Colorado. We'll stay there until this crisis is over."

President Caneman yelled at him in frustration, "You have any idea how much productivity has been lost due to this? What the hell do you know about this detonation? Are we missing any bombs? Have you caught wind that we're going to be 'rocked' again?"

"No sir, we don't know. The full staff agrees that relocating is the prudent thing to do, and just ride this out in safety."

"Oh, and that's a rich one. I can see the headlines now, '*President tucks tail and hides beneath mountain while taxpayers run around in circles!*' You get on top of this. Every rat in this town has jumped ship, and road traffic's jammed up between here and Texas. We aren't going anywhere until I know more about those announcements. You own the largest security force in this country... get out there and have them search every corner and inch of this city, do you understand me?!"

"Yes sir. We'll get right on it."

"And where the hell is McMinn?"

Marine General Burrister spoke up, "Sir, General McMinn called in and will be gone on a one week inspection of the port facility at Terminal Island. I'll continue today's brief. You're aware of the destruction of the power distribution system at the nuclear plant in Arizona. It's cooled with effluent provided by the waste treatment facility in Phoenix. If the moon people decide to hit that as they did our waste system here, they'll realize a two for one bonus there. The power plant would have to utilize backup cooling systems, and it's not known if those were designed to cool the plant under full power; we're looking into that now."

"Why that particular area? Why not a bigger city?

"For now, their campaign appears to focus on less populated areas. That system in Arizona is fifty miles out in the middle of nowhere. They've timed it for the hottest part of the year for that area of the country. Millions of people are without electricity or are experiencing slowdowns over a three state area and that loss is projected to last at least another week. We don't need to be concerned about hospitals, major industry, police, or the like. Most have emergency backup electrical systems fueled from buried tanks. It's the common man who is being affected most by these tactics, and every switchboard in the nation is jammed with their complaints and demands for something to be done."

Looking thoughtful, President Caneman asked, "Can't we station people around the power distribution stations? It looks like they're not interested in the main plants yet."

Glancing sharply at the President, General Burrister stated, "Using human shields would violate the Constitution and just about every legal and ethical standard this country was founded on. It's out of the question. Besides, nothing would prevent them from simply taking out the transmission towers themselves, a lot of which are located in almost inaccessible areas serviced by heavy lift helicopters."

Continuing, he added, "The debris parked alongside the ISS will have to stay where it's at for the time being. I recommend nothing be said publicly about that, it could become a morale issue for the people. Rail switching yards have been taken out in Houston, Georgia, and along the southern coast."

"What impact can a few train yards have on the big picture?" grunted President Caneman.

The Secretary of Transportation spoke up. "Houston is a large switching hub. Blocking movement there has stopped the ability to relocate freight cars between the Eastern U.S., Midwest, and West Coast. That's caused rail traffic to be jammed into one of the biggest gridlocks ever seen... shipments of petroleum, grain, foodstuffs, car parts, toys, passenger trains, you name it. Those rail lines normally move three quarters of a million freight cars a day. We're projecting delays up to thirty days or more. Some companies are looking at using rail cargo ships to move some of the backlog, and thinking about diverting cargo to trucking companies. Those options would erase all profitability and negatively impact the rail company's already significant financial woes."

"We've analyzed their plan of action. It's obvious they're waging a war of inconvenience against us," said General Burrister. "We haven't suffered a single casualty that can be attributed to them since their campaign started, but this country's economy has been staggered. As soon as we repair damage in one section of the country, they drop rocks on another. They've demonstrated creativity in finding unique solutions to slow us down. Land, air, and water transportation have all been affected. They control our satellites and communications at will.

"We can expect that all parts of the nation... north, east, south, and west, will be selectively targeted for similar interdiction. As soon as one region comes back on line, they take out another. They're staggering their attacks on the communications systems to affect all telephone systems, keeping regional areas silent long enough to really whip up a lot of anger and ill will... all of which is directed at us as soon as that area comes back on line. Why aren't we discussing options to sit down and talk to these people? Some agreement beneficial to us all could result in advancements to our technology that we won't see for another fifty years."

"Because," shot the President in return, "I've still got a few tricks up my sleeve. I'll be goddamned if I'll give up to a bunch of rock throwing crazies. Let me remind you, General, and everybody else in this room. Those people have declared war on us, and every other government on this planet to boot. Just be patient; we'll be answering their antics with some of our own very soon."

Edwina was conducting an all-hands update in the Starflyer briefing room aboard the New Hope when a call came in from Operations. Two conventional aircraft had been spotted moving south along the eastern coast of the United States. She was ordered to dispatch a team to intercept them. Grabbing Alahn, they were vectored by Prime to rendezvous with the targeted aircraft after entering atmosphere.

Spotting the aircraft, Alahn asked, "What do you make of that?"

"Looks like two 747's, one about fifteen nautical miles behind the other at an altitude of just over forty-five thousand feet."

"Seem unusual to you?"

"Not really. There's no rule about flying behind someone, as long as you maintain separation. Under the circumstances, I guess they can fly as high as they want. There's nobody else around to look out for."

"OK, Edwina. You head up front, and I'll get behind the first one," said Alahn, repositioning his Starflyer within range of the first aircraft.

"Horus, what do you have for scheduling and pilot assignments on this one?" queried Alahn. "I'd like to know who I'm talking to."

"There are no aircraft scheduled to fly this route, or pilot assignments from any available civil aviation data base," answered the AI.

"Can't understand why that would be. I can see "Express Air Aviation" clearly written on the vertical stabilizer, including the identification numbers "EAA612"."

"Nonetheless, there are no aircraft scheduled to fly this route, or pilot assignments from any available civil aviation data base," repeated Horus.

Transmitting on civil aviation plane-to-plane frequencies, Alahn ordered, "Express Air Aviation echo alpha alpha six one two, reduce airspeed and land at the nearest facility capable of handling an aircraft your size."

Not prepared for the unexpected lack of response, he removed the aircraft's winglets and repeated his transmission twice more with the same results. "Hey Edwina, this is odd. I'm not getting any reply from the pilots."

"Well, maybe they've been through this before and are hoping we'll ignore them. Go into the high-vis aspect. Shaking up bill-paying taxpayers should bring them around," she replied with confidence.

Moving to the port side, Alahn positioned his Starflyer close enough to make out individual windows, and was surprised to see they had all been lowered!

Something funny going on here, wonder what's up front?

Placed forward of the port wing, Alahn attempted to peer into the pilot's area, but wasn't sure of his observation.

"Horus, enlarge the nose area of the aircraft by a factor of six." As Horus complied, Alahn could clearly see that the pilot compartment was empty! Repositioning his Starflyer behind the aircraft, he spoke again.

"Edwina, you better get back here. I don't see anyone in the pilot's area, and all the passenger windows are closed."

"That's different. Tell you what. I'm already behind you; about eight nautical miles. Apparently they didn't respond to my turbulence either. Take a few centimeters more off the horizontal and vertical flight surfaces ... let's see if that gets a rise out of anybody."

Air Force Colonel John Mikelson normally flew first strike fighters, and was not happy to be commanding a wallowing air whale, even if it was reconfigured. It wasn't that he minded flying the newest toy in the inventory... it's just that it wasn't very fast or glamorous.

"Yo, heads up everyone," announced his co-pilot, Lieutenant Colonel Mark Platos, to anyone listening. "Just caught a radar spike up here."

"Whatcha got," asked Colonel Mikelson.

"Dunno. Just a few short flashes, as if something was there for a second and vanished. Whatever it was appeared at our altitude, then looked like it was descending. Poof! Gone."

"Descending? Gone? Damn, Mark! Maybe as if something fell off the lead plane? That's it folks, we've got a nibble! Beans to steak those moonies are here and they've taken the bait."

"No bet! Want to get closer so we can take a look?"

"You know the orders. We'll maintain separation and let the first plan work itself out, then go to backup if we need to... we're changing altitude now."

Colonel Mikelson pulled a grease pencil out of his shoulder pen holder. Sitting up and eye balling the view port, he reached forward and in-scribed a circled cross-hair in black on the glass at eye level.

"What's that all about?" asked Mark.

"A little insurance in case our big gun doesn't pick them up. Just a trick I learned a few decades ago in the jungle."

Keying the plane's interphone, he ordered, "All personnel, don protective goggles now. Recheck security of all equipment and breakables."

"Edwina. This plane doesn't have any open passenger windows or pilots, and no one's answering the phone. I don't like this," said Alahn.

Lost in thought as she tried to think through Alahn's description of the aircraft, she returned, "Just a minute, I'm going to take a look at the other one."

Falling back to trail behind the second 747, she noted it had initiated a gradual climb. There were no windows at all, and it sprouted a considerable protrusion on the nose of the aircraft. She could also make out what appeared to be exhaust ports along the belly... not standard fare among passenger airliners.

Jesus, an ABL!

"Alahn, get out of there! GO NOW! They've set a trap! This one's an Air Force Air Borne Laser, a YAL-1A!"

And a rather nasty one it was.

Boeing, Lockheed Martin and the Air Force Research Laboratory fielded a weapon system powered in the million watt range by a chemical oxygen iodine laser, nicknamed COIL. A standard 747-400F freighter was modified to carry the turret in its nose and the laser's computers, battle management systems, hardware and optics in the main compartment.

Housed there were half a dozen modules, each approximately the size of a small truck. Initially designed to detect and take out ballistic missiles during the boost phase of launch after takeoff, President Caneman had ordered the Air Force to alter its operational mission somewhat.

The lead bait aircraft was flying a computer generated course assisted by a remotely controlled autopilot. Its windows were locked shut to conceal ad hoc radiation shielding and ejection framework installed inside an otherwise vacant and stripped passenger compartment. Sensors configured to detect a pre-set level of damage to the aircraft's external structure now triggered explosive bolts which blew out a specially prepared panel at the airplane's rear, followed by the ejector mechanism coughing out a relatively small package... a B61 tactical thermonuclear bomb.

Modification number eleven, to be exact, capable of up to a 340 kiloton yield depending on configuration. Removing the parachute and fin assemblies from its hardened case took nothing away from its functionality. While its primary role was ground penetration, Air Force mission planners decided it painted with a broad enough brush to swat stealth ships from the air as well.

Detecting the object's radiation signature simultaneously with Edwina's shouted warning, Horus applied full power to the Starflyer's engines and was successful in gaining separation of almost four nautical miles before detonation. The device's full potential would normally be focused toward its ground target, resulting in the highest possible yield. That yield was reduced as a result of using the weapon in an air burst mode which generated energy in all directions.

Regardless, there was plenty left over for this job tonight. The lead 747 vanished in nuclear disintegration created by the initial fission stage of the nuke's birth. That and radiated heat energy caused by its second effect triggered automated dampening to shut off Alahn's visor before he could be blinded. The ship's exterior anti-friction high-heat construction was able to shed the greater part of it and save him from incineration.

The emersion envelope saved his life as the third and final effect, explosive concussion, compressed the atmosphere into a hammer that slammed and shattered virtually every system on the Starflyer, throwing it upwards and back in the ABL's direction while shedding pieces of its external frame and empennage.

Viewing the event with calm professionalism, Colonel Mikelson noted that wide field infrared scopes mounted on his fuselage would be useless in observing the moon ship, now somewhat silhouetted against a brilliant nuclear background. Also noted was the inability of the multiple beam track illuminating laser to pick up any range data for that same reason. A thousand watt beacon illuminating laser, designed to reflect light from a target and provide data used by mirrors for COIL compensation, was just as ineffective.

Residual radiation in the visible light range still glowed faintly around Alahn's Starflyer. His overwhelmed absorption systems where now being fried by electrical arching that snapped about the surface of his vessel, adding to its visibility. John Mikelson, also known by his fighter call sign as "Cowboy Jack," pulled the YAL-1A into a heavy-G climbing starboard turn, slamming the thrust levels to their stops and gluing all hands to their seats.

"I want full military on all engines, Mark, and you sit on those handles until I tell you otherwise!" With the airplane almost on its back at a climbing thirty-five degree angle, he guided the ABL towards its target which he judged to be at about sixty thousand feet. Locking down the COIL's killing beam targeting systems and noting they were now fixed directly ahead, he initiated the laser's systems. Energized oxygen was combined to generate excited iodine, which created photons capable of being amplified and projected as the iodine returned to its common state.

Judging his target to be at apogee of the ballistic curve it had been thrown into, he lined up his ersatz targeting reticule directly on the largest part he could see and triggered the COIL.

In what could arguably be described as the luckiest shot ever fired by a bronco-riding cowpuncher slapping leather, the COIL's beam burned a hole cleanly through the Starflyer.

Colonel Mikelson watched in satisfaction as the moon craft nosed over in its death plunge, resembling nothing more than a badly served badminton bird rotating around its axis and dropping toward the ground. His short-lived thrill at being the first to kill one of Earth's opponents was startlingly interrupted by an outraged voice pounding both of his eardrums.

"HEY, IDIOT!" screamed Edwina in fury on the ABL's operational frequency. "Forgot something did you? Does WINGMAN ring a bell?"

Enraged at the deception now laid bare before her, she had not been in position to counter the weapon prior to its firing. That failure drove her in frustration to line up on the ABL, removing portions of both wings all the way up to their ailerons. Fuel sprouted from ruptured cells as Colonel Mikelson fought his controls in complete surprise.

Recovering the aircraft to level flight, he was startled to hear, "Turn that damned Christmas tree light to a heading of ninety degrees indicated; due east. Do it NOW!" was punctuated by an increase in vibration caused by additional loss of horizontal and vertical control surfaces. Crew members from the main compartment reported mysterious leaks had suddenly appeared in the chlorine, oxygen and hydrogen peroxide tanks that power the COIL. They initiated an overboard dump of all tanks, hoping to neutralize gaseous and liquid chemicals before any catastrophic mixing could occur.

Colonel Mikelson had no choice. Once the now toothless ABL reached the east coast, it was ordered to proceed over the Atlantic Ocean. That same voice ordered all crew members to prepare for leaving the aircraft. At approximately ten miles off the eastern coast of New Jersey, all hands bailed out once their aircraft commander confirmed the number on board. After counting eight parachutes to verify the total, Edwina had Sidney cut the ABL into graffiti.

Returning to the area where Alahn was last seen, she was unable to pick up any locator information or determine where his Starflyer might have landed. Gautier's earlier warning of Starflyer shortcomings now came home to roost as intense feelings of guilt and self-doubt ran their course; her belief in the invulnerability of Starflyer technology badly shaken. The burden of having to return to the New Hope with such news weighed heavier on her than any other event in her lifetime up to that moment, and she dreaded her inevitable meeting with Jake.

Alahn was disoriented; his vision in complete darkness. Rerouting visor power into an emergency panel located within his environmental enclosure, he was happy to regain limited use. A review of that system readout showed that it was operating on system number five, last of four redundant backups to the primary system; literally a battery operated line to the visor and one remaining external camera which wasn't functioning normally. If this extremely limited capacity where to fail, he would be completely blind!

The harness devices securing his frame were developed to limit travel induced by relatively smooth changes during heavy acceleration. They were not designed to withstand shock forces transmitted by nuclear explosions. His brain pounded as if it had been a golf ball rattling around inside a pipe and he ached all over!

Realizing something terrible had happened, he spoke aloud, "Horus. Horus?" Receiving no answer, he called out to Edwina with the same results. Reaching down to the right of his enclosure gave him access to a lighting actuator. Looking around, he was startled to see a hole in the ceiling approximately eighteen inches in diameter, located at the exact spot where the AI hardware would normally have been. Following the trajectory, he could see that something had burned completely through his Starflyer; ceiling to floor!

Make a note; relocate the AI and its memory to somewhere safer. Yeah? And exactly where would that be?

Equipped with a manual recovery system, Alahn activated the ballistic parachute mechanism. Deploying once his altitude fell to fifteen thousand feet, he was relieved to feel the initial tug of its drogue chute followed shortly thereafter by operation of the mains. From altitude, he had been able to see lights that indicated falling toward a metropolitan area, but as he fell closer to Earth the lights became fewer and fewer. Sooner than expected, harsh, abrasive scraping noises were followed by a decelerating lurch, as if a giant's hand had reached up to pluck him out of the air!

Jerked to a halt, his craft came to rest nose down at about a twenty degree port angle. After a moment or two of swaying, everything came to a standstill. Detecting no further movement, he activated an emergency egress release. In a space of seconds an accumulator of compressed air forced out the liquid compound surrounding him, released his locking harness and blew the exit portal away. Glancing to his left, Alahn was surprised to see that he appeared to be in the air!

In truth, about thirty feet of it.

He fell straight down, hitting a large tree branch with the underside of his arms and impacting the ground on his side. His left shoulder separated, the elbow broke, and all his wind was knocked out of him. Rolling onto his back in anguish, his entire left side was awash in a sea of agony as wave after wave of searing red hot pain splashed over his eyes, stealing from him any ability to speak or make sense of his situation other than a vague remembrance of something or someone placing a hand on his chest and saying, "Bitte, sie sind verletzt! Thee ist verletzt! Lie still! Oh, please, thee is hurt!"

Alahn was unable to comprehend the speaker or assimilate the horrific pain coursing through his body. Darkness came and he heard nothing more.

"Grounded! What the blue-blazes do you mean, grounded?" shouted Edwina. She was infuriated by Jake's response to her report on the encounter with the ABL. They faced each other now in the New Hope's Operations room.

"You violated our principles, Edwina. You broke your vow of non-violence."

In angry indignation, she argued, "Well, you're going to have to explain that one to me, *Mister, Colonel, Jake, Sir,*" sarcastically emphasizing each honorific. "I don't seem to recall harming anyone in an attempt to save your son's life!"

Turning to face her, Jake said evenly, "In anger, you intentionally placed eight human beings in harm's way by overly damaging their aircraft. You could have allowed them to bail out over land for an easy retrieval, but instead choose to have it done over the ocean. You exposed those people to hypothermic fifty degree water, predator attack or worse. You're extremely fortunate they were seen landing close to a shipping lane and were picked up by a passing freighter, otherwise you'd be accounting for their deaths before the Council."

"That's unacceptable! I purposely ensured they would be picked up there. We're at war; they're alive and undamaged. So they got a little wet... my life was on the line too. Are you treating me this way because I screwed up and let your son get shot down! I don't understand you at all! Why aren't you sending a team to try and locate Alahn now?"

Jake took a deep breath, closing his eyes and rubbing one side of his temple with closed fist and thumb. "I'm not sure I wouldn't have done the same thing, but that's not the point; you were there, not me. We've dispatched a single TUG to the satellite coordinates recorded before Alahn's AI went off-line. We haven't found anything yet. In the interim, your access to Starflyers and TUGs has been revoked. The Council has decided you're to remain here on the New Hope until further notice."

Fighting to control her anger, Edwina looked hard at Jake. She could see that worry and stress were bearing down on him and realized she had added to his burden. That realization took the wind out of her sails.

He's as worried about his son as I am. Retracting her claws she apologized. "Jake, I'm sorry for my outburst. I didn't think they would be smart enough to pull a stunt like that."

Bowing her head in shame, she added, "I underestimated their cleverness. I'm confident the Starflyer's emergency systems got Alahn to the ground okay, although I couldn't raise him or his AI. I don't understand why Sidney or Prime have no signal on his locator disk."

"We'll address that tomorrow," returned Jake. I suggest you turn in and try to get some sleep. I have a very important visitor coming to Luna. I have to leave immediately to go there and be ready to deal with him. I'm taking one of the Starflyers to cut down on travel time."

Taking another sip of wine, Johnson McMinn settled back into his chair with relaxed contentment; staring at Jake with pleasure written all over his face. Shaking his head, he beamed, "I've never tasted anything so good. Synthetics, hydroponically grown food; unbelievable. Jake, you've accomplished a miracle here."

Setting the wine glass down, he added, "Of course, someone like Caneman won't understand or appreciate that. He'll take your wealth to conquer Earth, or at the least buy a small place to retire on, like the Virgin or Hawaiian Island chains… probably both if I'm any judge of character. And he'll have plenty of help from all his cronies, both domestic and international."

Jake had arrived early enough to meet Johnson at Cordial when his TUG landed; conducting a personal tour of Luna and showing him all its cities, resources, science, and industrial accomplishments. He had held nothing back. The TUG's AI had been instructed to answer all his questions during the trip. The two old friends had just finished an excellent dinner in the Nearside lounge and now discussed current events.

"He'll have to get here first. We can take out anything he tries to send while it's still in its boost phase. Johnson, Earth's military science is stale dated. Our research is decades ahead and that gulf will continue to grow. For Earth and its people to have any chance to evolve, fundamental changes in the way they're governed have to take place. Those changes will need to come about peacefully and with the population's approval. You must see that."

"Whether I do or not is irrelevant. I'm not the President, and Chairpersons don't change the world overnight. This little campaign of yours is shaking the economies of an entire planet, so I don't think you're going to win very many hearts over to your cause."

With concern aging his features, Jake answered, "War was inevitable, and not something any of us wants. The sooner we can conclude this, the better."

Glancing through the lounge's multi-layered crystal aperture at the rim of a rising Earth, Jake explained, "The World Court issue was an intentional distraction... an effort to introduce ourselves in a positive way; to show Earth we're here, peaceful, and pose no threat. We never intended that any outcome beyond staking our claim would take place, but felt that preparing for conflict was prudent planning. Our goal remains peaceful coexistence and exploration. We intended all along to include selected Earth representatives in those efforts, in furtherance of mutually beneficial discoveries."

"Noble ideals, my friend, but doomed in naivety. So long as have and have-nots exist, you'll never find the type of cooperation you're striving for. Who gets to come, who gets left behind? Damn, Jake, since the day the program started there've been taxpayers on Earth demanding rides on the space shuttle, claiming they own it. There's not enough room here to house every human being on Earth who would want a piece of your dream. And how are you going to assimilate the controllers and conquerors? Put drugs in their water to make them play nice?"

"Perhaps; in a sense. Remove the reasons that create controllers and conquerors, have and have-nots, and the playing field changes radically."

"You can get away with that in this sterile little colony you've established... for all practical purposes a controlled societal experiment in homogeneous association. Like it or not, the Earth in general, and the United States in particular, is one big shake and bake... only the ingredients won't mix."

Looking disgusted, Johnson went on, "People want privacy, Jake. They won't take public transportation because they don't know and don't trust the person sitting next to them. The world has surrounded itself in blatant me-ism, and capitalistic 'king of the hill' rules the roost in every direction. What you've got won't wash in the reality of what the Earth's population has to contend with on a daily basis. For example, look at the type of people you have here."

Interrupting his friend's thought, Jake interjected, "You're right, Johnson, take a good long look at them. They're Earth's throwaways; human garbage. Misfits that the average citizen of mother Earth wouldn't deign to sit next to on that same city bus you describe. Educated, nonviolent men… who by extraordinary circumstances alone are branded as heinous criminals condemned to rot in prison or die there by execution. Human beings challenged to understand their highest social functions barely rate an evaluation of "idiot" from passersby; doomed there to lead an unproductive life locked away from society at large for their own good. But you wouldn't be able to pick out a single one to place within those categories by simply looking at them now.

"Every human being here has exploded in a blaze of self-fulfillment… some of them with savant intelligences that can challenge your best computers on an intuitive level and win unassisted. While President Caneman and others like him plot self-enrichment and conquest, our citizenry have worked to the mutual benefit of humankind. You're surrounded by the results, one of which is that tasty meal you just enjoyed, and the antibiotic medication you took after boarding the TUG. I dare say you won't be suffering any more colds or flu problems, and I've asked Dr. Agave to prepare a package of the same for your family. You might want to go back and restudy the lesson of Australia for a better understanding of what a society's castoffs can do."

"Point taken," answered Johnson in a polite but more somber tone, taking no offense at the mild rebuke. "That robot thing of yours, 'Prime' is it? Impressive as hell. Do you intend to build an army of them?"

"You know better. I've known you for long time, Johnson. You're my best friend, and I can honestly say we've been apart far too long. I've truly missed our discussions; our… close interaction. There's a place for you and your family here when everything settles down, or sooner if you'll consider the offer. In the interim, if you have any of your people at the Walter Reed Hospital, or that county prison in Pennsylvania, I suggest they be somewhere else after Monday of next week."

Nodding in understanding, Johnson inquired about Alahn. "We haven't found him yet. He's somewhere in Pennsylvania, but we've narrowed the search area somewhat."

"Want me to help?"

"Better not. You'd have too difficult a time trying to explain what you're doing to Congress. You need to get back to your job, or I'll be bailing you out of jail as well," Jake said with a grin. The two friends shook hands and embraced.

Johnson pushed back slightly but continued to maintain his firm grip on Jake's shoulders. Looking directly into his eyes, he asked, "Anything to that detonation warning being broadcast all over Washington, D.C.?"

Impressed that his friend knew of the event, but not surprised that he had managed to contact his team and stay up on events, Jake smiled. "Even Chicken Little needs to be entertained now and then."

Johnson's hearty laughter boosted Jake's spirit considerably. Escorting him back to the TUG, Jake stopped at the entry portal. "I won't ask you to keep me informed, but here's a special phone just in case. Don't worry, it's keyed to you. Anyone else tries to use it and it'll simply go dead with all memory destroyed. The TUG will take you to the UN helipad—there'll be a glitch in all the security cameras lasting for several minutes when you arrive. I've arranged to have you picked up there discreetly and driven to your home. Give my love to the family."

The Walter Reed hospital complex located in Washington D.C. has a number of units in addition to an institute for research and new general hospital. The old original structure, now more a visitor center than medical facility, is fronted by a circular driveway enclosing a beautiful white fountain and pool. Surrounded by red ground cover and lush greenery, the pool reflects a powder blue sky perfectly complementing the stately, columned entryway standing almost as tall as the building itself.

Working in conjunction with Prime, Walwyn had fixed both Chateauleire and Iawy's locations as being there. He and his associates had successfully hacked into the military medical systems and downloaded their case histories, which were forwarded to Doctor Agave and his staff. The full Council, including Gautier, was present for the briefing.

"According to her file, they're being guarded in rooms 307 and 308, essentially the eastern most rooms on the third floor as seen from the building's front. That keeps them away from the hospital's general population and any other prying eyes. Chateauleire suffered a fracture of the C1 and C2 vertebrae, with some subdural hematoma or bruising of the frontal lobe and brainstem. She was saved from basilar skull fracture and soft tissue laceration by her helmet, and is extremely fortunate her spinal cord was not damaged. Her injury has been fixated with application of a halo brace, accomplished by insertion of four cranial pins drilled directly into the skull. Those pins are connected to a circular halo-type fixator through which are threaded four rods attached to a vest unit. Her neck and head are completely immobilized. The lung puncture was repaired and rib wired back into place."

After a pause to allow the Council to view projected examples of halo brace equipment and x-rays, he continued.

"Iawy's injuries are consistent with blunt anterior chest trauma. This may be associated with cardiac or thoracic problems as well, but are more usually linked with compression fractures of the thoracic spine. Similar cases of sternal fracture have resulted in high death rates usually due to involvement with pulmonary and cardiac contusion, aortic ruptures and the like. Most patients complain of localized pain in the sternum, and computerized tomography, or CT, is used to rule out these other problems. Of a more immediate concern is my interpretation of this next part. The human body's ribs are attached directly to the sternum, however, the two lower connect only to the spine and float in front. It's common to see subluxation or dislocation of the ribs in that area due to this type of sternal injury. A result of that subluxation is compression of nerve roots causing spasms in the muscle area between the ribs, a highly painful reaction sometimes confused with heart attack. I'm disturbed to see signs of intercostal muscle strain, which can generate excessive levels of pain due to twisting of the trunk and add to the perception of heart attack due to location and severity."

"Why would that be of particular concern, Doctor Agave?" asked Maralah. "His injuries would not seem to be as severe as Chat's."

"Trunk twisting is normally associated with common sports activities such as golf, baseball, or tennis. If Iawy is confined to or secured in a hospital bed, how is it possible that he would engage in the type of twisting activity that would produce such agonizing pain?"

"Simple," replied Gautier. "If another person were present and intentionally moving his body in two directions to aggravate his pain. It is called torture, Doctor, and I know Iawy well enough to know he would not do such things to himself."

"Enrique," asked Jake. "Can they travel now?"

"Chateauleire is young and will heal quickly with minimal scaring. Her hair will cover the small scars from the cranial pins, and her rib will be fine… the surgery having been performed orthoscoptically. Iawy owes his survival to excellent conditioning. Both will profit from our antibiotic regimen. They may also require counseling for the mental trauma they have been subjected too. Otherwise, with caution, I believe they can be moved."

Jake shared with all assembled his discussion with Johnson McMinn, to confirm Gautier's contention about Iawy and the fact he may have revealed the source of their mineral and other assets. Most of the Council members expressed dismay at hearing this latest, but Jake assured them the impact would be minimal.

"OK, everyone. We'll now go over the plan to remove and relocate our friends to safety."

Alahn swam up through darkness and dull throbbing pain to discover he couldn't move his left arm, hand, or side. Still in shadow, he slowly reached over with his right and felt hardness encasing his upper body.

I'm in a cast?

An unseen hand, small and tentative, wrapped itself warmly around his; guiding it back to his side.

Turning his head to the right, he asked, "Who's there, where am I," and was puzzled when no reply was immediately forthcoming.

That same gentle hand now touched his lower chest, then slowly moved up to just below his chin and hesitated. He could feel from the pressure exerted that it continued to move upward, but he wasn't able to discern the touch. A delicate, obviously female voice was able to make itself understood in a baffling way.

"Thy dress is strange; we know it not."

Slowly reaching out, he felt a slender arm. Allowing his hand to slide up to meet his benefactor's wrist, he moved it to feel below. Realization came to mind.

My helmet. I'm still wearing the Starflyer gear.

Relocating her hand to the left side of the helmet, he placed the index finger on a release trigger; moving his hand to the matching trigger on the right. Intuitively, she pressed it as he did. The lower part articulated, allowing him to reach in, grasp and lift the helmet. He could sense that she was assisting him, as it came off with less upward effort than he would normally exert.

Once clear, he removed the visor and heard a sharp intake of breath as she saw the interconnecting wiring leading to his eyes... but felt her relax as he pulled the inoperative black, high-definition contact lens-like discs free; laying the apparatus beside him; keeping both eyes shut against the light until they could adjust. Reaching up with a smooth motion he pulled breathing mask, throat microphone and nose-inserted high-G sensor array from his lungs. The assembly joined the other equipment at his side, and he could feel a damp cloth wiping away excess mucus from his face.

Alahn's head fell back onto the pillow as he took a deep breath. It was obvious even that small effort was taxing, and his companion again guided his hand to the side and held it. After a moment he managed to reopen his eyes to a squint, and could now discern that his covering had been cut away from the lower waist upward. However, the peculiarity of his new environment overcame any embarrassment at this point in his recovery.

He was in a small plain room that smelled crisp and fresh... painted in light blue with white trim. A peg rail on one wall was hung with articles of girl's clothing... a stripped water basin and bowl sat on a stand adjacent to a window crowned by a dark green shade. The bed appeared to be bordered by sturdy head and foot boards, with a diminutive one-drawer chest placed within arm's reach holding a small vase with flowers. Both the stand and chest were protected by knitted linen doilies. He was lying on a goose feather mattress, covered to his waist by a sheet and multi-colored quilt.

Up to this point in his life, Alahn's interaction with females was limited to research associations and gatherings of like-minded adults on Luna in furtherance of science. Somehow, his studies had consumed time that others would normally have used to pursue the more fair gender. Flitting about between the Earth and its moon wasn't an environment where young people would normally gather for social contact, and his work kept him much too busy to squander precious free time in the Great Hall. He simply had not met anyone that took an interest in him beyond that.

Turning now to face his benefactor sitting at bedside, his eyes were drawn to an exquisite vision... a cream complexioned face delicately inset with pastel blue eyes, framed by tender matching eyelashes and eyebrows now somewhat furrowed as if in worry. Mid-parted dark blonde hair with a hint of twin waves in front flowed back and disappeared under a white linen heart-shaped cap. A matching neck cloth broadened into a full apron which fronted a pale lavender dress with elbow length sleeves. Extending to just above her ankles, the dress was in sharp contrast to black stockings and shoes.

She was the loveliest person he had ever seen.

He was the loveliest person she had ever seen.

The room seemed to grow brighter as Alahn's warm open smile came naturally; being the one unexpected and freely given gift no man had ever bestowed to a flowering young woman... whose sequestered life up to that moment had been spent in helping to raise five siblings between chores within a religious farming household.

"Thee...," her voice caught as words tumbled out in helpless honesty, never before having seen any man with lean, muscled abdomen, toned and buffed body exposed in this manner.

"Thou... thou arte comely," she whispered, blushing fiercely.

First glances can be magical with promise, and two young hearts skipped the same beat. She suddenly realized her palms were damp and she was holding his hand more firmly than intended, and that his grip had tightened to match hers.

Time seemed to slow as one took in the other; two sets of eyes eagerly drinking in the visage before them... neither understanding what was happening or realizing its strength as behavior locked in the genes of humanity combined with hormonal chemistry to bond them forever.

"Thank you," Alahn replied in quiet sincerity. "I'm sorry if the equipment made you uncomfortable. I didn't realize I still had it on."

The youthful yet masculine timbre of his voice sent a thrill coursing through her soul. Self-consciously releasing his hand, she grasped her own in the folds of her lap as her legs and feet pointed inward; almost pigeon-toed with unease. Still somewhat embarrassed, she looked down at the floor and explained softly, "We knew not the manner of its attachment. Doctor Beiler and father felt it best to remain in place until thee could administer to it thyself. I... the other children, were frightened... that... oh, sie könnten eine wanze sein... that thou might be a wanze... a bug, and not a real man."

Grinning at her awkward disclosure, he replied, "My name is Alahn. Please, what's your name?"

Recovering some composure and bringing her head up to look at him, she responded in a more business-like manner. "I am Hulda, the oldest of six children at seventeen; soon to be eighteen," she added hastily. "Born to Henry Esch and Mary Beals. The others are twins Rachel and Hugh, fourteen; Abraham, twelve; and young twins Issac and Susannah, just turned six; we call them the twins."

"The manner of your speech and the way you're dressed are new to me," said Alahn with open inquisitiveness.

"My father is Amish, my mother Quaker. He is... shunned, for marrying outside the faith in this manner. Mother can be persistent and it was agreed that we would be taught both ways. We live and dress as the Amish, though our speech be of the old order Society of Friends. Wir sprechen Deutsch, that is, we speak German among ourselves."

"Hulda, where am I?"

"Thee is in our house, lying in my bed. I am staying with Rachel, and Hugh has moved in with Abraham; to be close while thee recovers."

"I mean what city or state."

"Oh, thee is in southeastern Pennsylvania, the county of Lancaster. This is our farm. Where is thy home?"

"That may be a little difficult to explain at the moment. Is your father or oldest brother available? I need assistance with another piece of my equipment."

"Father is out in the field; Hugh in the kitchen. I'll have him come right away." So saying she left and was quickly replaced by a bare-footed teenager wearing a bright blue shirt and black pants with buttoned suspenders.

"I am Hugh. How may I help thee, English?" he asked eagerly.

"Thanks, Hugh. My name is Alahn, why did you call me English?"

"It is the name given to all outsiders."

"I understand. Hugh, I'm wearing a waste recovery system, and need your help to remove it." Alahn talked Hugh through the steps required to remove the items, asking him to discard the remainder of the body suit as well.

"Thee is of a size with our father. I will bring thee clothing when thou arte strong enough to rise. I will see to the disposal of thy suit. Does thee wish me to bury the other items as well?"

"Thank you, Hugh. Yes, they may be discarded... they're of no further use to me at the moment."

Returning once Hugh had left, Hulda took on a more nurse-like demeanor and in a somewhat more haughty tone advised, "Thee must take medication left by Doctor Beiler... for thy pain and recuperation." She helped Alahn move to a sitting position. After swallowing the pills provided, she fed him a meal of heavy stock soup.

"What happened to me?"

Setting the empty bowl aside, it seemed instinctive that she took his unresisting hand.

"Thee took quite a fall from the tree. Doctor Beiler put thy shoulder back into place, and set thy arm... it has a crack at the elbow. Thy arms and ribs are badly bruised. Thy cast is set about the body to hold everything firmly while thee heals. Doctor says it may be replaced with just an arm covering in several weeks, but for now thee will have to suffer with thine arm up in the air."

The excellent soup combined with medication to infuse Alahn with a soothing feeling of pain-free fatigue. He drifted off to the melodious sound of Hulda's voice as she softly stroked his arm.

Awakening early evening, he found Hugh waiting there with clothing as promised. It required laborious effort to dress with frequent rests between items, after which he was assisted to the bathroom.

"Mother insisted on indoor plumbing, and we are one of few families locally to have such convenience. Come, we are to have dinner now, and father wishes thee to meet the family."

Hugh placed Alahn's good arm around his shoulders and helped him down a rather steep and somewhat narrow stairway to the kitchen, bypassing the living room. Gathered there were all the family members, and Hugh left him standing to take his place among them. Alahn was greeted to the sight of a typical Amish family... bearded father, mother, and six children lined up in perfectly descending height consistent with age, oldest to youngest.

"English, um... Alahn," corrected the father, after a short glance at the disapproving look on Hulda's face. "I am Henry Esch, and this is my wife Mary. Our children are Hulda, Rachel, Hugh, Abraham, Issac and Susannah. Welcome to our house."

"Thank you, Mister and Mrs. Esch and family. And thank you for the loan of your clothing." His following comment, "I apologize for dropping in on you as I have," brought smiles and several young mouths covered in vain attempts not to burst out in open laughter. He was helped to sit, unable to ignore the aroma of home cooked bounty that assaulted his senses and permeated every corner of the house.

While they ate, conversation was intertwined with both English and German as the children spoke to their parents. Henry explained the Amish spoke Pennsylvania Dutch, a form of Palatinate dialect, and followed the Ordnung, their code of church discipline. In the main, they were a totally self-sufficient and high-spirited people of good humor. One immediate benefit was the reward for tilling the land placed on the table before them, and fellowship evidenced by his unexpected but welcome company.

The warm summer evening permitted open windows and raised shades to invite an occasional breeze to join the gathering.

"Alahn," asked Mary. "Does thee have more than one name?"

"Yes, Mrs. Esch. My full name is Alahn Starnes, but we only use one name in our home and community."

"In like manner, I am comfortable to be called Mary, Alahn. Where doest thou call home?"

Knowing he couldn't delay the inevitable, and with trepidation, he lifted his arm and pointed. All eyes followed his movement to see him indicating the rising bright full moon framed majestically within the window. Alahn was pleasantly surprised at the response he received.

"Thee belongs to that group which has set up residence there? I thought as much. Thy vessel and manner of dress does not speak of earthly influence," remarked Henry.

"Yes, Mr. Esch. We went there almost six years ago. My friends and family live there, much as you do here. You may find we have a lot in common. How is it that you know of us?"

"Our newspaper, the Budget, has recently made mention of differences between thy people and ours. Not something we normally see in print there, but unusual enough to discuss among ourselves."

"Has thee and thy people been shunned?" blurted the youngest girl.

"Susannah!" admonished Mary. "Thee is impolite to ask such a question."

"Her question is open and without offense, Mary. No, Susannah, not as you think of shunning. We choose to live apart on our own. Our issues lay not with the people here, but with the manner of governments that have forgotten them. Like you, we wish to live our own lives free of intrusion—to explore and discover for the enrichment of all. Forgive me, Susannah, but I must change the subject and speak with your father."

"Mr. Esch, I feel we should discuss what is to be done with my Starflyer."

"Ah, Sternflieger… Starflyer. Aptly named, and please call me Henry. Thy ship does not a fitting ornament for yon oak tree make. The children climbed up and cut free the fabric holding it in place. I used the horses to pull it into our barn while Doctor Beiler attended to thee, so none but ourselves have seen it. It is remarkably lightweight for an object of its size. Hulda was walking to the barn when thy ship first confronted the oak, so was there to find thee. She and the other children took quite a fright when first met by water, followed by pieces of ship and thyself plummeting to ground. She had courage to see to thee before raising an alarm, so I have placed thy care in her charge."

Alahn took a moment to explain the emergency egress functions to the children, looking each in the eye and apologizing for their fright. His honest concern for their well-being won their hearts, leaving all of them with a desire to embrace his kindness.

"What would thee have us do with the fabric?" asked Mary.

"You're welcome to it if you can find a use."

Having finished the meal, Alahn turned to Hulda and asked, "Would you be kind and assist me in going to the ship. I must determine its condition."

"Thou should not exert thyself unnecessarily, Alahn," she fretted. "Doctor Beiler would not be kindly disposed to additional injury."

Nonetheless, the trip was made. He was able to ascertain the damage was greater than expected. The AI hardware and all of the communications circuitry was gone, along with most of the routing and automated emergency systems as well. What had not been vaporized had been fried, and the fuel tanks had vented until empty. There was no hope of using remaining components to attempt contact with Luna, and the ship was incapable of flight. He could see that decentralizing the location of so many critical components would be a priority when he got back and brought this to the attention of the engineering crews.

It was a wise planner indeed who had decided that manual emergency actuators should be installed as backups to the electronic functions. He retrieved an emergency packet that contained a portable Global Positioning Satellite receiver.

"Hulda, do you have a telephone?"

"There is a community phone used by all, located a goodly walk from here. Our farm is located quite a distance from the city proper, being one of the more outlying ones. I will take thee in the buggy tomorrow, but only if thou are rested."

Exercising her prerogative as nurse-in-charge, she ordered, "Now come, thee has visited thy wounded bird enough for one day."

Returning to the house, Alahn was pleased that Hulda helped him up the stairs. Neither complained about the length of time required ascending to the bedroom, and both were acutely aware of the other's closeness, sharing frequent pauses, glances and smiles along the way. They spent the next hour in pleasant conversation about life on Luna, not realizing or caring that she had held his hand the entire time.

Hulda took Alahn to the phone before sunup the next morning. Unable to completely close the door of the booth, Alahn felt somewhat self-conscious with his left arm sticking partially out into the open, although he was quite happy that Hulda was out there bracing it on her shoulder... her closeness was very welcome and gave him assurance. He was sure his cast, combined with ill-fitting blue shirt, black pants, coat and hat, presented a comedic appearance sufficient to draw more than a second glance from passersby. Thankfully, there hadn't been any this early in the day. He was able to place a collect call to a pre-arranged number.

"Dad, it's me. I'm okay."

"Thank God, son, where are you?" Alahn and Jake brought each other up on events that had transpired since his downing, including a full explanation of the Starflyer's equipment location shortfalls, the farm's location and GPS coordinates. Jake suggested that he remain where he was for the time being… he seemed to be in good hands and the change of scenery would be a well deserved break. They both agreed his fall in all likelihood broke the locator disc embedded in his wrist. Jake assured him he would see that replacement communication and locator devices reached him as soon as possible.

Despite her closeness, Alahn was able to speak discreetly. "Dad, there's more I want to tell you. Something new has been added… her name is Hulda." Jake listened with fatherly interest as Alahn described the family in detail, and asked for some ability to pay his way during the time he'd be there. Jake assured him he would arrange something for the short term, then asked Alahn to work with Mr. Esch to move the Starflyer into an open area the following night for retrieval by a TUG.

On return to the farm, Hulda informed Alahn she had chores to do. He insisted on accompanying her, over her protests.

"Staying active will improve the healing process," he explained in his defense. "Besides, you can show me how your farm functions."

Entering the barn Hulda could see that Hugh, assisted by Rachel and Abraham, had led a cow into one of the stalls not blocked by the Starflyer's bulk and had placed feed in its trough. The twins Issac and Susannah joined them. Washing her hands and the cow's udder with their assistance, she sat on a short stool, placed a pail beneath the udder and began to milk it as Alahn grabbed another stool and sat down next to her, reveling in the wonderful fragrance of nature permeating their enclosed environment.

"Does thee have farms on thy land?" she asked matter-of-factly.

"Yes, but not in the same sense as this. In the city of Selene, we have people who study our land and grow things from it. Hulda, you should see the result! Everything we plant grows in abundance! The soil there is sterile yet very fertile."

Issac piped up, "Does thee have cattle, Alahn; horses and cows?"

Having quickly grown fond of all the children, he replied, "Not yet," reaching with his hand to ruffle the boy's hair. "Perhaps one day. We have to be very careful that we don't introduce something into the new environment that doesn't belong there. That type of error could be potentially harmful to everyone."

Not to be outdone, Susannah moved next to Alahn. Placing her arm around his neck she brought forth her query in a wonderfully charming child voice, "But how does thee move thy buggy when visiting?"

"We have our own special buggy, one that doesn't need a horse, or use the type of engine forbidden by your church. And," he added, "our sidewalks move so that you don't have to," punctuating this last by touching the end of her nose with his finger and smiling. Encircling them both with his good arm, he gave the twins a hug and kiss which was just as quickly returned.

Taking advantage of the distraction and aiming carefully, Hulda squeezed one of the cow's teats and let fly with a thick stream of milk directly at Alahn.

Releasing the twins, he fell backwards off his stool, mouth opened in total surprise! Hulda and the children erupted uncontrollably as fresh warm milk splashed and flowed freely down the front of his astonished face!

Hastening to his rescue, Rachel slipped on a fresh cow paddy and with limbs flying akimbo found herself indignantly deposited just as helplessly to the floor. The joke was too rich for decorum with Alahn adding his own laughter to the merry chorus.

Pandemonium reigned as the twins fell to the hay-covered floor while holding their sides. Hugh and Abraham wiped streaming eyes and held on to each other for support, pointing and roaring in delightful hooting laughs and howls of glee at the hilarious absurdity of it all.

As their whoops of joyous mirth and hilarity subsided, Hulda and the older boys helped Alahn struggle to his feet; she using her apron to dab excess milk from his face as the boys and still giggling twins dusted hay and dirt from everyone's clothing.

Standing close, she grinned broadly up at him while straightening his hair. "Thine eyes smile as brightly as thy face, Alahn."

Reaching to take her hand, he drew it to his lips and kissed it gently… looking deeply into her eyes as he did so. Her gaze never wavered as this sign of promise passed between them, nor did she attempt to recover her hand. Not understanding the silent communication that was going on before them, the others left the barn to complete their chores, unable to fathom the change that had come over their sister. Alahn followed as Hulda remained behind for a moment to put away her milking items.

Turning in mid-step without quite realizing it, she stood silently and watched him walk back toward the house with the children. Leaning against the stall, her mind drifted into contemplation of events and feelings she had never encountered, unable to reconcile her puzzlement and confusion... her strong sense of longing for this robust young man a driving force; wanting him as she had never wanted for anything in her young life, yet fearful that he would be lost as quickly as had been found. She marveled at her own boldness in speaking so openly to him... as if by long association rather than mere days.

"Thy new friend is beautiful, is he not?" stayed that line of thinking. Unaware her mother had entered the barn but comforted by the knowledge, she leaned back into the only true comfort zone she had ever experienced as her mother warmly embraced her from behind. Hulda sighed deeply.

"Ach, mutter, I know not my own heart. He has fallen from the sky and stolen it as surely as a thief in the night. Ich bin so verwirrt, so confused."

Sensing her oldest daughter's internal turmoil, Mary hugged her closely, murmuring gently, "He has only received what was freely given. I judge he has given his as freely to thee."

Rubbing her mother's arms, Hulda lamented, "But mutter, I have completed rumspringa, my running around time... I've committed myself to Ordnung; our religious order. How can I have him and not be shunned by the Aeltesters; the elders and all that I love and hold dear? He and his people may feel as strongly opposed about us... and I will lose him to another." Weeping openly, Hulda pleaded, "Please help me mutter, what shall I do?"

Turning her daughter around to face her, Mary lifted her chin. Wiping away uncertain tears, she offered, "It was much the same when first I met thy father."

"Truly, mutter?" she implored, new hope springing into her eyes.

"Ja, meine schöne tochter, I was as strongly committed to thy father and felt my heart would break from the love of him. We faced questions as perplexing as what is before thee now. The Aeltesters saw our love, our promise." Mary paused, her face aglow with fond memories of those days.

"While not a usual arrangement, it could be seen that we both embraced similar commitment and would remain true to both communities."

With a humorous sparkle in her eye, Mary continued, "Yes, it is true Alahn's people are some distance away... but he has a marvelous buggy to visit with, and thy father's curiosity has leaped with the thought of it. I should say we both like thy young man very much. My advice is to not worry... all will work out as destined to do." Kissing her daughter's forehead, she finished, "Now come, we must prepare for the evening meal."

Following dinner and cleanup that evening, Mary shooed the children from the room, then invited Alahn and Hulda to remain in the kitchen and visit. She exchanged a knowing glance with Henry as he winked back at her.

Alone, Alahn gave Hulda a puzzled look. "I don't mind being here with you at all, but it seemed odd that your parents would suggest it as they did."

"It is the manner of our people," she replied, blushing openly. "We are given privacy so that we may come to know each other better. We will not be bothered."

Overcoming his sudden awkwardness in realizing the others had seen how the two of them interacted, he reached to take her hand. Moving close to her while gazing steadily into her inviting eyes, Alahn searched for words. "Hulda, I understand this may seem to be somewhat forward. I have never met or known anyone like you. I... I've never been with another woman. I don't think there's any doubt in your mind that something has passed between us—a strange and wonderful feeling. I don't know what to call it... I only know that for the first time in my life I have discovered something that wasn't there before, something named Hulda. I want to be with you."

"And I with thee, Alahn."

Each took in the natural scent of the other; powerless to resist the pull of genetics as in mutual attraction they leaned together with the innocence of first love. Lips touched lightly; brushing slowly back and forth as with closed eyes they savored that first brief, intimate closeness that would take them on a path of discovery spanning two worlds...

neither one having experienced such nearness before; lost in the wonderful rightness of the act.

Their kiss melded into full blossom, and both felt the quickening heartbeat of the other; the warmth and sweetness of their breath, the wonder at how their lips fit perfectly together. Faces tilted in unison as his lips lightly stroked her cheek, settling gently to kiss both of her eyes… tenderly bussing her forehead as unfamiliar strains of biological music played joyfully in both hearts. He took in the heady unspoiled aroma of her hair, the exquisite design of her ear as he gently nuzzled the side of her neck; the willowy caress of his exhalations a thundering waterfall cascading over the most receptive parts of her innermost being.

Amish children are not exposed to many realities of an outside world overdriven by electronic and printed media; catering to pre-pubescent young females in an increasingly open and permissive society at large. The Esch domicile contained neither television nor radio, and Hulda's formal education ended at the eighth grade. She was overcome with sensations she was unprepared for and never knew existed; both were in the grip of unfamiliar stirrings.

Such close embrace worked an enchantment on two young lovers as he became suddenly aware that Amish girls don't wear bras; her firm breasts and erect nipples now pressing hard into his chest!

Most farm children learn early on about mating habits of animals in their charge and accept such practice as common. Thoroughly lost in intimate embrace, she was suddenly aware of an awakening change in Alahn as her hand rested harmlessly on his lower chest.

"You… we… must stop," she breathed huskily, shuddering in delicious ecstasy at his touch; the feel of his breath on her neck and shoulder, desperately wanting the ambiance of his masculinity to go on forever.

The resonance of his whispered, "You didn't say 'Thee'," almost pushed her over the edge, demanding that she throw her arms around him to declare her betrothal body and soul forever; to hold him evermore and never let go.

With a remarkable effort to regain control while pushing him back gently, Hulda paused a moment to capture her full senses; blinking her eyes… inhaling fully, then resting her head on his shoulder. Alahn's right arm drew her closer and she relished the warmth of his hand resting snugly on her upper arm.

"'Thee' is reserved for elders and those outside the family. We are closer now, and I may use the familiar 'you,' if thee… if you will have it."

"I'll treasure its first use on this night always. I'm in love with you, Hulda Esch-Beals."

Turning her head to face him, understanding of her mother's words came as she realized his inviting eyes were a window to his soul. She could see plainly his desire was as strong as her own.

"And I as truly with you, Alahn Starnes," was answered with a second kiss as enjoyably binding as the first.

With hands and eyes locked together to cement this declaration, their all-too-brief foray into intimate togetherness was interrupted by a familiar whooshing sound. "It's a TUG, here for the Starflyer," explained Alahn, excitedly. "Come, let's meet it."

The two of them joined family now assembled on the porch to watch it circle and land, with the children standing behind and clinging to Henry and Mary in wide-eyed wonderment at the sight. Alahn walked over to greet the pilot, and was greatly surprised when Jake exited the craft! Father and son embraced tightly as two of Luna's E-suited engineers walked over to secure a lifting harness on the Starflyer.

"Dad, there's someone I want you to meet." Escorting his father to the house, Alahn introduced him to Henry, Mary, and the children. His introduction of Hulda was saved for last and was accomplished with somewhat more meaning than the others… a fact that didn't escape notice by the other adults.

"Our house has been blessed by the presence of thy son, Mr. Starnes," said Mary graciously.

"Please, call me Jake. Thank you for taking him in and caring for him as you have. He has spoken very highly of you all."

"Komm in, bitte. Come in," remarked Henry with enthusiasm. "Let us visit."

"For a short while only," responded Jake, removing his helmet after depositing a pack on the floor. Henry asked if he was concerned about exposure to Earth's infirmaries, and was told he had been inoculated with

Luna's medical protocols for a much longer time, so brief exposure to the outside world wasn't as much a concern as it would be for others. Several hours passed quickly as Jake answered everyone's questions about their life on Luna. The children were mesmerized by his colorful E-suit, passing the helmet around for close inspection; their imaginations going wild with the miracles being described. Jake was as interested in the accomplishments of Henry and his family, and listened with focused attention as Henry proudly discussed his farm and community.

When the time came for leaving, Jake shook hands with each family member and handed them a package from his pack, hoping the gifts would help to cement new friendships between their families that were formed that day. Everyone watched as the TUG lifted majestically into the night sky with the Starflyer in tow, eventually disappearing into the night sky.

Back inside, the family gathered around the kitchen table to ponder events and Henry gave the children permission to open Jake's gifts. He was wordless at opening his own to discover a gold card with the words "Luna" and "Admit One" engraved on one side, his name and an unfamiliar phone number on the other.

The box also held a jewel, in his case a perfect blue star sapphire almost one inch in diameter, and a solid gold nugget five times larger! All packages were similar, with the exception that a different representative of the jewel family was to be found in each one. All were speechless at the magnificence found within each box!

"How can we accept such treasure?" asked Henry with a look of open bewilderment on his face. "Thy presence and company in our house is payment enough, Alahn."

Reaching over, he handed Henry and Mary three additional blank gold cards each.

"The pleasure of my company doesn't feed hungry mouths. This should pay for the medical care and my stay here, with something left over for future needs. I apologize that we don't deal with currency as you do, so you'll need to have it converted."

The younger children had fallen asleep and were taken to bed. Having assisted Alahn upstairs and helping him to lay comfortably on his back,

Hulda sank to her knees then bent over the bed whispering, "Beyond doubt thy people live in a wondrous land. My head is full to overflowing with images painted by thy father."

Taking her hand to draw her nearer, Alahn found no resistance. The memory of effervescent-like tingling remained fresh on her lips as she willingly renewed their interrupted intimacy with another kiss as sweet as the others.

"There is a place on Luna for you and your family. I intend to speak with your father about this in the days to come. Please have Doctor Beiler come tomorrow, I want to have this cast removed."

"Sie haben mehr arme als ein krake!" squealed a happily embraced Hulda, as Alahn, done with his plaster casement, was now able to freely wrap both limbs around his new love and kiss her again. His remarkably speedy recovery was attributable to Dr. Agave's science team.

Mimicking her manner of speech and father's verbal mannerisms Alahn quipped, "Was, meine liebe? Thee doesn't desire my arms? Perhaps yon scarecrow would find them more comforting!"

Laughing, she interpreted, "Thee has more arms than a krake, an octopus," and with that announcement rolled on top of her lover while throwing both arms around his neck.

"Well, I only have two, and thee didn't say 'you' that time, so I get six more kisses," he returned just as gaily. They both lay on a quilted picnic blanket spread out under a gorgeously clear sky, and after slowly collecting a bounty of small pecks around her face and hands, Alahn sighed with contentment. Putting on a more serious countenance, he absorbed the marvelous perfection of this woman while running his fingers gently down the side of her face; tracing the line of her linen cap, basking in the delightful feel of her full body resting on top of his as she now gazed lovingly into his eyes. As he viewed his reflection in the mirrored liquidity of her soul, his heartfelt "I love you, Hulda," reinforced every emotional feeling she had for her young man.

Her eyes sparkled brightly as "I love you as well, Alahn," reinforced his pledge. With a slight pout she added, "And thee is unfair to take advantage of me in that way. I must have more time to learn new ways."

"And time will be given freely, but 'thee' must promise not to learn too many new ways. I love you as you are now, Hulda, and would ask that you remain true to yourself and your family's customs, including your manner of speech. It is a unique facet of your being and one of the reasons I love you so.

After a moment of studying her face closely, he added, "These past days have been like heaven for me." Reaching to brush a bit of hay from her hair, he added, "Your family has accepted me as one of their own, and I grow fonder of the other children with each passing day.

"Hulda, are you permitted to marry?"

Without responding she sat up, and as he did, brushed hay and twigs from his hair and clothes. Remembering her mother's words at the barn, she spoke with less confidence.

"It is the custom of Amish to marry within Amish. Shunning comes about when someone marries not simply outside the Amish family, but into another religious order. That would be a breaking of commitment to the Ordnung; the order and discipline of our community. Father strayed from custom in marrying mother. However, they were joined under God in civil ceremony, neither one entering into the Order of the other. In a strict manner of speaking, both are in good standing within their religious houses, so it is fair to say that we are only frowned upon a little."

"Hulda, will you join with me… marry me… be my wife?" all came out as one unbroken sentence.

"With all my heart I wish it and will say yes, my love, but I know not thy heart in matters of the Ordnung, or how our community will view us. I have made my commitment to our tradition."

"Let's go back to the house and finish your afternoon chores. I had promised to speak to your father previously on another matter. I'll speak to him at dinner about both.

The meal prepared by Mary was excellent, complimented by the happy banter of the children as each recounted their experiences for the day. Mary was perceptive in noticing that Alahn and Hulda seemed unusually quiet, exchanging numerous glances during dinner.

"So, how was thy lunch in the field, Alahn," asked Henry, smiling. "Hopefully not disturbed by too many wanzen?"

Somewhat hesitantly, he replied, "Oh, fine, Henry, and no… not many bugs at all." Pausing to collect his thoughts and with a quick look at a pensive Hulda, Alahn reached over to take her hand, then turned back to

Henry. By now, every family member knew that something different was going on and all grew quiet.

Alahn began, "I suppose at this point you must all be aware that Hulda and I have found something special happening to us." Pausing, he looked at both parents. "Henry... Mary, I love your daughter, and she has confirmed those same feelings to me. I have asked her to join with me, and she has accepted. It is my desire to wed Hulda and be a good husband to her."

At that announcement, Mary grasped both hands together over her heart, tears of happiness welling up in both eyes as Issac and Susannah both leaned over to embrace and comfort their mother, not understanding exactly why she would be crying.

"We are both apprehensive about how such joining would be viewed within your community." Taking a deep breath and with renewed confidence, he continued, "Henry... I ask your permission to marry your daughter, Hulda. I will seek the approval of your Ordnung leaders to bless our union. As far as it is possible for someone like me to become a part of that commitment, I will do so for the sake of Hulda and your family. With your approval, I will speak to my father as well."

The momentary silence that accompanied Alahn's declaration was broken suddenly by a widely smiling Henry jumping to his feet and grabbing Alahn's hand to shake it while happily mixing languages, "Mein junge! My boy! Sehr gute! Wunderbar! Wonderful!

As Alahn stood up, Henry embraced him in a bear hug and welcomed him into the family, pounding his back in congratulation as Mary and the children swarmed around them both.

"I will speak to the bishop and preachers. Having known thee and met thy father, I see nothing obvious that would act to keep thee and Hulda apart."

"Henry, please sit... there's more to discuss. My father and I want you and the entire family to come to Luna, to be our first farmers. You heard that we manufacture much of our own products and food, and are in that sense similar to your people in our self reliance. We have researchers that grow much of what we eat hydroponically, in an artificial environment, but we need actual farmers. A welcome augmentation to our synthetic food would be fresh vegetables and other items best provided by those with knowledge and skill at tilling soil, able to grow sustenance for a large number of people. You would be farming pioneers in our new world. In future, other farmers would join us on Luna and other places we may settle; building on what you have started.

"Your family can have all the land it can manage. Initially, you would have to farm using our equipment, which I assure you uses nothing but hydrogen and air, leaving only water vapor as a result. I find no conflict with that use in what you have shared with me about the restrictions you embrace. Later, if you desire it, you can work with our researchers in determining how to bring farm animals into the new environment. You would be welcome to maintain your faith and ways, and would be given a TUG-buggy dedicated to your family for visiting back on Earth."

There was much discussion leading into late hours of the evening. It was decided that Alahn and Hulda, accompanied by Abraham and Hugh, would journey to Luna for a first visit to see the land. If results were promising and their reports fair, then Mary and the younger children would go. Trips would have to be staggered in this manner as the farm still needed to be managed in the interim. Henry would make a final trip with the entire family. Once he was satisfied that all could be accomplished, the farm would be given to a good Amish family that had long desired to add it to their own, with the understanding they had a life-long invitation to return and visit. It was agreed that Alahn and Hulda would exchange vows at the Bishop's house on the day the entire family was to leave for Luna. After arrival there, they would again exchange vows to be duly recorded by Prime into the official logs of everyday activity.

Eleanor wasn't sure what woke her up. Exhausted from the day's efforts, she had tried to turn in early. The other inmates kept later hours and had the TV sets blaring right up until lights out. Warden Framer had continued to stop by on occasion but had nothing to add to his original assessment. She spent days reading as much as possible to stay up on current events, secretly pleased at the discord being waged by Luna's advocates.

The past few weeks had gone by pleasantly enough, other than missing her friends and unable to determine where they were in the prison. Neither had she worked out how she would get to them even if she did know. The ache in her heart for Gautier and Chat grew more worrisome with the passage of time.

It's three a.m.—why am I awake?

Flopping onto her stomach with one palm braced against the wall, her other arm dangled over the bed's edge. She opened her eyes in the darkened room, gazing through the cell bars at a somnambulant day room. A late night freight train punctured the night's silence by rolling noisily several blocks away.

How can anyone sleep through that?

As if the clatter of its passing was insufficient, the engineer laid on a raucous multi-tone horn melody at each road crossing, seemingly hell-bent on ensuring every citizen of the county knew he was in town regardless of the hour.

That didn't account for a noticeable increase in vibration she now detected with her hand, or the sudden ultrasonic screech that accompanied the engineer's horn blast and cut right through her skull... blasting away any vestige of weariness that might have clung to her now fully awakened and alert mind.

What is going on?

Climbing down from the top bunk, she noticed that no one else seemed to be aware of the disturbance she felt, or what appeared to be a small cloud of dust surrounding the barred window. Curious, she walked over to look outside, leaning against the frame as she did so. As it took her weight the window, metal frame, and approximately two inches of solid steel reinforced concrete disappeared!

In point of fact, fell outward and away to the ground below with a low dull thud announcing its arrival.

The darkness she peered into wasn't the envelope of night, but rather the light-absorbing vacuum of blackness making up the port side of a

TUG hovering perfectly still just beyond the window, the sound of its exhaust smothered by the passing train. Its open portal outlined an unrecognizable silhouette.

"Le bon soir, Manquer Ernst. Si vous n"êtes pas autrement engagé, soigneriez-vous pour me joindre pour le dîner?"

"Gautier!" Climbing through the opening, she launched herself through the TUG's portal; leaping into Gautier's open arms and causing him to sway as their bodies collided. Burying her face into his chest she wrapped her arms and legs tightly around him, shaking with emotion as he enfolded her protectively. The portal closed as the TUG climbed away from the prison.

"No, I'm not engaged in anything at the moment, and yes, I will join you for dinner. Oh, you beautiful man, I've missed you so." Kissing his face, then looking up into his eyes, she asked, "How are Chateauleire and Iawy?"

Allowing her to compose herself and slide to a standing position, he replied, "We'll discuss that later; your friends are here. Our strike was coordinated with a passing train and convenient virus for the prison's security computer system."

In confirmation, both Randolph and Jennifer rushed to embrace her just as tightly. Walwyn and Prime had compromised the prison's computer system and determined exactly where each one was being held. A Starflyer's finely tuned mining laser made short work of cutting out the windows in all three cells, allowing Gautier's TUG to do the pickup honors.

"Edwina and I will be taking you three to Luna, where you'll be met by Doctor Agave and his staff for checkups. We have set aside an area for your friends to complete the Q protocols there."

The Council had decided to allow Edwina to redeem herself by planning and conducting the rescue operations, and she now waved in happy recognition from the TUG's command position.

Warden Zachary Framer stood in silent contemplation while running the tips of his fingers over the inner wall of a missing window frame, wondering what sort of device could cut so smoothly without making a sound. There wasn't a metal burr or rock chip to be found protruding anywhere within the affected space. No foot prints or tire tracks... nothing on the ground except the window plug. No one on the roof and no methodology seen that would provide a way up there. And nobody in the adjacent area heard a damned thing... in cell blocks located in three separate wings of the prison!

Security camera tapes were just as vacuous, containing several minutes of blank static. A helicopter would have awakened the entire prison... besides the fact it couldn't have gotten close enough to the wall due to its rotor blades. Dismissing the thought that his prisoners had pulled an Icarus and flown away on their own, he turned to an associate.

"Get the Attorney General in Washington on the line. We need to have a talk."

"**Have** you given any thought to spending some time for yourself?" asked a smiling Maralah, interrupting a too-infrequent break in the solitude in the Nearside lounge. "After all, we've got Eleanor and her friends back and events seem to be running more smoothly now," she stated.

Turning to face his trusted friend, Jake answered somewhat pensively, "I've been contemplating that very thing, actually. There are a number of old friends I would like to reconnect with... perhaps persuade them to come here... we do need more agricultural expertise. I just don't see how I can make time to accomplish that."

"Don't be foolish. Everyone needs a break and you're long overdue. The Council can handle anything that comes up at this point. Go, right now. Take off. Don't tell anyone where you're going. I'll call you if we need you."

Involved with Jake Starnes from the beginning, Maralah had been a family friend for decades prior to the Luna adventure. Intuitively sensing his inner turmoil, she placed her arm around his waist as she did when a much younger man needed guidance. "It would do you a world of good to have someone to share things with. Why don't you look around? I'm sure there's lots of opportunities to meet someone new? It's time to stop mourning Natalia and move on with your life."

Grinning at her not-too-subtle prodding, he drew close to embrace and hug his dead wife's dearest friend. "What, at eighty-plus we become match makers? I've still got loose ends to tie up with the Esch family and Alahn's wedding... you know, the one I missed."

"Oh, stuff and nonsense. I've already spoken to Henry and Mary. They'll all be here next week. The children have already come and gone, and couldn't be enthusiastic enough about Luna. Alahn and Hulda exchanged vows in Lancaster and you aren't the first man to miss a wedding. I'll forgive you this one time… they already have." Shifting into a more serious stance, Maralah admonished her charge.

"Jake, they are as concerned about your well being as we all are. You can't carry the weight of two worlds on your shoulders. Let others help you. Now I'm serious… leave now. Go to Earth and take all the time you need. We'll handle any problems that pop up."

"Dad, are you sure about this?" asked Alahn, tugging the suit's collar upward for mating to the helmet, standing alongside a fully prepped TUG.

"Everything will be fine, son. I'm just taking some time to visit old haunts and become reacquainted with friends from my past, including recruiting. I'm disappointed that I missed your wedding."

"It's okay, dad. We met in Mr. Esch's house with families and their religious elders. It was simple, plain and heartfelt. I would not have had it any other way." Dropping his voice in a conspiratorial manner, Alahn's whispered, "I had KhenemetAhmose there as my cousin, 'Ken.' He recorded everything… you can view it later in private," was answered by Jake with a warm hug for his son. He had arrived too late for that festivity, but had lingered for one week to assist on the farm and become better acquainted with his new in-laws.

Now taking a closer look at both young adults, he noted with satisfaction a certain glow about their countenances; their mannerisms indicative of lovers at ease with each other as well as excitement of new intimate discoveries. Pleased with the closeness of their association, his own inner being was troubled for a moment with memories of losing what had been nearest to his heart… *Natalia…*

Abruptly closing a mental door on that thought, he refocused on the business at hand as his now daughter-in-law and son continued to assist him with the Starflyer gear.

She fretted, "Thou arte a personage of some importance now, Father

Starnes. It is not seemly to place thyself into such situations without assistance to protect thee. After all, thou has the interests of a new world to consider."

"The very reason not to do so, Hulda. I wish anonymity, and will not achieve that if constantly surrounded by armed security personnel. Maralah and Kelly can handle Council issues here for awhile. Donah is in the process of making some very special arrangements for me. I'm confident all contingencies have been addressed."

Warmly embracing Alahn, Jake said, "Thank Hulda's family for their company and the relaxing visit. I have truly enjoyed joining in with the farm work on Earth. I'm sure they'll be happy with five miles of fertile farm land here on Luna. And you, young lady," he said, lifting her chin and kissing her forehead, "will ensure my son is kept in one piece. No climbing of trees, if you don't mind." Both young adults smiled at his not very subtle reminder of Alahn's first encounter with the Esch family.

Jake had grown quite fond of that household; parents and children. Raised in an Amish community yet schooled and taught as Old Order Society of Friends, their speech and simple yet straightforward manner-isms had impressed him as it did his son. His departure was sealed with another warm embrace from Hulda and firm hand shake from Alahn.

"So, was ist sein name, dieser gefährte?" inquired Isaac Lengacher of those gathered at his house in the Southern End Community at Quarry-ville, Pennsylvania. He and his family were hosting this Sunday's bi-weekly religious service. The women were gathered in the kitchen preparing today's meal, children outside tending to animals in the barn. Men were left to discuss issues within the community at large. Word was that a stranger from out of town, perhaps as far away as the Indiana Amish, had recently leased old Chupp's small farm, southeast of Stras-burg in Cochranville.

"The name of dis fellow, as you say?" responded John Lapp in his usual matter-of-fact tone. "Ja, I heard from Daniel Stoltzfus's Samuel dis man comes to here from daht Indiana Amish, daht he is plain, and I believe he is called Yacob. Samuel has it from his paper but daht is all at this moment."

"Why has Chupp not given his farm to family or those of us?" inquired another in a slightly accusatory tone. "Das ist der weg unserer reihenfolge, the way of our order, is it not?"

Lengacher recaptured the conversational lead by reminding all gathered that Chupp's wife had died long ago, his two children grown and gone; none wanting the farming life, and neighbors close by had all they could handle with their own farms without taking on much more responsibility, times being what they were. Chupp's passing offered opportunity to this new plain farmer, also a widower if rumors held true, and income from rental of the farm added to a steadily declining community fund which existed to provide for all.

Herr Amos Wagler spoke up to advise he wasn't far from this Chupp's farm Yacob, would keep an eye on events, and promised to update everyone as they transpired. Conversation now turned to more immediate issues closer to hand, with talk of new members pushed aside by delicious kitchen aromas driving anticipation of the delicious meal to come.

Jesus pleases, why me? thought the boringly frustrated driver of a fully loaded refrigerated eighteen wheeler, stuck at an overlong red light behind a black, Amish horse-drawn buggy at a four-way intersection; stark multi-directional highway routing sign pointing toward freedom in every direction except the one he was on as if to say, "Sucks to be you, fella."

Be my luck to lose the reefer, he mused idly. *Might be interesting to see how the locals handle tons of melted ice cream lining their streets.* However, at minus ten degrees Celsius, local winter weather spoiled even that mental pleasure. *Drop the lot onto the pavement and the company wouldn't lose a penny.*

He knew it would be a mistake to take this truck route through Lancaster, Pennsylvania, but figured lady luck owed him one and he was calling in his marker. In a perfect world he could have cut several hours off the trip if able to avoid exactly the situation he found himself in at the moment. Ugly black with tall rectangular carriage, all he could see on the back of the thing was a bright triangular caution placard centered between reflectors and four-spoke wheels.

To pass time, he counted a backup of at least fifteen cars stretching behind him in his rearview mirror. Bent forward with right elbow resting on the steering wheel, forearm lifted with closed fist pushing against his distended cheek, he sighed in resignation... figuring the way his luck was going, the next five or six miles would be just as leisurely paced before reaching a point offering passing room. He suddenly realized the fingers on his left hand were unconsciously tapping the horn button. It took an act of true discipline to keep that hand off the truck's sonic alert, imagining the liability incurred if it spooked the buggy's horse or scared some old farmer into a heart attack.

After progressing through the intersection at change of traffic signal, the buggy swerved slightly to avoid an ice buildup on the road's surface. That small change in angle gave the driver a glimpse of the buggy's horse, which to his surprise wasn't a horse at all. Noting this as the first interesting thing to come along in hours, he sat upright in his seat and craned his neck to better view the target of his renewed curiosity.

The damned thing was being pulled by a box!

Less than one third the buggy's size but just as black and rectangular in shape, it too featured four smaller spoked wheels. Normal horse collar and hames tack was missing, replaced by sturdy traces appearing to be bolted to each side of the unit. A bar mounted horizontally at top rear of the contraption featured leather reins attached to each end leading back to the driver's hands. Pulling on one or the other acted to turn the box's front set of wheels in like manner to conventional steering.

Recalling what he had read about Amish people in general, he figured this particular individual had built a simple battery-powered box attached to an electric motor, now pulling along at a rate equal to any local animal. He mentally lifted his hat in tribute to a really clever man... coming up with such an idea, while noting the driver avoided all the pitfalls of administering to a live animal under such harsh conditions.

Wonder what his neighbors think about that? he mused, while signaling his intention to slowly pass the odd, rolling roadblock that had held him captive for so long.

Unknown to anyone else on Luna's Council, Jake had tasked the Council's Kelly and Donah to arrange something within Lancaster County as close as possible to the community where Alahn and his Starflyer had crashed. Having completed visits to a small, selected group of old friends, including General Johnson McMinn, he focused on recruiting efforts. Luna was in need of true farmers and it appeared from Jake's initial assessment there were plenty to choose from in that area to complement the Esch family's first efforts on Luna. More importantly was the observation that this particular community practiced farming in its most basic application; exactly the type of practice needed initially to jump-start land production on Luna.

Leasing an available bit of local acreage had been arranged through intermediaries, giving Jake a perfect venue for scouting out additional farming talent needed on Luna. Placing small notices of the purchase in local papers was a real touch, providing just enough information to cover his arrival and hopefully assuage curiosity of too-inquisitive neighbors.

The small Amish farm offered perfect concealment for his TUG; now tucked safely out of sight in its large barn. This was accomplished by a concealed landing pad built over a sliding track leading directly into the barn; balanced so well that one man could push the craft easily. Late night landing approaches were hidden by surrounding trees while the craft's already quiet engine exhaust was further silenced by creative engineering additions. There was sufficient room between farms to keep any remaining sound levels low enough so as not to disturb their animals.

Typical community clothing had also been provided but the real touch was his so-called 'buggy.'

The sides and roof of both the coach and engine cart were covered with cleverly constructed high efficiency solar panels, all but invisible unless very closely scrutinized. Wheels on both featured regenerative braking which could provide additional electrical charging, while an extra coach pedal installed adjacent to the footbrake controlled energy flow. Advanced lithium-ion battery packs stored under the buggy's floorboards and engine enclosure offered impressive stored capacity. The engine cart itself contained very powerful electric motors attached to each of the four driving wheels.

When coupled with the energy available, they proved more than sufficient to move the buggy about twenty miles in any direction at speeds easily exceeding any local horse-drawn convenience. In a pinch, Jake could also recharge the unit with power available from the TUG. For that matter, his ship's systems were capable of powering the entire community he found himself in, if it ever came to that.

Today's events called for a carefully planned 'coming out' high visibility ride to at least announce himself by supposedly visiting local markets for supplies. Given that the Amish openly utilized direct current devices driven by battery power, he felt his choice of mobility would not offend local customs while at the same time allowing him to limit his need for animal effort. It wouldn't hurt to generate an impression that he was good with his hands in building the engine cart, thus marking him as acceptable if somewhat eccentric. The farm itself housed a number of common animals in order to maintain his facade.

Spotting his turn, Jake was relieved to be off the main road so that a following interstate truck and its retinue of trailing cars could safely pass and be on their way. This particular road took him through some of the neighboring farms enroute to the closest market he could find. Off to his right stood a wonderfully picturesque farmstead, main and ancillary housing blending in with newly fallen snow, as if both had just been freshly painted a pristine white. Tall evergreen trees guarded both sides of a hard-packed roadway leading up to the main house, while an equally vibrant stand of large winter foliage stood sentry at the homestead's main entrance.

Directly across that roadway was placed the main barn, bracketed by two silos used for grain storage. Acreage to the rear was populated by a small forest, while that in front sported an unusually high growth of grasses for this time of year; stretching the full length and breadth of the farm's property. Thirty meters southwest of the main house was a large farm pond, about fifty meters by twenty meters. Now frozen over, it added stoic silence to complete a vision of inviting winter grandeur.

Looking somewhat closer, Jake detected signs of disarray about the property. House door ajar, gates left open, grass not cut; roadside fencing showing a fallen rail or two here and there. *Pretty place, but looks like someone's a little behind on chores,* he thought.

What he saw next caused him to focus intently on the pond as he brought the buggy to an instant halt. Two small children were playfully sliding on the pond's seemingly solid surface, about four meters from the bank closest to the house. As he watched in apprehension, one child slipped and fell on its bottom, causing the surface to fracture and break. Freezing water now reached up to embrace both in cold arms and drag them to a watery grave before either child could scream out in terror.

Jake applied full power to his energized contrivance, turned around and headed for the entry road. Due to his proximity, he arrived at the pond's edge in seconds. Leaping out of the still-rolling buggy while throwing off his coat, he rushed onto the snowy iced bank and lowered himself horizontally onto the pond's frozen surface to distribute his weight; pulling forward over the ice with both arms. One of the children had clung to a somewhat larger broken lip of the ice, but was rapidly losing strength and going under.

As he reached out and caught that child's arm, his own support was lost as the position he occupied split and threw them both into the bitterly cold liquid. The incredible shock of that indignant encounter sent a jolt of agonizing menace throughout his body. Using his free arm to backstroke and rotate himself vertically, he was surprised that his feet found bottom purchase and thankful the pond was shallow, leaving him chest-deep at the surface gasping with shocked breath.

Placing his burden on the ice and pushing that child toward the nearest bank, he ducked and reached below to find the other quickly. Breaking surface with this new encumbrance, he made a grab for the first child and with both arms now full, bodily pushed through broken ice and force-fully made his way to ground. Setting down the child still breathing, he became aware both were girls, apparently twins. Applying resuscitation to the other brought immediate response as the girl coughed and spit out a small amount of water. Jake realized the extreme cold acted in her favor by causing a breath-holding reaction while she was submerged.

Regardless, both were turning blue with hypothermia and in danger of going into shock. Rushing to the buggy carrying both girls, he climbed inside and shut the door. Placing them on the bench seat, he quickly tore off their deadly soaked outer garments and managed to wrap them in the buggy's large winter blanket. Placing the blanket's foot over a covered outlet on the floor, he turned on two hidden high powered common hair dryers, focusing their life-saving warmth on his young charges. While both were now shivering uncontrollably, one seemed more alert than the other.

"Where is your house?" he asked. Receiving only an uncomprehending stare for his effort, it came to mind this was a German speaking populace. Mentally reaching back to his foreign language studies in school, he managed to articulate his request in passable Deutsch.

"Bitte, Wo ist ihr haus?"

She lifted a badly shaking arm and pointed to the structure adjacent to the pond. With full electrical energy applied once again, Jake drove his vehicle at high speed and came to a sliding stop at the partially opened door that had been spotted earlier. Enfolding both girls still wrapped in his blanket, he ran up the short entry stairs and banged his foot loudly on the door frame. A small boy approached from inside the house and opened the door fully, standing there looking at a stranger holding two children... all three dripping wet with icy water running down and pooling at his feet.

The boy was suddenly pulled aside by a young woman... her initial look of curiosity now replaced with stark terror at recognizing Jake's two bundles. Her terrified voice rose with intensity at realization of jeopardy faced by her children.

"Gott in Himmel; meinen kindern, meine mädchen!" [*God in Heaven; my children, my girls*] she screamed while reaching to yank them both away from Jake. Ignoring him, she rushed from the room holding both children tightly.

"Quickly, place them in warm water," shouted Jake, not taking time to convert his message and uncertain if she understood. Looking down at the boy, he asked, "Was ihr name ist."

The youngster replied, "Ich bin Johann gerufen."

"Ich bin Yacob... Yacob, ja?" said Jake with quavering voice, now shaking almost as badly as the girls at being overcome by hypothermia himself, but noting the boy's nod in recognition of his name.

"Johann; geben sie ihrer mutter diese kleider. Ich muss jetzt gehen," asking Johann to give the girl's clothing to his mother, and that he must now leave. Regaining the use of his buggy, he immediately turned both refunctioned hair dryers to full heat and blower as he set a badly quavering course back to old Chupp's farm.

An armed guard posted outside rooms 307 and 308 at Walter Reed sat with his chair pushed back against the wall, feet balanced on the leg rails while reading a magazine. His concentration was interrupted by the unexpected arrival of two individuals dressed in medical lab coats.

Dropping the magazine and standing up, he stated in an officious tone of voice, "I'll need to see your identifications please.

"Of course," replied the older gentleman, as he and his accompanying male nurse both handed him hospital issued photo ID. With these balanced at the top of a clipboard, he ran his pen down the names of eligible visitors.

"I'm sorry, Doctor... 'Agave', is it? I don't seem to have your name or that of Nurse Anoki on my approved access list.

"Young man, that is an administrative issue, and not my concern. I have just been posted to this wing from the new hospital. You may contact personnel records and update your list at your convenience." Consulting a thick medical chart, he flipped through several pages, then turned it so the guard could read along. "Please note Doctor Capet's name and signature on this order placing me here. I'm aware he is the head of this hospital, is he not? Unless you are prepared to answer direct-ly for the care and condition of the two special cases, please allow me to see my patients."

Unable to refute the authenticity of the ID's or document presented, the guard unlocked the door. On entering, Doctor Agave was pleased to note both rooms shared common access. He headed for Chat's bed as Anoki went into the other room containing Iawy. Quickly checking her intravenous lines, bedside chart, and medical monitors, he bent over the bed and was puzzled to see indications of fresh bruising on her arms. Pulling back the blanket covering her, his distress peaked as he viewed bright fiery welts and more bruising on her lower abdomen and upper thighs.

What in God's name?

"Chateauleire, Chateauleire, it is Doctor Agave, can you hear me?" Her eyes fluttered as weak moans escaped her lips. Unable to move her head due to the halo brace, she struggled to lift a shaking hand, vaguely pointing but not having the strength to complete the act. The arm collapsed to her side as she sank into unconsciousness. Seconds later an unexpected voice broke the silence and sent a cold chill shooting down his spine.

"Waddaya know, come to pluck the chickens again and two more drop in to join the party!"

Doctor Agave turned around to see a man framed in the doorway between the rooms, holding a club in one hand and a bottle of liquor in the other. Swaying slightly, he motioned behind, his slurred speech saying, "Your friend had a little accident. Seems he got acquainted with my baton while I was practicing on King Tut back there. Quite a racket you moonbeams locked in for yourselves. Got enough gold and diamonds to buy planet Earth, and not gonna share any of it with your old friend Special Agent Darren Souser, are ya?"

It was apparent now why the guard outside hadn't seemed overly concerned about their coming in. Souser had been posted to the hospital guard detail immediately after the true revelation of his first encounter had come to light. He was speechless at learning of the assignment, thinking he was to be fired and jailed for his actions on the helipad that night. It came as no surprise when the anonymous calls started coming in. Seems his benefactor was highly placed and had heard that Souser could be quite persuasive. Obtain anything useful, and another promotion and pay raise might be in the offing. In the interim, he was granted a special bonus and a week's leave. He squandered the money on booze and every hooker he could get his hands on during that time; roughing a few of them up in the process.

Eager to get started at his new job, he had worked on Iawy at first... after all, what's a little payback among friends? He took particular delight in applying just enough pressure to elicit exquisite cries of anguish as he recalled the humiliation he had endured at this one's hands. Grinning wickedly with tongue lolling out one side of his mouth, he happily twisted Iawy's body, altering that action with manipulation of his damaged sternum.

The medical chart hanging from the end of the bed laid out everything that was broken, and while those facts took some of the fun of exploration out of his labor of love; it didn't take as long to break his victim as he had feared. Darren always did have a knack for this kind of work. His contact was impressed with the information he discovered, and another quite handsome bonus found its way into his bank account.

They were going to be mightily pleased after tonight to find out about the base these moonies had on that mountain top in Nepal. Yes, sir... that tidbit should be worth two bonuses plus the promotion. He would hold back on the corporation name for awhile. No sense milking the cow dry at just one sitting. Using his belt on the girl didn't get him much; she fainted. He had no doubt that the location of the three cities mentioned by the geek would be forthcoming from her, and he salivated just thinking of it. He was just getting started again on the old Egyptian when his two friends walked in.

Casually strolling over to Doctor Agave, Souser coldly hit him with the club, knocking him senseless to the floor. Reaching down and grabbing the Doctor's medical frock by the neck, he dragged him into the other room, dropping him next to Anoki. Souser fumbled turning the door's lock toggle as he returned to focus his full powers of persuasion on Chat, discarding the liquor bottle and pulling his pocket knife out as he transited the room.

"Hey, moon pie! We're gonna get real cozy now. Ole Darren promised you a trick or two, and tonight's the night." Staring intently through his drunken haze, Souser reached with the point of his knife to cut her, then was startled to see a uniformed hand intercept his arm with an iron grip on his wrist, stopping him from completing the act.

"Waddaya doin, idiot?" he snapped at the guard. "You're supposed to stay outside."

The guard's left arm now came up from behind and placed a lock around Souser's neck, seizing his throat—squeezing until his eyes started to bulge. "There was a shift change," said a calm voice with a strong French accent. "Why don't we let the little girl sit this one out, and you and I will dance, Oui?"

The rescue plan for Chat and Iawy was complicated by the fact that a number of very tall trees were located in front of the wing containing their rooms. It was unknown how their proximity would affect a Star-flyer's ability to get a direct shot at the windows. Gautier was the backup plan. Uniformed exactly as the guards now in place, it required little effort to fix the security company's computer to show him as available for that day. He was to remove the windows from the inside if necessary, by actuating the emergency interlocks and pushing the glass and frames out. Hearing Souser's inebriated ramblings, he entered the room to confront him.

Anoki's head was erupting with pain, but he ignored it as well as he could to assist Doctor Agave, raising him to a sitting position and prop-ping him against the wall. "Enrique, are you all right?"

The Doctor's eyes were pinpointed. Although non-responsive, he was breathing smoothly, so Anoki left him to look at Iawy.

"Iawy, my friend, it is Anoki. What has been done to you?"

Wrestling to make himself understood, all that came out initially were gurgling sounds as Iawy attempted to speak. Anoki located a water pitcher and filling a glass, helped him to drink.

"Ohhhh… Anoki," he uttered hoarsely; his face pale white with agony. "He hurt me… uhhh… the pain. I tried to be strong but could not… could not…" His voice failed again.

"Lay still, my friend. I know you're feeling somehow at the moment, but help is on the way. We'll have you out of here soon. The man in the other room is a monster, a *Skinwalker*, an evil spirit come to maim and kill. My *shimasani*, my grandmother, taught me about such things. It is part of my Navajo medicine. Gautier has him for the moment, but only I can deal with him."

"How will you accomplish that, Anoki?" said a now conscious Enrique Agave, holding his head with both hands. You can see that he is armed. He overcame us both easily."

"We were not prepared for his attack. His feet are in contact with Mother Earth, the source of his power. I will confront him there."

Gautier's hold on Souser seemed impenetrable, fueled by the need to avenge his daughter's mauling at the hands of this creature. Souser's right arm was locked in place and face turning blue, but he had enough presence of mind remaining to shift the grip of his left hand on the baton. Raising it above his head he drove it backwards into Gautier's ribs, temporarily knocking the wind from him and forcing his grip to loosen enough for Souser to break free, then seamlessly reversing the baton's direction to make a powerful sweeping lunge back that would have opened Gautier's head like a ripe melon if it had connected.

Ducking the blow as the baton whistled by, Gautier ripped the blanket from Chat's bed and wound it tightly around his right hand and forearm. Using this to shield a vicious backhand knife slash from Souser, Gautier hit him squarely with his left, breaking Souser's right cheekbone and causing him to stagger backwards in painful spasms.

Gautier rushed into Souser, continuing to back him up as he pummeled him mercilessly. They hit the wall together, grappling. Stepping back, Gautier executed a spin kick that caught Souser's left upper arm squarely, shocking that limb to the fingers and forcing him to relinquish the baton.

Neither combatant noticed Anoki enter the room, wetting the palms of his hands and tightly clasping the medicine bag hanging from a sinew cord around his neck. He began swaying back and forth to the silent cadence of his tribal mysticism.

Gautier hit Souser with an extended arm full-power right punch that shattered his jaw in two places, then a left to re-break his nose. Grabbing Souser by the throat with his right hand and fueled by adrenalin, he lifted him off the floor, again immobilizing the knife-wielding right. The broken cheek bone, accompanied by internal bleeding, caused the entire right side of Souser's face to turn bright red, offset by stark whiteness of the left side due to his injuries there.

The two-toned countenance was striking, clearly observed by Anoki as he sang in his native tongue, "*Skinwalker, your true self is revealed! You are not of the Dine. Your presence here upsets hozho, balance. You are against*

nature. *You cannot run away from my song, for I am Anoki, Navajo haatali.
The power of my tribe is with me... I am the singer medicine man who will
steal your evil wind.*"

Gautier thought not of himself or consequences of breaking his vow of
non-violence. All that mattered at this moment in time was that he rid
two worlds of a madman who delighted in fiendishly violating helpless
victims. Inches away from his opponent's face, he took in the stench of
drunken breath, foul body odor and perspiration as blood from Souser's
facial injuries ran over his hand; his own face screwed into a toothsome
snarl as he contemplated his adversary's upcoming demise. He squeezed
Souser's airway all the harder to prevent loosening of his grip.

In desperation, Souser let go of the hand around his throat and stabbed
his thumb as hard as possible into Gautier's right eye. Forced to release
his grip and step back, Gautier attempted to shift his balance in
preparation for another blow.

Taking savage advantage of the respite, Souser countered with an
uppercut movement of his right arm that drove his knife five inches into
the lower left rib cage of Gautier. Falling to his knees with the knife protruding from his side, Gautier was instantly paralyzed with the sharpest,
most intensely piercing pain he had ever encountered; overcome with
passionate loathing that his final act of choking the life from Souser
would go unfulfilled.

"Time to die, Froggy, then I'm gonna pay particular attention to your
little bitch. Your friends will fetch me a king's ransom before this night's
over, but all your moon faggot pals will get out of that deal is four more
bodies." Souser bent over to retrieve his baton, holding it like a baseball
bat in preparation to bash in Gautier's head.

In Navajo culture, song and action are intertwined. Twirling a full intravenous bag over his head like a lasso, Anoki let fly and caught Souser's
hands... wrapping the bag and drip tubes around his arms as neatly as
any bola-throwing Gaucho. As Souser struggled with this new distraction,
Anoki rushed over and kneeled, using the full weight of his upper body
and arm strength to drive two scalpels straight down into Souser's leather
boots; embedding the full length of the blades into cuboid bones at the
tops of both feet.

Screaming in agony, Souser attempted to hit back, but only succeeded in awkwardly turning around and shuffling toward the wall. Anoki grabbed Souser by his utility belt and lifted him with a strength driven by faith in his heritage, his mind in the grip of a potent tribal chorus led by the voice of his *shimasani*, the power of their combined medicine trapping the spirit of this *Skinwalker*.

The Starflyer was in place... the parameters of the frame cut within specifications. Prime had accounted for the safe location of Luna's participants in the rooms, and approved initialization of the cutting laser.

Darren Souser's fantasies had once again come crashing down in abysmal failure. Seeing his work and plans for riches slipping away, he reached deep inside and gave one final, mighty heave to be rid of the impediment that imprisoned him.

Anoki was holding Souser from behind, leaning backwards at approximately a fifteen degree angle to keep his feet in the air; removing the *Skinwalker's* source of power. Souser's yank caused him to stumble backwards. Refusing to let go, he caught his balance directly in front of the frame edge, still facing the wall with the window just at his right shoulder as the Starflyer's laser fired.

The methodology was to cut the bottom of the frame first, then the sides and top; requiring about two seconds per side total, given the size and composition of the window framing materials. This permitted the cut-out window plug to drop and fall away of its own volition, leaving an opening large enough for human egress.

The laser cut through both of Anoki's legs just above the knees, the strength of its beam acting to cauterize the wounds somewhat. He collapsed, falling away from the window frame as he released his enemy. With a rush of elation Souser dropped to the floor standing, then lurched back a step; now also standing sideways to the window but thankfully rid of his foe's interference.

Now he could complete his little side-scam, collect his ransom for the four, then see a doctor first thing to get his face fixed... hell, he'd been hurt worse in other fights. So that the night wouldn't be a total waste, he'd spend some quality time with little Miss Moon Pie... that was certainly worth looking forward to! Then look out D.C., here comes ole Darren to spread the wealth!

Suddenly realizing his arms were free as well, he looked to see why; glancing downward just long enough to see them both hit the floor as the first vertical cut was initiated. There was no pain or bleeding at first as his mind failed to comprehend the act.

Souser stared openmouthed at the results in horror, white bone ends from both arms now beginning to protrude through the fleshy stumps as cleaved muscle and tissue began contracting. With blood now flowing and spraying freely, he had little time to contemplate a life hindered by prosthetic science as the top horizontal cut neatly severed his head flush at the shoulder. The window and frame fell away, accompanied by Souser's body. There was enough blood left powering his brain for a final glimpse at the underside of the Starflyer and what seemed to be sounds of a large group of singers chanting in his mind before blackness took away his spirit, freeing Chateauleire and Iawy from the tyranny of Darren Souser forever.

Chupp's farmhouse was typical Amish; plain and simple. Jake found the simplistic arrangement of rooms to be fascinating but practical. Amish people did in fact utilize a number of modern conveniences, but operated by twelve volt battery power converted to standard house current by electrical inverters. Diesel generators recharged the batteries, an acceptable arrangement not in conflict with their religious guidance to live apart from modern society by not connecting to any local Utility's electrical grid.

Old Chupp had incorporated a surprisingly roomy kitchen pantry off to one side and partially under a steep stairway leading to the second floor. Installing shelves on the outside of its door acted to blend it right in with the wall, making it all but unnoticeable. Surreptitious late night visits by a few of Luna's more clever engineers had both enlarged and turned that room into an ultra-modern communication center complete with holographic projector and high-tech computer systems. A very powerful rotating antenna was installed in the upper reaches of the barn and interacted with Earth's communication satellites when not in direct position with Luna. The entire system was powered by one of the hydrogen fuel cells located on Jake's TUG.

It was mid morning that found Jake sitting at the system's console. "Is that the complete report?" he inquired of Maralah. Her colorful three-dimensional image stood in full size on the holographic emitter located adjacent to his computer station, making her appear as real as he was. She noted his plain Amish clothing, consisting of suspendered pants, white long sleeve shirt and high neck black shoes. She saw a black matching coat with no lapel hanging on a wall hook behind him.

"I see you're blending in quite well. And yes. Walwyn was assisted by Natalya and Yoshko in compiling it from sources provided by everyone involved, as well as all information that could be gathered from computer systems. We'll have it ready for distribution in a few days. It's as factual as we can make it. Due to the death of Souser and injuries he inflicted onto others, it would be best if you came here and addressed the Council personally."

"Okay. I'll cut this visit short and return, but I have a few details to work out yet. I'll be there in a few days." On that note, Jake ended the transmission and placed the system on standby.

As he exited the room, a light and somewhat tentative knock was heard. Carefully closing the panty, he walked into the small foyer and opened his door; quite surprised to see an Amish woman standing there fronted by three children... one boy and twin girls. Somewhat shorter than he, she wore a vermillion-colored dress with full skirt, an apron and warm cape. He noted her light brown hair was put up in a bun concealed with a small white cap of sorts. The twins had matching blue dresses, hair covers and warm coats, while the boy had simple pants, plain shirt, coat and hat.

All three appeared somewhat apprehensive. All four had delightfully bright blue eyes.

"Guteen morgen Herr Yacob. Ich wünsche zu vielen dank zum sparen der leben von meinen kindern," she stated as the boy stretched forward to return his blanket. Jake now recognized her as the young mother of the twins at the pond and the boy as her son, Johann. Her features required no enhancement to draw any man's attention to how alluring she was.

He understood she was attempting to thank him for saving the lives of her daughters and was impressed with her sincerity. Smiling at this unexpected but welcome appearance and searching for words, he did his best to reply,"Bitte, ist mein deutsch nicht sehr gute. Please, are you comfortable with English?"

"Ja, Herr Yacob... von schule, oh, daht is to say, from school. Mein name ist Marian Ella Fisher and here ist, are, mein, ah, my children. Johann has four years, Kristina und Kathryn have three years." All three watched Jake shyly, tentatively looking up at him as if to gauge his reaction to their unscheduled visit.

Remembering his manners, Jake invited them in, kneeling down to look into the eyes of each child while shaking their hands in greeting; welcoming them into his home. He was pleased to receive hugs and a kiss from each of the girls which he just as eagerly returned. He then stood to take Frau Fisher's coat, gathered up the others and asked them to sit and talk for awhile. After seating his guests in the kitchen, he prepared hot chocolate for the children, tea for her and coffee for himself. The kitchen's warmth, reinforced with welcome refreshment, invited verbal interaction.

"Are the girls better now?" he inquired sincerely as he sat down beside her at the table.

Somewhat timidly she responded, "Ja, because of sie they are safe und happy." Eyes suddenly brimming with tears, she continued with remorse, "Ich had only turned away moments... moments to ensure cooking. Then comes you to our door mit meinen kindern, my babies, close unto dying. Ach, Ich, I... was very frightened. Ich placed them in a warm bath as I heard you say, rubbing them both, until slowly they returned to me. I don't know how to thank you, Herr Yacob... don't know..." At this she lowered her head, covered both eyes with her hands and burst out crying in bitter self-reproach. The children ran to their mother's side, eyes over-flowing in uncomprehending sympathy with their mother's emotions.

For all of his battle hardened sturdiness, Jake could never sit idly by when another was suffering in anguish for any reason. He reached over and placing one arm around her shoulders, extended his other hand to gently cover both of hers. She offered no resistance as he pulled her to-ward him; embracing this sobbing, distraught mother close to him as her body shook with emotional distress.

After a moment, he offered kindly, "Seeing your beautiful children standing secure and sound of body in my home is thanks enough, Frau Fisher. I only did what anyone would have done. No one can be in all places at once. There's no need of blaming yourself and all is well now."

After a time she dried her eyes, composed herself and sat upright, then began talking. Words spilled out as if a floodgate had suddenly broken open... desperately needing someone to talk to, even if that someone was this kindly stranger unknown to anyone within her small community.

Her husband, Abram Isaac Fisher, was dead... murdered by the village idiot; her cousin Eli Yoder. That revelation confirmed Jake's observation that her homestead appeared unattended. He asked why no one was offering assistance under those circumstances.

Shunned by his own family, Eli had nowhere else to go or anyone to take him in. Abram was patient in attempting to teach Eli how to be helpful around the farm, but he seemed incapable of learning such things. His behavior, odd and eccentric, was too difficult for others to deal with and as the next closest family member, she accepted the responsibility. Eli's demeanor was acceptable around Marian and her children and no conflict existed in that regard; he was as a child himself, but his presence kept away those who would otherwise be more helpful, including her closest friends. Due to his obvious mental infirmity, he was sentenced to the State's mental hospital.

The twins were born just before Abram's death. With three children and a farm to run, it was proving almost impossible during the last years to keep things in order and she had no one to turn to. She had heard rumors about someone buying old Chupp's place and the name Yacob, which matched the name given to Johann by a stranger at her door. She concluded it must be him, Herr Yacob.

"Why have you come to our county, Herr Yacob? Is there no farming in Indiana?" she asked with open curiosity.

Her direct look into his eyes, filled with compassion, acted to draw Jake into speaking of a subject he had held closed for far too long. "Please, you may call me Yacob. My wife died long ago, Marian, an innocent victim of disturbed individuals reveling in destruction. Perhaps I simply needed to be elsewhere. My inquiries led me to this place, and I find it peaceful, perhaps an opportunity to meet new friends. I have a son, Alahn. He has married a wonderful Amish girl here, Hulda Esch. I am happy for them both.

"If you feel like discussing it, what where the circumstances of your husband's death?"

She explained that Abram and Eli were to take their buggy to market. Grain was needed for the animals and supplies for the house. Abram's habit was to carry his money in a pouch kept tied around his neck and hidden beneath his shirt; it was most of what they had saved. A passing car spotted them and called the police. He was found lying on the ground beside the buggy, obvious marks from Eli's hands plainly seen around his throat… the money pouch missing. While there were no direct witnesses to the event, it all seemed simple and straightforward to the police. Eli was charged with the crime. There is no law to terminate one such as Eli, so he was confined in the State's mental institution, perhaps forever.

Jake thought about her comments for a moment. At times, first appearances can be quite deceiving. He resolved to look into the matter when time permitted.

She and Jake talked for some time, finishing their tea and coffee. He offered to come by the following day to see what needed to be done. Her protests were easily overcome and he bid the family good day, escorting them out to their horse drawn carriage. The children were in a much better mood by now, and he gladly accepted their hugs of parting. He stood leaning against the door until they had driven out of sight, suddenly enveloped with an unusual feeling of loneliness at the silence that greeted him upon entering the empty house.

Shaking off such gloom, he walked back into his ersatz communications room, taking only a few seconds to make contact with Walwyn on Luna. Addressing his holographic image, Jake tasked Walwyn to provide a subliminal German language program, adjusted for local dialect, and obtain all the information available on a local felony murder case dealing with the Fisher family… Abram, his wife Marian, and Cousin Eli Yoder; from all sources including electronic. Also, be prepared to send KhenemetAhmose for a short stay; he had a job for him.

Marian Fisher was assisted in barn chores by three young but eager helpers. Feeding the few animals she hadn't sold didn't take long, and the children loved having those that remained. More troubling was recent talk around town that the Elders had been discussing what to do about her situation. Economics of a farm weren't difficult to understand, but with no husband to work the land, cover market visits, and the hundred and one other small details required to be fruitful, she felt it would only be a matter of time before she would be forced to consider selling and moving elsewhere.

Mornings come early on an Amish farm, so back into the house she went, trailed by three little chickens as if behind a mother hen. Removing outer coats and getting them situated in the kitchen, she began breakfast preparations but was startled by a knock on the door; secretly delighted to hope it may be Yacob come calling as she moved to open it.

"A good day to you, Frau Marian Fisher," offered a smiling Jake with a small, polite bow.

"Und gute morgen to sie also Herr Yacob," she replied, wiping hands on her apron. With a slight curtsey and return of his smile just as brightly, she offered, "Wird sie herein kommen to visit?"

Putting on his most serious mein, Jake intoned quite formally, "Ah, Frau Fisher. Fortune has surely smiled on your house this day. On my way to your settled homestead, I met the most astonishing fellow."

Pausing to glance down while leaning back against the stairway railing, Jake folded his hands across his lap, adopted a quite thoughtful expression, then looked up at Marian.

"A very insistent person. He would have me believe he was master of all trades, capable of the most unsurpassed craftsmanship in all these parts... and most compelling of all, was readily available to demonstrate such ability. He has arrived in yon buggy," finished Jake, with a slight wave toward his carriage.

Attempting to see beyond Jake for a glimpse at who that might be, she folded hands under her apron and with a distressed look on her face replied, "Ach, Herr Yacob. Bitte, ich habe nichts, oh, I have not to pay for such effort, my farm is poor and with Abram gone..."

At her awkward pause, Jake stood grinning to face her and broke in, "Well, Miss Marian. How about my working then, in exchange for nothing more than your good company and conversation?"

At suddenly grasping the joke, Marian's entire face lifted with a growing smile, impossible to contain, that now grew into delightful laughter at Jake's humorous presentation. Covering her mouth to hide embarrassment, she surrendered to his absurdity, dropped her hands and laughed right along with the wonderfully amusing man standing before her. Her children watched this exchange with happily smiling faces and much interest. It had been a very long time since they had heard their mother respond with such happy resonance.

Her face aglow with elated glee, she added, "Yacob, you bring to me laughter; such a gift." Reaching out to take his hand, she said, "Komm. Join my family to breakfast. Only after may you show to us these marvelous skills so recently spoken of."

For that day and the next, Jake worked to repair and set straight as much of the needed patching and refurbishing as he could. Little Johann wanted to be a big helper and followed Jake to each site, where he would be handed a tool suitable for his small hand and encouraged to assist. The work was simple and easy enough and he enjoyed the child's company.

Suddenly lifting him from behind under both arms, Jake swung Johann up onto his shoulders and ran to the next fence section. Hat blown off with wind in his face and hair flying, the boy squealed with delight at such rough play and urged Jake on to more; both laughing merrily as Jake ran a few circles with his exuberant bundle. None of this association was missed by a longing set of blue eyes watching from inside the house.

Unknown to Marian, he made arrangements for a local farmer's two sons to earn extra money by coming on the third day, weather permitting, and cutting all of the unruly grass noted when he first saw the farm.

As Marian would have no excuse but that he join her and the children for meals, Jake insisted that he provide market items and Marian was content to accept that, so long as she would do the cooking for her share of the bargain. They traveled to the local farmer's market in his horseless buggy, to the absolute delight of all members of the Fisher household. Johann stood on the seat between Jake and Marian as the twins sat behind, thrilled to view the world through the rear window. It drew admiration and comment from others at the market place as well, and Jake was pleased that the local Amish seemed to welcome him quite freely. On the way home, he hiked young Johann up onto his lap, giving the boy a thrilling turn at the reins. That act drew fretting comment from

Marian and the twins until it was seen that unknown to Johann, Jake was still holding them as well.

His timing of the return trip was perfect; the buggy almost halfway across her farm's acreage before she realized the fields had been cut level. She favored Jake with her warmest smile as they looked directly into each other's eyes; heartfelt appreciation of their separate endeavors shared with that affectionate glance.

After arrival and storage of their shopping efforts, she began preparing the evening meal, stirring a pot held in one arm balanced against her midsection. Hearing an uncommon but merry commotion from her front room, she peered around the corner to find a fully engulfed Jake, three children leaping onto, rolling, and tugging him to the floor. All four laughed with glee… Jake tickling each one to invoke joyous response from all. She smiled inwardly with true affection at noting sounds too long absent from her house; but welcomed back with open arms.

As her attention moved back to her stirring, more troubling thoughts intruded.

Marian, was ist it you do hier? Dis man is fremder, a stranger, only kommen to your haus since some days, she argued with herself. *Und so?* she shot right back. *Do I deny vaht my eyes see, vaht my heart speaks to me? How long since any happiness tür durch kommen… through that door kommen? Where ist mein family, die community, die helpers, some other single mann? Ich sees them not. Siehe, wie er mit meinen kindern ist; see how he ist with mein children.*

Ja, Marian, clearly visible before you dis gute… this good, but vaht of the Aeltesters, the Elders? Vaht is their role to be in this newness now komm to you?

It had been noted on many an occasion by her parents that Marian harbored a stubborn quality, and she proved them correct yet again.

Ich haben nichts… I have not married the Aeltesters, and not one of dem mit courage komm to hier since gone my Abram ist. They vant dis farm and me sent back to my mutter.

Only now dis good plain man kommen hier from another place. He wears not the beard, but if such is his way, it brings no harm to my haus. Und see him for how he ist, strong, kind, gentle, und as alone in dis welt, dis world, as I am. I will more believe die hand von Gott brings him to heir, rather than he falls from the sky to do harm.

Tears came to her eyes as fondest memories of her lost husband came to mind.

Meine liebe, mein herz... mein Abram, who had all my love... but he is gone for so long now. No other stands hier to fill mein empty haus... or heart.

Her thoughts solidified and ended that short internal struggle.

Ja, mein own mind will I keep.

She secretly hoped against hope that something bigger and better may spring from the beginning she was witness to, then refocused her thoughts toward the meal she was arranging.

After an excellent dinner and engaging conversation among all present, Jake bid the children good evening as Marian accompanied him to his buggy. The air was alive with the ambiance of nature, crystal clear and tingling with the sharpness of winter's tang. Sunlight fading and early evening now beginning to wake, they caught a glimpse of the moon's edge on the horizon, starting its journey heavenward to stake its claim among the stars. That brief look reminded Jake of his duty and last conversation with Maralah, something he had willfully set aside for a few days of uninterrupted happiness. It was as if weight of the world had lifted from his shoulders.

If Marian had noticed Jake's much improved use of her community language, she made no mention of it... it simply seemed natural. Reaching to take her hand, he looked slightly down into her inviting eyes.

"Marian, these past days have been wonderful for me. The presence of you and your children have taken my mind away from many troubles and left it free to truly enjoy myself for... well, it's been a long, long time. Thank you for having me.

Perhaps I may stop by again?"

"Ja, Herr Yacob. Meine kinder und I would like daht very much. Bitte, please komm soon, ja?" At that, Marian reached to hold both of his hands, then pushing up on tiptoe kissed a surprised Jake on his cheek! An unexpected but intense feeling shook them both, head to toe, as if a jolt of high energy had struck without warning! Marian's sharp intake of breath announced her recognition, in equal measure to the sudden questionable look on Jake's face!

It took every bit of discipline on both their parts to pull back as if nothing at all had happened. They saw wonder and truth in each other's eyes, the longing, the raw desire building up within two souls denied for far too long, an unfulfilled need to grab each other and never let go… but the children's closeness combined with an aura of commitment which surged forward to block further congress, and that incredible moment almost ended.

Almost.

Jake was helpless to stop his face moving within an inch of this resilient yet vulnerable woman; her openly inviting lips, the fragrance of her being acting to pull him closer.

He murmured softly, "I have to go now, but I promise, *I promise…* to return soon." His gentle squeeze of her hands was as instantly returned, and Jake let go to reluctantly turn and leave. As he drove away, Marian stood there watching until he was out of sight, overcome by intense feelings of melancholy as she wiped helplessly at tears running unashamedly down her face.

Jake the would-be swain ran headlong into former Army Colonel Starnes.

What the hell are you doing, Jake? he asked himself. *She's what, mid to late-twenties?*

So what. Age isn't the only criteria for successful relationships. I was eighteen years older than Natalie.

Natalie was an older woman when you met. Marian is younger than Nat was.

She needs me. Her children need me. I need them too.

You were supposed to come here looking for farmers!

I found one.

One! One what? An undereducated girl/woman from a devout farming village?

That 'woman' has been without a husband or man on her farm for more than three years, wrapped in grief over his loss and a family member in prison. Regardless, she's educated enough to manage the entire affair by herself, which is more that I can say for some of the so-called professionals I've had to deal with along the way. That's the kind of resolve and dedication we need on Luna.

Belay that you idiot. You're acting like some love-struck teenager. The Council needs you right now. Forgot about a little thing called 'duty' have we? Does the short phrase 'two planets' take any precedence at the moment?

To hell with that 'at the moment.' Where does it say I can't have some joy in my life?

She has a commitment to her religion, she can't just pull the plug and take off, you know.

Lost that argument before it got started, my little inner-head buddy. I listened to my son. Alahn and Hulda both assured me such a relationship can go either way, or stay both ways, as long as the commitment is there and so far I'm not aware anything we do offends anybody's religion.

Now get out of my head and leave me alone. I've got to get up to the New Hope.

Maralah looked at Jake as he finished reading the Souser report.

"You seem distracted, and have been since you arrived here. Something I should know?"

Glancing up to refocus on her eyes, he responded, "No, Maralah. Just a head full of new details in working out our latest farm acquisition. I'm fine. Just need to come up to speed on your report."

Maralah knew better. Something happened to him during his visit to Earth, she was certain enough of that. She resolved to be more attentive to ferret out the cause of his diversion. Events were moving too quickly now to lose sight of what remained to be done in earning Luna's freedom.

Jake stood in the briefing room aboard the New Hope, his holographic image addressing assembled members of the Council and citizens gathered in Luna's Great Hall's auditorium. He spoke in length and detail to explain the events leading up to the rescue of Luna's citizens and friends.

"Anoki is in the medical facility at Q with the finest international team of micro-circulatory and orthopedic surgeons we could assemble, in the process of reattaching his legs as I speak. Their prognosis is good due to his excellent physical conditioning and Doctor Agave's antibiotic research. Fortunately, these dealings took place in a hospital. Doctor Agave was able to immediately clamp the arteries and utilize tourniquets to minimize bleeding; ice was available with which to pack the limbs.

"As they had been freed with surgical precision by the Starflyer's laser, virtually no soft tissue loss was experienced. Iawy and Chateauleire have been sedated and are on their way to physical recovery, but will need time and nurturing for mental scars to heal. Doctor Agave and his teams are working with Gautier now, and I have been assured he will make a full recovery. Miss Ernst and her friends are fine, and have volunteered to assist with recovery of our wounded."

Allowing a moment for that portion of the report to be absorbed, he added that unfortunately, Mr. Souser's condition precluded any attempt for recovery and trial, having fallen victim to his own perverse schemes. Initial inquiries demonstrated that Prime was justified in authorizing the firing of the Starflyer's laser, as the position and location of all Luna rescue team members was precisely determined. The on-duty guard in the hallway was accounted for, but there was no record in the hospital security computer to indicate Mr. Souser's presence in the rooms, he had no locator device, and he had closed the window's blinds to prevent discovery.

Mr. Souser was directly responsible for placing Anoki and himself in the path of the Starflyer's cutting device and its resultant consequences. Video taken from security cameras located in the rooms provided corroborating evidence, and were assumed to have been overlooked by Mr. Souser in the arrogance of his drunken state.

"Therefore, I conclude that no blame will attach itself to the actions of our team members in defending themselves against Mr. Souser, and I ask for the Council's concurrence. A full transcript of the affair, with statements, is being made available to the Secretary-General of the UN and his people, as well as the International Court of Justice."

"Well, good morning, sleepy head, or should I address you as 'Your Highness', given the crown you're wearing?" teased Eleanor to a just aroused Chat.

With heart wrenching sobs Chat began crying, words spilling out in a rush of painful self recrimination, "Eleanor! Oh Eleanor, je suis désolée. I am so sorry; I tried to warn Doctor Agave… that man, he beat me, oh, it hurt, it hurt!"

Overwhelmed at the pitiful wails of anguish and her own sense of helplessness, Eleanor's tears now ran freely. Gathering up both of Chat's hands, she held them tightly to her breast with one hand as she brushed away the wounded girl's tears with the other. She kissed her face and forehead, holding her close as the young girl cried away her fear and apprehension.

"I'm here, sweetheart, I'm here... never to leave you again. Feel the strength of my hands holding you. You're safe now, Chateauleire. That man can never again harm you or anyone else. I will stay with you until you're well enough to leave this bed, then we'll be with your father together, I promise."

Mercifully, Chat had passed out in pain that night and was spared the sight of events that transpired. When her crying had subsided, Eleanor told her how brave and heroic her father and Anoki had been in protecting her from Souser. While both had been injured, they would recover. They would all be reunited soon and could look forward to lots of time together, but it was very important that she rest and get well. Eleanor couldn't very well play tag in the Great Hall by herself, now could she?

Her thoughts turned to Gautier, worried about his injuries and recovery. She had been informed he would require significantly more care due to extensive damage done to his internal organs. He would be under heavy sedation for quite a while and there was little she could do for him at this point.

In like manner Jake spent time with Iawy, offering him the same assurances; telling him he wasn't sure if he could have held out as long as Iawy had, given Souser's determination. No harm had been done to Luna or its citizens as a result of his revelations. His task now was to recuperate and return to his friends.

Affairs on the New Hope took most of a week before Jake could get away. He missed Marian and her children badly... wanting to contact her daily but unable due to lack of modern practicality, in this case, a convenient phone. They were uppermost in his mind after landing and putting his ship away, having decided that for the sake of expediency he would use one of the New Hope's Starflyers. While he still had to wear the Starflyer's specific gear, the short trip wouldn't require body waste systems. He was pleased that Walwyn's language program had allowed him to re-visit his university studies. While night had fallen, he just had to see Marian and hoped he wouldn't be coming too late in the evening.

Arriving at her farm, he hurried up the stairway and lightly knocked on the door. It wasn't long before his inquiry was answered. Marian stood there in night dress for all of two seconds before rushing to grab him around the neck!

"Yacob, oh Yacob, where have you been? Days go by und nothing is heard... I, uh... ummm..."

Before she could get another word out, Jake bent over, cradled Marian with strong arms and pulled her to him. He cut off any further questions by covering her neglected lips with his, drinking deeply and with hunger the fundamental being of this woman, strength and passion returned by her in equal measure—such was the urgency of their need!

Marian Ella Fisher was born slim and grew into a woman lissome in form. Child birth created a brilliant transformation... building on that lithe foundation to fill out this young woman to erotic proportion. As she pressed her full, unfettered breasts into Jake's chest, followed by wrapping one leg around his and embracing him all the harder, Jake was almost overcome by feelings deep within his loins he had thought long dead!

Pulling slightly away but holding her closely, he breathed huskily into her ear, "The children?"

"Asleep, mein liebe, my love... oh, how I've missed you so." So saying she renewed her passionate kisses and a thoroughly receptive Jake drank them all in with equal ardor.

There was no protest as he bent to pick her up, carrying her up the steep stairway to her bedroom; gently placing her next to the bed as he closed the door. Reaching back, he embraced her just as reverently as before, both their passions rising to the breaking point. Lost in his kisses, she responded to the thrilling light pressure of his hands exploring the full range of her back, her neck, her hair. She needed his touch, his presence, the feel of his body responding to hers as her hands caressed both sides of his face. His lips explored her face, eyes, cheeks, and throat. She was helpless to resist and had no desire to ever do so... surrendering herself fully to his ardent masculinity.

Reversing their positions, he sat on the edge of the bed while drawing her to him. Undoing the top hooks of her white chemise, luscious breasts poured out—nipples standing arrogantly taut with both breasts held out by the sides of her garment. Farm labor had toned her frame, acting to pull proud, firm breasts up and apart without sag. Placing her hands at the back of his head, she drew him closer. The invitation was immediately accepted as his lips eagerly closed around one nipple, then the other, his tongue working in circles while he sucked greedily, his hands wonderfully caressing both breasts. He cupped them both while forefinger and thumb gently pressed and pulled both nipples straight out. He buried his head between her delicious mammaries, pressing her warm, plump breasts against his face while massaging and kissing them.

Her breasts were very sensitive and Marian reveled in sensations she had never experienced, maternal sensations from nursing her children replaced by lovingly erotic attention from a man she wanted more than anything else in her life.

Abram had never given such interest to her. Both of them young and inexperienced, they had to learn together. He had left her wanting and unfulfilled far too often; his zeal driven by hormones more than knowledge.

This man, this stranger, this Yacob that she has found new love with; he was driving her insane with desire!

Stepping back with panting breath, she pulled him off the bed, fumbling with clothing held with unfamiliar attachment. Calming her hands, Jake removed his garments and let them slide to the floor. He then took one step toward Marian, fully illuminated by pearlescent moonlight filtering through light cloth covering her bedroom windows.

Ahh, such a mann! her mind shouted, eagerly taking in the visage before her; passion alive with anticipation!

She reached out to the top of his shoulders, tracing a path down both to marvel at the strength and solidity of his arms... abdomen flat and well muscled! Slightly changing to reach around his back, she continued her odyssey, gasping in wonder at tightness of his buttocks. Reaching forward, she saw he was entire and perfect in his manly parts, enough to overshadow any comparison with another. Cupping them in one hand, she wrapped the other around his manhood while slowly exercising it back and forth, pleased at the length and girth of its solidity, unable to close her small hand fully around his member. That act elicited a blissful sigh from Jake, as he moved slightly forward to hold her while she continued her delightful voyage of discovery. With his lips now resting lightly against her ear, the feeling of his warm exhalations against her neck caused her to echo his sound of enjoyment.

"Mein liebe, let me bring to you pleasure," she whispered breathlessly.

"Not tonight," he returned softly. "This night is for you. Come, lie down here." With her head at the top of the bed resting comfortably on a pillow, Jake gently moved her legs apart and placed himself lying on his stomach directly in line with her, noting she was almost devoid of hair in that region. Where he believed her breasts to be magnificent, he found the bright pinkness of her pudenda to be exquisitely attractive... so fresh and appealing as to drive his craving even higher.

Placing his hands on the underside of both thighs, he raised her legs up and allowed them to flow over his shoulders, crossing at that point to rest easily on his back.

Softly running one finger to trace the outlines of this sensuous blossom, his administration brought forth a smooth, sugary viridity, oleaginous to his touch. Replacing enticing digit with prehensile tongue and lips, he continued, slowly moving up one side and down the other, stopping only at the pinnacle of each journey long enough to pay particular attention to that receptive apex. She was sparkling clean, her essence untainted in any way... compelling Jake to carry his explorations even further.

With her hands situated on both sides of Jake's head, Marian moaned delicately as he applied a mature touch to the most sensitive area she possessed, guided in that effort by careful attention to her yielding responses. After lingering at her vulva, he readjusted and focused attention to the inside walls of this portal. She was highly aroused and almost swept away with erotic sensation driving her to heights of desire never imagined, much less experienced in her lifetime!

Jake now repositioned himself on his left side perpendicular to her, as if the top of a letter 'T.' He again lifted her legs and let them bend naturally over his right side. Marian was aflame with passion and without waiting reached down to his manroot and positioned it facing her convivial threshold. Jake accepted this enticement by delicately entering the gates with slow deliberate pace, pausing to ensure passage was well lubricated before moving ever deeper. The position he chose allowed for direct stimulation at the top of the tunnel's mouth as he slowly withdrew, and bottom-most part of the warren when fully entered. Every reversal was accomplished at leisure; permitting the tip of his probe to massage her button, then reenter and smoothly plunge to the depths. Each easy thrust raised her buttocks slightly off the bed's surface, resulting in alignment and simultaneous stimulus of each of the two most erogenous areas of her core. Every cell in her body, every fiber of her being screamed out in ecstasy as each movement by Jake drove her to ever intensifying heights of frantic extravagance.

Her soul surrendered as Marian was overcome by the most incredible sensory culmination she had ever known, head arched backward, calling out, "Oh, Yacob… oh, Yacob," as spasms of sheer rapture exploded and coursed throughout her body, causing greatly stimulated musculature to grip the full measure of Jake and hold him deep inside her.

Four times Jake withdrew and entered at the height of supreme passion, and four times Marian called his name as she slipped into a state of sensual unconsciousness, overcome by sheer intensity of this first intimate encounter with her new found lover.

Moments passed as she lay there, till panting subsided to slow easy breaths. Jake was filled with wonder at this woman's response to his attentive machinations, loving everything there was to love about her; her personality, femininity, soft yet firm body, her beautiful children… all aspects of this association affording the highest respect while embodying him with that one invisible characteristic that makes one, in every sense of the word, a true *Man*, privileged to provide such pleasure to another. Gently repositioning himself so as not to wake her, he too welcomed sleep's encirclement while holding her in his arms.

Somewhere in the wee hours of the morning, Marian awoke to find herself nestled up to Jake on her left side, her back to him in somewhat of a spoon position. She had captured his member which now rested between her legs, soft and docile; both of his arms wrapped protectively around her. She reached to move and place one of his hands over her breast, noting dreamily how wonderful that feeling was as she held it there. She was content to be enfolded in the masculinity of this man, savoring the warmth of his body against hers as well as his touch.

It was the exquisite aroma of her hair that gently pulled Jake into a higher state of awareness, not quite fully awake. "Marian," he murmured, in that soft bed-talk manner reserved for intimacy; his cheek laying against her head.

She turned leisurely to face him, demurely snuggling against his chest as her fingers played lightly over his lips, eagerly recalling the wonderfully intense and oh-so special 'kisses' they gave; still swimming delightfully in the afterglow of their coupling... wishing she could hold such feelings forever.

"Mein liebe... oh, my love... mein Yacob. Sie did some strange things that Ich, daht I never knew existed."

"Oh," he whispered sleepily. "Guess I shouldn't do that anymore, umm?"

"Ahhh," was her sighing reply, "Never stop. I enjoyed it more than I ever have in my life. Such wonderful feelings!" After a moment's reflection she became concerned about his gratification and questioned, "Were you... did you..?"

He calmly moved one finger to still her questioning lips. "I wanted this first time to be my gift to you. I gathered more pleasure pleasing you than I would have otherwise, and didn't want you to be preoccupied with other worries."

She reflected on his comment for a few moments, thrilled by his unselfish declaration. "*Yacob*," she whispered, as if to say something important, but nerve abandoned her and she lapsed into silence instead.

His hand moved up to delicately caress her forehead; fingertips tenderly stroking the outline of her face. "What do you want to say, Marian? Please speak it to me... there can be no shyness between us now."

That comment, his soothing touch, his very closeness threw off apprehension while embolding her to continue. With courage restored, she stepped off the highest emotional cliff she had ever climbed by affirming, "Yacob, I have fallen hopelessly in love with you. Vaht I felt tonight has drawn me closer to you than I have ever felt toward any other person. You are *my mann*, Yacob, *my mann*. I pledge myself to you, here and now, under God forever and ever, if… if you will have me."

For only a moment, her strong avowal created hesitation. Uncertain how best to articulate his own feelings, her special emphasis swept away any doubt he may have had while driving his lover's harpoon of commitment deep into his heart… wanting this woman and her children to be with him till end of his days. If possible to do so, he drew her even closer.

A comforting and delicate, "Marian," echoed back in response. "I have only known love once in my life. When that was taken away, everything died within me. I've been alone for more years than any man should be allowed. I have no idea how this has happened to me… to us. I don't care to know. It's important for me to believe that you have rekindled true love inside my being.

"You'll think me silly, but I fell in love with you the second you kissed my cheek, that first evening I left your house. I'm as deeply in love with you as you are with me. I will never leave you, Marian. As you have spoken, so I also say to you, that you are now *my woman*, also under God, and I pledge myself to you and your children forever."

Tears of joy burst freely from the eyes of Marian Ella Fisher, as she held tightly to this man… a new future of promise with this Yacob, her Yacob.

Having parked his buggy behind Marian's barn on arrival the previous evening, Jake made a show of re-arriving this morning, so as not to cause tongue wagging within the community.

After a satisfactory day of interacting with Marian, her children, and a number of chores around the Miller homestead, Jake returned to Old Chupp's farm that evening to attend to his animals. He then initiated contact with Luna.

"Jake, what have you been doing? You're late for this Council meeting and you opted out of the last one," stated a very concerned Kelly, Luna's Administrator. "There are some uneasy members here that feel you are ignoring us."

Jake didn't feel that time was yet ripe to reveal recent changes in his personal life. He could see some of the council members as well as Kelly in the holocamera's sweep of the Council chamber.

"There have been a number of incidents occur here in the past few days."

"And these require my personal attention? What of Alahn, Donah, and Maralah? Or any of the other Council members for that matter."

Kelly's countenance became one of worry and distress. Her voice took on a more urgent tone. "Jake, these incidents don't appear to be random occurrences. Maralah and the older Council members are investigating, but what they've come up with appears to be intentional. Each one, had it been allowed to proceed before we found them, could have had serious consequences."

That statement caught Jake's attention and he focused sharply on Kelly's image.

"Oh? Explain, please."

She made clear that one of the common airlock control pads seemed to have been tampered with. When activated, the interior door did not completely close, although the pad indicated that it had. That user had been observant enough to note the anomaly and stop their exit process prior to opening the outer door. Engineering repaired the fault quickly but wasn't able to pin down exactly why it failed. Those pads were simplistic and virtually foolproof.

"There's never been any problem with them, in use by every country's space administration since we first left the planet Earth. Maralah has Engineering checking them throughout our cities."

"Kelly, perfection exists only in the eyes of children. One slight failure among many thousands of units shouldn't be cause of much concern, should it?"

"If it were only one, I would agree with you, but Prime detected incongruities at other locations and sent Engineers to investigate. They in turn found signs that others have been tampered with, although happily not to conclusion.

"There's more. Unexpected power reductions and temporary loss of power at odd times, again throughout all three cities, leads us to believe at this moment we have an unknown saboteur among us."

Jake reflected on Kelly's report with heightened interest. "We've been quite thorough with our interviewing process. I'm comfortable the people we've invited to Luna were held to the highest standards of behavior, given the depth and breadth of our background and personal analysis. However, it would be foolish to assume that within our thousands of inhabitants that one could not have been turned. Not everyone thinks as we do, and promises of wealth, regardless of how they're presented, can act to overcome the strongest of wills."

After a moment of silent contemplation, he announced, "Effective immediately, I want you to issue a full alert. All inhabitants wishing to use airlocks for any reason will take a suited-up shadow buddy with them. That person will observe from the interior and be prepared to halt egress manually, then sound an alarm if any malfunction is seen.

"Couch the verbiage in such a way... as to seem that we're simply being prudent in performing required annual testing of all of our equipment, and this new requirement is part of that. Ensure that all E-suits are double checked by shadow buddies before going outside. All transportation devices, Starflyers, TUGS, and Hoppers are to be inspected and Level One diagnostics run by Prime before each use... any anomaly to be reported immediately. Find Walwyn and Alahn and have them contact me on our highest encrypted band. I'll standby."

It was a wait of only moments to have both men appear before Jake for his restricted discussion. The only other individual, outside these three, who knew of Prime's exceptional teacher was Doctor Agave. A very extraordinary teacher indeed, with special needs recruited from a small settlement of expatriates in the Kampala, Central Region of Uganda, located at the southeast extreme of the Earth's African continent.

"You and Alahn speak to Reatah Kobusingye. I want Prime's sub-routines to be given broader bandwidth and boosted to a higher level of priority. Any irregularity, no matter how insignificant it may seem, is to be elevated to highest priority and investigated by our Engineering staff with full reports forwarded to all Council members. This matter is to be given the highest level of priority."

Both young men suddenly glanced at each other, turned to face Jake and with excitement in their voices responded, "I've got an idea!" simultaneously.

Jake smiled fondly at them both. "Well, 'two minds think as one.' I'll task Maralah and Anoki to translate that into their Navajo language and induct the both of you into their tribe," he replied with warm inflection. "Now, what do you propose?"

"Dad, why don't we set up mini-cams at each location, placed for differing points of view," offered Alahn.

"That's correct," replied Walwyn. "We can capture video, sound, time and date from anyone using any device, portal, or wherever we choose. We've developed some really small ones. It would be more correct to call them micro-cams. They're self-powered, adhesive, and once placed will be virtually invisible. The signal they transmit is ultra high frequency and coded."

"Brilliant! That's an excellent solution. Ensure they're placed so as to clearly capture the face of all users as well. Get right on this, both of you. Work with Prime to set up a grid as well as a map of all locations where you've installed them, and that means outside as well as in-house. Include the external infrastructure also. Keep all of this close-hold; I don't want anyone else to know anything about what we're doing, including the Council members. Unless you believe my presence is needed there, I expect you two to give this your highest priority. Keep me in the loop on any developments while I continue my work here." As troubling as Kelly's report had been, Jake felt that Walwyn and Alahn were extremely competent and could handle this matter themselves as he ended the holographic transmission.

Unfortunately, other plans had previously been put into place by one who labored cunningly to overcome the technological gulf that currently existed between Earth and Luna. One who was successful in hiring another... an incredibly skilled 'another,' that possessed the necessary ability to turn one of Luna's own against her.

There are individuals born into this life; emotionless, hard, cold and unfeeling. Schooled in the most heinous fashion to hold nothing dear, such bipedal scorpions operate on the outskirts of humanity's existence; to view death as nothing more than a stepping stone to whatever ambition fuels those personalities to perform sadistic deeds of barbaric nature. Homosapic camelions living always in shadow; hints of their presence only guessed at by virtue of carnage left behind in the form of tortured, mangled and rotting corpses. If any hierarchy existed to rank humanistic parasites, this particular assassin would count himself at the top one percent of that calling.

An international purveyor of his gifts, he had found employment through a number of varying worldwide business and government contacts; speaking seven languages with fluency. He understood well that hatred came in many colors, forms, and ideologies; with cold revenge providing a ready market for his specific talents if one knew how to find him. It would be more proper to say *when he allowed himself to be found...* such was the arrogant level of deadly esteem he held himself up to.

Meticulous with preparation, weeks and sometimes months were spent to absorb significant information concerning each assignment, then executing that contract in precise application of detailed instruction as how to carry it through. Unscrupulous employers sometimes found it useful to utilize such talent; to send quite unique messages to those they wished to control and had the substantial wherewithal to pay handsomely for the expected results.

It also paid to be well-read. He stayed on top of local and international news events, focusing on those of special interest potentially worthy of his efforts. The moon issue had caught his attention, especially that aspect of it dealing with a certain Special Agent of a United States security department. This Agent's inept handling of an encounter at a United Nations helicopter landing pad was noteworthy. A computerized search program, initiated to capture any further aspect of that incident, coughed up a small press release sometime later. Its announcement of the untimely death of that same Agent due to 'an industrial accident,' intrigued him further. It was simplicity itself to combine those events and conclude another government may have use of his unusual skill set... a determined proficiency to find permanent solutions to certain types of problems. As this one had the potential to affect two planets, he found himself... *quite interested indeed.*

Given the level of his remarkable abilities, it required surprisingly little effort to entice contact by a new, unnamed, but apparently quite eager benefactor; one who promised exceptionally high reward to be rid of certain impediments. A complete record of all that had transpired, including an exorbitant retainer over-generous by even his morbidly elevated standards, was carefully forwarded through a series of supposedly untraceable intermediaries and oblique actions until resting in the assassin's hands.

Included in the materials was a complete list of all missing persons thought to be associated with the moon's new population. While initial reports assumed that entire families had left as well, the report included several names of family members who had declined to leave. Those names included addresses.

Of particular note was verbiage obtained during an agony-induced interrogation of one of the moon prisoners in a military hospital; something concerning agriculture and a name... *Lancaster!*

A company or person? An actor's name? An older military bomber? A location, perhaps?

Amos Wagler was a talkative old Amish farmer, telling everyone at the

Sunday gathering all that he had seen in the previous two weeks taking place at Old Chupp's place, including the Fisher farm. He was the center of attention today.

"Ja, daht Yacob is seen to hier haus most every day, working, fixing to dis and daht. To market he goes, taking Frau Fisher und ihre kinder mit his elektrisch wagen. It comes to me he saved hier girls, falling through ice at hier bauernhof, hier farm. Back to Chupp's haus he goes each evening."

This disclosure led to questioning about Herr Yacob's intentions. He seemed plain enough, though he wore no beard, but nothing more was known about that. He was from Indiana kommen, and other Amish communities did have some differences. Chupp's farm was small and it was common knowledge that not much effort was needed there. The Amish, as a people, were as curious as any other group. But that curiosity stayed within acceptable bounds, limiting itself to what is seen and heard. None would even consider the idea of taking a fact-gathering stroll through another's property without introductions and permission.

"Careful to keep die barn doors closed, he is, perhaps for his few animals. But I would let them out more often if left to me. Und sometimes, late at night, Ich hears wind blowing strangely, but nutting is seen." At that, the conversation turned to events closer to hand, leaving the Fisher-Yacob association to Wagler's next report in the near future.

Bi-weekly meetings are attended by many from the local community, and there was quite a gathering at this one with numerous men arranged around the porch's boundary. No one took particular notice of another presence situated at that perimeter's edge, listening attentively, taking in everything offered by Wagler. Anyone glancing in that direction would only see one more plain, bearded, Amish farmer who quietly walked toward his buggy as the meeting concluded.

The assassin counted fluent German among his verbal accomplishments, but prudently spent several weeks in and around Lancaster, Pennsylvania, becoming attuned to local inflection and mannerisms so as not to stand out. He was surprised at how open his target's activities seemed to be, as if taking a page from Poe's 'Purloined Letter' to hide in plain sight.

So be it. All the simpler to accomplish this mission.

He waited for the next moonless night to access Chupp's barn. Beyond the expected animals housed there; an expandable pad and rail system, as well as what appeared to be a high tech antenna and power system of sorts, added considerably to his understanding of the individual taking residence in the farm house itself. It was of no consequence to barricade himself behind hay piled up in the barn's loft and he was awakened hours later, but not surprised, to witness landing of one of the moon vehicles and its repositioning within the barn. His placement did not provide an angle sufficient to see the person who left the craft. He made mental note to correct that oversight.

Discreetly following an individual leaving the farm house the following morning, his reconnoiter revealed the location of a local widow and her children spoken of during an earlier community meeting. He captured crisp, high resolution digital photographs of them all for later identification. His employer was paying him for irrefutable proof, not guesswork.

Taking residence in his hay loft lair that night, he watched closely as the target entered the barn wearing a type of protective suit, but without helmet or gloves. Stepping up to his craft, something was uttered and a hidden panel opened to accept the pilot's hand. A dim light illuminated his face. At that, a previously unseen portal slid silently open to admit him, then closed just as noiselessly. After the ship left, the assassin reviewed his work, pleased at the quality of pictures he had obtained.

Take off the head and the snake dies. Straight forward enough and I believe I have exactly that, he thought to himself, after comparing his photos with those provided by his benefactor. There was no mistaking who his target was... Colonel Jake Starnes himself. Frau Fisher and her three brats were icing on the plot's cake.

An unexpected but appreciated bonus. I could retire forever on what's being paid for what I have in hand right now. Undeniably; paid very well.

But patience... yessss... patience. Work out the angles properly, and I should expect three or four more of those 'verys' nicely placed in front of that 'paid well.' I could be as Pharaoh ruling Egypt, anywhere on this planet I could dream of.

The following evening, the assassin waited with calm serenity for some hours after the target secured his ship and left the barn. The thought occurred to him that ability to capture the space craft could be a crown jewel in this assignment. Having photographed the machine from all angles, he approached the side from which he had observed the target make an exit.

Running his hand over the ship's surface, he found nothing there. No seam, no line, no protrusion or indent to signify existence of the portal he had seen opening and closing. *Yet, it was right here*, he thought. *I'm certain of it.* Relocating his hand to explore the area where he saw the smaller panel open for the target's hand, his results were the same. *Incredible technology,* came to his mind with some admiration.

Making his way to a hidden vehicle, the assassin returned to a small rented room located in an adjacent county. He completed his first update report and forwarded it as instructed to his employer. One part of his plan faced opposition. His suggestion to extort and squeeze the target by kidnapping the woman and her children was immediately overruled by his benefactor... they were all to be eliminated, period, and disposed of forever. He decided to withhold information about the spaceship for the time being, certain that his contact would be happy to forward an additional bonus for that juicy tidbit and one other offered by the assassin; his turning of an unnamed family member whose moon citizen son enjoyed somewhat of a well-placed position and believed to be, even now, of some assistance.

Simply amazing just how well and quickly one could enlist another to his cause, if that new associate was given a short view of his parent with a razor held to her throat. He had followed one of the Earthly leads provided by his benefactor, one that resulted in an older Asian woman easy to intimidate and break... who had the foolishly bad habit of too often staying in touch with her other-worldly son. She accomplished that interaction via a common, unsecured, laptop computer containing a social media program in use by most of Earth's population.

Not very wise. No, quite stupid, in fact, and more than likely in violation of instruction to do otherwise. The assassin took a dozen or so short videos using that same laptop's camera and memory; posing the old woman with various deadly instruments touching her body. In a couple, he nicked her slightly to show blood, ensuring he captured her vocal response from such tender application. He had applied appropriate pain during each pose to guarantee an expected horrified expression was easily seen on her face. These were for later use in allowing his new 'accomplice' to believe she was still unharmed and alive. He was quite thorough in ensuring no one would ever find the unidentifiable small pieces of what remained of her earthly existence.

Jake's nightly returns to Old Chupp's farm for Council meetings were starting to draw attention from Marian. They had both discussed the idea of a more open association, marriage within her community, and a combining of the farms. He was deeply troubled that he had yet to find an acceptable time or reason to bring her into his 'other life,' and used the need to care for his farm animals and grounds to justify the evening trips. The first hour or so of his nightly conferences was spent on general Luna issues, culminating with an update on unusual activities. Kelly and Donah were both in the other cities going over damage reports.

He shuffled over, yet again, an ever-growing, mundane and tedious stack of postings from Luna's Recycling and Sanitation Engineering staff as he waited for that final report.

"For reasons unknown, our incidents seemed to have taken a break, but we're no closer to discovering who's involved."

"Thank you, Maralah. I've initiated a number of actions that hopefully will assist in that area," responded Jake. "I'll keep you posted on results and ask that you and all Council members stay on top of this."

"We'll do that. Oh, before you sign off, Walwyn wants to speak to you." The holographic transmission now transferred to Operations. Walwyn stepped into view with somewhat of a worried expression.

"Jake, something's come up, and I thought it best that you speak directly to the analyst involved."

Jake was almost certain he knew who Walwyn was referencing. Thin, squeaky voiced, gawky, awkward, knobby kneed; any and all of these would correctly describe the love of Walwyn's life, Miss Meridyth Pitre-waitte... better know by her Operations herky-jerk moniker as "P-Way." This young woman was born with a so-called mathematical silver spoon in her mouth; an astonishing grasp of higher analytical abstraction. She was assigned to monitor activities of the Central Intelligence Agency at Langley, a community in McLean, Virginia, and had developed undetectable, untraceable and self erasing programs granting her unlimited access to every computer the CIA had in existence... anywhere. She acted to consolidate senior level reports found at the highest levels of that organization world-wide, and passed on such intelligence for review by Luna Council recipients.

What was good for the CIA was also good for Luna.

That kind of focused mental intensity required an outlet, and P-Way's one and only preferred method was an overwhelming obsession in a fantasy world of her own creation. Her relief valve, though different, brought no concern to Jake. His understanding and support of such activities was key to winning devotion from those that Earth populations, regardless of country, arrogantly labeled as social misfits.

Would that he had another hundred just like her.

He expected this shy and introverted young woman to appear on his holographic pad enveloped head to toe in extremely high definition, introvisionary three dimensional helmet, sensory apparatus, extensive wiring, and all such other trappings of Ops gear. Unprepared for the vision now standing before him, he was somewhat startled to observe a bright, lavishly colored, tall avatar dressed in riotously imperial regalia; gold scepter in hand and topped with a magnificently bejeweled crown... haughty affectation staring straight at him!

Working quickly to erase a wide smile beginning to conquer his face, he reminded himself he could find no fault in the kind of intelligence that could, and had, defeated the strongest of Earth's algorithmic encryptions. Inserting a representation of this nature into Luna's programming would, quite simply, be even less than child's play for an adolescent of such intellectual achievement.

He was aware that from her point of view, she was floating in a noncorporeal form; overlooking the fantasy world she had developed to encompass Luna, Earth, and the CIA.

"Prithee, Noble Jaathus. We seek audience with the Lord Most High," emanated from the dignified representation, verbal tones reverberating slightly as if bounced between walls of some long, under-populated royal hall.

Jake—Jaathus? I guess that fits... somehow. Noting she had also articulated her voice electronically to present a mature, regal persona; he searched his mind and concluded she had selected a beauty of mythical stature... the Roman Goddess of Wisdom. He approved her choice; it fit her perfectly, from a certain point of view. Not many knew of Jake's scholarly pursuits as a young man, one of which was President of his university's Concert Choir and Chamber Singers. While the Choir addressed compositions of musical masters from past eras, the smaller group performed lighter madrigal renderings in full period costume, complete with proper period anachronistic verbiage.

Drawing on those memories, he readjusted his posture while taking on a stately demeanor and responded in kind, "Well met and happily granted, Galactic Queen Minerva. Welcome. How goes your Realm?"

The sudden uplifting of the avatar's countenance depicted first surprise, then joy at his recognition of her digital presentation. Composing herself, she continued with renewed enthusiasm, "My people are well and labor contently, Ruler of the Known Universe. A minion protonic has approached Us. As it has found favor in Our eyes through past worthy effort, We bade it speak... its message may interest you, High Lord, if you will hear it."

Jake understood that P-Way's people existed in her computer programming world, while 'minion', one of her better search programs, had probably picked up something of value.

As if a king seated on lofty throne, Jake majestically leaned forward in sharp focus, "I attend most carefully, Precious Sovereign. Pray, what is thy message?" was followed with closed right hand raised to front his mouth in attentive concentration.

"Word from the outlands has come to Our ear, Great One, concerning an executioner most foul... confined not to one warring kingdom as is the wont of most such, but in practice of his heinous art throughout the realm immense." With that statement she made a wide sweeping motion with her gold scepter, as if to indicate this practitioner was far beyond her reach.

With genuine concern written on her face, she continued, "Mayhap his fetid adventures will find him close to thy Keep.

"We also take note of a most curious event. The admirable sky chariot of our Lord Jaathus, ever vigilant, has cried out in alarum, having been touched by strange hands but rejected forthwith. Filthy appendages of some common peasant, no doubt; come skulking about to seek plunder. Nonetheless, We urge thee to alert thy legions vast to be wary, and trust these occurrences do not portend greater peril to thy Exalted Self."

Interpreting her communication, Jake understood that a very dangerous person may be in his locality, and something or someone had set off the proximity alarm on his Starflyer. He would endeavor to determine if both events were related; dismissing the idea that one of his animals had blundered into the craft.

"Thy message is timely and efficient, Grand Queen Minerva." Glancing at the recent paper stack on his desk, an idea formed quickly as he continued, "While such duty never seeks benefit, it is incumbent upon a Lord, from time to time, to reward those in his service for exceptional undertaking. As Exalted Queen Minerva also stands high in my favor, know this. I expand your rule by granting dominion over the lands of Recycling and Sanitation. Rule wisely, and they will ensure health and happiness to you and your people."

Surprise enveloped the avatar's face at this unexpected boon. While those automated systems didn't require much hands-on management, Jake felt that Meridyth Pitrewaitte could accept a little more responsibility. He knew that by doing so, her stature within Luna's Ops world would tack on another point or two in the eyes of her peers. He felt this would go a long way to boost both her confidence and self esteem, regardless of the risk of starting a new royal fantasy trend.

With a stately bow of her head and slight curtsy, the avatar responded, "My Liege! Thou arte wise and generous beyond reckoning. On behalf of Our people, We thank thee!"

"Rather, Our thanks to thee, Gracious Lady Minerva. Now prithee, wouldst thou beckon thy Knight-errant, Sir Walwyn, that he may come into Our presence?"

"Immediately, Lord." At that, communication was switched back to Walwyn, who had monitored the full session with P-Way.

"Sorry, Jake. I've tried to talk her out of that, but…"

"No, Walwyn. Leave it as is. To tell the truth, I rather enjoyed it. A little imagination is useful and brightens up the place, don't you think?"

Walwyn grinned widely with relief. "You're right, of course. I just didn't know how you would accept her little play."

"Walwyn, listen carefully." Jake went on at some length to discuss upcoming events and a number of unique but timely plans.

"Mutter, Vahter Yacob! Vahter Yacob, Mutter!" brought Jake and Marian up from a sound sleep as three bundles of exuberant energy leaped onto the bed screaming their names with laughing glee. As Marian intercepted one wiggling boy, Jake found himself suddenly encircled by the twins… he hugged and kissed both, noting as he did the sun had just began to peek over the horizon.

"Daddy Jacob!" he inquired, bemused and only half awake. "When did that start?" Turning his head toward her, he lightly kissed Marian and Johann on their foreheads. "Und guten morgen auch ihnen," he said softy, wishing them all a good morning.

"It came to them naturally. They see us for how we are. Love has embraced them as it has you and I. Yacob, none of them truly knew their father; Abram left us too soon. They asked me last night as I put them to bed, before you came to kiss them goodnight. I told them to try it this morning to see if it would fit as wonderfully as your hugs. That is why they are so excited. Do you object?"

"Not at all. I love them as deeply as I love you." On that note, he pulled both girls up with a close hug which was just as eagerly returned. Not to be outdone, Johann jumped into the fray with Jake now laboring to entertain the bunch. Relaxing back into his pillow, he glanced over at Marian and winked one eye. Looking back at the children, he whispered,

"Aber ich habe ein problem, einen, die mich eine zeit lang jetzt geärgert haben [But I have a problem, one which has vexed me for some time now] he said, looking into the children's faces.

"Ein problem? Können wir helfen, vather Yacob?" [A problem, can we help, daddy Yacob?] asked Kathryn in her delightfully childish voice.

"Well, that is the worry, Kathy darling. I can't tell which one of you three I love the most! Is it you, Kristina, or Johann?" For just a second, the children looked at each other. Faces suddenly exploding with smiles of expectation, they all shouted, "Mich, ich sind das einer! Nein, ist es mich! Er liebt mich mehr!" [Me, I am the one! No, it's me! He loves me more!] were all thrown at Jake as each child vied for his affection, renewing their efforts to all grab him with loving hugs at the same time. With Marian laughing at the calamity, they both untangled the happily squirming offspring. Gently placing all three between Marian and himself, he pulled the bed's cover up to their chins, snug in the warm embrace of both adults with their arms crossed over the children. It was only a matter of minutes before they nodded off.

Jake reached over and gently caressed Marian's arm, looking directly into her adoring eyes. Taking her hand, he kissed the open palm, then closed it to capture and hold that memory. He uttered softly, "Marian, I have invited a cousin to visit. His name is Kenneth... Ken for short. He's pretty bright about figuring out puzzling events. With your permission, I would like to look into the circumstances of Abram's passing."

"If doing such would please you, it is acceptable to me, mein liebe. If you can add anything to the efforts of our police, it may go well with my cousin Eli if something new may be added."

Prime had obtained a full police record of the events of Abram's death after easily compromising their computer systems; including printouts and photos. They believed that Eli and Abram had struggled and during that action Abram was choked to death for his money, not yet recovered. Circumstantial evidence at the crime scene was enough for them, and no further investigation was initiated.

After daily chores, Jake left to pick up his cousin from town. In actuality, he returned to Old Chupp's place to get KhenemetAhmose, the robotic representation of Prime, which had arrived the previous evening.

Taking a moment to check his internal security systems, he noted no evidence of any prowler detected during that time period. Upgrades to Ken were sufficient to prevent all but the closest attention to see that he wasn't mammalian, while being dressed in correct Amish clothing for his age. Jake would ensure that Prime's physical representation kept a discreet distance from others.

Marian had kept Abram's clothing, and Jake now examined it closely, finding nothing remarkable other than the obvious fact she had cleaned and brushed both the coat and shirt. Ken however, closely focusing with adjustable lenses, studied the material at much higher magnification.

"Jake, thread fibers on this item have been crushed; I am able to detect a pattern here."

"Oh, and what do you make of that pattern, Ken?"

"Not possible to say at this time, but it appears to be circular, with an open end, approximately 139.7 millimeters in width, and 154.9 millimeters in length. The closed end shows deeper crushing than where it opens up. It's high up on the clothing items. I note a similar pattern on both pieces, although not so prevalent on the shirt as it is on the coat. It can be seen that the pattern has been imprinted on the left side of each as viewed from the back, and I've scanned it with ultraviolet as well as infrared. That data has now been forwarded to Prime Main for comparison and analysis. I will advise when study is complete."

Picking up Abram's boots, Jake noted the right one was still tied, yet the left appeared to be only partially so. The police report simply stated that Emergency Medical Service personnel had removed his shoes, probably by simply pulling them off.

One bit of good fortune was the fact that Marian hadn't yet sold Abram's horse. The children loved it too much and it was able to pull her buggy still. The Amish had taken to purchasing actual race horses, rather than commonly available stock. These animals had been raised well, exercised, and trained, and were also in the best of health. While past their race earnings prime, they still had years of good service left in them. They may have cost a bit more, but were expected to far outperform any other comparable animal... all in all, a really good investment. Abram bought this particular horse for a bargain price as the owner felt it had gone lame and could no longer race.

They walked to the barn and Jake led the horse out of its stall for examination. He had Ken digitally record all of their proceedings to keep excellent record of their investigation and findings. Ken, of course, was silently constructing a wire frame model in his central computer's memory, then populating that model with a complete three dimensional scan of the animal. This would complement full color photographs for later analysis of all aspects of size, weight, metabolism, body temperature, respiration, and other factors. Jake opened the horse's mouth so that Ken could record its oral condition, then checked its eyes and ears. Slowly walking around while running his hand over the horse's skin, he was alert for any imperfection or anomaly that may have an impact on the results. Their exam didn't appear promising as the animal, for all practical purposes, seemed to be in excellent health.

Coming around the left rear with Ken closely following, the restless horse danced its hind legs, jostling Jake. As he was facing the front of the animal, he unconsciously reached out with his right hand to steady himself, failing to note that as he did so his hand pushed on the muscle mass running down the rear of that limb. Without warning, that leg lashed out at an angle, missing Jake while hitting Ken's chest with sufficient energy to knock him tumbling to the floor of the barn!

After recovering from his surprise at that result, Jake assisted Ken in returning to an upright and standing position. "Are your systems functioning properly?"

"Yes, Jake. Impact from the equine's appendage was insufficient to penetrate my exoskeleton. All systems are functioning within acceptable parameters."

"What do you suppose could have caused such a reaction? I had not expected light pressure of my hand would have created that sort of result!

After a silent moment as Ken queried Prime, he advised, "Equine musculature is composed of a number of muscle and hamstring groups. I could list them all if you wish."

"No, Ken. Limit your report to just those facts which seem relevant to what just occurred."

"Yes, Jake. I believe the area where you placed your hand would demonstrate that the semitendinosus muscle, a hamstring grouping, causes an inward rotation of the leg. A common ailment associated with that rotation encompasses the digital extensor muscle which terminates as a major tendon. Trauma there is often misinterpreted as lame in that area, but it is not always so. If simply damaged or not functioning properly, the animal may compensate by flicking of the lower limb. I have reason to believe that is what caused the reaction we have observed... due to stimulus of your hand pressure."

"Thank you. If I interpret your report correctly, this horse may have suffered an injury to its left hind quarter sometime in the past... enough to end its days of racing, but still leaving it adequate for the job it performs on this farm; simply pulling a buggy."

"Your conclusion agrees with mine, Jake."

"This is a very interesting development, Ken. Please ensure you have documented every aspect of this event. Encrypt it under file name 'Abram Fisher,' please." An idea began to form itself in Jake's mind, added to his examination of Abram's clothing. It was taking a direction far away from the deduction that had been reached by the local authorities. He pushed it aside for further study and continued his search.

Marian had informed Jake that she and Abram owned two buggies; an enclosed one for market and an open wagon type for large loads... grain, feed, and such.

Jake and Ken pulled the wagon into an open area of the barn, noting how heavy it was. Marian had never removed all of the grain and feed bags obtained on the day that Abram died. She simply cut one open for access as it was needed, leaving the heavy bag on the wagon until empty. Selling most of the farm's animals reduced any need to unload, so there were still a number of such bags in place. Jake and Ken pulled all of these, stacking them for storage as they went. Lifting one corner of the last row of feed bags, he spotted a lump at the extreme back of the wagon's floor, reached down, and pulled up a large man's leather pocketbook with attached throng, which had apparently been hidden under the heavy bags of grain just removed. It was bulging with money!

After replacing the wagon, the two of them returned to Old Chupp's farm. The wallet was inventoried and determined to contain just over eight thousand dollars! Jake then set out all of the police photos for study.

Of note was discoloration around Abram's throat… somewhat horizontal at a slight angle. "Ken, how do you account for the marks on Abram's throat?"

"They can represent results of a laryngeal fracture. This would follow some type of direct trauma to his neck region that would have led to life-threatening airway obstruction."

"Look here at Eli Yoder's hands in this photograph. Now look at mine. If I place my hands in this manner." Jake mimicked crossing of his thumbs, as if his two hands were around a circular object. "Would you believe the width of my two thumbs could account for the width of that mark on Abram's throat?"

"I note your thumbs have crossed each other at an angle of approximately forty-five degrees each. The mark on Abram's throat is not angled to that extent or in that manner."

"Would you conclude that something other than Eli's hands may have made those marks?"

"Yes, Jake. Simple observation does in fact support your statement."

"What are the dimensions of the wheels on Abram's wagon?"

"My record banks contain descriptions of common steam-bent hickory used by Amish wheelwrights to manufacture heavy-load capable wooden wagon wheels, twenty-eight inches in diameter, with a one and one half inch steel rim."

"What is the width of the marks seen on Abram's throat?"

"Extrapolating dimension of the objects seen in the photograph based on known parameters of the camera and film used, and knowing exact nomenclature of the wagon, plus the victim's height and weight from Emergency Medical Service examination at time of death, I can state with some certainty they are approximately one and one half inches in width," replied Ken.

"And these smudges seen on either side of his neck, could those have been made by someone attempting to support his neck so he could breathe, given that his larynx was crushed?"

"Yes, it is possible they may have occurred in that manner."

"Now, Ken. Note Eli's hands. Are they clean?"

"No, Jake. Quite blackened... perhaps from physical labor of loading the wagon with heavy feed bags, and I note that Abram's hands appear to be similarly coated."

"Was Abram's body found at the front of the wagon?"

"No, the wagon had been moved forward, and one police photo demonstrates his body lying a short distance behind the left rear wheel of the wagon."

"Is the body parallel to the wagon?"

"No, it is perpendicular, lying at a ninety degree angle to the wagon's direction."

"Which direction is the head pointed?"

"Toward the wagon."

"Ken, please save and encrypt all record of our investigation and conversations. I want a complete printout of the entire affair as quickly as you can produce it, please.

"**Marian**, this is Lancaster County Police Detective Edward Brewster. Mr. Brewster was the lead investigator in the death of your husband, Abram Fisher."

After introductions in Marian's kitchen, Jake advised both Detective Brewster and Marian that he had discussed the details of Abram's death with a private organization that employed his cousin Ken, an experienced analyst of such issues who lived and worked in another state. That organization agreed to perform another very thorough review at no cost. "Given the heavy case loads of most police precincts, I felt my cousin and his associates could be of assistance if more time was taken to go over facts and some rather interesting *new information.*" Jake purposely emphasized that last for Detective Brewster's benefit while handing him a folder.

"You'll find a complete report of their findings, with supporting documentation, digital video as well as photos, and a rather startling new conclusion." Handing the Detective Abram's leather pocketbook, he added, "Here's the missing money. This wallet was found in the back of Abram's heavy feed wagon, hidden under the bottommost row of bags. It's apparent he placed it there due to its contents. It contains just over eight thousand dollars."

Marian's hands flew to cover her mouth. She turned to face Jake as her suddenly expanded eyes glistened with tears at this unexpected but happy revelation.

"Moreover, there's a more focused theory as to what actually occurred the day of his death, with detail now available that wasn't at the time of your investigation. Abram bought a race horse at auction, thought to be lame. It had suffered an injury to its left hind quarter sufficient to mimic that disorder on occasion, but in fact was not so obviously debilitating.

"Normal light pulling duty around the farm would not have demonstrated the horse's affliction. However, additional weight of the heavily loaded wagon aggravated its injury, causing it to tire more quickly than expected. Ken's investigation suggests that Abram stepped down from the left side of the wagon to allow the horse to rest, which would have left Eli still seated to the right with the reins in his hands. Abram would now be standing close to the horse's left hind leg, and noted that his left shoe was untied. Bending down to secure it, he was off-balance and placed his right hand against the horse's left hind quarter to steady himself. With that contact, its injury caused two reflex events to occur. First, its left rear leg turned inward slightly, and second, it flicked that leg outward with sufficient force to strike Abram in his left upper chest, knocking him backward and to the ground.

"We know this from crushed thread fibers on his clothing. The pictorial results, including analysis in ultraviolet, infrared, and x-ray, are included in your folder. The outline of those crushed fibers almost exactly matches the size and shape of the left rear horseshoe. The angle of impact matches the angle of the horse's turned leg as described.

"Having seen Abram knocked back, Eli would have now jumped down from the wagon, dropping the reins, in order to run around the wagon's right rear and then forward to assist him. He had to, as he would not have been able to see where Abram was on the ground due to height of the loaded bags in the wagon. However, now relieved of Eli's weight and release of the reins as he leaped, the horse lurched forward. As stated, the angle of impact of the horse's leg knocked Abram backwards beyond the front left wheel. He hit the ground on his back just as the rear wheel on that side rolled over his throat. That act alone would have caused serious injury, but was rendered extremely critical due to additional weight of the feed and grain bags loaded in the wagon. You'll find the marks on his throat closely match the width of the steel rim on the back on the wagon.

"Eli's inability to communicate would not have been a factor... he could only comprehend that Abram couldn't breathe, and placed his hand under his neck in a vain attempt to lift and assist him. That accounts for the smudged fingerprints you obtained, and incorrect conclusion that Eli's hands were on Abram's throat. You'll note that Abram's hands were just as dirty as Eli's... due to both of them loading the wagon, so other smudging could have come from either one. That would explain markings on Eli's clothing; not as a result of any type of violence, but Abram's arms thrashing about as he struggled to breathe.

"If your department agrees with this new assessment, I ask that Eli Yoder be released from confinement in the State's mental hospital and be returned to custody of his cousin, Marian Fisher. I also ask that you return her husband's money to her at this time, if you're satisfied it's her property. She's in desperate need and will sign a receipt after you count and verify it."

Detective Brewster thanked Jake for the assistance of his cousin, promising to immediately act to have the sentencing Judge overturn Eli's conviction. He accepted Marian's receipt for the wallet and its contents.

As Marian closed the door with his leaving, she turned to Jake, throwing herself into his arms, crying hysterically. He simply held her shaking body close; caressing her head while allowing her to vent years of bottled emotion through closure of the hardest event she had ever experienced in her lifetime. Her morose mood continued for the balance of that day and into the night. Knowing that time would be the only true healer of such deep wounds, he made no claim upon her. Gently awakened at some unknown hour of night's encirclement by touch of her breasts into his back, her arm slowly traveled over and across his chest; her hand reaching to tenderly nudge his face toward hers.

With quiet undertone she sighed, "Mein liebe, I have no words to thank you for my Abram." That said, she moved her leg and thigh up over his, pressing herself against her lover, to hold him in her manner of praising his efforts.

Jake cuddled even closer, "You have no need to, Marian. I understand your love of your husband, and what his death must have done to you. I'm happy to have been of some small help in sorting out the true details that occurred."

"Small help?" she answered, astonished. "My love, I would never have believed daht anyone could have done vaht you did. I can't sleep for going over and over in my mind vaht actually happened to Abram, and Eli... Eli will come back to us, where he belongs."

"I don't believe you'll have any financial worries for quite a while. You can buy new animals; hire workers. Your farm will become one of the more prosperous in this area."

"The only riches I want is you, Yacob. You are my liebe, my love now," she murmured, snuggling close to be with her man as sleep finally released her troubled mind.

It's impossible. *I can't do what he wants.* Robert Kyoung-Joo Kim stood alone in his room, hands shaking. Beads of perspiration oozing from stress induced pores ran unconfined down both sides of his head; frightened tears flowing down his face… wringing hands in helpless panic. His stomach was tied in knots; cold apprehension shaking him to his core. *My mother! God help me. God help us both!*

A Maxima Cum Laude graduate of Duke University in Durham, North Carolina, his Engineering degree had a strong focus in photovoltaic development and application. Believing he would apply his career toward improving the energy needs of developing countries, he was surprised by a caller offering opportunity at a place that truly defined the term 'developing.' Robert was directly responsible for the solar arrays that constituted the primary energy source for all of Luna. His father died while he was still very young, and his mother invested a lifetime of hard work to ensure he would succeed. She was extremely proud of his academic achievements, and happy for his decision to leave Earth, but strong Asian family ties dictated that she remain behind.

How did he find her? How can this be happening to us? I have no idea what to do now; who to turn to. He knows us here, knows where I am, what I'm doing. He'll kill anyone I talk to. Mom must have told him… what choice did she have? Death holds her.

It wasn't so difficult at first. Pull a little something here, shake another thing there. *'Just keep them off balance for awhile, and I'll let your mother live.'* That's what he had demanded, standing there with a blade at her throat. You never saw his face… only his hands and upper arms. The voice was muffled, but the same couldn't be said for his mother. Her frightened screams terrified him. He had never felt so helpless in his life… watching this assassin torture her each time contact was made. *At least she's still alive; there's got to be an answer somewhere for this!*

They had been told not to use commonly available Earth communication programs during his orientation at Q. They were too easily compromised and traceable. But his mother was not very computer literate. She didn't understand the security requirements, and the laptop computer system was much simpler for her. He spent a considerable amount of time in Operations, the central hub for control of his energy systems. It had been nothing more than simple chance that he had caught a whiff of conversation from Walwyn to an unknown person. The word 'mini-cam' stood out like a shout in his mind.

They're on to me, they have to be. Now they're installing cameras everywhere! Almost impossible to see, unless you were an Engineer, unless you worked in Operations, unless you knew exactly where and what to look for. Spotting the first one confirmed his fears. He had immediately ceased all covert activity; his efforts silenced lest he be found out.

This latest demand was unthinkable. '*Spill some blood,*' was the order, '*or she dies. I'll make certain it's done slowly over a period of days, recording all of it.*' He had no choice but to obey, and had open access to any number of items that could be used for deadly work. He had decided a section of structural reinforcement from one of the solar arrays, crudely resembling a baseball bat, should be adequate… *for whatever I'm going to do with it*, he thought. *Our entire society is completely open. Where, when, how, could you do anything without being seen? People walking around was one thing, but cameras all over the place now?*

Leaving easily discoverable, almost harmless little traps was one thing, but harming another human being? *How will I do that? How can I do that? Oh God… Oh God, what can I do? Someone help me, please.*

Even under such seemingly impossible stress levels, his highly educated mind momentarily pushed aside his mental panic to take a logical look at his plight and seek a solution. A possible answer had come after careful consideration. He was aware of some kind of vault door between Ops and his quarters. That it existed was no secret, and while he had seen an occasional visitor enter there, he had never developed any curiosity beyond that. *Maybe that's the answer. There's privacy… it's out of the range of prying eyes.* He resolved to pay much closer attention to that door, and do what was required to save his mother.

It had been a wonderfully glorious day for Marian and Jake. The family had visited a few local farms to enquire and inspect a variety of animals, but also to visit and share their plans for improving her farm. Returning in the early afternoon, they put the children down for naps. Just as tired from the trip, both returned to her bedroom. As she reached to pull her dress up over her head, it stopped at covering her eyes, surprised there by a manly hand extending around to cup a right-royal handful of her left breast, while the right hand moved slowly to lovingly press and search the center of her abdomen in small circles… then slide unhurried downward. Tilting her head to one side openly invited captivating lips to explore the side of her neck; her mouth slightly open to gasp in appreciation at the thrill of it all. Her body came alive with a spirit of anticipation, in broad daylight! To even consider such activity at this time was wondrous! She had never known such intimacy could be so lusciously exciting!

She stood immobile; enveloped with deliciously hypnotizing lust as that hand found, and explored with exquisite touch, regions too long neglected and hungry for attention. Releasing the dress, she reached both hands back to grasp and pull tight buttocks toward her, relishing the growing presence now touching her… feeling it grow and stiffen against her body as it reached maturity.

"Oh… Yacob," she breathed with questionable craving. "It's still daylight… someone may…"

"Oh, Marian," was his confident reply.

She awoke to a very late afternoon, noting that evening would soon be here. *We'll have to wake the children… such a good long nap!* Lifting both arms to stretch with a developing yawn, she reached for Yacob, then realized he wasn't there. Still glowing from their delightfully spontaneous union, she thought he may have gone outside to attend to some over-looked chore. *Ah, does that mann never rest? I will prepare a large meal for him to end this day.* With amusement in her mind, she tempered her proposed effort with the thought, *perhaps a smaller meal will do... he has more than enough energy for both of us!*

However, he had not returned by the time she had finished preparing dinner. Concerned but no longer diverted with cooking, she now noticed a note tacked to the inside of her kitchen door. "Marian, returned to Chupp's. Urgent business; an appointment forgotten in the magic of your distraction! I will return later. Yacob."

After feeding the children, he had not come back. Marian decided his business must have kept him overlong, but he would still be hungry. Resolving to put something together, she prepared a big plate of food, covered it with a small, clean towel and placed it into a picnic basket. She was happy that her nearest neighbors, the Waglers, were receptive to her again, especially since Yacob's coming. Amos Wagler's wife Emily agreed to watch the children for awhile. They had renewed their friendship and Emily was full of questions about her new relationship. Marian promised they would get together in time and to catch up on everything. On that, she stepped into her buggy for the short ride to Old Chupp's farm.

The meeting was overlong. All Council members were too eager to drag out details of their accomplishments, upcoming projects, recent problems; all too familiar, all too bothersome at the moment. But everyone needs someone to report to, and as elected head of the Council, he was it.

"No, we're no closer to finding out who has been the cause of our recent problems, or why, for that matter," reported Maralah. "As I had reported previously, they seemed to have suddenly stopped."

Jake mulled that over. Apparently his ploy concerning camera place-ment had been found out. All of the mischief ceased just after their installation was completed. Prime's daily reports came up dry for any information about the instigator. He would have to develop a better plan with Walwyn and Alahn's assistance.

He had rushed back to Chupp's to catch this particular Council meeting. The events occurring on Luna had been troubling... escalating in degree until the cameras had been installed, then stopping as suddenly as they had begun. The Council needed him back on Luna, this night, to personally take over and hopefully come to some understanding of what was going on. His presence would add confidence and assuage the apprehension that seemed to permeate all three cities with the discovery of damage being done. He had left a note for Marian... but had not anticipated the Council's decision to call him back. For now, he had no choice but to leave and would have to address the issue of Marian later.

That matter was taken from his hands in the worse possible way.

"You've got company," said Maralah, glancing past Jake at the open pantry door he had failed to close.

Marian had climbed down from her buggy, noting it was almost dark now. She reached into the picnic basket and removed her plate of still-warm food; aroma wafting up to assure her that Yacob would be delighted to partake of such wholesome goodness. Seeing that some light was glimmering in his kitchen, she entered, only to find it vacant. The illumination was coming from his cupboard area. Hearing voices there, she turned to her right and walked toward the pantry door.

Seventeenth century Amish culture collided head-on into plus-twenty-first century science with unanticipated ramification.

The plate fell to the floor, shattering with a resounding clatter at the sight which greeted her. Marian tried to get her baffled mind around exactly what she was seeing... an elder? An *Aeltester?* A woman older than old—sunken dark eyes and gray-streaked, untamed hair adding a hint of wild fury; heavily weathered visage standing before her in open condemnation of her unannounced presence... gnarled, hard, brown skin appearing as if bark torn from bitter winter's tree; that same wrinkled casing seeming to carry the weight of centuries. The small room and person standing before her were splashed with glittering rainbow dots generated by multi-colored devices never before imagined!

It vanished!

Marian stood there in astonished silence, wide-eyed, open mouthed, with empty hands held palms up as if still holding her burden, not understanding what had just occurred; her mind not grasping how a human being standing not five feet in front of her could have suddenly, silently, and without warning, simply disappeared.

It hadn't yet entered her mine who that strange entity had been talking to. Frozen in place, feet firmly rooted to the floor, her head now turned slowly to the left, stunned mind screaming *Run! Flee!*

But a morbidly fascinated psyche refused that act, forcing her to answer one simple question... who had that sorceress been talking to?

The answer stood there in mute silence, starkly outlined against a pallid green glow of mystery; a pale, milky white creature of unimaginable horror... misshapen body a mockery of the human form, large globular head with immense insect eyes, stabbing proboscis instead of a chin or mouth... unnatural bulges on its back and between its legs... deformed chest, hands and feet!

That terrible head turned, devouring her with its gaze. Marian's courage failed as water now ran tricking down one trembling leg. A shriek born of stark terror was torn from her throat as she turned to run away.

"Teufel! Ungeheuer!" [Devil! Monster!] she shouted in unnerved fright, rushing for the door and sanctuary beyond.

"Marriiiaan, NOoooo!" came a deep, moaning growl from behind her.

Gott in Himmel, it knew her name! The cursed thing was coming for her! In her panicked state she stumbled and fell from the now darkened kitchen steps, screaming as she plunged into cold, gripping unmelted snow and freezing, penetratingly wet slush... shock of that encounter only adding to the adrenalin-fueled distress of her plight and need to escape the deathly peril confronting her. She lost one shoe, then the other while laboring through the icy buildup... imagining in her fear-fueled rush that arms of clenching snow had grabbed her legs as if to pull her under. She threw herself into the buggy, desperately grasping for the reins.

Jake stood there for a moment, not immediately comprehending what Maralah had stated before abruptly ending transmission. Turning his head in the direction that she had been staring, his "Company? Wha..." was cut off at seeing Marian standing there, face twisted in horrified distress, hands now held to both sides of her face with mouth opened in silent dread.

As she screamed and ran away, he shouted after her, then came to his senses at realizing he was fully engulfed in Starflyer gear, and how extra-ordinary he must appear to one with no knowledge or understanding of what it was. Swearing silently at his lapse in judgment at not speaking to her when he had the chance, he frantically tore off the helmet and threw it down, struggling to remove the nose and mouth inserted tubing. With that much accomplished at least, he ran after the only thing, the only person that mattered more to him than any other factor of his life at that moment.

It caught her in the darkness! The monster had her in its clutches; death was upon her! She attempted to thrash it off with the reins... now suddenly ripped from her hands by an evil spawned from the depths of Hell itself. Screaming in blind terror, adrenalin pumping her heartbeat and respiration to dangerous levels, she hammered at it with her bare hands! Her overwhelmed nervous system ended the struggle by blowing every safely fuse in her body... Marian collapsed, unconscious.

Nightmare! Revulsion! Horror! Marian's cataleptic mind was swimming in chaos. It seemed that time stopped... was there a feeling of movement? Another retreat into psychological darkness. Wait! There. A voice. As she struggled to unravel her mental torment, her mind finally initiated a re-boot of sorts, aided by and focusing on a soothing sound that gently pulled her up from the depths of anxiety she had been driven to.

"Yacob? Yacob, nicht wahr sie? Is that you?" she muttered, slowly regaining some sense of her surroundings. She was naked, lying on a bed, wrapped in a dry, warm, comforter, being held by someone... by Yacob! She was secure! Rescued from demons by the one she loved and needed most! It was with a desperate sense of reprieve that she threw herself at him, arms grabbing him tightly as she buried her face into his chest, breathing deeply with relief.

It was then she realized that drops were splashing on her arm. "Was ist dies?" It was Yacob, and he was crying! As she turned her face to look upward, tears flowed from his eyes, splashing onto her face! It was his voice that had called to her.

"Marian, Marian… I'm sorry, I'm so very sorry," he repeated over and over, his face a display of profound emotional censure, cradling her in his arms, slowly rocking her back and forth as a child being safely held and rocked by its father.

Pushing aside her own troubled thoughts for a moment, she tenderly raised one hand to wipe away his tears, soothingly caressing him, "Nein Yacob, nein. Weinen sie nicht, weinen sie nicht meine liebe. Bitte, welche schwierigkeiten sie? [No, Yacob, no. Cry you not, cry you not my love. Please, what troubles you?] pleaded a now concerned Marian.

It was then she noticed the clothing he wore, or more correctly, the remnants of his Starflyer suit. Her gasping intake of breath at recognizing that much drew Jake's attention to the fact she had now fully awakened.

"I should have told you, I wanted desperately to tell you. I just couldn't find what seemed to be a good moment, a private moment to discuss this with you. I thought I would lose you once you knew… I, I fear that I've lost you now," he finished, head drooping downward at this declaration.

Her face lined with distressed worry, she gazed deeply into his eyes, gazing from one to the next, seeking truth. "Yacob, was hier geschieht… vaht is happening here? Daht, daht *woman?* A sorceress or witch? Some devil worship? Daht ungeheuer… monster." She shivered slightly at that recent memory. "Why are you dressed in this manner? Yacob, Ich bin, I'm so confused. Are you not plain? Not of our way?" Pausing, she pulled him down to lie beside her, their faces inches apart. "You once said to me there can be no shyness between us. Speak to me, my Yacob. Tell me vaht is in your heart."

"I have something to tell you, Marian. A long, long something."

It was almost sunrise before Jake finished. After she fainted and once inside his house, he had seen to her horse and buggy, now resting warmly in the barn. Marian had, for the most part, remained silent throughout the telling, listening attentively as the most astonishing tale she had ever encountered unfolded before her. Jake answered her few questions as simply as he was able, to explain the more intricate parts of some aspects of his technical world.

"Marian, I love you before and beyond all things in this life. With all my heart I say to you how truly sorry I am to cause you such fright. I pledge that never again will you face anything of that nature from me. I need you, Marian, more than you could ever know. You have every right to be angry with me. I understand you may not want to be with me, now knowing the truth of my past and how I came to be with you."

He was in pain, the events he shared a terrible burden to carry alone. She could see that clearly in his pleading eyes. Here was a true mann, a worthy person... one who cared deeply for his people, their cause, and for her in equal measure. His philosophies were closely associated with those of her community, and not opposed to the teachings of her elders... just, arrived at from a different direction. And the Esch family! Wondrous! From hier kommen, von Lancaster... and now farming with his people! His heart was breaking at the thought he may have hurt her... that she would leave him and he would be alone again.

Running her fingers delicately against the side of his head, her sweet breath lightly brushing his lips, she sighed, "Ja, Yacob. It will need some time to take in all the new ideas you have shared with me. But there is no lie in you, in your heart. I knew daht the moment we first met. I will never leave you, Yacob. If it is possible to be so, I love you even more, now than before. God has brought us together for a purpose. I do not fully understand it yet, but I will accept it. We will work together to solve die questions before us, ja?" She moved up to kiss tears away from his eyes; her lips taking in his with new promise as they held and caressed each other tightly.

His confidence restored at her reaffirmation and pledge, his tone became even more serious as he responded, "Come, Marian. I have made a decision," He helped her dress, having set out her soaked clothing to dry before wrapping her as he did. Leaving his bedroom, they returned to the panty communications room.

"These are very powerful computers," he pointed out; arm sweeping to take in all of the electronic equipment that had been installed there, filling the room with its bulk.

"Ja, Yacob, but vaht is all of this for? Vaht does it do?"

"For lack of any better description, Marian, this is... a telephone."

Holding his hand and looking at him, she grinned, "Nein, Yacob. We have a telephone over to Herr Lengacher's farm... it is in a small cupboard outside, hanging on the wall. It is for use by everyone in our community."

"Yes, you're correct of course. This telephone allows you to actually see the person you are talking to, but in a much more complete manner. I'm aware you know what a television set is. This device," he said, pointing to the floor and ceiling holographic imaging emitters, "acts as a television set, but in a much more complicated way. I'm going to turn it on now, and ask that the full Luna Council be present. It will be strange and new, at first. Please don't be frightened; these are my friends."

As the emitters came online, an image began to form, then solidified into a human form, three dimensional and in full color... as real as if the person actually stood before them. It was the female elder that had so frightened Marian. Regardless of Yacob's explanation, she still felt a cold chill run up and down her spine at viewing this apparition, and moved even closer to him in apprehension. The other Council members could be seen arrayed around her.

"Marian, please meet Maralah, a Native-American of the Houck Navajo nation, located in the city of Houck, state of Arizona. She is one of our oldest members, and a long time friend of my former wife, Natalia and our families."

Looking closely at both of them with narrowed eyes, Maralah stated in her direct, matter-of-fact style, ignoring any pretense at political correctness or manners, "Well, at last we all learn the reason for your distraction;

the reason you've missed important Council meetings. Taking time off to look around was never intended to be abandonment. You need to be here NOW, Council Leader Jacob Starnes, not jumping about like some wild stallion in heat chasing the nearest filly to ground," she scolded.

Jake was taken somewhat aback at the directness of that statement, but even more surprised at Marian's passionate response.

How dare such a one speak to her Yacob in that manner! Suddenly moving to place herself in front of him, she faced the target of her fear with courage and arms spread wide, as if to protect Jake. Her voice an arrow of conviction aimed directly at the target of her fear, it struck dead center with, "Nein, nie! Er ist meiner! Sie können ihn nicht haben! Wenn sie ihn geliebt haben, würden sie verstehen!"

Glancing at Marian with a look of disgust on her face, Maralah looked at Jake. "I don't understand her tongue anymore than I would expect her to know mine. What did she say?"

Gently pushing her arms down and positioning Marian to his side, he grasped her left hand. She leaned against him, wrapping her right arm and hand around his to hold him close. "Her words were 'No… never. He's mine. You can't have him. If you loved him, you would understand!' That's pretty close to how it came across." Moving his eyes to take in all of the Council members, he addressed the entire room.

"And it's important that you all know and understand that I love this *woman*," he carefully emphasized, "in equal measure." Moderating his tone somewhat, he continued, "This has been a true adventure for all of us. Begun and continuing for all of the right reasons. I don't need to stand in front of you with some bombastic pontification about accomplishments or future goals, you already know all of that. So, I'm keeping this simple. You have a freely elected full Council that administers to all of Luna's needs, plans in place for sovereignty and internal growth. No one person is more important than that. Therefore, I tender my resignation as Council Lead. I quit."

Every face in that room was stunned into silence! Quit? Resign? What does that mean? After a few seconds of anxiously looking at each other for an answer, the room erupted in pandemonium.

"Jake! Dad! Jacob! Colonel Starnes! What? NO! You can't do that! We can't do this without you!" shouted voices across a distance of more than a quarter of a million miles of space. Maralah's position in the holographic camera's space was now occupied by Kelly Akamatsu, Luna's Chief Administrator. Motioning for quiet, she directed her attention at the founder of all their dreams.

"Jake, when you came to me years ago as owner of Akamatsu Industrial Manufacturing in Sendai, Japan, you proposed a grandiose plan, one that had the highest ideals. Moreover, you presented a workable plan and had the people to make it happen. I committed myself, my family, my resources, my life... to that plan, as did thousands of others here. I don't recall anywhere in that meeting the idea that you would one day, just at the moment of achieving our greatest success, act to pull the rug from under our feet and walk out on us. You owe me... all of us, a better explanation than what we just heard."

After a moment of contemplation, Jake addressed the assembly. "You're right, of course, Kelly," Not surprised at the reaction to his announcement, he continued. "War, as a concept and action, is obsolete. Limited and unrenewable resources, both material and human, squandered over something as intransient as national pride has never made any sense. The idea that a nation has to use an army rather than have it sit around is equally useless and wasteful. My own personal loss pushed me over that line. It's what started our program here. I wanted to move us away from all of that. Perhaps it was arrogance on my part to believe we could escape the violence of Earth. Instead, insane jealousy has driven an entire planet to covet our successes. It isn't enough for them that I would be the only target, but now my vision has placed everything we've worked for in jeopardy, including all of you.

"I've also got a very selfish reason now to be even more concerned. Marian Ella Fisher has pledged herself to me, and I have done the same to her and her children. The position of Council Lead has absorbed my life, to the exclusion of any personal happiness I could ever have. That's changed now. I will not relinquish Marian."

After a moment of thoughtful silence, Kelly responded, "Jake, regardless of my so-called position here, I've got more of a personal stake in founding this society that anyone else. I think I speak for everyone here in saying we do not accept your resignation, nor will we permit you to quit and walk away. Give us some time to consider everything that's happened. We'll get back to you." On that, Kelly ended transmission.

Robert Kim followed his man from a discreet distance, certain he wasn't attracting attention. He had watched this individual for over a week while noting his routine was relatively consistent. He also knew there were no cameras installed in this location. Opening the vault door required knowledge as well as biometric scans, something he didn't have security level clearance to accomplish. However, like most who felt safe in their environment, his intended victim was lax in not closing the vault door completely before continuing inward; allowing it to close slowly behind him. It was an easy task to confirm no other presence in the hallway, then simply piggyback his target as he walked through the vault door entrance.

As he now did so, he smoothly pulled his club from the front of his jump suit, raised it over his head and with all his strength brought it down on the head of the hapless person walking just in front of him. The man collapsed, falling to the floor with a thud, scattering the materials he had been carrying.

That should be enough. Word will get around… the assassin will see that I've done what he wanted; he'll have to let my mother go now. As he turned to leave, he spotted a shadowed glow in the otherwise darkened room.

What's that? A light, over there beyond that small stage… past the seating. What can that be, a lab? Someone in there may have seen me. No alarm yet, I can't take any chances.

Robert made his way quietly to the lab's entrance. Not immediately detecting any movement inside, he entered, only to be stunned into frozen silence at the sight that greeted him. His troubled thoughts attempted in vain to form a cohesive answer in his mind at what the distorted figure in his field of vision could be.

What in cosmos is this? A being? Could this thing be alive?

He easily recognized some items; helmet, wiring, sensors. The intro-visionary helmet, similar to those worn in Ops, was much larger in size than any he had seen before and was in the process of raising to its parked position. Tubing and electrical cabling ran from medical equipment and other apparatus arranged in a semi-circle around a cylindrical glass enclo-sure two meters in length. That tubing terminated at various positions into apparently living flesh inside that cylinder. It was difficult to deter-mine structure of the body, if that's what one wanted to call it, but one part was at least fairly recognizable—it had a head. A huge head! And the eyes in that head were looking straight at him!

Reatah Kobusingye was born into a body of troubling mutation. Limbs grotesquely atrophied; bent into uselessness, a body wasted almost to the point of death... more resembling a dying insect tossed onto its back than anything that could possibly be breathing air. That was the state of her existence until a chance encounter with a doctor doing charity work in her village. His examination revealed a brain seemingly swollen to almost three times normal size, but more remarkably, also functioned significantly more rapidly than anyone he had ever known. The disease that ravaged her body at birth spared her the living hell of being locked into her own mind... she could speak! Moreover, her mental processes and comprehension of mathematics was noteworthy in one so obviously challenged. Word of her eventually made its way through medical jour-nals to the attention of a Doctor Agave, who just happened to know someone needing such talent.

Reatah was arguably the most extraordinary computer authority ever produced by human interaction. Her intuitive grasp of electronic memory function and fractal design algorithmic calculation was at the heart of all of Luna's technology. She would pit herself against several Cray supercomputers and still come up an easy winner, so strong was her computational intuition. Every individual recruited for Luna's electronic requirements studied her work. She was directly responsible for Prime... call it her 'child,' if you wish, for that's how she saw her creation. Khene-metAhmose was one physical aspect of Prime, and self-realization, or self awareness, was her highest goal for that creation.

Her salutation, "Hello, Robert. What can I do for you?" emanated simultaneously from two directions! The creature enclosed in glass, and another person; a woman, now moving from the room's darkened corner into the light.

No! Witnesses! They know who I am? How can this be?!

Robert was on stress overload, pushed to, and beyond, normal limits of human mental endurance over the torture of his mother, commands of an insane assassin, and knowledge of the harm that had almost befallen his friends and associates over actions he had already taken... and other actions not yet concluded. Now the man he had just hit in the other room; certainly dead! Nothing mattered anymore. Adding more to the list would not increase the penalty he had already incurred.

Make it quick and painless, were his thoughts... his face twisted into a scowl; thoughts only of saving his mother. *It's them or my eomma!*

This one first, quick and easy, then the woman. Moving to stand next to the head, he raised his club. Tensing his muscles to strike again, he brought his arms forward and down with all his strength for the smashing blow.

The assassin was careful; oh so very careful. He had lain in his hay-wrapped den for all of a day and a night, his only absence from vigil the breaks he had taken beforehand to report his progress. He wore a waste recovery bag and subsisted on high-caloric, high-moisture food tabs. The space craft returned; pilot exiting and walking to the house. After a short time, he had emerged again sans flight gear and took his automated buggy toward the woman's farmstead. That was some hours ago. This life-ender, now repositioned, studied the Fisher house with professional interest, starkly outlined by luminescence of technological headgear he favored. Having already entered and mapped out the floor plans during one absence some days ago… he knew exactly how many steps led up to the second floor, which ones creaked and those that did not, adding to that knowledge the layout of bedrooms and who slept where and on what bed.

Terminally stupid to leave the doors unlocked.

His tool of choice for tonight's work was a handgun built on a reputation of solid reliability; an alloy chassis Ruger Mark III .22 caliber automatic handgun with 4.75 inch barrel, 10-round magazine and complete with highly developed sound suppressor, which fired a 1.9 gram bullet with 70 foot pounds of energy. Traveling at 1,045 feet per second, up to two inches of solid wood could be penetrated. Absolutely silent and guaranteed deadly.

Pastel light from a full moon shown through the bedroom's window, sufficient enough to illuminate his victims. He was as a ghost finding itself hovering over two sleeping bodies, his wraithlike silhouette reflected in the bureau's mirror.

First things first, he thought. Placing the weapon's barrel under a chin, he pulled the trigger. An almost indiscernible *puff* announced the end of former Colonel Jacob 'Jake' Starnes as the body jerked slightly. The killer had skillfully cut four grooves into the lead bullets in all ten rounds loaded into the magazine. This first one accomplished its deadly task by slicing four trails through the braincase of its victim. Instant death.

Under the chin was a good idea... very little bleeding. Frau Fisher just as quickly followed, as her body jerked with impact of the second round fired as accurately as the first.

There was no regret, no sympathy, no remorse... no human feelings whatsoever as he fired similar bullets into the brains of three sleeping children.

Having collected and accounted for shell casings in the children's bedroom, he removed his night vision goggle apparatus, cautiously noting his camera had captured each act without him being seen in the picture frame, and saved the content to a secure flash drive. He then returned to the adult's bedroom to collect shell casings there, and ensure his work had been as complete as he could make it. Satisfied that all five targets had been neutralized, he left to file this last report and collect the bounty he had earned, thinking, *Hell of an easy way to win a war!*

Prime occupied the room with Reatah and Robert, or did *He? She? It?*

Conceding the masculine and ignoring the bi-pedal representation for a moment, then the question remains the same... was he, the thinking part of him, present in the room or in a box locked away somewhere in the secure bowels of Luna as nothing more than a clever program? After all, both held memory capability. Was he self-aware; aware of himself as an individual?

Did he possess his own thoughts and actions?

What is sentience anyway? Strict definitions deal with aspects of perception or feeling, states of consciousness; both undifferentiated and elementary, or the manner in which an external world may be sensed or held. Philosophical debate among the world's elite could stretch forever attempting to dissect the various definitions down to their root meanings and never reach consensus. While they wage their battles of verbal intelligencia, sentience could walk right by them and they would never see it.

Given that, one could say the bi-pedal aspect was Prime's hand, or finger, or whatever appendage you care to name that provides input for consideration. Or, simply accept him and don't dwell on the layers of his physical being. After all, when holding a telephone receiver, one's mind doesn't consciously differentiate between the handset and the person being spoken to.

Just how fast is the human brain? At what speed do the human brain's biologic neurons fire one to the next? Does it matter? Is that speed relevant to perceptions of how smart or intelligent or sentient one is? Prime's processing function could be measured by teraflops... trillions of calculations per second, all very good if he was constructed to simply calculate.

At any given moment he was engaged in managing numerous electronic systems having to do with every facet of Luna's operation including life support, transportation, sanitation, sustenance, and so on... in that sense compatible to the autonomic or self-governing functioning of the human body and managed by relatively low level sub-routines; transparent to his higher cognitive occupation.

Reatah, assisted by Walwyn and his friends, understood that programming logic lacked intuition, and they set out to provide that or some semblance of it to their creations. The Starflyer AI's were an initial result. Factoring in the concept of humor was a work in progress, and some advancement had been made. It wasn't too difficult to write a comparison program to review verbiage against a standard of skill, ingenuity, or congruity; especially if the result could be observed to evoke laughter.

The concept of absurdity was incorporated as well. The AI Sidney which controlled Edwina's Starflyer was their first success in that endeavor. Human brain function is not remarkably dissimilar to computer functioning. Something is perceived, choices provided, and a selection is made. Rather elementary process, actually. The result is cataloged as {Experience}, and filed away until needed the next time.

Prime observed the actions of an individual entering the vault room... an individual rather oblivious to the fact that the vault door, the rooms and everything attached to them, including the floors and ceilings, where virtually alive with sensors, cameras, and scanners dealing with every detectable frequency that existed in the electromagnetic spectrum. His data files, or memory, already contained recognition patterns of Luna's participants, so in that regard he was aware of who was present... Robert Kyoung-Joo Kim; that his presence was unauthorized and this area was not within his normal working environment. Running a simple comparison program against facial patterns allowed him to conclude Robert's mood, and review of social verbalizing gave him the clues needed to predict what Robert was possibly involved in doing.

He wasn't always right in his conclusions, but didn't need to be at this point in his existence. After all, children learn given time, experience, and good teachers. In the case of Prime, he had at his disposal the complete history of mankind, as well as the individual AI personalities available for any of the transportation vehicles, and thousands of Luna's inhabitants. He could access, compare, analyze, and conclude to his heart's content.

Noting Robert's physiological aspects, excessive perspiration, highly elevated heartbeat, breathing rates and stress levels of his voice; he dutifully recorded it all and reviewed each interaction several million times, correlating relations one against the other. A conclusion was reached that was not a pre-programmed choice. The unique selection of programming variables that formed Prime's first original thought came seemingly unbidden, and he greeted them without emotion. Passing the revelation against his computational matrix and experiences of the various AI's, he reviewed available options for all of one nanosecond:

[Unknown item held by Robert: no discernible function in vault/lab room]
[Robert's act in front area; aggression: deduction that Robert will repeat aggressive act]
[Can not harm Robert: can not permit Robert to do harm via no action]
[Must obey orders from living beings, unless orders conflict with first requirement; Second requirement not applicable: no orders given… ignore]
[Can protect himself, unless such is in conflict with first two requirements]
[He, She, and/or It, and Reatah, are all one and the same. Can not permit Robert to harm him, her, it, us; but in equal measure, cannot harm Robert]
With a leap of insight and true intuition, the answer sprang forth:
[Action required: impound Robert's item]

Robert's hands slipped off the end of his weapon; the force of his effort causing him to overbalance and stumble forward slightly. Turning around, he was astonished to see his bludgeon hanging in midair! Even more astonishing was the undeniable fact the man he had just killed was standing there holding it, his head tilted unnaturally to one side from the force of Robert's blow! And the other woman in the room now coming toward him!

His mother repeatedly tortured; horribly twisted humanity laying before him; a man supposedly dead standing in full view with yet another person about to capture him… his mind was stressed to the point of irrational incomprehension, as if trapped between some nightmarish B-movie freak show world and zombies coming back from the dead! Letting out an insanely high-pitched squeal of incoherent mental anguish, he bolted from the room.

At Reatah's command of 'down,' her helmet began to lower itself. "Jonathon, come over here, dear. Did that bad man hurt you?"

"No, Mother, my systems are fully operational," returned the anthropomorphic being standing there smiling crookedly down at her. He reached up with both hands and reinserted the stem of his cranial frame into its mating aperture, returning his head to acceptable elevation. "I'll retrieve medical items dropped in the foyer and proceed with your normal administration."

"I will assist him, Mother."

"Thank you, Krista. You're such good children. Please continue your work. Momma has to talk to Operations now." Reatah explained events just occurring and issued a full alert for Robert Kim.

KhenemetAhmose had siblings.

"Alahn, where are you?" queried a distraught Kelly. She was in Cordial's Operations with Donah, Maralah, and a number of other Council members close enough to come running at her call.

"I'm in Prexus with Edwina Lewis, going over expansion plans with engineering staff. Is there another problem?" he asked with exasperation, knowing the issue concerning his father's recent resignation still begged resolution.

"You can certainly call it that. Both of you drop what you're doing and get here as quickly as possible; Robert Kim is in Selene's main entrance airlock and he's strapped explosives all over himself!"

Alahn didn't waste time asking questions. He and Edwina suited up, grabbed a Hopper, and pushed it to full speed. While enroute, he keyed Ops, "Where's my father, Kelly? Have you alerted him to this danger?"

"We don't know where he is, exactly. We can't contact him. Our calls to his communication center go unanswered, but his identifier puts him somewhere in that same town you were in on Earth. We don't have time to send someone for him and this crisis won't wait for his return."

Kelly wasn't initially aware of who Reatah was, but Walwyn was adamant in vouching for her with assurances that both Jake and Alahn knew her personally. Kelly explained that Reatah had issued an alert and synopsis of Robert's actions in her vault laboratory. She had also disclosed unauthorized entry into the seismic and mining explosive storage areas, with inventories now demonstrating shortages.

Edwina broke in, "Kelly, contact this Reatah. Find out exactly how many explosives are missing by type. Then look at Robert and try to determine if he's wearing them all. If not, we can conclude he has set them in place to destroy something other than himself."

"How will I do that, Edwina? No one will go near that airlock in fear of him detonating himself."

Figuring he now knew who was responsible for all the incidents occurring on Luna, Alahn told Kelly about the cameras he and Walwyn had installed in secret on orders from his father. "If you're still in Ops, have Walwyn bring up the cameras installed there. You'll be able to see and talk to Robert; we put cameras inside the airlocks also."

Once video was established, it was disappointing to discover that explosives adhering to Robert did not account for all that were missing and this was passed on to Alahn with Edwina reacting instantly. "Listen carefully. Have Council members contact the three cities… full alert. Have all inhabitants go to the nearest shelter and seal it now. Wait! Have everybody complete a visual search while they're headed for their shelters, and let us know immediately if anything unusual is spotted, anywhere, no matter how trivial it may seem,"

In the space of only moments, a habitat-wide alert was generated. It was hoped the crisis narrowed to only focus on Robert, his state of mind, and what brought him to this point. Unfortunately, Operation's next message was chilling.

Lloyd Boxe, Luna's premier horticulturist, had contacted Ops from the security of his now buttoned down shelter, located quite close to Selene's Great Hall main entrance. There was a rather large group of adults and children on a field trip to the lake area adjacent to the main glass viewport, who had apparently not heard or understood the alert message. Moreover, he had spotted black dots now situated in one area of the viewport... to the side closest to the main airlock. By now, Alahn and Edwina had arrived at Cordial and been brought up to speed on events up to that moment.

Alahn contacted Selene. "Lloyd, stay in place. Ops is attempting to link a number of the shelter audio systems together. It's hoped that combined, they'll produce a high enough sound pressure level to overcome the noise at the lake and pool so we can get a warning to them. We can't risk anyone leaving their shelter to physically go there.

"Walwyn, patch me through to Robert."

He was backed into one corner of Selene's main air lock, perspiring heavily, his face displaying a cycling kaleidoscope of extremes; anger, fear, terror, hurt, remorse, anguish, as he wrung his hands in extreme psychological distress.

Unknown to Robert at that moment, he hadn't actually harmed anyone. Under the circumstances, he could be forgiven for the mischief he created. The most important facet had to be an attempt to have him regain his composure, so that rational discussion could take place... to quite literally defuse both the mental and physical aspects of this situation. As calmly as he could manage, Alahn keyed his mic connection to the airlock, "Robert, it's Alahn. I'm in Ops; you might be able to see the camera I put in the airlock there, look up into the corner across from you."

In doing so, his face contorted into a look of incalculable hatred and anger... his response hurled at them with that same high-squealing intonation, "You're responsible for this! You, Jake, all of you! You did this. That fiend, assassin, that murderer... he's killed my mother. He tortured her for weeks! Ohhhh. My mother... my eomma. None of this would have happened if you had left me alone... if you had never come to me at all. He wouldn't have found her otherwise. Alone, she was alone. No one protected her! I was coerced into acting because of you... YOU... ALL OF YOU!"

It was obvious that in his altered state of mind, Alahn wasn't going to be very effective in calming Robert down. No one in Luna, not even Jake, could have predicted an event of this nature ever occurring... and most certainly, not what instantly followed.

The camera caught disintegration of Robert's body as the explosive's pressure wave simultaneously distorted and removed the airlock door before going dark... as did the camera in the precautionary second air lock as it too was relegated to destruction. Seismic explosives placed on the glass viewport removed about fifty feet of six-inch thick quartz glass, leaving the balance fractured and inculcated with growing fissure lines. The main viewport metallic shields, designed for closure in the event of loss of pressurization, were a matter of high tonnage and mass, even in Luna's lighter gravity. While mechanisms controlling those doors were robust, it still required time to move that much weight.

Eighteen miles of pressurized air carried considerable force, now increased to incredible velocities at the point of decreased area... an exit through what, in relation to size, was the tapered end of a small funnel. There was no resisting the incredible jet effect of the venturi force placed on anything within reach of that greedily sucking orifice. Every human being within close range of that opening was wrenched through and consigned to oblivion.

Explosives placed at the main junction line connecting power relays to the three cities were severed just as quickly.

The catastrophic sisters of death, destruction, and darkness had just wrought havoc upon Luna.

"**One** hundred and fifteen; seventy-seven adults and thirty-eight children. That's the best count we've got on who's missing so far," reported Lloyd Boxe. He had suited up immediately after the blast to assess damage to the viewport and airlocks. "We've arrived at that by using the intershelter system to ask everyone to tell us if anyone's not home, hasn't reported in, or they believe they're missing, so the total number can go either way, Alahn. We won't know for sure until crews have gone outside to pick up the remains."

"Oh nooo, dear God, madre de dios," and similar mutterings of severe emotional distress in other languages came unbidden from any number of those in Ops, heads dropping with shock and remorse as details of the devastation rocked some there into silence, and others to tears and crying. Even the Operations herky-jerk's normal animations were stilled at hearing this staggering report. Personally relieved to know that Hulda and her family were safe, Alahn realized he didn't have the luxury of one family... his view had to take on the welfare of the entire population of Luna, which at this moment had all of its citizenry in fear of their lives.

"Lloyd, what about air pressure?" queried Alahn.

"Once the shields locked up, it settled down. Should be up to acceptable levels in an hour or two after you get the systems back online. Eighteen miles of air takes a long time to empty out, so we got lucky there. No casualties in the shelters themselves. Your alert was in time, so we got closed up pretty quick. Good planning on the part of Engineering that the shield doors were on their own power system, as are the shelters in here. There's enough food, water, and air in each one for about two weeks if fully occupied, longer if we have to ration.

"Bad news? We lost the lake water and main supply... all of that was sucked out with everything else close to the hole. That includes every bit of plant life, dust-cover ground matting, and I'll bet enough actual dust for Earth to pick the cloud up. It's also pitch dark outside the shelters, so crop loss is a possibility. We're locked in here, Alahn. No airlocks. How soon till we can get Engineering over here to fix them?"

"Give us a few minutes to contact Cordial and Prexus to get their reports. Then we'll assign specific teams to address each issue as it's identified. Beyond that, I'll look to you to be the contact person there, and keep everyone up to speed on updates. Start by polling every shelter individually through the full length of Selene. We need to pin down a correct headcount as some families may have been traveling to the other cities."

Turning to take in the faces now staring at him, Alahn took in a deep breath, then straightened while squaring his shoulders. Grim determination set his youthful countenance to hard features as cold tentacles of inconceivable accountability wrapped firmly around him.

In a dejectedly somber tone, he instructed, "Edwina, contact Prexus. Get teams out to the solar arrays now, and you go with them. Have them determine extent of damage and why the alternate systems didn't come on line. Robert didn't have enough explosives to take out the entire solar array system, so he may have targeted the relay junctions themselves. Have those teams prepared to deal with that before they leave the city.

"Kelly, Maralah, get with the other Council members. All of you, I want damage reports on the status of all three cities as quickly as you can get them. Don't say anything about our casualties yet. Let's keep morale up as high as possible until we're fully up and running again. I'm going to put a team together to search for the remains of our people."

The President was working late. His Chief of Staff had just left to retrieve tomorrow's VIP listings from the protocol office. In a moment of reflection, he swiveled in his chair to look out a window of the Oval Office, noting it was just after nine p.m. Located on the first floor of the west wing, he viewed more vegetation than civilization per se as the exterior White House profile was minimized by landscaping. The presidential and domestic staffs had left for the day, and all was quiet in the family quarters on the second and third floors. Hearing footsteps enter the room, he pushed his chair back toward the desk and turned around.

"Well, that took long eno—"

Standing before him was an individual dressed in a dark gray protective suit; seemingly at ease with hands at his side; face somewhat obscured by color reflections from instrumentation within his helmet.

For all his faults and personality quirks, President Caneman was not a stupid man. The White House contained one hundred and thirty-two rooms spaced along six stories, over four hundred doors and almost one hundred and fifty windows; eight staircases and three elevators. As a result, the building itself was surrounded by security fencing and concrete barriers that restricted vehicular and pedestrian access. Armed agents constantly patrolled numerous guard points, coordinated and controlled from a Secret Service office located on the west wing ground floor. There were people on-duty and staffing the Presidential Emergency Operations Center in a nuclear bomb proof bunker beneath the east wing. The same was true for the Situation Room in the basement of the west wing including the Secret Service office on the ground floor.

For this person to be standing before him, something terrible had to have happened, or the most implausible set of circumstances ever in the existence of mankind left the front door open to uninvited passersby. Dismissing the latter explanation, he stayed with his intuition.

"My security people?" he queried.

"Ineffective. Unharmed."

"Well... thank you for that," responded the President, slowly moving his hand toward the edge of his desk.

"You're welcome to attempt activating your security systems, or try the phone, Mr. President. I assure you those actions will be equally ineffective."

Resting his elbows on the desk, President Caneman grasped his hands together and leaned forward, focusing a cold, hard stare at his uninvited visitor.

Impossible. This can't be. I read the reports, saw the photos and video... dead is dead. The Assassin is the best in the business. We paid him a gosh-damned triple fortune worth half the gold in Fort Knox to be certain! Without revealing his thoughts, ice-cold perspiration now ran down the back of his neck.

"Colonel Starnes. Come to gloat, have we?"

"No... I've come to bring you to justice."

Dropping any pretense at cordiality and with a condescending chuckle, the President leaned back into his chair with a self-satisfied smirk. "I get a lot of damned egotistical fools in here on occasion; you're right up there at the top of the list. You've come a long way for nothing, you arrogant piece of work. How in hell did you get in here anyway?"

"Our engineers and medical staff came up with quite a novel approach... rather ingenious, actually. You'll notice the shoulder-mounted protrusion to the left of my helmet. It's a pneumatic device capable of sending a one-inch compressed powder dart a significant distance. The dart itself is about the thickness of a human hair... composed of a quite powerful muscle relaxer and tipped with an anesthetic; targeted for the carotid artery by the helmet's AI. It dissolves instantly on contact and the victim doesn't even feel the impact. It also contains a neural trigger that activates the body's own natural sleeping mechanisms. The gentleman that left your office, the security staff and others we've encountered are resting peacefully. The exterior guards have been replaced by our people, and we won't bother anyone that's sleeping upstairs."

Jake's strike force had closely coordinated replacing the exterior guards. Once that was accomplished, several TUGs had landed clandestinely in the open Eclipse area, carefully avoiding the rather large crater that still hadn't been filled in. Aided by a clever computer virus that led the interior security monitoring teams to believe they were still seeing actual real-time images of business as usual, it had been a relatively straight forward exercise to replace them as well.

Jake had been impressed by the alertness of the first interior guard he had encountered entering the White House from the west executive drive entrance. Walking through the foyer and lobby, he had been confronted before he could gain access to the stairway leading upstairs.

"FREEZE! Put your hands where I can see them; do it NOW!" was accompanied by a military stance and two-handed brandishing of an M9 service pistol aimed directly at Jake's head. Walking forward, the agent's eyes blinked swiftly as he lost his grip on the handgun.

Jake caught the rapidly fading young guard… lowering him gently to the floor with, "Rest easy, soldier, we haven't come to harm anyone." He retrieved the weapon and replaced it in the guard's holster.

Returning his attention to the President, Jake advised him, "You have a lot to answer for. We're aware that every switchboard in the country is overloaded with constituents looking for your head. That stunt of yours with the tactical nuke and ABL… innocent lives placed at risk and many millions of dollars worth of defensive weaponry lost to remove just one opposing craft; not a sound military decision or very effective use of scarce taxpayer money. Detonating a nuclear weapon over a populated area must have required a great deal of explaining, as well as the one you fired at us. While I'm surprised you're still in office, your legal problems have only begun."

Pausing for effect, he went on, "It's remarkable, Mr. President, the amount of trust people put into electronic media… and given that, not at all startling at what you find if you have the ability to access it. I believe that even you would be impressed. For example, the person you selected to head up the Secret Service security detail is a very distrusting man, and has a bad habit of surreptitiously recording his phone calls. We've retrieved all the originals, by the way, leaving him with nothing to show for his efforts. Of particular interest are those placed to him from the executive restroom. Our sound analysis researchers assure me the electronic voice print exactly matches your own. We have the bank records for the payoffs, and you'll be hard pressed to explain how an entry-level employee got promoted to Special Agent virtually overnight without support or required training, in that we also have his psychological profile and extremely marginal performance evaluations.

"The link between you, your Security Chief, and Special Agent Souser is ironclad, as are your instructions on how to handle the two 'special cases.' I believe that's the term you used. We have the results of his attentions to an eleven year old girl and seventy year old man on video. Suffice it to say your days of frightening children and old men are over."

President Caneman responded true to form, "It'll be a cold day in hell before you prove anything, Starnes. You can't stand there forever. The next shift will be along to deal with you shortly, and I own the legal system of this country right up to the Supreme Court. Let me point out that you declared war on us, so take your best shot, pal; you and your monkey boys are history. I'll build a base on the moon with my name on it, take everything you've got and wipe the surface with your worthless carcasses and do it all legally," he snarled.

A blue aiming reticule with crosshairs suddenly appeared before the President. He watched in silent fury as it slowly moved across the desk, marching up the right side of his suit jacket until lost to his peripheral vision.

"We have a totally open society on Luna. All facts and details shared in full with every member of our citizenry… young and old alike. However, due to the special circumstances being dealt with here, I made the decision to hold on to the information I've shared with you for the moment." Taking a small object out of an external pocket on his E-suit, Jake tossed it on the desk. "Here's a CD containing all the evidence I just spoke of… you can judge it for yourself at leisure. I have the original.

"I'm going to make you an offer, Mr. President. You and I are going to take a short trip over to the UN building. I will afford you the respect of allowing you to walk out of here with me. Or, I will carry you out. Either way, you will be coming. What's it to be?"

With an ugly scowl on his face, President Caneman got up from his desk and was escorted to a waiting TUG for the short trip; unaware that Colonel Starnes had arranged an even bigger surprise for a soon to be ex-President.

UN Secretary-General Baruti Harakhty was at the General Assembly Hall with as many delegates as could be summoned on short notice when Jake entered with his guest in tow. As they walked up the aisle, President Caneman was asked to join the group seen sitting in the front rows. On closer inspection, he recognized the leaders of the G8 nations! Standing or sitting on the raised platform fronting the audience was a group of people in plain jump suits, composed of adults and adolescents. A now helmetless Jake took his place among them.

"I apologize for the lateness of the hour. It's necessary that we gather and discuss resolution of the difficulties that face us all. The course of action forced upon us is abhorrent, violating our philosophical values and causing unnecessary stress to all of our populations. We have made our salient points within each of your countries and the Council of Luna feels it isn't necessary to prolong this any further. Allow me to introduce Miss Eleanor Ernst, Chief Executive Officer of Ernst, Long & Stein. You're aware her law firm is representing our interests."

The German Chancellor leaped to his feet, shaking his fist and shouting, "Ich werde diesen frevel nicht darstellen! Ich kann nicht zulassen, daß dies fortsetzt… release uns sofort!" being extremely vocal in expressing that he wouldn't stand for this outrage and clamored to be released immediately… followed on his heals by the Russian Premiere just as passionately screaming; demanding to know who they were to kidnap leaders of the free world and bring them here against their will!

The French President threw in his opinion with as much fervor, 'Si ceux-ci sont des affaires d'Etat, sont pourquoi là-bas des enfants ici?" pressing to know why affairs of State were being attended by children. By now the other G8 leaders were just as agitated, jumping up and vehemently shouting to be heard.

Jake walked to the front of the platform and gestured for silence. When it wasn't forthcoming, he spoke up for all to hear. "Ladies and gentlemen, we have declared war on you and have chosen to prosecute that action as a matter of inconvenience rather than outright destruction."

That got everyone's attention. As they quieted and some sat down, he continued while sweeping his hand to take in the full assembly, "You cannot attribute the death of a single citizen in any of your countries as either a direct or indirect result of our campaign. We have shaken your economies, leaving your citizenry berserk with anger at your inability to counter our actions."

Raising his voice to be more clearly heard he stated, "I urge that you listen to what is being discussed this night. Choose to do otherwise, and we have it in our ability to inconvenience you back to the sixteenth century. Please, be patient and take your seats."

As they began to comply, no one took particular notice of blue-helmeted and fully armed United Nations soldiers discreetly taking positions at every entrance and exit in the building. A number moved quietly up the aisle close to the U.S. President. When no further interruptions were forthcoming, Jake motioned for Eleanor to continue.

Stepping to the dais she stated, "We petitioned the International Court of Justice on behalf of the leadership and citizens of Luna. Allow me to introduce the Honorable Hidetada Funabushi, Chief Justice. Seated to your left are the other fourteen sitting judges from the international community."

Justice Funabushi, now almost eighty years old, walked slowly to take his place and addressed the impromptu gathering of Earth's leadership.

"We have reviewed the petition provided, and are aware each of you has access to the same documentation. The assumption is made you are fully read into the matter before us. Unable to locate any precedent in existing law, international or domestic, it was necessary to adjudicate the matter in the light of existing fact. The petitioning Council and leadership of Luna graciously invited us to view their accomplishments for ourselves, and we did so over a three week period. During that time of personal inspection no question was spared, nor did we accept anything less than full disclosure and detailed explanation. All was revealed to us openly.

"Speaking on behalf of the full Court, I can assure you the endeavors listed in their petition have been vastly understated. In the near term, each of you may be invited to form delegations and see the miracles for yourselves. Now, back to the question before this Court. In a way, the deciding factor was a recent decision by the Supreme Court of the United States. You must be aware that decisions made there have far reaching consequences, and influence law in other countries to a great degree, even when the outcome may not be what was intended. The ruling I refer to removed the citizenship, birthright, and legal protections of all individuals inhabiting our moon, or Luna, as it is now acknowledged."

Pausing for a drink of water, he continued his summarization by stating that expeditious writing of a few words on paper in the heat of political decision cannot be utilized to initiate legal genocide against a group that wishes to live apart peacefully. Nor can it justify taking action to imprison or bring harm to their citizens, confiscate their lands and property, and take from them all they have accomplished here. Close precedent existed in examples of religious communities granted immunity to remain true to their own beliefs. Under those circumstances, such a group would have the same right to self defense under international law as any nation represented in this room tonight.

Additionally, every nation gathered here has had the opportunity to travel to and build upon the moon for decades, either singly or in cooperation with other space-faring nations. The fact that they elected to do otherwise provides no justification to decide today to take what others have worked hard to achieve. Therefore, the action of the U.S. Supreme Court begs the question... if they are not citizens of this world, what world are they citizens of? The Court found the answer to that question to be simplistic, obvious, and rooted in common sense.

"They are citizens of the place they inhabit. It is the unanimous decision of this Court of International Justice that the Petition of Sovereignty be granted, and we recognize the ruling Council of Luna to be the legitimate leadership of that planet. The Court apologizes to the leadership and citizens of Luna on behalf of the nations of Earth for recent suffering and loss inflicted upon its people by unprincipled elements of this planet, regardless of nationality. The Court also applauds their remarkable restraint in waging arguably the most humane offensive action ever seen in the history of mankind."

As the Chief Justice gathered his documents, a wave of ice cold apprehension ran unfettered up and down Stewart Talefer Caneman's spine at noting a too-familiar CD among the papers in Justice Funabushi's hand. Before he could leave the dais, President Caneman shot to his feet.

"This is meaningless. Wave your papers for all the good it will do you. I have no intention of honoring any pact you've made. We're the big dog on this planet, and you have no ability to back up anything you've said here so far tonight, so stuff it!"

"Sit down, Mr. President. You haven't been granted the right to speak at this assembly," ordered Chief Justice Funabushi with authority, not at all impressed with or intimidated by Caneman's outburst. "The matter of sovereignty is concluded, and we move to another issue of even graver import." So saying, he moved back as Jake walked over to stand at the podium.

"As we have done in the past, these proceedings are being made available to every country on planet Earth capable of receiving them, with simultaneous translation. They are being recorded and will be re-broadcast throughout the next few days. Those broadcasts will include documented proof of the abduction and torture of our people by agents of the United States Government, as well as attempted illegal use of nuclear weapons against an unarmed civilian populace. Failing in their attempts to wrest any useful information in that manner, a new direction was initiated."

At that statement, a heavily chained and secured individual was brought kicking, fighting, and dragging his feet to the front of the stage by four armed UN soldiers. His weathered complexion, dark hair, eyes and skin spoke to mid-eastern culture. President Caneman, now realizing the trap he was in, canvassed the large room for possible escape routes. If he could gain the outside, Secret Service personnel could whisk him to safety. Seeing they were all blocked by armed personnel, his expression took on a heavy look of troubled concern.

"The person just brought before you is Anwar abd-Alahad, also known as 'the Assassin.' He's wanted in fourteen Earth countries for capital crimes against civilian, industrial, and political targets. Please watch the following."

The picture changed to show everything the Assassin did. Unknowingly, Earth's International Criminal Police Organization, Interpol, had been breached as easily as its CIA to identity him and his nefarious activities. From the moment he had set foot in Lancaster, Pennsylvania, he had been recorded. Every move, including his hideouts, had been tracked; his reports intercepted. A crystal-clear line of progression from his hand right up to his anonymous benefactor was documented. His visit to the Fisher house and assassination of Colonel Starnes and his family was presented in full color and exquisite detail. That bit stood Anwar abd-Alahad straight up, with "How did you…" getting out before one of the UN soldiers twisted his shackles painfully to silence him.

Had he completed a more thorough job of studying the environment he was operating in, he would have realized a number of rather obvious facts; Amish bedrooms don't have mirrors… a prideful acquisition. Nor are window coverings quite so translucent as to permit as much light as was available that evening. Had he listened more attentively, he would have noted an absence of breathing from any of his victims, and a closer inspection of the rooms may have disclosed the cameras. Luna's engineers didn't have much time to prepare, but were counting on hubris to blind the Assassin. His arrogance took care of the rest.

At that moment, another Starnes strolled casually to stand beside Jake… an identical twin in every way. "Knowing his intentions, we fashioned avatars of my family… my wife, three children, and me. They are virtually undetectable from their living counterparts. Sensors were installed to react correctly to several forms of attack, and my family was relocated to safety. Ultra low light cameras were installed throughout the house, capturing this man in the act of committing five more murders for hire. We intercepted the rather generous payoffs sent to his secret bank accounts, which will be returned to the American taxpayers.

"Unfortunately, we were not aware his benefactor had provided him with information of family members remaining on Earth. He found one such, an elderly Asian mother whose son was a member of our community. He tortured her to turn him against us, then murdered and dismembered her body. We have the computer he used and videos he made to compel her son to violence. Chief Justice Funabushi and his delegation were on Luna collecting their evidence for our sovereignty petition when the following transpired."

Planet Earth was then given a front row seat to the terrible events that came about as a result of Robert's actions. At conclusion of that presentation, all eyes now followed Jake as he turned his head to view the full assembly. Looking directly into the cameras, his face took on a combat-hardened aspect. As his gloved fist struck the top of the podium, his voice carried an edge of sharpened steel.

"We came to you in *Peace!*" boomed from one wall to the next. Allowing a few seconds for that to settle in, he followed, "*With Open Arms!*" reverberating throughout the hall strong enough to rattle everyone's composure. *"With offers of science that would have moved your industries ahead more than fifty years!"*

After a short pause to regain some composure, he continued. "Our reward? Abduction, imprisonment; torture of our young and old. Nuclear weapons fired at us. Attempted murder of my family and me, followed by callous destruction to one of our main habitat cities with the deaths of one hundred and fifteen non-combatant innocent citizens; thirty-eight of which were *CHILDREN!*" he roared!

"*THIRTY!—EIGHT!—CHILDREN!*" pounding the podium heavily to emphasize each of those three words, the crack of those impacts echoing in the stunned silence that followed. When the resonance of his thunderous proclamation had died sufficiently, he lowered his outburst. Not a sound issued from startled throats of the world's leaders; realizing what they had witnessed could just have easily occurred within their own boundaries, their people, their families and children, and to themselves.

"I have, with the assistance of Chief Justice Funabushi, prepared an indictment of crimes against humanity; illegal torture and use of nuclear weapons, collusion with a known assassin to commit interplanetary and domestic murder, and a number of slightly less charges of a felonious nature, brought to the full Council of Luna acting in the capacity of Grand Jury. On that authority I now order the arrest of United States President Stewart Talefer Caneman III. He'll stand Earth trial on these charges before the World Court. Assassin Anwar abd-Alahad will be remanded to Interpol for prosecution. The Vice-President of the United States has been brought here and will be sworn in at the conclusion of these proceedings."

The soon-to-be ex-President Caneman was successful in bolting up and knocking over two of the UN soldiers blocking an emergency exit. He wasn't aware that guards had been posted on the outside of all such and he was easily recaptured. As he and the Assassin were led away, his exit was punctuated by profane epitaphs hurled at Jake, who now refocused on the assembly at large.

"As the elected Council Head of Luna, and with full concurrence of that Council, know this. We renounce planet Earth."

His next proclamation, "We renounce all plans to share any of Luna's technology with Earth," came as no surprise to those watching; simply adding one more brick to a wall of 'what could have been' being built before them.

"Luna will become our Embassy; only those passing the most rigorous vetting process will be permitted to visit. We are expanding and will relocate initially to Mars, now renamed 'Pax' by our children after the Roman Goddess of Peace. Our scientists are in the process of determining how best to begin terra-forming. Our plan is to build a fresh society based on a nucleus city concept.

"Each city will stand alone, similar to existing structure on Luna; providing everything needed for its residents while focusing on a specific societal project benefiting the whole. Intercity transportation requirements will be met by moving sidewalks. Transport to other cities will be accomplished by using systems such as maglev trains, moving both above and below the surface. There will be no need for personally owned transportation, as use of all transport systems will be a guaranteed right to every citizen, including unlimited movement between Luna and Pax.

Photoelectric and nuclear power only will be utilized, and the use of fossil fuels prohibited."

He concluded the Luna Council's presentation with, "We will not petition for sovereignty of Pax. We claim that planet for our own and will defend our right to be there against any aggressor move from Earth." On that announcement, they left.

EPILOGUE

"Chateauleire!" was the first word spoken by Gautier as he shook off the effects of long-term anesthetic from his surgery, struggling weakly to continue his conflict with Souser. His movements were held in check and gently restrained. Focusing, he could see that he was in a hospital bed, wired to medical monitors and intravenous lines.

"She's fine, Gautier, just fine," said Eleanor. He realized now that she was holding his hand and stroking his head. "You were taken to Q initially. Doctor Agave and his surgical staff stopped the internal bleeding and repaired the damage. They have kept you sedated for the journey back to Luna so you wouldn't reopen some of the more delicate work that was done. You've been in a sustained coma for that entire time so your body could heal properly."

She explained everything that had transpired after he had collapsed in Chat's hospital room, including the events at the UN. "The war's over, and Luna has won. Your actions at the hospital were very brave. Given the horrible circumstances, the Council has forgiven your anger."

"Remercier Dieu, thank God for you... Eleanor, mon amour. Anoki saved my life, and Chateauleire's as well. And thank God for Jake and his Council. I owe them all a debt that can never be repaid."

"Don't concern yourself with that; your friendship and commitment to Luna is payment enough and no one expects anything else. Gautier, I love you, and my intuition tells me you feel the same... that you love me as well. There can be no doubt that Chateauleire and I have bonded very strongly. I can't take the place of her mother, but I can be the best friend she ever had, and I love her as deeply as if she were my own. I'm not going to stand on ceremony, nor attempt to travel this life's adventure any longer by myself. Gautier Devereux, will you marry me?"

"Oui, la Madame," he said without hesitation, a humorous glint in his eye. "But I must insist that in future only I may select the hotels where we will stay. This last one you graced with your presence; very bad taste, poor view... and I'm sure the service was not up to standard, oui?"

"Oh, you horrible man, what am I getting myself into?" she answered laughing, bending over to hug him, certain that Gautier and Chateauleire were the fulfillment of her life's dreams.

The next meeting of the Luna Council found Jake and the others going over the details of Luna's administrative change to an Embassy posture, Pax settlement, Venus mineral exploration, and the United Nation's agenda for upcoming talks.

"I'm sorry for the necessity of deception... subterfuge," said Jake. "The fewer of you that were aware of our plans meant less chance of discovery. Maralah, there were only four others beyond me... Reatah, Alahn, Walwyn, and Kelly. We met secretly to work everything out... and each acted their part admirably without knowledge of the others involved. Marian was an unexpected surprise, and I'm thankful to all of you for accepting her as you have."

I echo Jake's comments," added Kelly. "The danger was extreme. A known international assassin, the issue with Robert and his attempt on Reatah's life. Our losses could have been even more disastrous had Robert's plans not been interrupted in time. His design was to plant explosives in all three cities. He was revealed when all harmful acts ceased almost immediately upon installation of the cameras. Only someone in Ops could possibly have known that, so we initially focused our search there. He had covered himself so well that we simply weren't aware of just how far he had progressed with his plan and were late in confronting him. While I hope we never have to encounter situations like this again, we'll be better prepared next time."

"The assassin was too close," said Jake. "We set up his confrontation in order to isolate him; make him become careless. Once he completed his mission, it was relatively simple to capture him; the Chinese brothers Zieng and Wiang had little difficulty in disarming him as he exited his rented room. I can assure you all he was quite surprised.

"The avatars were constructed in secret. I'm glad to know we no longer have to hide Reatah's assistants." On that, Jonathan and Krista came into the meeting room. Jake explained that Krista was autonomous when performing general housekeeping duties, but was available to Reatah as her own personal avatar otherwise.

"Thank you, Jake," spoke Reatah through Krista. "And thank you all for your assistance and cooperation throughout our crisis. We'll be adding to our growing line of anthropomorphic children, now that we're so much closer to our goal of awareness than before." Her request, "Please, feel free to come and see me. I'll leave the vault door open!" was met with good natured laughter all around with numerous promises to do exactly that.

Repairs to Selene had been completed. Remains of the dead were all accounted for and buried with deepest respect. Planning was in place to ensure such tragedy could never occur again. As the course of business now changed direction, a newcomer was invited to speak at the Council meeting.

"I thank you and your associates for inviting my friends and I to this wonderful place, Mr. Jake," said a highly enthusiastic UN Secretary-General Baruti Harakhty. "And thank you for allowing me to participate in your government processes today. What a glorious experience, to sit and discuss the future path to be taken without animosity from anyone! Oh, I only wish it were so in our own dealings with representatives from other countries on Earth."

"You're welcome, Baruti. I'm sorry your first trip was delayed. I'm sure that one day you'll find a more positive viewpoint from your constituents, which brings us to the matter at hand. The Council and I would like to offer you the role of first Luna Ambassador to planet Earth. You may select your own staffing. Caretaker personnel will continue to maintain operations in all cities... we still have mineral, manufacturing and agriculture interests. But you will be the sole contact for all Luna and Pax interests with Earth."

Former UN Secretary-General Baruti Harakhty, overwhelmed by Luna's generosity, was staggered into speechlessness. He rushed over to shake the hands of each Council member in gracious thanks for such an opportunity... promising faithfully to uphold the highest standards in performance of such duties.

Maralah asked to speak, and expressed her concerns for Luna science that may have been compromised during their troubled times with Earth. "I meant to bring this up earlier. Some of us are still not confident that Earth's factions won't revert to form and attempt to corrupt our science toward violence and conquest. We have only the tentative and somewhat shaky word of those leaders in position today and no assurances future leaders will honor those accords. Earth's history is replete with examples of broken treaties and dishonored agreements."

At an indication from Jake, KhenemetAhmose joined the group. "I have been granted permission to inform the Council members, including Mr. Harakhty that at the heart of all programming existing within our systems is a very special code, one which can't be accessed by anyone but me. It's an algorithmic representation using fractal encryption to constantly change itself at a rate of transaction far beyond the ability of any computer system presently existing on Earth. Given their rate of progression in that area and the gulf that exists between their science and ours, I'm confident Earth will never discover it or understand how to affect it in any way."

Appearing puzzled, Abigail asked, "What's it for, Ahmose?"

Jake grinned and responded before Prime could answer. "In simpler terms, what he said is that a failsafe has been embedded in every program and mechanical device we have. Anyone attempting to convert our science for other than what is intended will suddenly discover the item in question will no longer function. Tampering will cause a program to either terminate and delete itself or initiate contact with Prime. He'll take it from there, simply turning it off if necessary. They will be unable to reverse engineer any of our programming or equipment they may have come into possession of during our conflict." With Council members nodding their understanding, Jake adjourned the meeting and thanked all participants for their efforts.

Later that day, throughout three cities of Luna, parents and children gathered to reflect on events shaping two worlds. Safe in the security and comfort of their habitats, far from strife and worry, families and friends joined in fellowship over a sumptuous evening meal. Tensions of the past months evaporated as an almost party-like atmosphere seemed to permeate the whole of their lives.

Unfortunately, governance had no such respite, and many found themselves still working hours later to lock in resettlement planning. One in particular found himself deep in thoughtful wonder at how all they strived for had been achieved.

Jake had reserved the Nearside lounge for some quiet time. The entire family had gathered on a long couch whose back was pushed against the expansive viewport. "Do you like the view?"

As Jake sat sideways watching the children visually explore Luna's surface, Marian kneeled on the couch and pressed herself against his back, wrapping both arms around him while resting her chin on his shoulder. She kissed his cheek lightly to answer his query, "Vaht I see in your eyes is dearer to me than die welt hanging outside daht window!" The children stood three in a row on the booth seat ogling and pointing at the planet Earth, floating serenely in splendor before them.

Jake reached for and kissed one hand. "Well, soon they'll have another sky to amuse them. We'll be traveling to Pax once the resettlement teams have our first shelters in place."

Raising one finger enough to point at Earth, she asked, "Do you regret leaving daht place… your people?"

His answer was firm with commitment as he turned to face her. "I have no regrets, Marian. We've decided to leave our front door open. We'll continue to recruit. Small delegations will be permitted to visit Luna, once vetted by our new Ambassador and his staff. It may be that in time, Earth will solve its problems. We'll be here to help them when that day comes.

"Your cousin Eli Yoder has settled in nicely, don't you think?"

Eli was quite a surprise, to say the least. His first few days back on the

Fisher farm found him right back at his old habits... wandering all over the farmland, muttering incoherently. It wasn't until finalization of much of Luna's transition business that Jake was able to spend more time with Marian and the children on the farm. Initially busy with other projects, he hadn't taken much notice of Eli's mumblings until he went to gather him for lunch, then focused intently on Eli's small voice, "Ein hundert zwei, drei tausend zwanzig drei, achtzig vier [One hundred two, three thousand twenty-three, eighty-four]." He concluded Eli must be repeating some type of children's counting game and had mentioned as much to Marian over the noon meal.

"Nein, Yacob. Daht is vaht drives everyone away. All Eli does is numbering. Dere is no reason to his habit, he simply makes die numbers." That comment drew Jake's immediate attention. After lunch, he guided Eli out of the house.

Pointing to a small flock of sparrows winging overhead, he asked, "Eli, schauen sie die vögel an [Eli, look at the birds]. As he did so, Eli instantly said, "Fünfzig sieben [Fifty-seven]." Asked to look at a tree close by, he just as quickly uttered, "Vierzig tausend acht hundert sechzig einer [Forty thousand eight hundred sixty-one]." There was little doubt that Eli had just correctly counted the number of leaves on that tree. Jake concluded Eli Yoder was a mathematical savant, and would be treasure if he could be persuaded to join Walwyn's group on Luna. Marian was receptive, and both Walwyn and Reatah were excited to welcome a new genius into their close-knit herky-jerk community.

Jake brought his focus back into the Nearside lounge. "Eleanor Ernst, Gautier and Chat will be coming to Pax. Her two friends will continue to represent us in legal affairs here. The others who were injured on Earth are all healing or fully recovered by now. Doctor Agave will relocate with selected members of a medical staff competent in a number of fields. Most of the existing Luna Council wants to go, so we'll elect a similar Council to replace them. Lloyd and Emma Boxe will stay... though Lloyd will come for a while to get planting started. Alahn and the Esch family have decided to remain here for the time being. Walwyn will select volunteers from Ops. My close friend Johnson McMinn and his family will initially stay on Luna... perhaps he'll be interested in leading the new

Council, but that remains to be seen. He wants to explore the universe one tiny step at a time. Hopefully he will join us on Pax in the future. Of course, there's no lack of families wanting to come along on our adventure. We're just about full on the New Hope for this first trip. I'm confident we've addressed everything needed in that regard. And, we're even considering tourism after we get settled in on Pax. Might be worth a tour there to see what we've accomplished.

"You and the children are my people now."

Jake stood and picked up both girls while Marian lifted Johann. All three rested very tired heads on their parent's shoulders, worn out from a wonderful day of excitement.

Moving to kiss his beautiful Marian, he ended, "It's been a long day. Come, let's go home.

"PAX"

Coming soon: "PAX," the exciting sequel to "LUNA." Mars, now renamed Pax by the children of Luna after the Roman God of Peace, carries on a cornerstone tradition of non-violence established by the citizens of both worlds. Earth, consumed by over-population pressures, petty rivalries and conflict, has never turned completely away from the successes achieved by those inhabiting their moon and neighboring planet. Ever-increasing resource depletion and environmental poisoning are only a small part of the continuing challenges that face the governments of home world... now standing at the precipice of global disaster but frozen into inaction by dissenting political factions. Yet again, an eye turns toward the heavens seeking to take what can't be achieved through productive effort.

About the Author

J. CARL HUDSON traveled nation-wide growing up in a military family. A degreed professional encompassing both U.S. Government Executive Office and military careers, he's earned two U.S. Department of Transportation President's Council on Integrity Efficiency Awards as well as the Chairman's Team Award. As a highly decorated combat veteran of three wars, he has been the recipient of numerous military accolades. Carl has military and civil flight ratings in helicopter and fixed wing aircraft (both single and multi-engine), holds teaching certifications and in retirement taught for local school districts. Having written and instructed throughout his career, "LUNA" marks his entry into the realm of sci-fi writing. After spending years sailing the San Francisco Bay and related areas, Carl now calls Sierra Vista, Arizona home.

51325411R00209

Made in the USA
Lexington, KY
02 September 2019